Praise for

JUDITH JAMES

"Judith James fearlessly bursts through the ceiling of the historical romance genre and soars to astounding heights. Her writing is intriguing, daring, exquisitely dark, and emotionally riveting."
—*USA TODAY* bestselling author Julianne MacLean

"This emotional, well-written novel has characters that are far from conventional; they're complex, heartbreaking and endearing. Readers will be enthralled."
—*RT Book Reviews* on *Broken Wing*

"Sarah and Gabriel's heart-wrenching struggle to keep their love alive…will really keep readers entranced throughout this epic read."
—*Publishers Weekly* on *Broken Wing*

"All I can say is WOW!"
—*All About Romance*

"*Broken Wing* is a grand story of love, acceptance and forgiveness. One of the best romance books of 2008… and quite possibly one of the best love stories I've ever read."
—*Romance Book Wyrm*

"Heartbreakingly lovely and passionate, the story of Gabriel and Sarah will stay with you long after you close the cover…beautifully written…Judith James creates a poignant story of loss and love that you won't be able to put down."
—*Romance Junkies* on *Broken Wing*

JUDITH JAMES

Libertine's Kiss

HQN™

Recycling programs
for this product may
not exist in your area.

ISBN-13: 978-0-373-77505-7

LIBERTINE'S KISS

This edition published by arrangement with Harlequin Books S.A.

For questions and comments about the quality of this book please contact us at Customer_eCare@Harlequin.ca.

® and TM are trademarks of the publisher. Trademarks indicated with ® are registered in the United States Patent and Trademark Office, the Canadian Trade Marks Office and in other countries.

www.HQNBooks.com

Printed in U.S.A.

To Audrey, who along with my Mom and Aunt Joyce is one of the three wise women of a wonderful extended clan. Thanks for sharing your passion, your humor, and your down-to-earth advice. Thank you for the incredible feasts and fascinating conversation, but what I'll miss most are your wonderful hugs. You lived life well and left the place better than you found it. I hope one day I can say the same. I love you.

Acknowledgments

A big thanks goes to writing buddies and stalwart friends Pat Thomas and Anne Cameron, for taking the time to do an early read, for all their encouragement and for being there whenever they're needed most. Thanks also to Julianne MacLean for her always generous and savvy advice, and Heidi Hamburg and Bev Pettersen. Your encouragement and support have meant more than you know.

Thanks as always to Bob Diforio who has taught me so much. And what can I say about HQN? From the beginning they've made me feel welcome, and somehow they manage to do everything with a personal touch. My thanks to all, with a special acknowledgment to my wonderful editor, Cassandra Dozet, for her patience, support and encouragement as well as her always thoughtful edits, and Mike Rehder and the art department for a gorgeous cover.

Finally, thanks to the fascinating John Wilmot, Earl of Rochester, whose often scandalous, surprisingly modern and sometimes sublime poetry helped give voice to William. In return, I hope that for modern readers, William helped give voice to him.

Libertine's Kiss

CHAPTER ONE

1658

NIGHT HAD DESCENDED hours ago. He wandered a dark wilderness that was almost void of form. The sound of musket fire and the shouts of his pursuers had faded in the gathering storm. Now a mounting wind moaned and whistled, snapping off branches and rattling trees as thunder rumbled in the distance. The ice-cold rain, driven by angry gusts, fell in stinging sheets that raked his cheeks and turned the ground beneath him slick and treacherous. Thick oily mud squelched under his feet, gulping greedily at his ankles and clutching at his boots, and the torn bits of cloth wrapped tight around gashes in his arm and thigh were heavy with water, mud and blood.

He labored forward, fighting the elements and his own fatigue. His ragged breath strained in his ears. He clasped his injured arm tight against his chest, protecting it and the battered leather pouch strapped snug beneath his shirt. It was an unconscious act. For the past hour, all his attention had been fixed on a lonely flicker of light, wavering in the distance. Friend or foe, for now it was his only beacon. His exertions had opened his wounds. He was losing blood and heat and soon he would lose consciousness.

He limped to a halt at the edge of a small clearing. The rain had eased a bit, though the wind still battered in sudden whooping squalls. The feeble light had resolved itself into a warm glow that cast just enough illumination to coax shape and substance from the shadows. It emanated from the windows of a substantial cottage. His eyes flit here and there, coolly assessing. Isolated, two stories tall, built of brick and tidy stone; it was fitted with a solid slate roof and bay windows, and was too fine to belong to a simple farmer. A wealthy merchant or a gentleman's hunting retreat perhaps, and potentially dangerous depending on who was at home.

He listened intently. The house was quiet. No shouts, no laughter, no sounds of brawling or signs of horses, supplies or armed men. No signs it had been commandeered by Cromwell's forces. His teeth flashed in a predatory grin and the fingers of his good hand twitched, then reached to caress the hilt of his saber. He needed shelter. Weapon drawn, keeping to the shadows, he crept forward.

There was no watchman, not even a mutt to raise an alarm. The only thing guarding the place was its solitude and a heavy wooden door. The latch seemed simple enough. He tried it with his free hand, but there was no strength in his arm and his numb fingers could barely feel to lift it. Cursing under his breath, he sheathed his sword and began working the latch with both hands as he pushed with his shoulder. The damned thing would not budge. His exertions were taking their toll. A wave of dizziness assailed him and he leaned back, letting the door take his weight as he waited for it to pass.

He lost his balance anyway, whirling to right himself,

scrambling for his sword and fighting to stay on his feet as the door swung open suddenly on its own.

"Most people use the knocker or pull on the bell."

He gaped in astonishment. Her voice was calm with a hint of irony, her demeanor self-possessed, but her fine gray eyes were as wide and startled as if she had just seen a ghost. Straightening and swallowing his own surprise, he looked carefully about the room as his heart steadied.

"Other than a handful of servants, I am here alone."

Leaning against the doorjamb for support, he examined her as thoroughly as he had the room. She was a tiny thing, dressed in drab woolens and wrapped in a shawl she hugged close to her breast. Her hair was drawn into a severe bun hidden tight beneath a linen cap, accentuating a pale face that looked worn and tired. Her gaze was probing and wary. She reminded him of a brave little bird, torn between curiosity and the impulse to take flight. Collecting himself, he removed a wide-brimmed hat with a rain-soaked plume, and performed a courtly bow. "Good evening to you, madam. My apologies for the rude intrusion, but I've traveled as far as I may this day, and 'tis wicked cold outside."

She noted his height, his disheveled appearance, his sodden bandages, and his cavalier's clothes. Her eyes met his…searching…and then looked pointedly at his sword.

He sheathed it as if at her command.

A gust of wind slammed the door against the wall and sent a sheet of water spattering across the flagstone floor. She took another step back and motioned with her hand. "Come inside. I'll give you shelter from the storm." He let go of the doorjamb, took one step, then another, and toppled into her arms.

HE AWOKE sometime later resting precariously on a dainty settee that was all but dwarfed by his length. Covered in warm blankets and settled in front of a cheerful fire, he was no longer cold, but his arm throbbed in time with his pulse. His leg burned like the fires of hell, and he ached all over. Grimacing, he tugged at his coverings, pulling them back to survey the damage, only to find he had been stripped of breeches and shirt, and other than a clean dressing and his boots, he was naked underneath. His lips quirked in amusement and he scanned the room, searching for his nurse.

She sat in the corner in a well-appointed chair, haloed by candlelight, frowning in concentration as she stitched his shirt. He watched her unobserved, smiling when she bent her head, lips parted, and snipped the thread with sharp little teeth. Though her hair and clothing made her appear severe, that unguarded gesture made her seem younger than he had first imagined. *I doubt she's any older than I am.*

She was not so plain as that, either. Long a veteran campaigner in the lists of love as well as the field of battle, he was somewhat of a connoisseur. Sometimes the quiet ones burned brightest. The little abbess had full lips, a becoming pout, and a mouth that begged to be kissed. Fine cheekbones would serve her well in old age, and he was fascinated by her eyes, intent now on her sewing. They changed in the light when he tilted his head, from a smoky gray to hints of stormy blue. *Sirens' eyes. A daughter of the sea.* He smiled, wondering what she would look like with her hair unbound.

His sex stirred and he grinned, forgetting for a moment the gnawing pain in his bicep and the angry stinging in his leg. *What is she doing here by herself? No father. No husband. She can't be married. No man would be so foolish as to leave her unprotected in these dangerous times. Perhaps she's been widowed by the wars.* Perhaps he should release her stays, loosen her hair and pull her down for a tumble. How long had she been alone? What depths of fire and passion simmered beneath that prim exterior, just waiting to ignite? He chuckled to himself and shook his head. He must be jaded indeed to imagine a houri from his tight-bound little wren. Still…there was something about her—

His heart lurched in his chest as he suddenly remembered his mission. Tossing blankets and pillows aside, he began a frenzied search for the pouch that could mean so much to his king. He subsided in relief as suddenly as he had started, when he found it still strapped to his side, but his movements alerted the little wren, who looked up curiously from her stitching.

"I am not in the habit of rifling the belongings of sleeping guests. Your secrets are your own."

His secrets. She had no idea. He thought back to the chaos and fury of the young King Charles's stand at Worcester nearly seven years ago and the mad scramble as Charles's loyal cavaliers and Scots strove to defend him, then fought to give him time to escape. The king was amiable, informal and an easy man to love, but at six foot three he had not been an easy one to hide. Dependant on the help of royalist supporters and a network of Catholic sympathizers versed in moving wanted men, they had lived as commoners for six weeks, eluding Cromwell's ferocious grip. They had experienced life in a way kings and courtiers never did, and grown close in a way only those who shared adventure and danger ever could.

He had bonded with Charles, not only as king to subject, but man to man. There was nothing he wouldn't do for him and no task more important than seeing him safe to France, but none of them had expected their exile to last for years. When they had crossed the channel to France he had been filled with hope and pride. He would help his king fulfill his destiny. They would reclaim the throne that Cromwell and his ilk had stolen from him in an unimaginable act of regicide. But when they had arrived in Rouen, bedraggled and spent, they had to borrow money and clothes before an innkeeper would rent them a room. It was a theme that had characterized their years in exile.

Despite his charms and graces, Charles had become the poor relation who embarrassed everyone, and no one knew what to do with. He lived on credit, charity and promises, until the goal was no longer to raise an army, but simply to pay for their bread. William had been sent repeatedly to different places in halfhearted efforts to gain support. It was a humiliating and dispiriting task, one for which he was ill suited. So when he tired of being kept waiting in the great halls of Europe, or seducing women and playing cards, he left for England and took to the roads. It was a welcome distraction at first. One that provided himself and his grateful king with some much-needed funds, but lately he had grown as weary of it as he had of everything else. The sense of purpose he'd felt as a fugitive cavalier protecting his outlawed king was with him still, but the idealism and sense of exhilaration had long since waned.

This time, though, there was news. The Old Pretender Cromwell was rumored to be gravely ill and his son ill equipped to grip the reins of power. There was talk of rebellion, offers of support, and a very important missive from a man who could help put Charles back on his throne. His pursuers thought they were chasing another of the hundreds of disgruntled cavaliers turned highwaymen who bloomed like wildflowers along England's roads since the end of the civil wars. If they had known what he carried they would have—

"Here. Take this." Gentle fingers brushed back his hair.

He blinked up at her in surprise and reached out to accept a tumbler full of brandy. She had snuck up next to him, bearing gifts, and her casual touch suggested she might offer more. *I need to rest and regain my strength. I'll stay the night, and be on my way by morning.* He grinned and nodded his thanks, then tossed back the sweet liquor. It tasted of apples and warmed his insides, spreading through him like liquid heat, and he handed her the glass, motioning for more. She refilled it and watched in silence as he emptied most of it in one swallow.

His gaze quickened with interest and his lips curved in a slight smile as he noted a stray tendril of hair that had escaped its bonds to tumble down her cheek. It gleamed in the lamplight in fiery hues. Something stirred within him, akin to faint remembrance. Mesmerized, he reached a finger to tuck it back but she stepped abruptly away. His smile widened to a grin. Fire and ice, bound tight in a plain brown wrapper. How intriguing! *I wonder what she'd look like clothed only in jewels. I am grown fanciful. It must be loss of blood.*

He tugged the blanket aside, baring his leg, and she lifted the dressing, probing gently, her fingertips brushing his naked flesh as she checked the wound. He hissed on indrawn breath and she looked up, concerned.

"I am sorry. Am I hurting you?"

He reached for her hand and held it a moment, his fingers stroking her palm as his thumb caressed her knuckles. "I am swollen and aching, little bird, but I feel certain your touch can relieve me."

She looked at him uncertainly, tugging her hand to free it.

With a knowing smile, he let it slide from his grasp.

"That is some very fine stitch work. You are skilled at nursing, madam. You did it while I lay sleeping?"

"I tended the sword wound while you were unconscious, yes. You were very lucky. You've lost a fair bit of blood but 'tis not as bad as I feared. The cut missed any major arteries and it appears to have bled clean. Provided there's no infection, you should be fine. I will tend to the swelling soon."

He choked on what remained of his drink, covering it with a cough. When he had recovered himself, he raised his empty glass and gave her a charming grin. "Won't you join me in a toast first, to my speedy recovery and your formidable skills?"

"I don't think that would be wise," she said primly.

"Come, lass. Share a drink with me. It's a bitter night and just the two of us here, cozy by the fire. There's no one to know," he coaxed.

She snatched his glass away and set it on the mantel. "I've seen to your leg. I've yet to attend to your arm. There's a bullet to be removed and more stitches, I'm afraid. Surely you would prefer I attend to it with a steady hand."

"Yes, actually, I would. But one wonders why you didn't complete the task whilst I slept…instead of darning my shirt."

She pursed her lips, a little put out by his ingratitude, but managed a patient reply. "Attending to your leg took longer than expected, and I was afraid you would regain consciousness while I worked on your arm. Any sudden move would be…well…best avoided. Now that you are awake, we can start. This may sting a bit, but I need you to cooperate and stay very still."

He nodded, holding out his hand for his glass. She refilled it and waited while he took another swallow. He closed his eyes and offered her his arm, nodding again for her to begin. She knelt beside him, the soft curve of her breast brushing his shoulder, and his lips curled in a smile as he settled his head against her bosom. He could feel her heart beating, slow and steady beneath his cheek, and he thought he detected a faint scent of lavender. Perhaps it was her soap. She stiffened, and he opened one eye to see her regarding him suspiciously.

"What? If you had put me someplace proper I could sprawl out in comfort, but I am stuck on this flimsy thing, and I need you to balance me lest I tip over the edge. How did you manage to move me here anyway?"

"With the help of my servants. You were too heavy to carry far, and are lucky we didn't leave you lying on the wet floor, or toss you back outside."

"I am most grateful, madam. And where are they now? These servants of yours?"

"Hiding."

"Ah! A cowardly lot, are they? But you are not afraid."

"No. I am not afraid. Now please be quiet and make no sudden moves." Biting her lip in concentration, she began working on his arm, probing carefully for the bullet. She labored in silence for several long minutes. His body was clenched tight from his teeth to his toes and a cold sweat beaded his brow, but other than a few muttered curses, he obeyed her.

"Aah!"

He turned his head to look. She waved her tweezers triumphantly, the fugitive bullet clamped securely within their grasp.

"All of that with naught but your sewing kit," he managed between tightly gritted teeth.

She gave him a broad smile, her eyes sparkling, and patted his shoulder, making him flinch. "You did very well! The danger is past and we're nearly done."

He replied with a weak grin, grateful that his hostess was a capable country lass rather than one of the decorative dolls he had grown accustomed to, but when she set to cleaning and stitching, he couldn't stifle a groan. He held his breath, eyes closed, one hand gripping his glass, clenching and unclenching as she worked a neat and tidy cross-stitch on his arm.

"Why aren't you afraid? Don't you think you should be?" he managed hoarsely, desperate for any distraction.

"Think you so?"

The thought occurred to him that she had never asked his name, nor where he came from, how he got his wound, or what he had been doing outside her door. In fact, she was curiously incurious. He continued clenching and unclenching his fist.

"You are out here by yourself. It is lonely and dangerous in the woods, little bird. Do you feed every wolf that happens upon your door?"

She pulled the stitch tight. He winced and swore under his breath.

"There! All done. You can relax now." She grasped his fisted hand and unclenched it, removing the glass from his grip and placing it on the floor. She massaged his palm briskly with her own to bring back his circulation. Holding his hand in her lap, she traced a faint scar that patterned the base of his thumb, and then looked up with a pensive gaze. His eyes, as green and layered as the forest depths, gleamed feral in the firelight. "Is that what you are? A wolf?"

His breathing was ragged. "Perhaps. A tame one though, madam, I assure you."

She released his hand abruptly, as if only now aware she held it. "Meaning you will not piss on the furniture and chase my chickens?"

He gave a bark of laughter. His abbess had a salty tongue. Perhaps she wasn't the cloistered innocent she appeared. This day had gone from bad to better to promising indeed. "Meaning I will not bite the hand that feeds me."

"Good! Marjorie will be glad to hear it." She rose to her feet, abandoning him abruptly. He watched in amusement as she straightened her apron and adjusted her slightly skewed cap, returning her stray curls to their prison before tugging on a bell cord and bustling about the parlor tidying up.

He closed his eyes and listened to her soft humming. The brandy had dulled his senses as well as his pain, but there was something vaguely familiar about the tune. He felt a pleasant ache, a yearning sense of melancholy, but though the melody teased at his memory he was unable to place it. His ponderings were interrupted by the arrival of a stout, white-faced maid carrying broth and bread, and a posset of milk, herbs and spices. Despite her considerable girth, she seemed as skittish as a mouse, and when he caught her eye and grinned she squeaked like one, too.

"There's no need to fear, Marjorie. He's as weak as a kitten and harmless for now. I am going to need your help to move him once he's eaten, so please stay close."

He grinned at the maid again and licked his lips, as if reminding her that kittens ate mice, too. Finding her courage, she lifted her chin and glared back.

"Please don't tease my servants. They've been through an ordeal and it's kind of them to share my exile."

"Your exile?"

"Never mind. 'Tis none of your concern. Drink your

broth. All of it. And the posset Marjorie has made you, too."

He wrinkled his nose, but directed a nod of thanks toward the older woman, who stood poised by the door, ready to take flight. She nodded back, giving him a careful look he found somewhat disconcerting. He pulled his gaze away and returned his attention to his hostess.

"I should rather have more brandy."

"That was for the pain. I should think you well insulated by now. You've lost a good deal of blood and you need your liquids. You can have more brandy with your posset once we have you tucked into bed."

He gave her a wicked smile, diverted by the thought of her wrestling his naked body into bed, and obliged her by drinking the broth and tearing into the hearty loaf of bread. He hadn't eaten in two days and he devoured it all, even the warmed milk. It was laced with tincture of opium as well as honey, herbs and spices, and the pain from his wounds quickly faded to a dull memory.

His hunger eased and his thirst slaked, his appetite was whetted for other things. Unfortunately, the abbess insisted, along with maid Marjorie's determined help, on slipping him back into his long shirt before assisting him to his feet and down the hall to a proper bed. It appeared he really was as weak as a kitten, or at least too weak to protest.

She sat beside him a moment and drew the blankets up to his chin. "Sleep now. We are deep in the forest. No one ever comes here. It's safe."

It worried him that she asked no questions. It was clear from his clothing what he was, and her kind were no friends to royalist cavaliers. He was also mightily

annoyed by the smug and watchful presence of her maid
by the door, precluding any attempt at seduction. There
seemed little point in fighting the effects of brandy,
fatigue and the old woman's posset. Waving them both
away with a yawn and a languid hand, he allowed their
ministrations to do their work and slipped gently into
sleep.

ELIZABETH SAT in the parlor wrapped tight in her shawl,
feeling cold and strangely hollow inside. His coming
had been so unexpected. She had feared at first it was
Benjamin at her door until she remembered he was dead.
Perhaps it was shock that left her feeling numb. She laid
her head back and listened to the rain, softer now, pattering on the pane. The fire had died to coals, its merry
crackle now nothing more than the occasional hiss and
pop. She blew out the lamp, and as darkness engulfed
her, her loneliness did, too. She turned her head as if
she could see through wooden door and plaster wall to
where he lay sleeping, and then she stood and started
down the hall.

CHAPTER TWO

SHE PERCHED on the bed beside him, her head turned to one side, examining him by candlelight. His hair was dark, almost blue-black. It gleamed in the firelight as his eyes had done as he watched her, a wicked grin on his lips, in her parlor. She lifted a strand in her fingers, raising it to her lips to kiss before tucking it back behind his ear. Her fingers, curious, as if with a will of their own, traced his straight nose and full lips. There was a thin scar running from cheek to jaw that failed to mar his beauty, and she traced that, too. She felt his brow with the back of her hand. It was cool to the touch. Satisfied he slept soundly and had no fever, she reached to draw the blankets back to his shoulders—

He caught her wrist in a viselike grip, forcing her down on top, and then beneath him, moving so fast she barely had time to squeal.

"Quiet!" he hissed.

She gulped at the feel of cold steel against her throat.

"If you wish to disarm a man, little bird, always check his boots. Is this what you were looking for?" He waved a wrapped packet in front of her nose and, wide-eyed, she shook her head no.

He eased off her, but didn't let go of her wrist. "No? Something else then?"

"You don't remember me at all, do you?" she blurted out.

"Should I?"

"You killed my father." She regretted saying it instantly.

"I've killed many fathers, uncles, brothers and sons. You cannot have failed to notice we are at war. It is what one does. I've yet to kill a woman, though." He removed the knife from her throat and regarded her quizzically. "So are you here now seeking revenge? You've come to kill me in my sleep? It seems a waste of all your earlier embroidery. If you had been patient and left me to it, I might have obliged you by expiring on my own."

"If I wanted to kill you, I could have let slip the scissors while removing the bullet and you would have bled to death in a trice."

"Well then, naughty abbess, I know of only three reasons a woman comes to a man's chambers late at night. If it's not thievery or murder…then it must be this."

He let go of her wrist and cupped her jaw and, half-surprised when she made no protest, he guided her into a gentle kiss. *God's blood perhaps this* is *what she came for!* It seemed strange given her accusation, but there had been many casualties in a civil war that had turned brother against brother and father against son. By *you* she must mean the royalist forces. Doubtless she was lonely. Doubtless she grieved. He was the man to help her, if only for one night. He deepened his kiss, sighing in satisfaction against her lips, and shifted his weight, parting her legs with his knee as his fingers tugged at her stays.

She began to struggle, pulling away and shoving at his arms in an effort to slide out from underneath him. "No! Stop it! Please! Please…I…I didn't come for this. I came to check on you. To check for fever and see if you were comfortable."

He caught her hands and pressed them back against the mattress, leaning over her, his upper body resting on his elbows as his groin lay heavy in the cradle of her thighs. He bent his head to lay a feather-light kiss on the tip of her nose, arching his hips just enough that his rigid cock ground against her warmth. His lips traced her cheekbone with soft kisses, and his tongue flicked the tender skin beneath her ear. "Are you certain, little bird?" he murmured. "*I* am very comfortable at the moment."

"Please let me go."

He let out an elongated sigh and released her. She was lying to herself. She was flushed and eager. He had felt her heat, could smell her excitement. Still…you didn't capture little birds by chasing them. You left a trail of crumbs, enticing them, and waited for them to come to you.

"You don't know what you are missing, love. You're as cold and lonely as I am this night. How often will a handsome soldier fetch up on your door? I'd be good to you," he coaxed. "And tomorrow I will be gone. No one need ever know."

She turned into his arms with an incoherent cry. He fumbled for her cap, impatiently tugging at pins and untying ribbons until her hair tumbled free, spilling down her back in a thick cascade. He buried his hands in it, groaning in satisfaction, gathering silken locks in both fists and drawing her closer into a fevered kiss. She moaned low in her throat and opened to him, generous and welcoming, her tongue meeting his, tentative, inexperienced, but eager to follow where he led. His lips and tongue danced with hers, as his hands worked busily to loosen her stays.

She arched against him in unspoken invitation and his expert hands slid past corset and lace, freeing and petting, squeezing and caressing, until all that lay between his naked flesh and hers was a linen chemise. He trailed hot kisses down her throat and plumped her breasts with his hands, brushing their stiffened peaks with his thumbs. He kissed their tips, pulling them into his mouth and wetting them through the thin material, his hot tongue flicking back and forth as she whimpered beneath him.

She grasped his shoulders, pulling him closer. He sucked her nipples through the fabric as his fingers slid under her shift to find bare skin, working with his mouth and tongue, tugging and teasing. Her breath came in little gasps and soft moans. Her heels dug into the mattress and he could feel her slick heat as she thrust against him. She was as hungry for it as he was, and her body responded to his every touch with ripe abandon.

Biting gently on a nipple, his hand reached down for the hem of her shift and tugged it above her waist. He felt her sudden hesitation. It reminded him that although she seemed eager and willing, she might be lacking in experience. He kissed her lips in reassurance, then slid down her body, his hands on her waist as he kissed her belly, then her soft wet curls. She stiffened and pushed at his shoulders and he relented, returning his kisses to her velvet mouth, wishing he had more than one night with her. Wishing he had the time to teach her. She would be well worth the effort. Even untutored and hampered by whatever constraints her upbringing had taught her, she was a sensual, receptive and giving partner.

His hands ran up and down the back of her thighs, tickling and stroking, rising to cup her firm behind. He moved his fingers to where his mouth had briefly strayed. They played with her curls as he distracted her with hot kisses, and then they reached farther. His knuckles pressed hard against her slick heat and she sighed, opening her legs wider. He slipped inside her and she clenched around him as his thumb and forefinger found her little nub and gently tugged.

No words were spoken between them, but her body arched and twisted, practically sobbing her need. He positioned himself above her, resting his straining erection a moment against her heated core, and then he entered her, very slowly. She was hot, incredibly tight, and he moaned his pleasure. She stiffened and he withdrew, even as his lips claimed hers in a fierce kiss. His tongue stroked hers with sensual abandon and she relaxed and joined in the play.

They thrust and ground against each other and he entered her again, only partway this time. She offered no resistance and he continued, entering her and withdrawing, slowly and repeatedly, until she bucked and ground against him, wanting more. It was she who raked his buttocks, rocking hard against him and rising to meet him, pulling him deep inside her until they were locked in a pulsing, pounding spiral of pleasure. Her rhythmic spasms gripped him tight and spurred his own release.

As he sank against her, lost in a moment's bliss, he held her close to his heart, wondering who she was and why she should affect him so.

Sated and relaxed, he tilted her chin to kiss her face, and was surprised to taste tears on her cheeks. "I didn't hurt you, did I, love?" he asked, dismayed.

She shook her head no and turned away from him, hiding her face as she tried to gather her shift and dress.

Poor little bird. After all she had done for him, the last thing he had intended was to cause her pain. He had hoped to give her pleasure, not guilt or regret. He had hoped to see her smile. He hadn't thought of consequences. In truth, despite her stern appearance and cool manner, from the moment he had seen her he hadn't thought of anything but being with her like this. It had felt so natural, seemed so right. "Don't fly away, little bird," he whispered, staying her with his hand. "Lay with me till morning. Don't be shy." He tossed aside her clothing, kissed her tears and pulled her close, nuzzling the back of her neck.

> *"Small is the worth*
> *Of beauty from the light retired:*
> *Bid her come forth,*
> *Suffer herself to be desired,*
> *And not blush so to be admired.*

"Were you mine, I'd work diligently to make you comfortable flaunting this bounty," he said with a grin. Nevertheless, he tucked the sheet around her, hiding most of her charms. He combed his fingers through her hair, drawing it out in a thick ribbon that glowed red in the candlelight. "You should never hide this. It's glorious. Do you see how it shimmers?"

When she didn't answer, he sighed and tightened an arm around her waist. "Fret not, little bird. We've done nothing wrong. Tomorrow I'll be gone and this will be naught but a pleasant dream. For this one night we have stepped out of time and into another world where we've long been lovers. This night I am a prince from a distant land and you my long-lost love, stolen from me years ago. Cursed by our separation, we have both been slowly freezing. I've searched for you, braving every danger, even these haunted woods. Now I have found you and we can both return to life."

She smiled in the dark, her heart torn and bleeding. His casual kindness had shattered her, destroying her hard-won peace. She had come, a stranger to his bed, and he had treated her not as his whore, but as gently as a much-loved bride. Now he held her close, his voice beguiling, lulling her to sleep as he whispered fairy tales in her ear. But it didn't make things better, and it couldn't stop her tears.

ELIZABETH WOKE to a cold room, a cold bed and a cold dawn. She was alone. Her clothes were strewn about the floor. Red faced, she gathered her shift and skirt and hastened to dress. Hopping from one foot to the other, she struggled to pull her sturdy stockings on, hoping he hadn't left yet, desperate to see him one more time. She shoved her hair under her cap, fastening it with what pins she could find, and hurried down the hall to find him.

He had found his way to the kitchen, and Marjorie had found her courage, clucking at him and plying him with food as he pulled on his boots and coat and adjusted his sword. He stood when he saw her, seeming awkward and shy.

"Good morning, little bird. I must thank you for your help and hospitality, and then, I am afraid, I must be on my way."

She nodded gravely, her eyes asking a question he didn't understand.

He reached into his coat and withdrew a small purse, placing it on the table. "Please accept this, madam, with my thanks."

Her eyes flashed, a storm brewing in them. "Just what do you think happened between us last night?"

He tilted his head, fascinated. In the morning light he could see her clearly. She had a slight dusting of freckles he had failed to notice before, but otherwise she was just as he had imagined. Her eyes were a stormy gray that reminded him of the North Atlantic in winter, and a strand of flame-red hair escaped her bonnet, hinting at the fire he had discovered last night. An unfamiliar longing stirred within him and, unthinking, he reached out to tuck her hair back beneath her cap.

She tossed her head and stepped away and he had the grace to flush. "I meant no offense. Yesterday you took me in when I was in dire need. You offered me shelter, fed me and tended my wounds. Last night was... unexpected. A sweet memory I'll always treasure. I owe you my thanks. I should chop you a season's supply of wood, bring you venison and hare to help you pass the winter, stay here and protect you, but I cannot. I must see to my duty. This—" he gestured helplessly "—was just my clumsy way of trying to repay you."

"Keep it. You'll need it more than I."

He took a step toward her and was amazed when she walked straight into his arms and laid her head on his chest. The awkwardness past, he sighed in relief, and they hugged each other like the very best of friends—or long-familiar lovers. "What's your name, little bird?" he whispered against her temple.

"Elizabeth."

"I am a fugitive, Elizabeth, as you've no doubt surmised, and my first duty is to my king. Though I am generally accounted a scandalous rogue, I *am* known as a man who keeps his promises. I will not forget your help. If ever you have need of me, you've only to ask. I will always do my best for you. You have my word."

"I keep my promises, too," she said gravely.

He was out the door and halfway down the path before he realized he had never offered her his name. Ah, well, 'twas best for all concerned she didn't know. Something else nagged at him, but he didn't stop and he didn't turn back. She was already in the past, a place that was dead to him. A hunted man didn't dwell in the past or imagine the future—he lived in the present. Right now his king had need of him and that was that. He hunched his shoulders and put her firmly from his mind.

Elizabeth stood on the doorstep. The air was crisp, fragrant with the perfume of autumn. Though the sun was only half risen, brilliant shafts of light pierced the trees, painting them in the same fiery reds, golds and yellows that carpeted the ground. It promised to be a

glorious day, but every step he took away robbed it of
its warmth and color.

Her hands clenched into fists as she watched him go;
the childhood friend who'd shared her fascination with
incredible tales and grand adventures; the comrade with
whom she had shared secrets and laughter and her very
first kiss. A man now. One who had no memory of her.
A man who'd killed her father. Her right palm itched
and she released her fist, spreading her fingers to look
at the faint scar still visible on the fleshy pad below her
thumb. She traced it with a forefinger and sighed. When
she looked up again he was gone. When she spoke, it
was barely a whisper.

"God be with you, William de Veres, and keep you
safe from harm."

CHAPTER THREE

ELIZABETH SAT on a bench in the kitchen, her elbows
resting on a trestle table centered in front of a cavernous
fireplace recessed in the wall. It was a low-ceilinged
room of whitewashed plaster and a stone-slab floor.
Utensils, pasty pans and hemp nets for boiling veg-
etables hung from the ceiling beams and walls. Galley
pots, porcelain cups and pewter plates lined the shelves.
A great log set on iron firedogs crackled merrily in the
hearth, warming her face and bathing the room in a soft,
flickering glow. She closed her eyes and sipped her tea
as she listened to Marjorie's humming. It was tuneless
and off-key, but comforting.

Marjorie, bless her soul, hadn't said a word all day
about their unexpected guest or his hurried departure.
Instead, she had set to work making a savory stew in
the large cauldron suspended over the fire, and was
now baking corn cakes and cranberry apple crisp. In
Marjorie's world there was no hurt or sorrow a comforting meal, a warm hug and a cup of tea couldn't set
to rights. When Elizabeth had been a child, motherless
and lonely, Marjorie's ample lap and her offerings of
hot gingerbread had often done just that. She, Mary,
and her husband Samuel, were all that was left of those
days. Or so she had thought until last night.

The shock of seeing William again had yet to subside.

It had taken all her will to remain calm and focused as she'd treated his wounds. Their last encounter she had been eleven years old, about to leave the world of childhood behind her. But she had still believed in magic and promises and heroes, and she had believed in love.

She wondered if he knew that the Parliamentarian general he slew during the fierce fighting at Preston was her own father. There was no reason he should. Though her father knew who William was, the two of them had never met. Her father had been a distant figure even to her, and when she'd blurted out her accusation, there'd been no flicker of recognition in his eyes. It was that as much as anything that had stopped her from saying any more.

William's deed hadn't changed the outcome of the battle, but it had changed the course of both their lives. It had been the only victory the Royalists snatched from a devastating and bloody three-day engagement. It made the brash and daring young William de Veres a hero, and left her orphaned in the charge of her father's stern and rigid younger brother. How strange that the childhood friend she had worshipped had killed her father. She couldn't hate him for it, no more than she could have hated her father if it had been the reverse.

She blushed crimson and bent her head, fighting back a bitter wave of shame as she remembered last evening. No…she couldn't hate him…but what woman with any self-respect would fling herself into the arms of a man who was not her husband? A man who didn't know or care who she was? When had she turned into a faint-hearted wanton? *The moment that I saw him standing at my door, and he didn't see me.* His smile had burned as bright as she remembered, and she had been drawn to his light as she'd always been. Too cowardly to confront him for not remembering, she had feasted on his warmth, no matter how casually it was given. *He called me "little bird."*

As she lay down to sleep she clutched her pillow, remembering a day years ago when a drab and lonely world had suddenly burst into color, full of promise and adventure.

The year her mother died in childbirth, she had lost her father, too. He didn't die. He simply went away. It was only for a few months at first, but with the loss of his wife and long-awaited heir, Hugh Walters's passion had turned to politics and military affairs. He shared Cromwell's distrust of the arrogant and inept Charles I, and his dream of an English republic. He'd been an earl by inheritance, a Parliamentarian by conviction, and a Puritan from expediency, well aware it was the mantle of those now rising to power. It was a severe religion, but as long as Elizabeth observed the proprieties in public, her father paid the rest of it little mind.

She dressed in somber browns and grays, fastened her apron firmly over heavy woolen skirts, and hid the hair that preachers railed against as sinful, under a linen cap. But Puritanism chafed her soul much as her clothing chafed her body: too confining, too restrictive and too tight. Lonely and craving adventure, she engaged in her own private rebellions. With her father away, her governess obsessed with study and prayer, and Marjorie and the servants occupied with running the household, it was seldom anyone noticed.

At first, it amounted to nothing more than escaping

the house to run through the pastures that surrounded her home. Over time, however, she began exploring the extensive woodlands that girdled her father's property, and one hot and hazy late-spring day, she slipped past pasture gates draped with pale roses, and followed a leafy corridor to a tumbling moss-banked stream.

Drawn by distant sounds of conversation and laughter, she hiked her heavy skirts above her knees and ventured across the fast-flowing water, wincing as she stubbed her toe on a submerged rock. The far bank was curved in a hollow around the roots of a giant oak, forming a shallow pool fringed by gracefully swaying cattails. The water here was warm and limpid, and tiny tadpoles tickled her toes. She grinned and stood very still, pretending she was a giant statue, and then splashed her feet and watched them dart away.

A far-off shriek made her look up, but her view was obscured by the riverbank and the surrounding trees. She scrambled up the steep slope, clawing at roots and tufts of grass and muddying her skirts. She knew she was trespassing, but she had come this far, and it only added to the thrill.

When she reached the flat rise beneath the oak, she collapsed in a heap, catching her breath as she surveyed her surroundings. Sunlight dappled the leaves above her, the stream danced and sparkled below, and milk-white clouds sculpted in whimsical shapes drifted by overhead. Soft pink dog roses climbed through a nearby hedgerow and the meadow immediately to her left was painted in brilliant hues. Yellow buttercups, blue irises, white daisies, and a sea of purple orchids swayed with each breath of wind. A light breeze cooled the back of her neck, and the air swelled with the scent of spring-time and freedom, a wild spice to match the unnamed longing in her heart.

She closed her eyes and settled back against the tree trunk, listening to the breeze sighing through the tall grasses. A lark sang close by accompanied by the chattering stream. A sharp little bark that could have been greeting or warning made her open her eyes just in time to see a copper-hued fox slip into the shadows of the thick hedge. She sat up straight and listened intently, wondering what had alarmed it.

Curiosity piqued, she looked up at the oak. Substantial, densely leafed and perfectly symmetrical, its broad branches spread wide like open arms, inviting her to climb. She wrestled with her skirt, brushing off dried mud. By pulling the back hem between her legs and using her apron as a belt, she was able to fashion a clumsy pair of petticoat breeches that gave her some freedom of movement.

Standing on her toes, she hugged the closest branch with both arms, grunting and cursing like one of her father's stable boys as she struggled to flip a leg up and haul herself into the tree. She heard a ripping sound and cringed as her heavy skirts caught on something sharp, but she persevered, twisting and scrambling with elbows and knees until she lay panting, her legs and arms clutched around the lowest limb.

Heartened by her success, she began to climb higher. She tested each branch carefully as she went, though there really was no need. The tree must have been ancient to have grown to such a height, but it was strong and healthy. She inched out along a sturdy limb almost two thirds of the way to the top, one hand gripping the branch above her for support, and parted the foliage. She gasped in surprise and excitement. The view that had been hidden by hedgerow and hills was laid out before her.

She could see for miles. The roof and steeple of the parish church was visible to the north, peeking out from a small copse of trees. To the west, beyond the stream, was a valley surrounded by gently sloping hills and a forest of beech, ash and oak. Its centerpiece was a substantial redbrick manor house that had to be the home of their neighbor, Henry de Veres. Her own home was not that different, though it lacked frivolities such as statues, a tennis court or a bowling green. It was something else that excited her.

She adjusted her position, settling more comfortably in her perch, sprawling out the length of an outstretched limb as she peeped through the leaves, watching with avid interest.

She knew from the kitchen that Lady de Veres was a Puritan just as they were but, according to Marjorie, she had married Henry de Veres, a hard-drinking cavalier, to guard her lands by keeping a careful foot in both camps. Her father grumbled that the lady's lands had become a center for Royalist activity since her marriage, and she was no longer to be trusted. Both Marjorie and her father claimed it not unusual to see elaborately gilded coaches trundle up the drive from London.

It was this that entranced her now. A fascinating world she had often dreamed of, but had never seen up close. She was too far away to hear anything other than the occasional shout of welcome and the distant barking of dogs, but she could make out three toylike coaches. They glittered in the sunlight as tiny horses pawed the ground and tossed their heads, and doll-like men and women, in clothes rivaling the flowers in her meadow, alighted in the courtyard amongst flowing ribbons, jaunty hats and luxuriant plumes.

Closer to her, several men and women wearing gold-and-silver-trimmed riding coats were wending their way up a wide path into the tree-lined hills, accompanied by servants and a pack of dogs. When the breeze shifted in her direction, she could hear them laughing and talking and she assumed it was this that had drifted to her from across the stream. They seemed to be heading in the wrong direction to be after her fox.

She watched it all with fascination, her eyes alight. These elegant, laughing strangers were so foreign to her they might have come from a far distant land. Indeed she supposed they did, for to her and many other country folk, London was an alien, exotic and wicked place, filled with danger and vice, brimming with adventure and excitement and—

She nearly tumbled from her perch, clutching for the nearest bough to save herself as a group of jostling boys tore through a gap in the hedgerow and burst into the meadow, laughing and shouting and hurling insults at one another as they raced across the field. She scrambled backward, hiding in the deepest recesses of the tree, and stayed very still. The tension sweeping the land as Royalists and Parliamentarians argued matters of church and state was ever present in her home in Kent, and idle gatherings of young boys needed little encouragement to be cruel.

These boys were dressed much like adults, bedecked in ribbons, silks and velvets, with white lace at throat and wrist. They must have come from London with their parents. She didn't recognize any of them, except Anthony Seville, who had come to visit with his father once. She had tried to strike up a conversation with him, but his eyes had flicked over her freckles with distaste, and he'd turned his head away in dismissal.

Her attention was drawn to a tall, handsome, sullen-looking boy with long, dark hair and a wicked laugh. He walked with an angry swagger and was quick to shrug off anyone who dared touch him. One poor lad who threw an arm around his shoulders was knocked flat with a closed fist, then flayed with a comment that made the other boys howl with laughter.

The tall lad removed his coat and neckcloth, dropping them negligently on the ground, and came to sit right where she had been sitting only minutes ago. Though he didn't join their games, electing to observe as the other boys insulted one another and ran up and down the meadow, it was clear he was their leader. Wrestling or racing, they turned to him time and again to settle disputes and call the winner of closely fought matches.

When one boy challenged him for calling a race in another lad's favor, his acid reply elicited gasps of shock and nervous titters. Elizabeth edged back out along the bough, straining to hear better. She squealed in alarm as something skittered across her calf. She lost her balance and caught at a tree limb, struggling to maintain her hold, but her toes could find no purchase and her desperate fingers slowly lost their grip. One quick glimpse of a curious squirrel and down she went. Branches bent and snapped, catching at her skirts and slowing her descent, but they didn't stop her from falling in a heap, her skirts about her head, into the arms of the sharp-tongued, dark-haired stranger.

She batted at her skirts, frantically tugging them down to cover her legs as her unwilling captor grunted and strove to replenish the breath she had knocked from his lungs. She scrambled off him, kneeing him in the groin as she escaped, and lurched to her feet, ready to run, only to trip and fall again.

"Well, look what just fell from the tree. A little brown wren that thought she could fly!"

It was the caustic voice of her accidental pillow. She might have been badly hurt if he hadn't broken her fall. It was a wonder that *he* hadn't been, and that he stood there now, towering over her. They all stood there, in a semicircle around her, their startled surprise changing to mocking laughter with a menacing edge. They glanced at him, and at each other, as she righted her skirts and scrambled backward on her elbows. One of them bent to retrieve a small stone, then threw it at her, grazing her arm.

"Begone, you ugly pockmarked creature. Your kind has no business here."

There was nothing she wanted more, but they were crowding her on all sides and she was so frightened her limbs had turned to jelly. She bit her lip, trying not to cry as they closed in on her. One of them picked up a stick and waved it menacingly.

"Are you as stupid as you are ugly? We told you to leave. Best you run, girl."

She knew it was another game. A vicious one. They

wanted her to run so they could chase her. Not that it mattered, her frozen limbs refused to move. She blinked back tears, held up her chin and stared them in the eyes. At the moment, it was the best she could do.

Anthony Seville, who had dined at her table, took a step forward and poked her with his foot. "Maybe she's no wren. Maybe she's a spotted duck. What say we throw her in the water and see if she can swim?"

"Enough!" His voice cut through their taunts and snickers like a knife. "Leave her be, Seville. I've seen you fight. You're ugly enough as it is without some girl breaking your nose."

Embarrassed in front of his friends, her red-faced tormentor tried to save face by turning his fury on her. "What? You are still here? I told you to run, you stupid cow! This is *our* place, claimed in the name of England's rightful king. Go and don't ever come back!"

He bent to grab another rock and hurled it at her, grazing her temple and cutting her scalp. A second later he was thrashing on his back in the sharp gravel of the stream, coughing and screaming for help as water streamed past his mouth and nose. His enraged assailant straddled him, pounding him with his fists. Elizabeth watched, blood trickling down her forehead, openmouthed with shock at her unexpected defender's sudden burst of violence. It took four boys to pull him off his beleaguered prey.

He rose to his feet, shaking Seville's rescuers off with the water. "You'll tell her you are sorry now, you craven hedge-born little shit." He reached for the cringing boy, pulled him from the water, and dragged him up the bank, then threw him down at her feet. "I told you to leave her alone. You should have listened. Now apologize!"

The other boys watched, white-faced and silent.

A dripping and battered Anthony Seville didn't look up from the ground. "I'm sorry," he muttered, whether to her or her new protector she didn't know.

"Now *you* take yourself off and don't come back. This is not your place. It's mine. I say who comes and goes here."

He kicked Seville's rump and the boy fell face-first in the grass, then scrambled to his feet and ran, tears streaming down his face.

The other boys looked about uncertainly. "How now then, de Veres?" one ventured tentatively. "Shall we repair homeward to play at bowls?"

"No. I'm tired of the lot of you. Go someplace else. Maybe you can find a small pet to torture." They looked at him, uncertain whether he mocked them or not.

"Go!"

They hurried off, glancing back and whispering as they slipped through the hedgerow and disappeared from view. Only then did he turn his attention to her, looking straight into her eyes for the first time. For a moment, she stopped breathing. To call his eyes green was to do them an injustice. One moment clear and bright, one moment darkly shadowed, they were as deep and changeable as the forest.

Chuckling, he plucked leaves and grass from her hair, and then he offered her his hand. "Stand up, girl. You are a right mess. Let's see if we can fix you up a little."

She let him pull her to her feet, her heart hammering,

and closed her eyes, blushing as his fingers brushed her hair aside so he could examine her temple.

"Hmm. You are a muddy little warrior, but the wound is not a deep one." He felt around in his pockets. "I've no handkerchief to clean it. Wait for me here." He jumped down the bank to the streambed, tore a piece of linen from his shirt and dipped it in the water, and was back by her side a moment later.

Her heart fluttered as he cleaned her temple with a gentle touch.

"I see you've been sprinkled with pixie dust," he said with a smile, noting the delicate mist of freckles that brushed her cheeks. "What's your name, little bird?" He had a man's voice, smooth and deep despite his youth.

"Elizabeth…Elizabeth Walters."

"My name is William de Veres, Elizabeth. We are neighbors, I believe." He plucked her bonnet from where it lay, forgotten on the ground, and fit it over her hair, tying it snugly in place. "So what were you doing perched in my tree, Lizzy Walters? Are you a Parliamentary scout? No? A fairy perhaps? Maybe you really can turn into a bird," he teased.

"I…I climbed up to see what was over the hedgerow, and then I was watching you and your friends play."

"Ahh! So you are an adventuress! I shall tell you a secret, little bird," he said, leaning in to her. When she bent her head closer he whispered in her ear, "Those aren't my friends, and I don't like them. Not one little bit." He straightened up and took her hand, helping her down the bank and back across the stream. He continued talking as they walked.

"Have you no friends of your own? You should seek

your own adventures instead of watching other people's, Lizzy Walters…and you should stay on your side of the stream."

They had reached the shaded drive that led to her door. He let go of her hand. "Go home, Elizabeth, and stay there. Play with your dolls, if your kind has them. None of us are nice boys, and should you return you might find more adventure than you bargained for."

She struggled for words to thank him, but he had already turned his back and was loping away.

CHAPTER FOUR

ELIZABETH SIGHED and rolled over, wrestling with her blankets and punching her pillow. Her heart ached in old familiar ways. She wanted things she'd never imagined before last night. William's lovemaking had introduced her to an exquisite pleasure she had not known possible and he had awoken longings inside her that refused to go back to sleep. He had also left her feeling hurt and confused. Should she have told him who she was? Well, it was too late for that now. Had he meant anything he'd said the last time they met, all those years ago? How could he and not remember her?

Nevertheless, for one night he'd been hers again, even if he hadn't known it, and if she went the rest of her life without seeing him, nothing could take that away. But there was no denying that right now she felt as lonely and heartsick as she'd ever felt in her life. Sleep was going to be a long time coming. *Just like it was the first night we met.*

Only then she'd been giddy and full of excitement, replaying the events of the day over and over in her mind, repeating his name. William de Veres...William de Veres...Elizabeth Walters and William de Veres. He was handsome, charming, gallant and kind. He had rescued her from her enemies and carried her away like a knight of old. That morning she had embarked on a grand adventure, and along the way she had fallen from a tree, made a new friend and fallen in love. She closed her eyes, resting them, and surrendered to a tide of unruly memories.

He hadn't told her she couldn't come back, only that she shouldn't, and she had chosen to take his words as a dare. She hadn't had the chance to thank him properly, and it was only fitting that she do so. The next day, armed with an offering of sugar cakes from Marjorie's kitchen, she followed the heavily wooded path to the stream, her basket in her arms, chanting "Please let him come…please let him come…please let him—"

She stopped at the edge of the stream. It was a challenge to manage her skirts, her basket and her shoes, and she wobbled dangerously several times, wincing as sharp stones dug into her tender feet. The bank on the far side presented another obstacle. She put her shoes and basket down, and stood with hands on hips, pondering. It was too steep to climb without using both hands and she was not about to leave Marjorie's sugar cakes by the streambed for her wily friend the fox to rifle through. Struck by a sudden inspiration, she crested the bank on all fours, her shoes stuffed deep in her pockets and the handle of her basket clenched tight between her teeth.

"Ahem."

Startled, she lifted her head. He was seated comfortably beneath the oak, using it as a backrest, his hands folded behind his head and his long legs stretched out. His eyes sparkled with curiosity and amusement. She scrambled to her feet, shoving the basket behind her back with one hand while the other frantically captured loose locks of hair and shoved them back under her cap.

He regarded her with a slight smile and one brow cocked. "Well, well. Yesterday you were a little bird, spying in the trees. Today a little red fox stealing baskets. It seems, fair nymph, you are indeed fay, though sylph or sidhe, I cannot say."

Her face broke into a pleased grin. "You made a rhyme."

He returned her smile and tilted his head. "Some kind of water sprite, I should think. You've silvery eyes that sparkle like yon stream."

She blushed and ducked her head. "You really shouldn't say such things. The preacher says talk of fairy folk and magic is wicked and sinful."

His voice turned cold. "*I* am wicked and sinful, in ways you could never imagine, little bird. You are not welcome here, Elizabeth. This is my private place. I come here to be alone."

Her face fell. She shivered as if the sun had gone behind a cloud. She took an awkward step back, her bottom lip quivering, not sure what she had done wrong. "I am sorry to have bothered you. I…I just brought you these. To thank you for your help the other day." She laid the basket on the ground, avoiding his eyes, and turned to go.

He reached for her hem, tugging on it to stop her. "Lizzy, wait."

She turned to face him, uncertain.

He struggled to smile, clearly trying to put his black mood behind him. "Where are my manners? You came bearing gifts. Sit. Show me." And as quick as that, the sunshine was back and the dark clouds gone.

She sat beside him, cross-legged beneath her skirts, and opened the basket.

"Sugar cakes!" His enthusiasm was clearly genuine and she beamed with pleasure. He devoured three of the spicy almond confections before thinking to offer her one. She shook her head no.

"They are all for you. It's the least I could do. Some people think our Marjorie makes the best sugar cakes in all the world," she added proudly.

"Your Marjorie is the sugar cake queen," he agreed, licking his fingers.

"That is very kind of you to say, though I am sure you can have sugar cakes whenever you wish."

"I hardly ever have sugar cakes, Lizzy Walters. I was handed over to the family chaplain as soon as I could walk, and my mother is one of you. Neither she or my... tutor...approve of anything sweet."

"One of me? What do you mean?"

"She may dress in peacock's clothes and strut with the rest of them, but underneath she's as strict and cold as a Puritan clergyman. She doesn't talk, she preaches. When the company leaves, our house is as quiet as a tomb. The servants whisper, one risks a whipping to laugh or joke, and indulgences such as sweets are forbidden."

"But I'm not like that!" she protested.

"No, you are not. But you're hiding behind your clothes, too. You and my mother are both impostors."

She adjusted her bonnet, tucking in a lock of hair that kept escaping, and he reached out a hand to stop her.

"Why do you do that? I like your hair." He gave the errant strand a gentle tug and she blushed to her roots.

"The preacher says a woman's hair is sinful, and that red hair is the worst."

"Is that so?" He snatched her cap from her head, and long coppery curls tumbled down her back.

He grinned in appreciation. "So that's what you've been hiding!"

She wrestled with him, mortified and almost in tears, trying to get her cap back, but he held it just beyond her reach, laughing even as she punched and hit him.

"Give it back! You're a bully."

"No, I'm not," he snapped, tossing it back to her, the black mood on him again. "I hate bullies. You saw what I did to Seville."

She wrapped her hands around her legs, hugging herself, and rested her chin on her knees. Her cap trailed between her fingers, forgotten. "I was afraid you were going to kill him. They all were."

"I have a temper, Lizzy, but it doesn't rule me. I use it. I seldom fight, but when I do, I win. I wanted him to know what it felt like."

"Do you think he'll be nicer now he knows?"

"No, little bird," he chuckled. "But I think now he will leave you alone." He reached out a hand to smooth her hair. "Sometimes, those who are supposed to be men of God lie, Lizzy. There's nothing sinful about your hair except in the mind of jealous old men. The great Iceni queen Boudicca, who united the tribes and drove the Roman legions from ancient London, had hair like yours. So did your own namesake, Good Queen Bess. Gloriana they called her. Some say she was the greatest ruler England has ever known. *She* was likened to a fairy queen, and there was nothing wicked or sinful about her." He rolled over onto his stomach and plucked a stalk of cowslip, tickling her chin as he recited.

"Upon a great adventure he was bound,
That greatest Gloriana, to him gave,
That greatest Glorious Queen of Faerieland,
To win him worship, and her grace to have,
Which of all earthly things he most did crave."

"What poem is that?"

"'Tis called *The Faerie Queene*. It's filled with elves and dwarves, knights and dragons and grand adventures. It was written by some fellow named Edmund Spenser, in honor of Queen Elizabeth, who is said to have liked it very much. Gloriana, the fairy queen, is meant to represent Elizabeth herself, as is Britomart, a beautiful maiden who falls in love with a knight she sees in her father's magic mirror. She becomes the greatest knight in faerieland as she searches for the man who stole her heart. So you see? Flame-haired beauties may be powerful and dangerous, but just like nymphs and fairies, it doesn't mean they're evil."

"Does your tutor teach you this?"

"Oh…Master Giffard has taught me many things, but not this."

Something cold glittered in the depths of his eyes but it was gone so quickly she wondered if she'd imagined it.

"I should like to hear some more of this poem, William, if you please."

"It is a very long poem, Elizabeth. Perhaps some other time. Right now, I've a mind to teach you how to fight." He jumped to his feet and held out his hand, snapping his fingers.

She ignored them disdainfully. "I am not a hound for you to snap your fingers at, William de Veres, and ladies don't fight."

"Redheaded ones do. Boudicca fought from a war chariot and burnt Londinium to the ground, and Elizabeth dressed in armor, her hair unbound, to face the Spanish Armada when they menaced England's shores. Besides…girls that can't fight get thrown into streams to see if they can swim like ducks."

She made a face and pelted him with a tuft of grass, but his grin was infectious and she allowed him to pull her to her feet. "If I am a queen of faerieland, do I not have knights to protect me?"

He made a courtly bow, waving his hand as if he held a Cavaliers hat. "I shall be Arthur to your Gloriana, Artegall to your Britomart, even your Redcross Knight, but I shan't always be around to protect you, little bird, particularly if you insist on wandering away from your home."

"Are all of them from your poem?"

"Yes, they are, but if you wish to know more about them you must show yourself worthy. Faerieland is a place for the brave and the bold. It is no place for a silly girl who can't even wrestle her cap back."

He reached out and snatched her bonnet from her fingers, laughing as he backed away, dangling it just beyond her reach. She narrowed her eyes and charged him but he darted to the left, reaching one arm out to hook her waist a moment before she would have hurtled down the bank and into the stream. As they tumbled to the ground in a heap, he was laughing so hard he couldn't speak. She had landed on his chest and she shoved against him hard, pushing herself to her feet. She stood with arms folded, glaring as she waited for him to stop.

He wiped his eyes, raised himself on his elbows and took a deep breath. "Well, Lizzy Walters…you really are a redhead it seems. I think it safe to say you make up in enthusiasm what you lack in technique." Clearly amused by his own wit, he collapsed in helpless laughter again.

"I don't think you are funny at all and I don't think it's fair," she snapped. "You are a good deal bigger, taller and stronger, than I am."

He rolled onto his side, leaning on one elbow, and rested his cheek against his palm. "So are most men. What if I were to tell you there are ways you can use that to your advantage?"

"I don't see how."

"Britomart is the most important knight in *The Faerie Queene*. People were always underestimating her. She was a young and beautiful girl, but she defeated every knight she met except her own true love, and even then, only because their fight was stopped. She traveled the world, met Merlin the magician, took on six knights at once and bested them, and even rescued Artegall and the others from slavery."

"She is just a girl in a story." Despite her words, Elizabeth was fascinated.

He shrugged and began trailing his fingers through the tall grass, looking for a stem to put between his teeth.

"Show me."

He gave her a brilliant smile. And then he taught her how to make a proper fist.

She returned the next day and he was there waiting, sighing in mock exasperation as he reached down a hand to pull her up the slope. "Back again, are you?"

She looked at him uncertainly. "Would you rather I didn't come here, William?"

"You can come, little bird. I'll share my kingdom with you, provided you obey its laws."

"What laws?"

"No bonnets are allowed," he said, plucking her cap from her head. She shrieked and gave chase, pummeling him with a well-formed fist.

"Ow! Ouch! Enough!" He laughed as he rubbed his shoulder. "You've learned that lesson well enough. Here. Have it back. Just don't put it on."

"I am *not* a girl who can't get her cap back," she said triumphantly.

"Indeed you are not. You are Britomart in the flesh. But even she had her nurse with her, acting as her squire. How is it you roam so free? Is there no one to watch over you?"

She flopped down on the ground and shook her hair loose, removing all the pins and putting them in her pocket. "There are servants, but they have work enough to do without following me around. My governess is very attentive when my father is at home, but that is not very often, and my mother died three years ago."

"I'm sorry." He settled down beside her. "Do you miss her still?"

"Yes. She was always there to talk to and she used to tell me stories just like you. I find it hard to remember her face sometimes, but she was always humming. She sang to me before I went to bed, and sometimes at night, I close my eyes and hear her still. My father and Marjorie say I shouldn't be sad. They say she's in heaven with my brother, but at her funeral, the preacher said she died in childbirth as punishment for the sins of Eve, and we must all pray for her soul."

"Bah!" He snorted in disgust and folded his arms, nudging her shoulder with his. "I told you before you can't believe everything that priests and preachers tell you. My tutor is a chaplain. When I was younger, he used to sleep in my bed, to keep me safe. He was always telling me what he did was for the good of my soul."

"And did he keep you safe?"

His laugh was harsh. "He was a hypocrite and liar. How do you know your preacher is any better? If you are going to believe in fairy tales, they should at least make sense. The Spartans thought women who died giving birth were heroes, just like men who died in battle, and they put special markers on their graves. Why would God punish someone for something they didn't do?"

"So you think my mother is in heaven, too." Her face lit with a happy smile.

He was about to correct her, but she seemed so pleased he didn't have the heart. "I think you should listen to your father."

"I wish he was with us more."

"I don't even know mine."

"I don't know mine anymore, either. He never talks or plays with me since Mama died. He's always do—"

"No, little bird. I mean I've never met him."

"How can that be? Do you miss him?"

"How can you miss someone you've never met? He married my mother, left promptly on the king's business, and never came back. He sends a letter now and then."

"Well, I am sure he's very proud of you. His business must be terribly important. Doubtless he will come to see you soon."

He chuckled and mussed her hair. "It has been twelve years, Lizzy Walters. He's not that interested. I don't think he and my mother liked each other very much."

"Well, at least you have your mother and your tutor to watch over you."

"No one watches over me. Not anymore, and that's the way I like it. My mother thinks me an unruly child and gave me to my tutor to correct. He's a small fellow and I am grown too big for him to chastise. I can lay him flat—" he bent his elbow and made a fist "—and I have. And do you know what, Lizzy?"

"What?" Her eyes were round as saucers.

"God didn't strike me dead. He dare not complain to my mother. He knows I have secrets to tell."

"What secrets?"

"None fit for your ears."

She sniffed her annoyance and changed the subject. "So your mother and father didn't love each other?"

He scoffed. "No one marries for love, except in stories. People marry for property and position, and one day so will you."

"I will not!"

He chuckled and tugged on her hair. "Yes, you will.

It's a woman's lot. Men go into the military, the church, or they manage estates, and women marry and raise children. Your family is not that different from mine. Your father is a landowner and an earl. He sits in parliament when it's open and has a large estate. You are an heiress, Lizzy. You'll be married in just a few years."

"I shall never marry and let some brutish fellow rule me, take my land and money and leave me behind."

"My mother's done well enough by it," he said with a smile. "There's no man dares rule her, including my father."

"Well, Marjorie says the happiest women are widows. They own themselves and their property, too. *That* is what I am going to be."

He snorted in amusement.

"It is not funny! And it's rude to laugh at people the way you do."

"I am sorry, Lizzy. I've laughed more since I've met you than I have in all my life I think, but it *is* funny. You clearly haven't thought it through. You *have* to marry in order to become a widow," he pointed out reasonably.

"Well…" she folded her arms across her chest and pouted "…perhaps I shall marry you, Will." He collapsed in helpless laughter and she elbowed his side, annoyed. "What's so funny now?"

"If you marry me, you'll have to kill me to become a widow, little bird, and to do that you'll need to fight a good deal better than you do now."

She growled and jumped up, wielding an imaginary knife. "Think you I cannot, de Veres? I will teach you to regret those words!"

He hooked an arm behind her knees and dragged

her down. They wrestled in the lush green grass and he tickled her mercilessly until she begged him to stop. When he did, he was lying on top of her, and there was something more than playfulness in his eyes. She closed her eyes, her heart thumping, waiting breathlessly for him to kiss her, but he leaped to his feet instead, pulling her up beside him.

They spent the rest of the afternoon play fighting and wrestling. He taught her where she should put her elbow and knees to incapacitate a man, how to strike at his throat, how to twist and shift her body so a man's greater weight worked against him, and some interesting things she could do with her hairpins. When she accidently gave him a black eye with her elbow, he only grinned.

He recounted more of Britomart's adventures in faerieland as they lay recuperating and savoring the late afternoon sun.

He tugged at her heavy skirt with one hand as he spoke. "Britomart didn't fight in her skirts, you know, but in a fearsome set of armor from her father's treasure hoard 'that bore a lion passant in a golden field.' If you had armor, I could take you on adventures through yon hawthorn bushes, to faerieland itself." He tickled her chin with a daisy.

She grinned. "I have never met anyone as fanciful as you, William de Veres."

"Pfft! It is not I who named them fairy thorn. It's said they guard the entrance to the otherworld itself. But if you are too scared to see what's on the other side—"

"I am *not* too scared! I climbed this tree almost to the top all by myself."

"All right, then, Lizzy Walters. Meet me here tomorrow and we'll go on an adventure."

The next day, with clothes filched from one of her father's stable boys hidden beneath her dress, and equipped with a sturdy branch to serve as a sword, she crawled through the hedgerow with William. And so the adventures of Artegall and Britomart began. Throughout the summer and into the fall they climbed trees, fought invisible enemies, explored the nearby woods and hills, and trapped minnows in the dammed up pools they built in the stream. William taught her how to fish, how to throw a rock and how to send a flat stone skipping across the water. Boon companions, they built a raft that carried them past two villages and all the way to the River Medway, where they abandoned it rather than be swept downriver to the Thames. They didn't get home until well after dark, earning William a whipping and Elizabeth a scolding from both Marjorie and Mary, who were the only ones who'd noticed she was gone.

In quieter times, they lay in the hollow beneath the great oak, watching the sky and talking of matters great and small. Sometimes William would pull his knees up and she would use his legs as a backrest, humming as the clouds passed by overhead. Sometimes he would mention his tutor, and his face would go hard and his eyes grow cold. She knew there was something eating away inside of him. His disdain for the church made her suspect something evil, and though he always changed the subject, she gleaned enough to guess that he had been trapped in something vile.

One day he reached for her hand, and their fingers tangled together as they lay shoulder to shoulder on the moss-covered ground. With her hand in his, she felt anchored to something enduring, and yet so light she might float upon air.

One blustery day he gave her his coat and hugged her against him to keep her warm. They spent many a crisp afternoon, cuddled together under his coat, sharing their warmth after that.

As the shadows grew longer, the nights grew cooler, and the hills gleamed flame and gold, William took to visiting her in Marjorie's kitchen. There they would sit in front of a blazing hearth, heads bent together in earnest conversation while playing at cards, cribbage, and Nine Men's Morris. Marjorie watched them with a careful eye, but it seemed to please her to hear Elizabeth's laughter and see her smile.

Her father came home in late January to say a quick hello and goodbye again. The king had issued a charge of treason against five members of the Commons who opposed him, and all across the country people were declaring themselves for Parliament and against the king. It was the excuse those who looked to Parliament and Cromwell had been waiting for. He was preoccupied, but not too distracted to surprise her at table.

"Who is this lad I've seen skulking about the courtyard and kitchen?"

She opened and closed her mouth, at a loss for words. It was so long since her father had noticed anything about her she was completely unprepared.

"He's William de Veres, one of the neighborhood lads. He visits our Lizzy from time to time," Marjorie said, stepping in with the easy familiarity of a lifelong retainer.

"I thought as much." He returned his gaze to Elizabeth. "He's not for the likes of you, my dear. War is fast approaching, and he's not our kind. He and his ilk will soon be our enemies."

"He's just a boy, Father, who lives across the way. His mother is—"

"His mother is a duplicitous harpy who switched her allegiance to further her own ends. The boy is wild, ungovernable and prone to violence, a petulant lad I am told, full of wickedness."

"But, Father, he's not like that at all, I—"

"Enough, Elizabeth! Remember to whom you are speaking. I heard it from Master Giffard, who is his tutor and the family chaplain."

The family chaplain? Her outrage at the accusation made her forget herself. "That man spoke with you about William? When? Why?"

"You question your elders? Your own father? The warning was well advised. It seems you are already under the influence of this boy's evil nature. You are young yet, but it will be time to arrange a suitable marriage soon enough. I will have no hint of scandal attached to your name. He is not to come here again. Do you hear me?"

She understood the implicit threat and his words frightened her. Why was everyone talking about marriage? First William, and now her father. She didn't want to think of such things. If there *were* a path to faerieland she would gladly take it, and never grow older.

"Elizabeth?"

She nodded and bowed her head. "Yes, Father, I understand."

Appeased, her father placed a hand on her shoulder and gave it a gentle squeeze. "It is for your own good, my dear, as I am sure you'll appreciate someday. Let there be no more unpleasantness between us, daughter. We shall speak of it no more."

She rose and curtsied, intending to retire to her chamber, but stopped on the stairs when she heard her father speak.

"She is not to see him, Marjorie. Do you understand? You will tell him she is not receiving if he comes to call."

"But he seems a good lad, Master Hugh, and she has no one to play with. She's been lonely since her mother died."

"The boy is a bad seed, Marjorie. He was a sickly child, prone to fits of anger and disorders of the stomach and the mind, and from what I am told things have not improved. He does what he pleases no matter the consequences. He will not obey his mother or his tutor, though he be whipped and starved for it. He even took his fists to the man! He is dangerous, Marjorie, perhaps to her person and most certainly to her reputation. See that he does not visit here again."

She crept up the stairs to her room, keeping her anger and rebellion mute. She had lost her mother. Her father was in residence at most two months a year, and he wanted to take away her best and only friend. *No matter. He'll be gone again soon. He says William may not visit here? Fine! Then I will visit him.* She was not about to give him up. A wild and troubled youth he might be, but not a wicked one, and to her he was a hero. He had rescued her from those who would harm her. He brightened her life with laughter, stories and adventures, and in her world he was the sun.

In March, as tender buds swelled tight on swaying branches and the first slender shoots of spring poked through the earth, Parliament seized the country's militia, the only armed body of men in England. In June, Parliament called for a new constitution, demanding that all church and military affairs, as well as the appointment of all ministers and judges, come under the control of Parliament instead of the king. None of it mattered to them. They slew invisible dragons, rescued unsuspecting villagers and defended castles sprung from boulders and wind-felled trees. When they lay together side by side, chewing on blades of grass and watching as processions of fantastical shapes and figures paraded overhead, her posture matched his exactly, right down to the way she clasped her hands behind her head and the angle she bent her knee.

Then came the day he told her his mother had decided he had outgrown his tutor. He was going away for a gentleman's education. He would be leaving soon for school. His face was lit with excitement and relief, and the silent strain that she barely noticed but was always with him had lifted. She was happy for him, she enjoyed his excitement, but the pang that filled her heart nearly stole her breath away.

He noticed her white face and grinned, ruffling her hair. "Don't worry, Lizzy Walters. I'll not forget you. I'll be back to visit so often you will not even know I am gone—I'll prove it to you if you're brave enough."

She watched, round eyed, as he pulled a silver-hilted dagger from his pocket. The razor-sharp blade was a fearsome weapon for anyone, let alone a twelve-year-old youth. He cut himself first, resting the blade against the fleshy pad of his thumb and slicing in a quick downward stroke without even wincing. She held out her hand, trembling but brave, and he smiled his approval and handed her the knife. She did exactly as she had seen him do, though she closed her eyes when she made the stroke. He clasped her hand in his, joining their palms and their blood together. "We are bound by blood now, Elizabeth Walters. I pledge you my friendship unto death. I promise to aid and defend you, never to forsake you, and to only speak the truth. I promise to return."

She swallowed and took a deep breath. A blood oath was a solemn thing. "I, Elizabeth Walters, pledge you my friendship unto death." She lifted her chin, caught up in the moment. "I shall brave any danger, face any foe, to protect you, and I shall always stand ready to give you my aid. I shall keep all your confidences though I be tortured, and I shall always speak the truth. I promise to wait for you, never to forsake you and to always bid you welcome."

Taking hold of the dagger together, they carved their initials and the date into the oak. Then he did something wonderful. He put his hands on her waist and pulled her into a tight hug. It lasted a very long time. "There's nothing here I'll miss but you," he whispered into her ear. "I love you, little bird."

"I love you, Will," she whispered back, her heart welling with joy and sorrow. She leaned her head against his chest and held him closer, savoring the warmth and feel and scent of him, knowing that once she let go, he would be gone. She felt him kiss her hair, and she turned her head to kiss his cheek. He put two fingers under her chin and lifted her face to his. She closed her eyes, trembling and shy, and felt his breath against her lips. He brought his hands up into her hair and leaned his forehead against hers, and then he kissed her. It was hesitant and awkward and he stepped back right away. She opened her eyes to catch him blushing and her heart soared.

She waited for him long past the time he was meant to return, visiting the meadow whenever she could escape her new governess, her heart thrumming every time, in the hope of finding him there. She climbed the ancient oak tree and perched within its branches to watch his house for any sign that he had come home. Coaches came and went, but he was never in them. In August, King Charles raised his banner, formerly declaring war. Months passed, then years. Battles were won and lost, the war ended and then it started again, and he never returned. When her father died, and her uncle came to take her, she could wait no more. She had never seen him again. Until last night.

CHAPTER FIVE

ELIZABETH WOKE to Marjorie's panicked screams and the crack of splintering wood as booted feet kicked down her door. She leaped out of bed and raced down the hall in her bed-gown and nightcap. Mary and Samuel huddled in a corner as soldiers in breastplates, pot helmets and buff leather coats ransacked the kitchen and parlor, breaking furniture, slashing cushions and ripping down curtains with their swords. Marjorie made a stalwart defense of the kitchen with nothing but a broom, until a hard-faced soldier cracked her across the jaw with the back of his steel gauntleted left hand, sending her crashing to the floor.

Biting back a scream, shaking with shock and fury, Elizabeth gestured for Mary and Samuel to stay where they were. Heart hammering, sick with fear, she dashed to Marjorie's side. Soldiers were all around her, overturning flour kegs, cutting open sacks, and tearing shelves and cupboards from the walls. Her fingers pressed against Marjorie's neck, just beneath her jaw, and she exhaled in relief when she detected a faint pulse. A moment later, a grinning soldier with a bulbous nose and a scar that twisted half his face, grabbed her arm and wrenched her to her feet.

"What are you doing? What is wrong with you?"

she shouted, struggling to break free. "What kind of cowards attack servants and old women?"

"And who might you be, girl?" he growled.

"It don't matter. She's young is what she is," a grinning pikeman sneered.

"This be your house, mistress?" the scarred man asked, shaking her.

"Yes! Yes, it is. And you've made some kind of mistake! We are for Parliament here. Why do you invade my home?"

"We are for Parliament here," he repeated in a mocking voice. "Over here, Sergeant! I think we caught the mouse you're looking for." He shoved her toward a beefy man with close-cropped hair and eyes that glittered like ice. The sergeant righted an overturned stool with one foot and shoved her down hard on it.

"He's right? You are mistress here?"

"Yes. Yes, I am. And you have no right to—"

He slapped her so hard he loosened a tooth and painful lights flickered at the edge of her vision. "I will do the talking, woman. You'll keep your mouth shut except to answer questions. Where is he?"

Her heart sank. Her cheek burned as if it were on fire, but her jaw was numb. She closed her eyes and gathered her strength. If she admitted she had knowingly harbored a Royalist cavalier they would all be lost. Though she was almost choking on it, she swallowed her fear. "Where is who?"

He hit her again, knocking her off the stool. "Where is the pretty gentleman you sheltered here?" he growled. "You say you are for Parliament? Then it is a traitor or a liar you be."

She was on her hands and knees. Her face was bruised and one eye already swollen shut. She looked up at her tormentor with hatred in her heart. He wasn't the first bully she had known. Her hand closed over a long shard of broken glass and for a wonderful moment she remembered a tale from long ago, of a warrior maid and a magical spear. She imagined rising to her feet and stabbing him through the throat, but she couldn't take on six armed men, and if she tried, her people would surely die. She let go of the glass, but fumbled at her bonnet, freeing a silver hairpin to hide in her sleeve, knowing full well they might decide to kill them all anyway.

The sergeant grabbed her by her hair, hauling her to her feet. "You'll tell us where he is, mistress, or we'll kill the lot of you, only you'll be last and longest."

"I don't know where he is or who he was!" she shouted. "He was wounded. A stranger. He appeared at my door. I tended him as I would any wounded man and then he left. He never even gave me his name."

"I am thinking maybe the lass needs another kind of persuading," the scar-faced man said with a wide grin.

"What's going on here, Sergeant Lewis?"

A tall, broad-shouldered man in black silk breeches, velvet coat and a tricorn hat stood in the doorway, slapping his gloves in his hands. He might easily have passed as a cavalier. His sand-colored hair was tied in a neat queue and although he had pleasant, easy features and spoke in an even tone, his gaze was sharp and his voice and bearing marked him as one accustomed to being obeyed.

"He was here, Captain. The man we've been hunting."

The sergeant reached for a metal cup and overturned it on the long oak table. A rust-colored musket ball skittered across the table and fell to the floor. "We was just persuading the *lady* to tell us all about it."

"You'll not be molesting women under my command, Lewis," the captain snapped. "Release her immediately! How are we to maintain discipline amongst the men if you show none? What is her name?"

"Uh, we haven't got round to asking yet, Sir."

"What is your name, woman?"

Two hands steadied her shoulders. Her vision was blurred but the voice sounded familiar. "Captain Nichols?"

The captain frowned and took a step closer, examining her battered face. He brushed back a mat of tangled hair to get a closer look. She shuddered and flinched as his gentle touch left burning trails of pain on her bruised and swollen skin. "Hell and damnation! Elizabeth? Elizabeth Walters?" He turned to face the sergeant and his men. "Do you have any idea who this is, you fools? This is the daughter of General Hugh Walters! One of the Lord Protector's closest friends. I will see you all whipped for this!"

"The one that got killed? How was we to know?"

"I swear, Lewis, if you and the rest of these fools don't get out of my sight this second, I will have you all hanging from yon tree by morning."

"Aye, Captain!" It took closer to ten seconds and a bit of pushing and shoving, but in short order they had left the room.

Captain Nichols shook his head in disgust. "I am sorry to see you and your servants so ill used, Lizzy.

Most of my soldiers are God-fearing and righteous, but Lewis and his men are a bad lot. They will be punished severely. I promise you it will not happen again." He wet a cloth and began dabbing at her face.

Elizabeth didn't know if she was more shocked by his sudden appearance and unexpected rescue, or the fact that she'd heard him swear, something he'd never done in any of his visits to her father at their home. But she did know that Marjorie needed her help. She pushed him away. "Captain, I beg you. Please! Let me tend to my servants."

"Brown! Wilcox! Pick up the cook, carefully, mind, and settle her in what's left of the parlor. Then fetch the surgeon to attend to her." He returned his attention to Elizabeth. "Rest easy, Elizabeth. You have been injured yourself. Our surgeon is very skilled in these matters. One or another of us is always getting bashed in the head. He will soon set her to rights. She is your Marjorie, isn't she? I remember her well."

"Yes," Elizabeth managed, fighting back tears. She was unaccountably grateful he had noticed. One of her father's most trusted men despite his youth, Captain Nichols had been a frequent guest whenever her father had been home. Perhaps ten years older than she was, he had always been kind, making a point of smiling and winking when he saw her and often including her in conversation as if she were an adult. Once he had even let her ride his horse. Now there were lines of weariness bracketing his mouth and a sadness to his eyes that hadn't been there before, but in the middle of this sudden terror and chaos, his familiar face reminded her of her father, safety and home. He embraced her gently, careful of her battered face and respectful of her person, and for a moment she sank against him, taking shelter in his arms.

"Sit now, Elizabeth." He placed his hands on her shoulders and guided her to a chair by the table, and then took off his coat to drape over her shoulders. "I shall make us some tea."

She watched as the surgeon tended to Marjorie and the commanding figure of Captain Nichols filled a kettle and hung it over the fire to boil. When the tea was ready, he brought them both a cup and sat beside her, grinning at her incredulous perusal.

"What? You needn't stare at me as if I were a two-headed calf. A good soldier has many of the same talents as a good wife. He can make his own dinner, mend his own clothes and even do his own laundry." His voice became serious. "Elizabeth, let me help you. I need you to tell me what went on here. The man you aided was a spy and agitator for Charles Stuart. He was carrying some very important documents. We believe he is involved in a scheme to foment a new rebellion."

Oh, William. What storm have you wrought? "All I did was help a wounded stranger, Captain Nichols, as was my Christian duty. I'm afraid I can tell you no more than that."

"Cannot or will not, Elizabeth? I can wait another day for your Marjorie to improve, but then you will have to come with me. You are in a great deal of trouble, I am afraid. You may trust that I shall do what I can to protect you, but it would help a great deal if I knew exactly what went on so I can present it in the best possible light. Perhaps he held you at gunpoint. Threatened your servants. Maybe he—"

"I am really very sorry, Captain Nichols. I am most grateful for your help, but I have told you everything I can." Her voice was emphatic. She was tempted to confide in him, at least in part. She was so tired of carrying her burdens alone. But though she trusted he would try to protect her, he was one of Cromwell's men. Anything she told him to save herself would certainly be used against William. Her palm itched and she made a small fist as she thought back to the oath she'd made to William under the oak. It would mean nothing to Cromwell or Captain Nichols. It only had meaning for her.

THEY STAYED two extra days, until Marjorie was up and about again. When word came that the Lord Protector himself would examine her in the next county where he was reviewing troops, the captain escorted her, riding beside her and chatting as though she were not a prisoner but a guest. They talked of Kent and her father. He strove to put her mind at ease, telling her she'd made an innocent mistake and that her father's name would protect her.

When they arrived at the makeshift military tribunal set up in a field, he stood beside her. Her knees quaked and she could barely stand, but the captain winked and took her by the arm, escorting her into a tent filled with hard-eyed soldiers who regarded her with varying degrees of contempt. She clutched his arm as if it were a lifeline. "Fear not, Elizabeth. He does not make war on women and his bark is much worse than his bite."

Elizabeth was not sure she believed that. Though known for his courtesy to the fair sex, Cromwell was a hard man, one who had risen from captain to lieutenant general in three years, and minor country gentleman to ruler of England in ten. A man of deep religious convictions, he was a mild-looking figure, with a long, gentle face, soulful eyes and a high brow. But she was well aware he had been responsible for the ruthless massacre and starvation of hundreds of thousands of his Irish subjects. At the moment he was glaring at her and he looked severe, disapproving, tired and ill.

He motioned for Captain Nichols to take a seat, and then began barking a series of questions. She tried to imagine she was Britomart, strong and brave. Squaring her shoulders she looked him in the eyes and tried to answer honestly when she could.

"This man? William de Veres? How well did you know him? Was he your lover?"

She flushed and stiffened her chin. *Does one night make a man your lover?* "I only met the man that night, Lord Protector."

"So you claim you had no idea who he was or what he was about?"

"I didn't ask his name or his business, nor did he offer it."

"Why not? He knocked on your door, you say. Wouldn't an honest person ask him his name and his business before bidding him enter? Do you make any stranger welcome in your home? Even those who arrive in the dead of night?"

"There's a name for women who do that," an overstuffed colonel sniggered. Cromwell quelled him with a look.

"No, Lord Protector. But I had barely opened the door when he fell on the floor unconscious. He was wounded and bleeding. I tended to him as an act of Christian charity. Something I would do for any wounded creature that happened on my door, just as my father taught me." The last was spoken with a hint of challenge. It was a defense and a reminder.

"Ah, yes. Your father. He was a good friend. A fine man and a mighty warrior. It pains me to think of the shame he would feel to see you here today, knowing you aided a man intent on overthrowing the very cause he gave his life for."

At that moment Elizabeth hated him. She hated all of them. Ruthless men. Ambitious men. Greedy men. Men who brought whole countries to war, trampling over farms and villages, killing women and children and tearing families asunder, and then dared to talk to others of shame.

"Did you know, Elizabeth Walters, that this man you aided is the very man who slew my friend and your father?"

A small sob escaped her. *You slew my father! He'd be alive today if not for you and your naked ambition.* She knew better than to say it. She bowed her head to hide the anger in her eyes. "No, my lord...I did not." Though she lied, the tears she blinked back were real enough. Captain Nichols stepped forward to give her a handkerchief and she thanked God he was there.

Cromwell steepled his fingers and regarded her carefully. "You come here pleading ignorance, madam. Yet you are clearly not an ignorant woman. I am mindful of your father's great sacrifice and service to our cause, but I am Lord Protector of this realm, not its king. England is governed by law and merit now, not favoritism and privilege. Even if I am inclined to believe your story, there is no doubt you would have recognized the man as a cavalier if only by his dress. If you did not ask his name or business it was because you did not wish to know. The man was in your power. You could have treated his wounds and then bound and held him until help arrived. Willful ignorance is no defense for failing in your duty to protect your country as a loyal subject should. It can't go unpunished. I am ill inclined to condemn my good friend's daughter to a traitor's death, but imprisonment and transportation will serve to—"

"My lord!" Captain Nichols jumped to his feet and caught Elizabeth's elbow, steadying her as she swayed, ashen faced with shock. "Surely you can't be serious!"

"I am not known for my merry pranks! What business is this of yours, Nichols?" Cromwell snapped.

"I apologize for speaking out of turn, Lord Protector, but the lass has no one to speak for her. General Walters was my friend, mentor and commander, sir, and I am well acquainted with Elizabeth. I had the pleasure of watching her grow up. She is a fine young lady, my lord, and though she is far from ignorant, her youth was protected and secluded. She is not well versed in the ways of the world. She has lost mother, father and husband, and has had no one to guide her through these difficult times. If she is guilty of anything it is of having an overly trusting and compassionate nature. These might be grave failings

in a soldier, my lord, but aren't they virtues we encourage
and admire in our women? Surely we should not expect
a soldier's duty from an isolated and unprotected young
widow who has lost her father in our cause. I submit,
Lord Protector, that it is not Lady Elizabeth's duty to
protect us, but our duty to protect her."

"Were you not a gentleman you'd have made a fine
lawyer, Captain Nichols, but whether from ignorance or
naïveté the offense was a grave one. Though it may be
the girl didn't know who and what she was helping, it is
clear to me she knowingly aided an enemy of the state.
I cannot favor the offspring of my friends. All must be
treated equally. You raise a valid point, however. One
that mitigates the circumstances somewhat. Nevertheless
it is clear that an unsupervised young woman is no fit
steward for her husband or her father's lands. Elizabeth
Walters, step forward."

Elizabeth took a deep breath and stepped forward.
Transportation, imprisonment, death. Could she possibly
have imagined such things when William stumbled into
her cottage and back into her life just a week ago? No,
and even if she had, she'd not have done any different.
How could she? She stood straight and proud, her head
held high.

"Elizabeth Walters, I judge you guilty of harboring an
enemy of the state. Given your tender years, your lack of
experience and supervision, and the great respect I have
for your father whose guidance you lost in service to
the Commonwealth, I leave you your freedom and your
life, and I shall not banish you from England's shores.

Your lands however, including your dower lands and those left you by your husband and father, are herewith forfeit to the Commonwealth of England."

CHAPTER SIX

PLANNING, FORESIGHT and flexibility were the key elements to any well-executed criminal endeavor. William de Veres, waiting along the side of the ancient southern highway between Brighton and Crawley, preferred to think of this current venture as a patriotic duty rather than a felony, but he *had* expected it to be a bit more entertaining, and not so damnably cold. A lacy web of frost coated the slick carpet of brown and yellow leaves, and a metallic wind bit his face. Overhead, a small flock of geese, stragglers on the journey south, flew in a ragged V silhouetted against a sullen sky. They saluted him as they passed with mocking cries. Last evening, cozy and warm, huddled in a corner of Crawley's aptly named Highwayman's Inn; he had planned for everything but a sudden drop in temperature. *Bloody hell! I'll freeze to death if I don't soon expire from boredom.*

The shadows lengthened. He blew on his fingers, warming them, and then tucked them under his armpits as he shivered in the cold. It would be full dark soon, but it could be hours yet. He hunched his shoulders and settled in to wait. The little bird's house wasn't far from here. He had passed the overgrown track that led to her door yesterday…sought it out in fact…he wasn't sure why. He seldom returned to a conquest and it wasn't his habit to think back, but something about her tugged at him, some quality had aroused his interest.

It couldn't have been her lovemaking. She was hardly the sort of woman he frequented. She was far more skilled at needlework than sporting in bed. But she had given him aid, shelter…*and comfort, too,* he thought with a grin. It was a harsh world and such gifts were rarely offered freely. It must be that peculiar novelty that fixed her in his thoughts. What harm in stopping by to visit once his business here was done? He had offered her his aid after all. Not a pretty recompense when he hadn't given her his name. He could give it to her now and…

It's been almost two years. She's likely married with a husband and a squalling brat. A righteous Puritan goodwife who will not thank me for knocking on her door. He shrugged his shoulders and putting her firmly from his mind, turned his attention to the road.

The full moon had risen in all her glory, bathing the woods in an opalescent glow. Other than the bitter chill, it was a perfect night for pillage and adventure, but his quarry should have passed this way by now. Perhaps he had misunderstood. Maybe they had decided to stay another day. Perhaps they had taken a different route, though back roads were particularly tricky this time of year and this road was the best route to Brighton. He leaned against his tethered horse, his eyes still on the road as one hand reached back, searching for—

"Is this what you be seeking, milord?"

"Lord thundering Christ, Tom! What in hell do you think you're doing?"

"I'm staying right behind you, milord. 'Tis the safest place to be in these woods is what I'm thinking."

William accepted the proffered flagon of brandy, taking a long swallow before handing it back to his servant. Its sweet heat coursed through him, thawing him from the inside out, waking his brain and loosing his tongue. "How many times must I tell you, there are no headless horsemen, ghosts, goblins, trolls or witches in these woods?"

"That is not what they say in the village, Master William."

"And you will believe a gaggle of rustic blockheads over your own lord?"

"Begging your pardon, milord. But them that lives here might be expected to know. And even if you'll not credit it, they say there be murderers and villains and highwaymen, too."

William put an arm around his anxious servant's shoulders, pulling him close to speak soft and low. "Have you yet to notice, dearest Tom? The highwaymen and villains would be you and me."

"Just so, sir. And if they are right about that, who's to say they are wrong about the rest?"

William clapped him on the shoulder. A lanky tow-headed young man with a charming gap-toothed grin, Tom had followed him from England to France, and though at times he was decidedly obtuse, he was always loyal. "Your logic is impeccable, Tom, but I assure you, the only thing you have to fear in these woods tonight is me if you fail at your commission. I need you farther up the road to give warning as our quarry nears. You know the plan."

"I do, milord. But I don't understand why we are risking our necks out here when we could be safe and warm back in Bruges. You were almost killed the last time you came this way, and you'd have lost your head had you been captured, Master William. Hanged maybe even, and that's not very dignified for a lord."

"Indeed! I should have hated to embarrass you so, Tom."

"If you're bored, milord, surely there are other ways to ease it?"

"We are here," William answered with exaggerated patience, "because *my* master is an indigent itinerant beggar, who is sometimes mistaken for a monarch, and sometimes for one of his own menials. His own mother charges him for meals. *He*...cannot pay his servants, and he walks the streets unable to afford a coach. All the princes of Europe have turned their backs on him, and someone has to feed him. I can only hope you'll take from this the appropriate lesson, my dear Thomas, and someday do the same for me. Now hie yourself off to yon bushes as we agreed, or I will strip you naked and tie you to a tree for the banshee to ravage."

Sighing, Tom covered his features with a scarf and pulled his hat brim down over his eyes. "You should do the same, Master William."

"I am not ashamed of what I do. Now shoo! Go away!" He motioned toward the bushes with an impatient wave of his pistol.

"It is a good deal warmer like this, milord."

"I am happy for you, Tom. Off you go before I shoot you." Tom's superstitious fears reminded him of a poem he had been working on, and he played with some verses, to wile away the time.

His reverie was interrupted not twenty minutes later by a low whistle and the rumble of a carriage traveling at a full speed. It was a tactic meant to discourage men such as him, but it was a foolhardy one to use at night, and it would not work against the surprise he had in store. As the coach rounded the bend and barreled straight for him, he stepped out onto the highway waving a lantern, one booted foot planted firmly on a sturdy log he and Tom had wrestled across the road. Any attempt to jump it or swerve around it would result in a wreck, and he was gambling the coachman would not take that risk.

Now the fun begins. His eyes lit with excitement and he didn't flinch as the coach careened toward him, lurching sideways in a spray of dirt and stones. William put down the lantern to draw his pistols as the cursing coachman fought with his team, laying them back on their haunches in a desperate scrambling stop.

"I do beg your pardon. I've forgotten *le mot juste,* but I believe it's 'Stand and deliver!' or… Ah! Tom. There you are. What is the other phrase one uses?"

"I believe it's 'Your money or your life,' Sir."

"How very trite. Your money or your wife would be more amusing. Perhaps we'll try that next time, just to see what happens." Though he spoke to Tom, his eyes were fixed on the driver. "You there! Coachman! That was nicely done. Now keep your hands where I can see them. I am not in the habit of shooting competent servants, they are far too hard to find, but I will put a bullet between your eyes right now, friend, do you reach for that blunderbuss you've been eyeing." His words were clipped and cold. The coachman, a grizzled fellow with a wiry frame and the steady eyes of one who'd been a soldier, eased his hands away from the weapon and raised them in the air.

"Good fellow. Now down you get. You will kindly remove your boots and clothes and hand them to my man."

The coachman surveyed William's thigh-high leather boots, his silver-trimmed coat and matching cape, and his broad-brimmed, long-plumed hat. "I am one who fought for the young king, too, milord. But not every man can abandon kith and kin and follow him to foreign shores. It's colder than a witch's tit this night. If you leave me bare-arsed in the woods, I'll not see morning."

"What's your name, man?"

"Alan Jackson, sir."

"Fair enough, Alan Jackson. You may cut loose one of these nags. Make for Brighton rather than Crawley, mind. And when you get there, use this to drink His Majesty's health." William reached into his purse and flipped the man half a crown. "You needn't worry for your master." He spoke loud enough so that the heretofore-silent passengers could hear. "Provided he is polite and accommodating, he shall come to no harm."

Alan Jackson looked doubtfully to the coach. He had survived two rounds of civil war, had a wife and three daughters to provide for, and wasn't paid near enough to warrant being trussed naked in the woods on a freezing night. He doffed his cap, cut loose one of the lead horses, and was soon galloping down the road toward Brighton.

"You are aware he will double back once he thinks we're gone, and alert the watch in Crawley, Master William?"

"The thought had crossed my mind, Tom. But no matter. We'll be in Brighton by then, and someplace else soon after that." He clasped Tom by the shoulder, and nodded toward the coach. The remaining three horses shuffled and snorted, clearly still alarmed, but there wasn't a peep from the carriage. "Shall we take a closer look at our prize?"

William strolled over to the horses, murmuring in a soothing tone as he righted traces, patted withers, and rubbed ears and noses. When the animals had settled down, he directed Tom to the left side of the coach with a brusque nod. He approached from the right.

He tore aside the leather window flap, raised his lantern and peered inside the carriage. A portly gentleman with bushy brows and beetle-black eyes glared back. William thought he looked rather like an angry badger but for the too-tight clothes and the pistol waving back and forth.

"You didn't expect this, did you, sirrah!" the badger challenged with a triumphant sneer. "Make one move, you cowardly cur, and I shall shoot you through the heart."

Ignoring him, William leaned against the window frame, angling his head to get a better look at the badger's companion. She was a pretty chit with tumbling blond curls, pouting lips and naughty blue eyes that couldn't hide a flash of excitement. He grinned and winked at her.

Her chaperone, bristling with indignation, raised his pistol and aimed it with shaking hands.

Tom spoke from the window on the far side. "I would advise against that, sir. Your barrel is not loaded and mine is primed and ready. It might distress the young lady to see your blood spilled all over the carriage." *His* hands did not shake, and his weapon was pointed directly at the man's temple.

"Well met, Tom! Look you here. We've plucked ourselves a fine Sussex squire and his beautiful daughter."

"She is not my daughter—she is my wife, you plaguey bastard!" the squire sputtered. The girl watched William wide-eyed, her bottom lip quivering.

"My apologies then, sir. And my condolences to you, madam." He motioned with his pistol. "Now if you would both be so good as to step from the carriage?"

Tom, one leg through the window and already halfway in the coach, snatched the man's pistol, then gave him a hard shove that sent him tumbling out the door.

"Allow me, madam." William reached in a hand to help the young lady descend.

"Blasted highwayman!" the badger cursed, dusting off his hands and knees. "Rogues and rascals the lot of you! Spineless cowards who hide in the dark rather than do a good day's work. I shall see you hang at Tyburn. Mark my words!"

"There seems to be a misunderstanding. We do not hide, sir. We are king's men. I am William de Veres." He performed a courtly bow. "We are here collecting funds for His Majesty, King Charles II. A small donation that will be remembered kindly if you will...or a tax you shall forfeit to contribute to his cause, if you will not."

"King? What king? There *is* no king, unless you speak of that degenerate wastrel! That…that debauched whoremonger who was rightly cast from England's shores."

Tom cocked his pistol and the girl shrieked in alarm.

"Tsk tsk, Tom. There's no need for that." William reached out and lowered the barrel of the weapon so it pointed at the ground, and then returned his attention to the badger. "No king you say? Be careful, sir. You mark yourself a traitor. Now you may consider it a fine, and count yourself lucky to escape with your hide."

"You are a royalist cavalier, sirrah? I suppose 'tis only fitting you represent your outlaw king by robbery and pillage."

"I represent *England's* king. And yes, of course we rob and pillage. Only the lazy ones do not. This is growing tedious. Let's finish the thing, shall we?" William cocked his pistol and the squire peeped in fright. "Your purse, your jewelry, and whatever is in that box, if you please. And not another word if you value your life. You may insult me, but I will not allow you to insult your rightful king."

The squire hurriedly divested himself of rings and pocket watch and tossed his purse at William's feet. His face went white and he moaned, almost crumpling to the ground, when Tom pried open the locked strongbox revealing more jewelry, silver candlesticks and cups, and an impressive quantity of newly minted gold and silver Commonwealth coins. A pleased grin split William's face as he sifted through them. He had hardly believed his ears in Crawley when he heard the man tell his wife it was safer to move their valuables at night without an escort, so they would not draw attention to themselves. *'Tis true what they say. A fool and his money are soon parted.* How fitting that Cromwell's coin would soon be keeping Charles in wine and whores.

He threw a couple of gold coins to Tom, who caught them deftly. "Keep a horse to carry this lot, and use the others to move the coach off the road before you cut them free. Do you fancy his wig and coat, Thomas? They will be of no use to Charles."

"Aye, if it pleases you, milord. They will fetch a pretty penny from a pawnbroker."

William waved his pistol at the shivering couple. "You heard him. Down to your shirt and drawers, sir. You may keep your boots. You'll have need of them."

Puffing and sputtering, the corpulent squire began removing his wig and coat. The girl started fumbling at her stays. William laughed and stopped her with a hand on her arm. "Not you, *ma belle demoiselle,* though I assure you, His Majesty would look upon the gesture most kindly." He chucked her under the chin, and then ran an expert finger along her décolletage, stopping to fondle a lovely amethyst gold-and-pearl pendant that hung between her breasts. Moving to stand behind her, he unclasped it, trailing his fingers along her neck and shoulders as he did. He tugged gently at her earrings, removing them, too, and murmured hot against her neck, "Is there ought else you would contribute, my dear? For your king?"

The squire gasped in outrage as his mesmerized bride

turned to face her handsome assailant, seemingly offering her lips to be kissed. William smiled and took her hand instead, bending to kiss her knuckles as he carefully examined her rings. "Is there one in particular you would like to keep, love?"

"Ahem!" The voice came from the side of the road.

"Yes, Tom?"

"There could be another coach along here at any moment, milord."

"Quite right! Keep your favorite, girl. And hand over the rest. Quickly now."

The woman's smile was much older than she was. She handed over three rings, keeping the one that was clearly the most expensive.

"You've given him your wedding ring? My mother said you were little more than a strumpet and I would not believe her!"

"Shall I kill him for you after all, my dear? They say the lot of a young widow is much happier than that of a young woman married to an old man." William laughed out loud when she seemed to consider it. Before she could answer, he jumped into the ditch and slapped the horses on the rump, sending the startled animals galloping into the dark.

"Cold-blooded blackguard! You will abandon us here like this?"

"I am a gentleman, sir. I would never do that to a lady. You, however, are a different matter. You have your boots, and Crawley is but five miles south. If you run you should stay warm enough."

"Eh?"

"Run."

"What's that you—"

"Run!" William raised his pistol and fired it just over the man's head. The half-clothed squire hared off down the road, his white shirttails flapping behind him like ghostly sails in the moonlight. William took off his coat and wrapped it around the girl, and then he and Tom loaded the remaining horse with their booty. "Well done, Tom. We'll be off now," he said, once they were finished.

"What about the log, milord?"

"The log?"

"It is a hazard, Master William, to any who pass this way. Someone might be killed."

"Tom…Tom…Tom." William sighed and shook his head. "You don't really grasp the concept of being a villain, do you?"

Together they grunted and heaved, rolling the heavy obstacle off the road, and then William leaped onto his horse and held out his hand. "Well, girl, will you sit and shiver until help comes along? Or shall I drop you at an inn in Brighton?"

She grasped his hand and placed a foot in the stirrup, and he pulled her up to ride pillion behind him. He wheeled his horse to look north. They could just make out a fluttering white form disappearing round the bend. "Your man runs well, my dear." Laughing, he turned his horse in the other direction, and took off at a gallop down the road.

The lovely Mrs. Badger held him tight about the waist for the first few miles, but when they slowed their horses to a walk to rest them, she slipped her hands inside his breeches. The bold move startled him and he sprang instantly to life. He tightened his reins, and his horse snorted, stepping sideways in protest.

"You don't mind if I warm my hands against your body, do you, sir?" she murmured against the back of his neck.

"It would be churlish of me to refuse, madam." He leaned back in the saddle, relaxing his knees, and she clasped her hands around his erection, interlacing her fingers together in a hold so tight he might have been inside her. A soft groan escaped him.

"It's not that much farther, Master William. We'll be warm and well fed within the hour."

"Thank you, Tom," William grunted.

She began to move her hands up and down his shaft, from the base to the head, with a firm elongated stroke. It seemed that the badger's mother was correct. The girl *was* a strumpet, and a very skilled one at that. He urged his horse into a canter, leaving Tom and the carriage horse he was leading behind them. The girl didn't let loose her grip. His hips thrust forward and back with the animal's movements, and she twisted her hands, wringing him gently with each stroke. Just as he was about to find his release she withdrew, settling her hands demurely around his waist.

"Bitch!" he ground out.

"We are almost in town, milord. Find us an inn," she whispered in his ear.

Tom caught up with them as they approached Brighton. There were still a few hours before dawn, and William arranged for two rooms, one for Tom, and one for himself and his female companion. He had yet to ask her name. It was Jane Shore, she told him, as she divested him of his shirt and boots. She was a gold-smith's daughter who'd been married just over a year, and had yet to conceive a son with her stout and elderly husband. She was promised a manor house should she give him an heir, a thing far more valuable than jewels, and once the thing was done, she would not have to lie with him anymore and she could expect a good deal more freedom, too.

William had seen the spark of interest in her eyes when he first stopped her carriage. Many women had fantasies of being gently ravaged by a handsome high-wayman. She would not be his first, but he had expected to have to calm her and woo her a bit. Instead, she had managed him expertly, almost professionally, on the ride to Brighton, and the minute he latched the door to the room she yanked his breeches down to his ankles and pushed him onto the bed.

He leaned back on his elbows, enjoying her minis-trations and the view as her fingers circled the head of his shaft and her knowing tongue stroked the underside just below it. Within minutes, his cock, still swollen from their moonlit ride, began to twitch. Her eyes shone with pleasure and she purred low in her throat. She pushed him onto his back and straddled him, gripping him tight with her legs and inner muscles, riding him like a horse.

"I know what you are about, my lovely," he chuckled, gripping her hips, lifting her off him, and flipping her onto her back, seconds before spending on her belly with a low groan.

"Bastard!" she hissed, striking his face.

He grabbed her hand to stop her from scratching him.

"I see you are used to having things your own way, fair Acrasia, but not this time."

"Acrasia? I told you my name is Jane, you witless fool."

"Acrasia was a seductress of knights, my dear. The title is apt." He hadn't thought of that poem in years, and he wondered why he did so now. It teased at other memories long forgotten.

"You are no knight! You are a useless, worth-less—"

"And you are no lady. I am not about to foist a bastard on your husband and have him raised a cuckoo in someone else's nest. Neither of you are fit parents for any issue of mine. I take care of my own, and if I ever have a son or daughter they will surely know who I am. I will pleasure you if you like. But you'll need to find another stallion to help you with your heir."

"You are no stallion! Doubtless I am too much woman for you. One hears you are all sodomites in the Beggar King's court."

His eyes hardened and a muscle twitched along his jaw. A part of him wanted to strike her.

She held out her hand. Imperious. Demanding. "Give me back my jewels."

"No."

"I'll cry rape! I will have the local watch on you in minutes. I will see you hang at Tyburn, you misbegotten son of a whore!"

"Don't make me shoot you, Jane. And pray try not to sound like the latest novel."

She made ready to scream and he clamped a hand around her mouth, cursing as she bit him. He tore off a piece of linen from his shirt to gag her, and then he ripped strips of blue satin from her discarded dress to tie her hands above her head. Her eyes blazed with impotent fury as she kicked her little heels in rage.

He was exhausted, but he picked up his clothing and got dressed. It was no longer safe to spend the night. When he was ready, he performed an elegant bow, sweeping his plumed hat so that it almost brushed the floor. "You pleased me somewhat, my dear, part of the time. Your skills are adequate, though you would be better served by keeping your mouth closed unless it's being used to please or swallow. I must go now. I regret I cannot bring you with me, but alas, I have almost more than I can carry with your jewels." He let the door close on her muffled shrieks and curses, and crept down the hall in search of Tom.

"Master William?" Tom ventured, as they made their hurried escape from town.

"What's on your mind, Tom?" he managed through gritted teeth.

"I've been searching for the right moment to say this…"

"And you think it is now?"

"I…yes…that is…I wish you would not use my name quite so freely, milord, when we are going about dangerous business," he blurted out.

"Why ever not? There are thousands of Toms skulking about the country. In your clever disguise you are well hid amongst them."

"If we ever return to England to stay, I've no wish to be known as a wanted highwayman."

"If we ever return to England, I will be at the king's

right hand, and all will be forgiven." *But we won't.* Their grand cause had become a grand farce. Even when old Cromwell died, the spark of excitement lasted barely a week. Young Cromwell replaced him, and they were still no closer to going home. The only good thing to come from his mad dash through the woods with letters from General Monk had been a night with the little bird in his arms. Had he known, he'd have stayed longer. Eight long years in exile and for what? There was nothing to show for it but wasted lives. Even Charles, once so full of promise, had stopped trying. *We shall all grow old and die having spent our lives waiting. It's time to go home. There are worse things than losing oneself in alcohol, sex and pleasure.*

He had one thing to do first, though. Mistress Shore had left a sour taste in his mouth. Another meaningless encounter with a spiteful venal woman. He sent Tom on to Bruges, where the exiled king and his court of beggars awaited, and the next day he stopped his mount by a familiar track in the woods. He wasn't sure what strange siren's call had brought him here, but his pulse quickened as he traveled down the path. He stopped at the edge of the clearing. The front path was overgrown with weeds and the house was boarded up. It looked to have been abandoned for some time. A pang of disappointment took him by surprise.

He broke a window and let himself inside. There was nothing. No chair in the corner of the parlor, no settee by the fire. There was no sound of her, no scent of her. She was gone. He shook his head in disgust. He was being ridiculous. He lived his life surrounded by courtesans and grand ladies, anything a fashionable rake might desire. Why had his attention fixed on a little brown wren? How had she remained in his thoughts all this time? He remembered her lavender scent. He remembered the feel of her hair, silky smooth as he had combed it out with his fingers. He remembered the sound of her voice, humming quietly as she tidied around him.

He shrugged and opened the door to let his horse inside. It was going to be a raw night and there was no reason for either of them to be uncomfortable. He collected some deadwood and lit a fire in the hearth, then curled up in his greatcoat on the floor. He had a sudden vision of summer and laughter, but it was gone as soon as he tried to capture it, elusive as a dream. As he settled down to sleep his lips curled in a self-mocking grin. The little bird had flown. The only way he was likely to find her again was if he happened to stop her in a coach.

CHAPTER SEVEN

WILLIAM OPENED his eyes and groaned. He rolled over onto his back and pushed away the arms entwined around him. His head ached, his eyes burned, and his stomach roiled. It seemed he had drunk too much sack again. A sharp pinch to his nipple made him sit up straight, slapping busy hands away. "Good Christ, Barbara! How is it that whenever I get drunk I end up in bed with you? Do you stalk me? Waiting for my steps to falter and my words to slur?"

"Nonsense, William!" She sidled up next to him and trailed her fingers down his abdomen to his crotch. "The important parts never falter, and wine does for you what jewelry does for a woman. It makes you sparkle and shine. It is only when you are drunk that you'll admit how much you want me."

"You *are* very beautiful, my dear." And she was. Famous for her vicious temper and hearty sexual appetite, Barbara Villiers, now Palmer, was tall and voluptuous, with slanting violet eyes, glorious auburn hair, and a full sulky mouth. She was a fit meal for any man, even a king. She was busy kissing the insides of his thighs and he placed his hands on the crown of her head. "You are voracious, too. One wonders that Charles is not enough for you. He is said to be a considerate lover, well made and well endowed."

"Oh, darling, he is!" she said, looking up. "But so are you!" She gave him a firm squeeze and grinned. "And it never serves to let a man think he owns you. Next thing you know you are not being treated as a mistress but as a wife! He abandons you for new challenges and soon the gifts dwindle and eventually they stop."

"Is that why you are with him, Barbara? For his gifts?"

"Well, it is certainly no hardship, William." She licked his swollen cock as if it were a sweet, and he lay back, taking a ragged breath. "I daresay I'd enjoy him king or no. But I am not foolish enough to fall in love with him. No man wants a woman who clings, but he will remember who it was that comforted him in his exile."

"You…" he gasped. "Along with many others."

"Pfft!" She waved her fingers dismissively. "No one else understands his needs as I do."

"What if he never regains his throne? What gifts can you expect from a landless, penniless king?"

"Oh, he will. He will be king in England, and sooner than you think. And when it happens, he will take me with him. He will owe me. He will owe all of us. You, too. Isn't that what keeps you here?"

William sighed tiredly, pushing her away. "He will make a good king if he's given the chance and the wait doesn't destroy him. He has wit and intelligence, grace and charm. He's generous and brave and he—"

"Good God, don't tell me you are in love with him, too! Next thing you'll be scribbling him pretty poems. One hears it is the fashion amongst the merry gentlemen to dip their wicks in both—"

"Shut up, Barbara. You have the morals of a street whore."

"So have you, de Veres. We make a fine pair. That is why you like me, darling."

"I don't fuck women I like, Barbara. It gets much too complicated." Even as he said it he knew it wasn't true. He had liked his abbess well enough.

"Pig! Swine! *Cochon!*" She slapped his face with a stinging blow and began kicking him with her feet, forcing him from her bed. He slid to the floor in a heap of sheets and blankets, laughing as he ducked her blows. She threw a silver brush at him and he caught it deftly. "Arrogant cur! I would not fuck you if you were—"

She squealed in outrage as he pulled her from the bed, down to the thick carpet, but in a few short minutes her squeals were replaced by breathy moans and soft sighs of satisfaction. Their wild gyrations toppled a side table, sending candlestick holders and silver cups crashing to the floor, and as they both neared their release, William had to cover her mouth to keep her cries from resounding down the hall.

Passion spent, they lay together side by side, gasping for breath. "One needs to be an acrobat to keep up with you, Barbara."

"Charles does well enough. Don't you worry that he might find out you are fucking his mistress?"

He shrugged. "It would not be the first time. Do you really think he doesn't know? He's generous with his castoffs and not averse to sharing. He even seems grateful to have them taken off his hands. How many offspring has he now?"

"Fils de bas! Lecheor!" She clawed at his face. He

caught her arm in a tight grip and squeezed it until she let it drop.

"You know it's true, darling. He knows you have lovers and he prefers it that way. He will not begrudge you yours so long as you do not begrudge him his. And why should you care? It is an arrangement that suits you both, is it not?"

"He will marry me, cousin, and make me his queen, and you'll regret your impertinence."

William burst out laughing. "Our cousins were cousins, not you and I, and he may make your bastards dukes and duchesses, Barbara. But you'll never be queen. Besides, isn't your husband likely to object?"

"Charles is in love with me. I have him wrapped around my finger, and my husband is old." She reached for her robe and pulled it on.

"Your husband is complacent and richly rewarded for it, and may be around for another twenty years. As for Charles, you lead him by his prick. You may rule his bed, but I assure you, you don't rule his head. You just aren't terribly useful, Babs, other than for the obvious reasons. If he returns to England, he will marry for money and to secure his throne. He will seek a useful wife."

Barbara leaped to her feet, returning with a lovely foot-tall blue-and-white chinoiserie vase. "I hate you! Get out!" She hurled it at his head.

Laughing and ducking, he reached for his clothes, hopping on one foot as he pulled them on. "That would have bought us all a month of dinners, love."

She shrieked in rage, reaching for its twin, but he circled around her and caught her from behind. "You

are a sex goddess, Barbara. You said yourself that is
far more powerful than a wife," he breathed against her
neck.

"But not a queen."

"Even a queen, love, do you not become too
greedy."

"You are an insufferable boor," she sniffed.

"I know," he said, pressing against her from
behind.

"I have always hated you, you know, ever since childhood. It is no wonder your mother pawned you off on a
clergyman."

"No wonder at all." His voice turned cold and his
eyes glittered dangerously.

"Have I offended you, darling?" Her voice sounded
pleased, but she turned in his embrace and put her arms
around his neck, pulling him into a torrid kiss. "You
really must learn not to vex me. Charles is good to you
because your father died helping his own. Do not pre-
sume too much, William."

It was true that his father had died fighting for Charles
I. It was the only useful thing Henry de Veres had ever
done for his son and heir. The letter he had sent two
months prior to his death, commanding William to present himself for what was in effect, a second civil war
in defense of the king, had raised him from obscurity.
It had turned him from an eager stripling finishing his
education in Europe, to a young captain who belonged
to the royal circle. His father's death before he had even
arrived proved a greater boon, marking him as one who
had already sacrificed much in defense of England's
rightful king. It was a last gift from a man he had never

met. If he were prone to tender feelings, he supposed he might even feel sentimental. "Charles is good to me because I share my women and fill his purse, while he takes his fill of you."

"He will never have his fill of me."

"Would you care to make a wager on that... cousin?"

"You shall see soon enough. Word has it that while you were out playing rascal and thief—"

"Patriot, my dear."

"Highwayman, patriot, call it what you will. It seems that word has come from General Monk."

"What? Again? And no one told me? His promises are those of a feckless suitor practicing his wiles on gullible sheep as he paws through them in search of the richest heiress, and I assure you that's not our Charles."

"Ahem!"

They turned their heads as one. A very tall, dark-complexioned man with lively eyes and coarse sensual lips stood watching from the doorway. "Someone would have told you, William, but you were snoring in the arms of Bacchus and a whore."

Barbara turned bright red, something William had not thought possible. He let go of her and made a deep bow. "Good day, Your Majesty. I was just greeting my dear cousin after returning from abroad."

"Ah, yes, one has heard of your latest adventures. We've been expecting you for the past two days, but as lovely as your dear cousin is, I suppose I must forgive you for paying homage to beauty before your king."

A beaming Barbara abandoned William without a

backward glance, and stepped purring into her royal lover's arms.

"And so, Your Majesty?"

"And so, dear friends—" Charles put an arm around them both "—the Old Pretender's son has stepped down. We are going home."

CHAPTER EIGHT

1661

GREAT CITIES HAVE their own voices. They talk and exclaim, screech and roar, and sometimes, late at night, they sigh and softly moan. London under Puritan rule was a sullen behemoth. It rang with the sound of booted feet tramping over cobbled streets, its heart beat with the steady pulse of prayer and commerce, but it lacked music, joy and laughter. It was rare that a city changed its tune as quickly and emphatically as London did when King Charles II was restored to his throne. Since his arrival in London, music seemed to float from every window in the city, winding through the streets, sweeping along the waterfront and swirling through the market squares. Everywhere people strummed and sang and the streets echoed with the sound of drunken laughter late into the night.

Great cities weren't necessarily filled with great men, though. It was the eve of His Majesty's coronation and William was already disenchanted. Any hopes that a shining and glorious future might balance a tarnished past were already abandoned. He rose, shirtless and disheveled, and slammed the window shut. He was restless and irritable and his stomach was clenched in a cold knot. It was curious how the tyrannies of the past could chase a full-grown man from his sleep. Though long past and all but forgotten, they still held sway in dreams. The roar of cannon, the stench of battle, and his mother's oft-threatened Puritan hell, had all found a comfortable home there, but what he resented most was the pestilent presence of Giffard. By day he could be banished with a flick of the pen, a quick tumble or a couple of glasses of sack, but at night he skittered through his sleep like a fat black spider. *Much as he did in childhood.* His lips curled in a self-mocking smile and he tossed back his wine.

He turned around and contemplated his empty bed. Luxurious dark blue curtains edged in gold braid were drawn back, revealing tangled blankets and rumpled silk sheets. A high-backed walnut chair was tipped on its side and a bolster lay draped, half on the bed and half on the floor. It looked like he had enjoyed himself before he had fallen asleep. He could only hope so, because the giggling jade who'd warmed his bed was long gone, and his purse with her. *Damn the chit!*

He went to pour himself another glass of wine, only to find the flagon empty "Tom! Blast it, man, where are you? Thomas!"

"I am right here, sir. There's no need to wake the palace." Tom stopped by the door to the outer parlor in his nightshirt looking somewhat sheepish.

"The wench has gone."

"Shall I find you another, milord?"

"No. And don't think I've not noticed you have one of your own stashed in your room. Did you see mine leave? She took my purse."

Tom's cheeks reddened. "Ah, no, milord. I was

distracted. I apologize. You had said I might retire for the evening. I thought your guest was a lady, milord."

"Aye, so did I. Bring me pen and ink, will you? More sack, too. I might as well salvage something from this adventure. I think I shall immortalize her in verse."

Of over fifteen hundred rooms available in the warren of courtyards and alleyways that was Whitehall Palace, William had been assigned four. It was a respectable allocation given the vast numbers of courtiers, ministers and servants who lodged there, and the fact that so many rooms were dilapidated or uninhabitable. It was true that the king's favorite mistress had twenty-four, but though William's bedchamber was cramped, his apartment was luxurious and well-appointed, with colorful hangings, murals on the walls, a view of the Thames, and a brick fireplace in every room. He had given one room to Tom, and once he was settled at his desk with pen, ink and wine, he gave him leave to go back to it and his lover, though he stopped him as he reached the door. "Thomas?"

"Yes, sir?"

"Do you truly wish to be a rake you must stop blushing."

Tom bobbed his head as the crimson stain on his cheeks spread to his throat. "I don't wish to be a rake, milord. I like just the one. She is comely and sweet and—"

"Yes, yes. Well? Don't stand there like a buffoon. She is waiting."

He watched Tom leave with an indulgent smile and a twinge of envy. His first experience with a woman had been at school when he was all of thirteen years old.

She was a prostitute, coarse and vulgar, but she knew what she was about and he'd had something to prove.

He had left for grammar school at the age of twelve, with Giffard begging his mother to be allowed to accompany him. For once she had listened to her son. Perhaps she had heard the desperation in his voice; perhaps she had been swayed by his vow to kill him. In any case she had sent him on alone. It was well she did. Even though the man had died several years ago, the thought of him still made his skin crawl. *If he had tried to crawl into my bed one more time, I'd have surely cut his throat.* That would have been difficult for his mother to explain.

The thought of Giffard brought on a familiar rush of black rage and he tossed back another glass of wine to tamp it down. His mother's influence had seen him enter Oxford at fourteen. By then he had thought himself a man. That year he discovered the joys of sex and wine. Although it seemed every sweet bit of sin he indulged in left a bitter taste in his mouth, while under their influence he forgot both past and future, leaving him almost content. He had never imagined himself in love and he had never experienced the wonder and excitement he had seen in Tom's eyes. *Well…perhaps once, but that was just a dream.* The one sweet memory from a childhood that never was.

At least there was always liquor and women to fill the void, because nothing had turned out as he'd hoped, including his idealistic notions regarding Charles. It had started with such promise. They arrived in Dover to cheering crowds. Bonfires lit their way to London, wine flowed from fountains, and throngs of well-wishers crowded the roads. When Charles made his triumphal entry into the capital on his birthday it took them seven hours to traverse the city. The streets were hung with tapestries; bells rang from every church; and trumpets sounded along their flower-strewn path. After eighteen years of Puritan austerity the English were overjoyed at His Majesty's return. Every window and balcony was strained to capacity with ecstatic onlookers, and the very air breathed liberation and a fresh new start.

Anything seemed possible. Charming, informal and debonair, Charles was a charismatic, athletic and witty man, at ease with himself and others in a way few kings ever were. He was everything his subjects, weary of years of gloom and civil strife, could have wanted, and they were eager to celebrate. They wanted to enjoy life again, and Charles Stuart, the Merry Monarch, was just the man to lead them in the dance. He had quickly repealed those laws his subjects found most noxious. Gambling, holiday celebrations and Sunday sports were once again allowed. He reopened theaters, permitted women on the stage, and endorsed a theatrical genre characterized by bawdy language, cynicism and wit. Though it shocked some, it delighted most others. William doubted any king had ever begun his reign with more popular support and such goodwill.

It seemed at first that Charles was set to become the king William imagined he could be. He had gathered a group of learned men to establish a Royal Society for scientific research and thought. He had issued a declaration of toleration and pardoned all his enemies except those directly responsible for his father's death. All others, including Richard Cromwell, were allowed to keep both property and position. It had all been very exciting, but it hadn't taken long for the honeymoon to end.

Like many of his courtiers, the king had read Hobbes's *Leviathan,* which argued there was no reality beyond that experienced through one's senses. It offered a brand of sensual atheism that his majesty embraced, and appealed to a generation of courtiers sick of the hypocrisy of their elders' wars. Pragmatic and cynical, he was a canny ruler who understood his people's love for their Anglican Church. When faced with an anti-Puritan movement on one hand and anti-Catholic sentiment on the other, his promise of religious toleration was quickly abandoned.

It can't have been easy for him. Parliamentarians besieged him, fearful of losing their lands while Royalist supporters entreated him, begging for the return of theirs. He sympathized. He nodded and graciously promised. And he responded by doing whatever was best for him—defending his powers and taking on Parliament in an endless quest for funds to keep his women and his throne.

William had little cause for complaint. Charles had been good to those who shared his exile. Barbara Palmer was now Lady Castlemaine, even as Charles finalized the details for a Portuguese bride. William, newly created Lord Rivers, had been returned his father's confiscated properties in Maidstone near Kent, though they could rot for all he cared. His mother had remarried and moved to the northern borders, but he had no desire to return to the country. He'd been awarded an annuity as court poet and named a gentleman of the bedchamber along with Buckingham, Newcastle and Lauderdale, planting him firmly in the circle of those closest to the king.

It was a place he'd once dreamed of being, but years in exile had honed Charles into a shrewd man governed by self-preservation, and the careless hedonism that had kept hopelessness at bay in exile was now a celebratory creed. Within one short year, all their dreams of justice and glory had devolved into an endless round of sex, pleasure and scurrying for favor.

It angered him to see such promise go to waste and he was baffled he should care. What did broken promises to old enemies matter to him? It was a foolish fancy, a relic from his childhood. Of all the sins of which he was guilty, idealism was the one that cost him most dear. *But shouldn't a man, particularly a king, have some care for his word? Shouldn't he care more for his country than his pleasures?*

Bah! Come to that, husbands should be faithful to their wives, preachers live by their words, and politicians do what was best for their country instead of themselves. He'd been caught in some mad delusion, pretending it all had meaning, but there was none. Nothing mattered but the moment. Men lusted so they fucked, they hungered so they ate, and they were governed by base desires. Kings and preachers were men, too, and there was nothing more to it than that.

He poured himself another drink, and began scratching pen to paper. As he did, his thoughts turned to his Puritan miss. He had taken to holding on to her like a talisman. She had given herself and her aid, asking nothing in return, one pure memory, burnished in his mind to a lustrous glow. She was like a figure from a fairy tale. A magical creature found hiding in the woods.

He smiled as he remembered Spenser's *Faerie Queene,* a poem he had long forgotten. An image came unbidden of a silver-eyed girl and a great oak tree. For a moment he felt uncomfortably tender, a ludicrous emotion in this court and time. He shrugged her away, returning his thoughts to the abbess. What had happened to her? He hoped she was all right. He regretted he hadn't left her his name. It would be cleansing somehow, to fulfill a promise to someone. He returned to his writing, banishing her from his mind, but the idea of her, something about her, snagged at his sleeve and clung to him like a burr.

TOM LAID OUT a white linen shirt, a forest-green coat with upturned cuffs of golden braid, and a matching pair of breeches. That done, he fetched a silver pot of coffee and thumped it on the desk by his master's head.

"Eh? What?" William blinked and groaned, letting the pen fall from stiff fingers and massaged his temples with his palms. "What time is it?"

"Barely time enough for you to make it to His Majesty's coronation, milord, which is at eleven."

William yawned and stretched, cracking his neck. "What an ungodly hour! He has been ruling for a year now. One wonders at the fuss." He sipped his coffee and nodded at the clothes. "Shall I get you a new livery, Tom? Are you overshadowed by your peers? We can't have that. You mustn't be demeaned in the eyes of your lady."

Tom's face flushed its familiar shade of crimson. "I

prefer to be inconspicuous, milord. Besides, it is better I blend in the background given some of the tasks you set me."

"Indeed, you are my muse, Tom. Your nighttime ramblings fuel many a pointed verse." He reached into a desk drawer that his high-breasted felon had missed, and found a gold half sovereign. He played it through his fingers before tossing it to his man. "If you'll not buy a suit then get gloves or ribbons for your lady. They tend to be impressed by things like that."

"Thank you, sir!"

William shrugged. "Consider it a gift on His Majesty's coronation. You risked life and limb the same as I to get him here. Good Christ, man! Are you trying to feed me porridge?"

"You cannot live on wine alone, milord."

"It has served me well enough till now. Bring me some more of that, and a bite of bread and cheese."

WESTMINSTER ABBEY WAS crowded to the rafters, with scaffolding laid across the north end to allow some lucky spectators a bird's-eye view. Buckingham, who'd latched onto William shortly after he arrived, told him those eager souls had been waiting since four in the morning. A raised dais covered in red and a majestic throne took center stage, waiting for the arrival of the king. He came accompanied by his brother the Duke of York and a coterie of bishops in capes made from cloth of gold. A train of nobles in their Parliament robes followed behind, and William and Buckingham inserted themselves in it unnoticed.

After a sermon and service, Charles stood bareheaded

in front of the altar to complete the ceremonies of office. The crown was placed on his head and a great shout rose from the crowd. Three times the master-at-arms called on any who could show a reason why Charles Stuart should not be King of England, and then, amidst a swell of music and the cheers and excited chatter of over ten thousand people, the king and his escort left the abbey for Westminster Hall. The crowd was there before him and when he entered with his crown on his head and his scepter in his hand, some wept tears, some shouted with joy, and everyone partook in the celebration.

William and Buckingham were seated at the far end of the hall, next to the king's table. The ceremonies continued throughout the meal, as heralds led people up to Charles to bow before him and be greeted in return. Buckingham, who'd shared Charles's nursery as a child, snorted when Sir Edward Hyde was brought forth as Earl Clarendon. "Now there's a problem, my dear William. Sir Edward is a relic our new king should have left in the past. He pines for the court of Charlie's father, and will be naught but a canker to us all."

William enjoyed the duke, who used his brilliant mind to mock anything serious, including politics and religion, but he made a better jester than advisor. "Clarendon is a joyless pain in the arse, George. Believe me I know. But he is the only one amongst us, including our beloved king, who puts his country's interests before his own."

"And that, dear boy," Buckingham said, clapping him on the arm, "is what makes him such a dangerous man."

Charles, already grown bored, spotted them and

waved them over to join him at his table, but the spectacle wasn't over yet. Dymock, the King's Champion, rode into the hall in full armor, with his spear carried before him. He threw down his gauntlet, challenging any who might deny Charles Stuart was lawful King of England. The king drank his health, the crowd cheered, and the public celebrations drew to a close.

The skies poured open as they left the hall, drenching them in a cold rain. Thunder rolled around them from towering columns of black clouds, and the air was rent by the crackle of lightning. It didn't dampen anyone's mood; quite the reverse, and as the common folk of London hastened to continue the celebrations in taverns, inns and private homes, the king and his company repaired to His Majesty's withdrawing room at Whitehall, to begin their celebrations in earnest.

Unlike many courtiers who occasionally drank to excess, William was an elegant drunk. He never spewed, grew ugly or passed out under tables. Though he was often distant when sober, something inside him loosened and soared when he drank. He was amiable, easy and daring. His wit danced like sunlight on water, or flayed like a serrated blade. It was then he was most likely to shock, scandalize and delight. It thrilled his companions, who in the interest of entertainment, were always inviting him to dinner, and always plying him with drink.

Charles, who had one arm around Barbara Palmer's shoulders, leaned into William, ready to be amused. "That was a pretty trollop you brought home from Oxford Kate's last night, Will. Are you inclined to share her?"

"She is yours, Majesty. If you can find her. She made off with my purse, but I daresay she would still cost less than the one seated in your lap. What will you do with *your* pretty trollop when your new queen arrives?"

Charles spoke mildly. "Barbara has a temper, William. Don't test it. I find you diverting, but not nearly as much as her. Now…I pay you to write pretty verse, do I not?" He raised his voice so it carried through the room. "Ladies and gentleman? Shall we ask our court poet for some words to mark this day?"

The room erupted into cheers and clinking glasses. William rose, a mischievous grin on his face, and raised his cup. "Ladies and gentlemen…a toast to our king on his coronation!

"God bless our good and gracious king,
Whose promise none relies on;
Who never said a foolish thing,
Nor ever did a wise one."

There was a moment of utter silence, followed by gasps of outrage and a smattering of nervous titters. Charles took his time framing a response, then raised his own glass and gave William a wolfish smile. "Thank you, dear William. As always, you speak the truth. For my words are my own, but my actions are my minister's."

The room erupted into laughter and applause, and the party continued well into the next morning.

CHAPTER NINE

ELIZABETH DROPPED her pen on the table and crumpled the sheet of paper she had been working on into a tight ball. She hurled it into the hearth and watched as blue flames licked at its edges, coaxing it open. Fiery fingers blackened, then devoured the stubborn numbers she had been wrestling with for hours. It was a terrible waste of paper, something they could ill afford, and it had given her no satisfaction at all. Whichever way she calculated them, the results were always they same. Unless something changed soon, they would not have enough coal to see them through winter.

Southwark was a lifetime away from her dower cottage in the woods of Sussex or her late husband's home on the coast, and though only a day's journey, it was an impossible distance from the gently rolling hills and valleys of her heart's home in Kent. They had all been stripped away from her, punishment for aiding and abetting the fugitive king. She had been allowed to keep some personal belongings, to make shift as best she could, but that hadn't amounted to much. Not with four mouths to feed. She was a widow. The worst kind of widow. One without adequate funds. But at least she was free.

Captain Nichols had been more than kind. He had helped her find a small timber-framed tenement house

just off St. Olaves street, a bustling area east of London
Bridge that was home to laborers and lesser tradesmen
and, at the easternmost end, the city's poor. The three-
story house was long and narrow and equipped with a
small garden and a chicken coop in the yard. It straddled
the divide between those who were destitute and those
who made do, but was still within the realm of the gen-
teelly poor. It was the best she could afford.

And so it was a childhood dream come true. She was
living in London, though it was nothing like she had
imagined. The roads were choked with carts and people.
Iron wheels rang harsh on cobbled streets. Chickens
squawked, turkeys gobbled, and lowing cattle ofttimes
blocked the road. Sometimes they stampeded, trampling
crowds and crashing into storefronts with half-wild dogs
yapping at their heels. Ship bells clanged, calling from
the docks, and everywhere people shouted, looking for
business or cursing those who got in their way. The
yodel of the milkman, the howl of the ragman, there
was a different cadence to each trader's cry.

Enveloping it all was the constant black dusting and
eye-watering stench of burning coal. More often than
not it joined the heavy fogs that rolled up the Thames
to grip the city in a choking black fist.

Elizabeth longed to hear the babble of a country
stream or the rustle of a breeze through autumn leaves,
but any such sounds were eaten by the city's dull roar.
She yearned for quiet and childhood and home; but all
that remained of home was here with her now, and she
was doing the best she could to keep them sheltered and
fed. Marjorie had survived her injury but sometimes
forgot what she had said just a moment before. Mary had

assumed the roles of housekeeper and lady's maid even though Elizabeth dressed plainly and by herself. And Samuel fancied himself the butler, though they had no guests; groom, though they had no horse and carriage; and groundskeeper of their small garden plot.

She had done well enough up till now. At first she had sold her jewelry, piece by piece. She had a brooch and a pair of earrings left her by her mother, a pearl necklace her father had given her, and a small collection of simple rings. She had begun taking in sewing, they were frugal with food and fuel, and they had taken in a lodger who was quiet and timely with his rent. The chickens provided eggs and an occasional tasty dinner and the garden kept them supplied with carrots, turnips and beets.

But two months past she'd sold the last of her rings, leaving only some china plates and what was left of the silverware. If she had only herself to worry about she would seek a job as governess or lady's companion, but neither position would allow her to live at home, or to bring what had become her family, who were too old now to earn a living on their own. Marjorie talked of opening an ordinary. One thing she never forgot was how to cook. But they didn't have the funds or the room to make that possible. They had taken to calling the kitchen Marjorie's Bake House though, which always made Marjorie smile.

She stared glumly into the fire, her elbows resting on the table and her hands wrapped around a mug of ale. Samuel's shoes had holes in the toes. Mary and Marjorie needed bonnets and stockings and cloaks to protect them from the winter's chill. The coal bin was nearly empty. She could fill it once, but it would not last them through till spring. *Now what?* She sighed. She still had some things left to trade besides the silverware: her independence, her childish dreams and her freedom.

Captain Nichols had begun a halfhearted campaign to win her hand shortly after he saw her settled. He would be coming to visit in a few days, as he had the third Sunday of every month since they moved to Southwark. There was no benefit to him in it that she could see. She had no lands, no annuities and no dowry. She supposed he made the effort out of a feeling of responsibility based on his friendship with her father. So far, she had refused him, but he insisted all she needed was time.

He was a good man, and it was an excellent offer. One a woman in her position would be a fool not to accept. A minor baronet with a small but comfortable estate, both he and his lands had been left untouched under the general amnesty proclaimed when the king was restored to his throne last year. He would take care of her and her servants. Marjorie, Mary and Samuel could retire in peace and comfort. They could all return to the country and leave the foul air of London behind.

And yet she hesitated. Captain Nichols—she had yet to call him Robert—was a sober and serious man from all she'd seen. He was kind. He would not be anything like Benjamin, but he didn't have William's mocking laugh, his flashing eyes or his devilish smile. She had only to close her eyes to conjure a picture of their life together, he noting crop yields and wool prices in his ledger while she sat in her bonnet embroidering by the fire. It stretched out in front of her, comfortable and quiet, boring and safe. She felt no passion when she was with him, no thrill when he spoke her name, and no spark of excitement when his hand grazed her shoulder or he took her by the arm. Without those things, she couldn't imagine any joy from their marriage bed. Perhaps that was an unusual, unreasonable thing to expect from a husband, but after spending a night in William's arms she just couldn't settle for anything less.

She shook her head in disgust. It was *his* foolish tales of magic, adventure and love that had infected her like some fanciful disease. She cursed him for it, not for the first time, but she couldn't see how marrying the captain would offer a cure. The year and a half she had known William had been the happiest time of her life. He had brought joy, but also great sorrow into her life, and that she could forgive him. But he had also taught her to dream and to dare. When she was young and full of hope she had dreamed he loved her. She accepted his words as truth and dared her father's wrath. She dreamed that they would somehow be together, and believed him when he promised he'd come home.

She traced the scar that tingled along the base of her thumb and snorted, then lifted her tankard of ale. In the end it had meant nothing at all. Pfft! Silly goose! William was no Artegall and she was no Britomart and life was certainly no fairy tale. Her late husband Benjamin had taught her that and her dreams had ended when her father died and her uncle came to take her home.

It was her uncle who'd told her that their neighbor, William de Veres, was responsible for her father's death. It was said without malice or blame, though if the mother had looked to the son instead of her holdings, the lad would be a sober Parliamentarian and they would all be better for it. A great tragedy indeed when neighbors who should be sharing fields and game were forced to go to war. He married her off quickly. She was seventeen. Her uncle had no wife and knew nothing of young girls, and he didn't want the bother of finding a chaperone.

Benjamin Horace was a preacher of the worst sort. Convinced of his own self-importance, he was a harsh, unbending man with a passion for enforcing his own will. In marrying Elizabeth he had reached far above his station, and though he had taken her family name to add glory to his own, he seemed compelled to remind her in any way he could that as his wife, her place was beneath him.

Forced into marriage with unseemly haste and no time to mourn, Elizabeth stumbled through her first year in a state of numbed shock. It was just as well. Her marriage was a nightmare. After her mother's death she had been raised in an atmosphere of benign neglect, but there was nothing benign or neglectful about Benjamin. He examined her coif, her nails, her dress, looking for any imperfection. He forced her to read page after page of scripture, ready to pounce on any mistake, and he set her to work like a kitchen menial, to cure her of any false pride she might harbor from her exalted birth. Any small rebellion was punished severely, with prayers on bare knees on hard stone, days without food, or a rod applied smartly across her naked shoulders and back. She pled for mercy once, near the beginning, but it seemed to give him pleasure, and she did not so much as whimper after that. She became his idea of a proper Puritan wife, her hair bound tight, her knees bent in prayer, her voice silent and her spirit stilled.

He drank often. It was a sin that would have shocked his flock but he blamed her for it, claiming she drove him to it with her willful manner and seductive ways. She quickly grew to hate him, and if she prayed, it was for him to be gone. She thought of leaving many times, but she feared for her servants and herself. She had seen the ducking stool and scold's bridle put to use. She had seen women die from the one and have their tongue's torn open by the other, and Benjamin, determined to crush her spirit, had threatened to ask the magistrate to use them if she dared oppose him.

She didn't think he really would. Those punishments were saved for the lower sort, and by publically humiliating his wife he would demean himself. Nor would he want to risk her life. Her uncle had been sickly and obese, and so long as he didn't marry or produce a son, she remained heiress to the lands in Kent. Benjamin was an ambitious man. He wasn't content with his holding in Brighton, and his only claim to Kent was through his marriage to her.

She bore it all stoically for seven long years, as one who was tired and friendless and had nowhere to go, but after one particularly brutal beating for leaving her hair loose and uncovered, she barred him in his room while he slept, took all the money from the locked box on his desk, and gathered Marjorie, Mary and Sam, and fled into the night. Imagining she was the fearless Britomart, she calmed her servants and kept her panic at bay. They walked through the night to the nearest market town and

she secured them passage on the early-morning stage.
The next day they reached the dower house.

She was fairly certain her husband knew nothing of it,
but she passed her first few weeks in constant fear. She
need not have worried. It was a peaceful haven. Once
a month, Samuel would walk to Crawley for news and
supplies. It was there he heard sometime later that the
preacher Benjamin Horace had been waylaid and killed
by murderous thieves. She hadn't shed a tear. Benjamin
had no living relatives, and the one thing she had somehow refused him was a son. She'd been content to stay
at her dower house, though. Even when news came that
her bachelor uncle had died. It seemed she had become
what she once told William she wanted to be, a wealthy
widow.

She was a practical girl and life had taught her the
best way to keep her freedom and what was hers was to
hide, but it had felt good to finally take charge of her life
and become not a girl who dreamed, but a woman who
dared. And so when William turned up at her door after
all those years she had reached for what she wanted.
She couldn't have done it if he had known her. It would
have been awkward and uncomfortable and there would
have been far too much to say. She supposed it was that,
as much as hurt and anger that had stilled her tongue.
But a handsome stranger could offer a lonely widow
comfort on a stormy night, if only she dared. And so
she had, though it tore her heart that he greeted her as a
stranger. She wondered if she had ever lingered longer
than a moment in his thoughts.

*Well, at least I captured a moment that will live in
mine. Damn it, de Veres! What am I to do? How can I*

marry the captain when the only man I've ever wanted was you? There was another possibility, though. One slim chance that required she dream *and* dare. Less than a year after stripping her of her lands Cromwell had died and his son had abdicated power shortly thereafter. It was Charles Stuart who ruled England now, and it was said he was a generous and gallant man, particularly when it came to women. She could seek an audience and join the crowd petitioning him for the return of their lands.

She could ask for her father's lands, her husband's lands, and her dower lands, too. If he chose to return any part of it, they would be able to get by. She would not be asking for charity. The king had granted amnesty to those who had opposed him and she was no soldier who had taken up arms. She was a young widow who'd suffered and whose lands had been confiscated for aiding his cause.

It was worth a try. If she failed, she would sell what remained of the furniture and offer her services to Captain Nichols as housekeeper instead of wife. He had been kind to her servants and would likely accept them. It was one of his soldiers who had injured Marjorie after all. He would be disappointed, but despite his kindness and apparent interest, the sadness and distance in his eyes hadn't lessened in all the time she'd known him. He was an intensely private man who seemed unable or unwilling to confide in her, and not terribly concerned that she confide in him. In all the time she'd known him their conversation had never approached the intimacy she'd shared with William. She wanted more from a marriage. Anything less would be unfair to them both.

Pleased to have a plan in place, she finished her ale and thumped the tankard on the table. Better to be a servant than to marry without love. With a tired smile she rested her head on her folded arms and fell asleep.

MARJORIE WAS DELIGHTED with her decision, but she and Mary could not seem to appreciate the gravity of their situation. All they were concerned about was that Elizabeth was going to the palace to visit the king and must look her very best. They brushed and aired her black woolen skirt and bodice, and sold what remained of the silverware to buy lace for her neck and shoulders and a satin overskirt of rich burnt gold. Elizabeth was appalled. They had so little left.

"Hush, child," Marjorie scolded. "If you are going into battle you must do so fully armed. You can always sell it after. Besides...what if *he* is there?"

"He will not be. This is none of the captain's business and I've not asked him to accompany me."

"Not the captain, Lizzy girl! Your William! The one who ate my biscuits and came to call in Sussex. The one you pretended not to know."

"You knew him? But you never said a thing!"

"Knew who?"

"William!"

"The de Veres boy? Of course I knew him. Don't you remember? He lived just across the way. They say he's called Earl Rivers now, and is always with the king. You must look your best. What if he *is* there, Lizzy?"

Elizabeth gave up. "Marjorie Dobbs, I think you are a sly hen who only forgets what she wants to. If William didn't know me in Crawley, he certainly won't remember me now." Despite her protest, the very mention of his name had made her heart jump, and the thought that she might see him again made something flutter deep inside. She made no further protest as Marjorie fastened her bonnet and arranged her skirts in front of the mirror. She could sell the skirt later, but for now it did look very smart.

ELIZABETH'S HEART THUDDED so loudly it drowned out everything around her. The clatter of the hackney coach and the hubbub of the city were distant echoes, muted by the thoughts that clamored in her mind. She was crossing the bridge into London to visit the king, like Dick Whittington and his cat. She worried how one approached a king. How deep should she curtsy? How did one make an appointment and where did one find him? What did one say? She rehearsed her plea…no, her *case*…for the return of her lands, over and over in her mind until the palace came into full view.

Despite living on the outskirts of the city, she had only ever seen it in the distance. She had thought it best not to risk Cromwell's displeasure, and in any case, they had neither the time nor the money for pleasure outings. Now she gaped out the window in amazement. Whitehall Palace was a rambling assortment of twenty acres of gardens, parks and buildings, set along the north bank of the Thames. It was a gilded wonder, with soaring turrets, imposing battlements, and architectural elements borrowed from Italy, the Middle East, India and France. Its outer walls of black and white were painted with fantastical creatures, and its pinnacles were crowned with lions and unicorns that glinted in the morning sun.

It might have been a fairy castle from one of William's stories. *Oh, how he must love it here!*

Well her William would. She had heard a great deal about the new Earl Rivers. Everyone had. The profane court poet whose lampoons toured the city on broadsheets. In Southwark, like elsewhere, gossip about the new king and his scandalous courtiers was a pastime everyone loved. He was said to be a man of wit, charm and devilishly handsome appearance, one of the king's close circle of decadent rakes. They also warned he was a danger to women, devouring and discarding them, wooing them with passionate words and a cold heart. His description bore no resemblance to the William she had known or, for that matter, to the one who hadn't known her.

Oddly enough, though he was said to be one of Charles's close friends, he was also one of His Majesty's harshest critics, and much of his satire was directed against the king. It was a wonder he hadn't been arrested, though rumor had it he had already been banished twice. Somehow he managed to remain in favor and keep his good-natured monarch under his spell. It spoke well for King Charles's sense of humor that he seemed inclined to give his poet free rein. The latest ditty making the rounds was certainly no compliment.

She could not help but smile, remembering what her father had once said. *The boy is wild, ungovernable.* Perhaps it was true. If he wasn't chasing strumpets, actresses or ladies of the court, he was writing sacrilegious, satirical, or slanderous verse. *Angry verse.* She had to admit she had read some of it, and it really was quite good. The bold and scathing humor with which he dared rebuke his king seemed very much like him, even if the stories about him did not.

She took a deep breath, wondering, despite what she had said to Marjorie, if he would remember her. Not as his childhood friend, of course, but the woman who had…the woman he had met in Sussex. *Ridiculous!* It didn't matter in any case. He certainly wasn't the gallant hero she had idolized in her youth, and if he did remember her, which was highly unlikely, it would simply be as one of many women who had graced his bed.

She was through the main gates now and approaching the inner courtyard. The chaos and bustle of London crept up to the palace walls and passed right through them, following the public thoroughfare that ran through the palace grounds. Her heart pounded louder with every hoofbeat that took her closer to her goal. As she passed hawkers and produce stalls, grand carriages and fine ladies, her heart caught in her throat. She told herself it wasn't at the thought of seeing William again—it was the fear of failing when so much was counting on her success.

CHAPTER TEN

"TOM! THOMAS!"

"Yes, sir!" Thomas came rushing into the room, straightening his coat and cravat.

William regarded him through narrowed eyes. "It is not yet noon. It's a bit early to be about that business, is it not?"

Tom blushed but didn't answer.

"She is a kitchen maid?"

"No, a lady's maid, milord."

"Ah! Be careful, Tom. Too many days with the same wench will lead to boredom or marriage, and a lady's maid seeks higher than a manservant. If you don't get rid of her soon I shall have to make you my steward and you'll be forced to learn your sums. Who is her mistress?"

"Miss Temple, sir."

"Ah, yes, I've met her. She seems a relative innocent, pleasant enough and new to court. But have a care she's not sent the girl here to spy."

"I doubt it, milord. My Jeanine says Miss Temple believes you are the very devil, and several ladies of the court have warned her away."

"Indeed? Bring us a brandy and tell me what they say."

"Isn't it a bit early for *that,* milord?"

"No, Tom. In fact you must hurry. I am already half-way sober and if I don't have some soon it will be too late."

"Yes, milord." Tom returned a few minutes later with two glasses of brandy, and sat across the table from his master, eager to share his gossip. His ear for it and his delight in spreading it were two talents William found most useful at court.

"Well, sir…according to Jeanine, Miss Hobart has told Miss Temple, who had formed an attraction to you, that you are one of the most dangerous men at court, and any woman who speaks to you three times is accounted your mistress, as none can escape you, should you set your mind on it."

"Aha! I knew it! I am a greedy devil indeed!"

"Indeed, sir!" Tom nodded his head vigorously. "She claimed, that is Miss Hobart, sir, not my Jeanine, that there is nothing more dangerous than the artful insinuating way in which you gain possession of a woman's mind."

"And by what magic do I do that, Tom?"

"She told Miss Temple that you applaud a woman's tastes, submit to her sentiments, and at the very moment you do not believe a single word you are saying, you make her believe it all."

"Well, it certainly worked on Miss Hobart, but she is a vain creature with very little sense. Your Miss Temple would be wiser to have a fear of her. She has a preference for her own sex and is doubtless working her own magic. Such is the fate of innocent lambs at court."

"My Jeanine is very innocent, milord. She has expressed a desire to meet you."

"Fear not, Tom. Should our paths cross I shall have a care to be argumentative and disagreeable. If she says the day is fair I will call for rain, if she prefers the guitar I will extol the flute, and if she tells me how manly and handsome you are, I will insist you are as fat and ugly as a boar."

Tom grinned and raised his glass. "Thank you, Master William."

"Now that you're here, Tom, I'd like your opinion on my latest work. I'm having the devil's own time finishing it."

"Certainly, milord, though I am no learned man of letters." Tom took the proffered page and began to read.

> *"I rise at eleven, I dine about two,*
> *I get drunk before seven, and the next thing I do,*
> *I send for my whore, when for fear of a clap,*
> *I dally about her and spew in her lap;*
> *Then we quarrel and scold, till I fall fast asleep,*
> *When the bitch growing bold, to pocket does creep."*

"What happens next, milord?"

"A valuable lesson for any man, Tom, though one few enough heed. But I can't seem to find the words to end it. She leaves the hero bereaved of both his money and the pleasure he paid for and then— Ah! I've got it.

> *"If by chance then I wake, hot-headed and drunk,*

What a coil do I make for the loss of my punk!
I storm and I roar, and I fall in a rage.
And missing my whore, I bugger my page.
Then crop-sick all morning I rail at my men,
And in bed I lie yawning till eleven again."

William waited several moments. "So...? What do you think?"

"I think it captures you at your best, milord. It's about you and your lady friend the other night?"

"A pox on you!" William snatched the page back from him and scribbled down the words before he lost them. "It is not *actually* about me. I use myself as allegory you see...to capture the irony of... Bah! Never mind. As you say, you are no man of letters. Your reading is restricted to racing forms and filthy pamphlets."

"But isn't that what this—"

"I am grown bored of your prattle, Tom. Tidy up here and then what say we take a gallop out of town and play at highwaymen again?"

"I will not, sir! Not unless your very life depended on it."

"But I tell you it does! I am about to expire from boredom."

"It will have to be a worse fate than that, milord, to make me risk my neck again."

"So your loyalty only goes so far. Very well. Take your lady fair on an outing and see if you have more fun."

In truth he *was* bored, of everything. He picked up his

pen to begin a new diatribe against his king, knowing full well it would have no effect at all.

In th' isle of Britain, long since famous grown
For breeding the best...

"Damnation! He threw his pen on the table. It was too early to go back to bed and he didn't feel like writing. Maybe he should amble down to the palace proper and see what news was making the rounds at court. The walk would do him good. Perhaps he might find a new conquest, someone to ease the tedium, but it was so difficult to find a challenge when they all toppled over with a pinch and a poem. He yawned and rose, and with nothing better to do, left to stroll the grounds of Whitehall and see what was happening in his majesty's chambers.

ELIZABETH STEPPED from the hackney, lost and bewildered. The driver stopped just long enough to wave impatiently in the direction of the Great Chamber, the outermost room of the royal suite, before trotting off to collect another fare. She entered a large paneled room with a carved ceiling and stained glass windows. A steady stream of people entered and exited, all intent on their business and all seeming to know where they were going except her. She elbowed her way through the throng, hoping to find an official she could ask for direction, and tripped on the hem of a very elegant lady's satin-lined velvet cloak.

"How dare you!" The woman gasped in outrage and

turned to slap her, only to be stopped by her beribboned companion who grabbed hold of her hand.

"Pay her no mind, my dear. She's a boorish country rustic without manners or style, or else she's somebody's servant. Either way, it's beneath you to address her, and if you strike her and she belongs to someone's household, heaven knows who you might offend."

"Well, I shouldn't let one of my servants leave home dressed like that! Imagine! Coming to the king's Great Chamber dressed like a common drudge."

Face burning, Elizabeth bit back a rude response and tried to slip back into the crowd, but her awkward stumble and her affronted victim had already made her the center of attention. People were whispering and pointing and craning their necks to see her. She stuck out her chin and clenched her fists, refusing to be cowed, but the remarks about her dress made her feel like a child again. The suit they had all sacrificed so much for was a mockery amongst these jeweled and glittering creatures, unfit for one of their menials to wear. She fought back tears and the urge to give up and go home. How foolish she had been to imagine she could just walk right in and see the king. Her lower lip trembled. She was *not* going to fail.

Ignoring the titters and amused looks around her, she squared her shoulders and shoved her way toward an imposing man in red-and-gold livery. She had come to make an appointment, and she wasn't leaving without one.

WILLIAM PASSED through the Grand Chamber on his way to Charles's suite. He had some plans to discuss regarding his latest play, and if anyone was awake yet, he hoped to arrange an expedition to Newmarket in the next few days. The racing was always exciting and God knew he needed a change of scene. Besides that, he hadn't seen His Majesty since his latest ditty had begun making the rounds. If Charles was in a black mood and intent on banishing him from court again it was best to get the thing done now, in the hopes of being called back before winter made the roads impassable.

He wended his way through a crush of supplicants, hangers-on and gossip seekers, ignoring the hands that reached for his sleeve to stop him and greeting those who tried to engage him in conversation with a polite, disinterested nod. He brushed by Lord Stanley and his friend Darnley, who were strutting with several other silken cockerels, adorned with enough colorful ribbons to supply half the peddlers parked outside the palace walls. They were squawking in excitement over something. He couldn't help but catch part of their conversation and he checked his stride to listen.

"Good heavens, Stanley, who is *that* creature?" Darnley asked, loud enough for his voice to carry.

"Don't you mean *what* is that creature?" Stanley tittered in reply.

William looked about the room. If there were a new personage at court he had yet to hear about it.

"Why 'tis a shapeless lump of mud, wrapped round in cloth of gold!"

Cocking his head, William was just able to discern a gold overskirt navigating a sea of ruffled knees and red-ribboned shoes.

"Or a plain little partridge hoping to pass for a swan.

What else can one expect from our boorish country cousins? Doubtless she's some Puritan miss come begging for alms. Why has no one shown her the beggar's gate?" There were snickers all around.

William stepped into the circle, resting a lace-trimmed cuff on Stanley's shoulder. He could see her now. They had crowded her into a corner and she looked desperate for a way to escape. "Stanley, my dear, you have never had the eye to discern the classic lines of a true work of art. Observe the fine bones of her visage, those plump lips and the saucy lift of her breasts. She may come in a plain wrapper, but I vow there's something exquisite underneath." *Poor little bird. No doubt she has scrimped and saved and wears her best to our soulless, shallow court.*

"Ha, de Veres! As if you have any interest in a country miss lacking style, funds or beauty. It's an insult for her to show herself here."

"And yet you bring your own half-naked doxie."

"Here now, Lord Rivers, Mistress Duvalier is an actress of great renown! Why the king himself—"

"Has fucked her senseless. Yes I know." He took a closer look at the girl. All he could see was her profile, but something about her intrigued him. A defenseless girl surrounded by hectoring bullies. He had a sense that he had lived the moment before.

"Surely you do not intend to pursue her, Rivers?" Grammont asked him, perplexed. "If so, you must be jaded indeed. It seems both dangerous and cruel. She will present no challenge. Awed by your beauty, charm and wit, she will tumble into your lap like overripe fruit, annoy you within a day with her breathless prattle, and embarrass you with her country manners. Then when you leave her, she will run crying to some burly relative you'll be forced to kill in a duel."

Tumble into your lap like overripe fruit. How many times had he dreamed that very thing? Memories jostled in his brain, tugging and teasing and then she turned around. Her eyes were bright and alive, though they sparked with hurt and anger. They glittered as the light caught them, changing from silver-gray to stormy blue, just like the sea in winter. *Sirens' eyes.* It seemed his little bird had come to call. His face lit with a slow smile.

He watched with amusement as she waved her arm, struggling to catch the chamberlain's attention. That wasn't going to work. Not unless she had a purse attached to it. *What is she doing here?* Suddenly her voice, frustrated and desperate, rose above the din.

"Excuse me, sir! You are the chamberlain? I should like to make an appointment for Elizabeth Walters to see the king, please."

William stood rooted to the spot, flooded by memories, oblivious to the gasps of outrage and disapproval. Elizabeth Walters. Lizzy Walters. The lass in the meadow who fell in his lap, wrapped tight in her skirts and bonnet. A shiver traveled up his spine. He could see the grave-faced girl with her wary silver-blue eyes and a straying flame-red curl. He remembered his teasing, he remembered her laughter, and he remembered her friendship as the best part of his youth.

Britomart...Lizzy. The only light in a dark time he still fought hard to forget. *She was the first girl I kissed, the first one I claimed to love, and it was the only time I meant it. Good Lord but I was young.* His heart quickened with a warmth that had been alien to him for some time, a warmth he had only ever felt for her. He had trusted her more than anyone in his world. There were secrets he had hinted at, almost told her.

As he watched her now, just a few feet away, he struggled to contain his emotions, and then he remembered something else. *"You killed my father."* Of course! Hugh Walters! *He* was her father! And his pretty little Sussex abbess was also his little bird. *Why didn't she tell me? And what in God's name is she doing here now?*

ELIZABETH WAS close to tears. A group of fashionably dressed courtiers, one who looked more like a maypole than a man, had surrounded her in a corner of the room, exchanging gibes and sallies about her appearance as if it were a contest. They seemed to find themselves terribly amusing, and their voices carried across the room. *I am not the clown. They are!* She looked straight ahead, ignoring them, standing on the tips of her toes straining to find the functionary who seemed bent on ignoring her. If he wouldn't even acknowledge her, what was she supposed to do?

She almost jumped when she felt a hand on her elbow. Before she could jab her assailant with a hairpin, a pleasant, cultured voice spoke from directly behind her.

> *"Full brimmed with spleen, and armed with pen*
> *These strutting, crowing, cowardly, men*
> *Forsake the cock and attack the hen."*

She turned around slowly, her face a deep crimson, her heart hammering in her chest. William de Veres was right in front of her, bent in a deep bow, the plumes of his hat sweeping the floor. He rose to his full height, towering over her, and gave her a lopsided grin.

CHAPTER ELEVEN

"ELIZABETH? It's been far too long! What a great pleasure it is to see you grace our court." His mocking eyes glinted with humor and his engaging smile tugged at long-buried emotions, locked deep in her wary heart.

"Ah…I…" Elizabeth stared at him, speechless, her pulse racing, her breath caught in her lungs. *He remembers me!*

In a room full of brightly colored fops and gallants, each trying to outdo the other as they sailed past in clouds of lace, trailing ribbons at elbow, wrist and knee, he stood out. He towered above most of the men in the room, but it wasn't just his height. Where others primped and postured, getting every detail right, his style was casual, bordering on negligent. He disdained both wig and powder. It was his own raven hair that fell past his broad shoulders. His clothes, other than a white linen shirt opened at the throat, were in shades of rich chocolate, the breeches just a shade lighter than his boots and coat. The coat was worn open exposing a tan silk lining, and his only ornamentation was some lace at his wrists and some bronze and charcoal embroidery on his buttons and sleeves. It was understated, elegant and impossibly rakish. For a moment she felt as if her knees might give way.

This was Earl Rivers, seducer of women and kings.

His smile still pierced her heart. She was dimly aware of that treacherous organ, thudding heavy and clumsy in her chest. She had stepped into his world and should not be surprised to see him, but it still came as a shock. That he should see her like this! A drab hen in a menagerie of exotic birds. She felt small and plain and wished desperately that she could sink through the floor. A tumble of emotions threatened to overwhelm her. Vivid sensations flooded her body as wanton images of lying naked in his arms flashed through her mind. She shivered to recall his warm breath brushing the nape of her neck. Her lips burned, remembering his heated kisses, and her skin tingled at the memory of his gentle touch.

"Don't you recognize me, Elizabeth? Surely you know who I am."

Her face flushed, burning and pricking as if bitten by tiny sparks, and then a horrible thought crossed her mind. *He was standing right there. He was standing with them. Was he one of the men who were mocking me?* "I know who you are, Lord Rivers."

"Come now. Surely you can do better than that?" His voice teased but his eyes were intent.

"You scribble naughty verses and seduce the wives of your friends." She had no idea why she blurted that out, and desperately wished she could take it back.

"A scribbler!" He seemed genuinely taken aback. "I hope you at least account me a talented one. Do you mean to say you don't remember our meeting near Crawley? You were of great service to His Majesty and myself."

There were rude sniggers from behind them and she

lifted her chin. "I remember you sought my help, my lord. But I do not believe we were formally introduced."

"I was a fugitive at the time, madam, and not in the habit of formal introductions, but I promised you assistance if ever you should need it. What business brings you here to court? Perhaps there's a way I might aid you."

"I mean no offense, Lord Rivers, but had you meant to keep that promise, you would have given me your name at the time. You needn't worry. I didn't come here to claim your help." She lifted her head, looking pointedly over his shoulder at the group of interested courtiers behind him.

"But I did come back to offer it, Elizabeth, only to find your path overgrown, your windows and doors boarded, and you long gone." He offered her his arm. "Walk with me. Let us speak somewhere private." When she hesitated, he leaned closer and lowered his voice. "Take my arm, Elizabeth. 'Tis no insult I pay you. I am an intimate of our monarch and, I am told, not without a small modicum of personal charm."

The thought of touching him made her tremble. To know that he had returned for her fanned dangerous illusions she should have long outgrown. But because of him she had lost her father, been forced to marry Benjamin, and then forfeited all her lands. She had lost enough already. She would have to be a fool to risk her heart. "I've no doubt you seem charming to some, but to talk with you in private is to risk one's reputation, my lord. What could you possibly want from me now? You are surrounded by court beauties who swoon as you pass."

"That is hardly entertaining, is it? They are of no use to me supine upon the floor."

"That is not what one hears."

He gave her a wolfish grin. "I'm relieved to see that *you*, my dear, are made of sterner stuff."

Her heart caught in her throat and she fought to suppress a foolish grin of her own, alarmed at how easy it was to slide into the easy banter they had shared as children. "Do they lie?"

"They exaggerate…somewhat. I am a gentleman by name and birth, sweetling, but not by nature, and I have never claimed aught else. It is only you who ever thought otherwise. In any case, no gentleman can help you in Charlie's court. They are very rare creatures and universally despised."

"Why?"

"Because they ruin the fun for everyone else." He nodded toward his arm, which was still extended, and looked at her expectantly. "I refuse to believe you are ruled by the opinions of people you've never met…or is it a husband you fear?"

"No. My husband is dead."

"How unfortunate! My sympathies, madam."

"They are not required. He was not a nice man and we were not close." *Why did I tell him that? It's none of his business.* Yet as a child there'd been no one she was closer to in all the world. It seemed a part of her still responded to him as the friend with whom she shared all her secrets. It was foolish and dangerous; something she must curb. This man wasn't her old friend William. He was the decadent and outrageous Lord Rivers.

He slid his arm through hers without waiting for

permission. A frisson of electricity charged her every nerve. Leaning into her shoulder, he spoke close to her ear, the intimate gesture causing heads to turn, "Congratulations then, Lizzy Walters. You are the widow you always said you wanted to be."

Her mouth dropped open and her startled eyes met his knowing ones.

"Yes, little bird. I remember everything. That surprises you? Come." He tugged at her elbow. Too shocked to protest, she allowed him to guide her to an alcove in the corner.

"Why didn't you say anything when we met in Sussex, Lizzy? Why didn't you tell me who you were?"

It took her a moment to gather her wits. Suddenly he *was* her William, yet she knew that was impossible. Life had changed them both, tearing them apart and washing them up on far and vastly different shores. She was a respectable impoverished widow who still clung to quaint notions of love. He was Earl Rivers, notorious libertine and court poet who lived in a magnificent palace and sat down to dinner with dukes and kings.

"Elizabeth? It's too late to pretend we don't know each other. Why did you do so then?"

She closed her eyes a moment and sighed. However the years might have changed them, in five short minutes they'd been stripped away and they were speaking as freely they had years ago.

"It had been too long. So long you didn't even recognize me. Not even when I…I don't know. I felt that if it was important to you, if you wanted to, you would have remembered on your own." There was a hint of challenge in her voice.

He sighed and closed his eyes a moment. "There were things I wanted to forget, Elizabeth, but you weren't one of them. Yet how was I to know you? When I saw you last we were children. You were a pretty child, full of life and laughter and you had changed so much. What happened to you?"

She was stunned by his casual cruelty. *You happened! Benjamin happened!* "You used to be a gentleman!" she snapped, close to tears. "What happened to you?"

He saw the hurt in her eyes and immediately regretted his choice of words. "I'm sorry, Lizzy. That was clumsy of me. It wasn't meant as it sounded. You were just so quiet and…careful. It is not as I remember you and I wonder what had made you so grave." He reached out a finger to curl it around a loose strand of hair, but she jerked her head away and took a step back.

"And now?"

He dropped his hand and shrugged. "Now you resemble a pretty bird who has wandered into an exotic—"

"Zoo."

"I was about to say garden. Why are you here, Elizabeth?"

"I am here to make an appointment to see the king."

"I am on my way to see him now. I can introduce you. What is it you want from him?"

"I shall tell him when I see him."

"I'd forgotten how mule-headed you can be. There's a very long line to see the king. Look to your left." He placed his hands on her shoulders and pointed her in the direction he wanted her to look.

Mulish! It's what every man calls a woman with a

mind of her own. The weight of his fingers warmed her shoulders and his breath stirred the hairs on the nape of her neck. She cursed her traitorous body as it responded to his touch.

"The fellow in the fine suit and glorious wig by the door you were shouting at earlier is the chamberlain. You must join a very long line to speak to him, and should you manage that, there's an even longer one to see Charles." He turned her to face the center of the crowded hall. "Take a good look. Everyone here is on the same mission as you. There are mothers with small herds of children, soldiers who've lost arms or legs in his cause, men with inventions, disputes and investments, and beautiful widows who would cry in his arms. He can't satisfy them all. Well, perhaps the last group. But unless you've changed a good deal more than I expect, you can't count on that.

"He is poor. Lady Castlemaine and his other pretties keep him that way. It is easiest to say no and he is an easy man in almost every way. Still, his largesse can be gotten if you know how to appeal to him, but you can wait here for days, even weeks or months trying to get in. You must bribe someone or know someone to get through that door, and if and when you do, you'll have only a moment to capture his interest. *That,* my dear, is why you need my help. So I ask you again…what is your business with our Merry Monarch?"

"You can get me past that line and in to see him?"

He groaned in exasperation, giving her shoulders a gentle shake. "I can, Lizzy, and I will. I made you a promise and I owe you much."

The day she left Benjamin she had taken her fate in

her own hands. Though she had made mistakes, they were *her* mistakes, and she felt she had proved reasonably adept at handling herself. She had vowed to never ask permission, never defer, and never leave her fate in someone else's hands again. *But I can't get any further without aid.*

"Let me help you, little bird," he murmured, his breath so close it tickled in her ear.

She jerked her shoulders from his grasp and stepped away. She turned to face him, ignoring his charming grin. "Very well, Lord Rivers—"

"William."

"I have come to court to see the king and ask him to give me back my lands."

"Your lands? I don't understand. Charles is careless, but he's not vengeful. He hasn't been confiscating property and even if he had, he would have no reason to take it from you."

"He didn't. Cromwell did."

"But why? Your father served him well and…" It was his turn to flush, perhaps the first time he had done so in years. "Elizabeth, I *am* sorry. I had no idea he was your father. It was war. The field of battle. I had no idea who he was at the time. In Sussex when—"

She raised her hand in a motion for him to stop. "Please, William. Not here…not now."

He let the subject drop immediately, greatly relieved, only to be struck by something else. "They came to your cottage?"

"The very next day. They were doing a search of all the homes in the area and found evidence you'd been there. By aiding you, they felt I had aided your king."

"Did they harm you?"

She hesitated a moment. "A friend of my father's was their captain and he intervened."

She'd been placed in danger and lost her home because of him. He felt a sick knot in his stomach and he took a deep breath, tamping it down. *It's simple enough. All I need to do is fix what I've broken and make things right.* "I regret that I brought them down upon you, Elizabeth. But you did well to tell me. I am determined to get you your lands back. Indeed, I've been hellish bored of late and I shall set all my talents to it. It won't be easy. Charles might be generous but his advisors are not, unless they're lining their own pockets. He *is* particularly fond of those who helped him during his exile, though. If you listen to me and follow my lead, you'll soon have him eating from your hand."

Elizabeth blinked in confusion. As a child, she had noticed his mercurial swings in mood, but in less than a heartbeat he had changed from William de Veres to Lord Rivers again. How could she trust her fate to a man who—

"Come along, Elizabeth. We've work to do."

He offered his arm and this time, feeling slightly dazed, she took it. He reached behind a pillar and snatched an elegant ebony walking stick with a lion's head grip that some careless owner had left leaning against the wall.

"William, that's stealing!" she hissed.

He smiled and winked, then twirled it experimentally. "I must tell you someday how I spent my time in exile."

He maneuvered her expertly through the crowd, elbowing those who didn't step from his path and poking those poor unfortunates in the back, head, or shoulders, who failed to step quickly enough from hers. It took them less than two minutes to cut through the throng and she gaped in amazement when the imposing chamberlain scrambled to fling open the doors to the king's inner sanctum.

William took a quick glance over his shoulder as they left. It seemed no one had missed their lengthy tête-à-tête. Satisfied, he pulled her close against him, and together they left the room.

CHAPTER TWELVE

"THESE ARE the king's private chambers?" Elizabeth craned her neck, gaping in wonder as she took it all in. Luxurious carpets muffled her footsteps and gilded ceilings with blue-and-gold moldings soared high overhead. Artwork was everywhere. Gorgeous Mortlake tapestries, paintings of mythical scenes by Titian and Rubens, and royal portraits by Holbein and Van Dyck were just a few that graced the walls. Each room they entered seemed more richly decorated than the last.

William glanced down at her and smiled. "Yes. These are all part of his private suite, little bird. This is his presence chamber. Would you care to sit on the throne?"

Elizabeth looked wide-eyed at the magnificently carved golden throne and William's lips twitched with amusement. Her gaze flicked to the far wall where four guards stood at attention in full armor and livery, pikes in hand. She looked back at William uncertainly.

He placed a hand on her shoulder, leaning close to whisper, "I dare you."

She felt a giddy thrill she hadn't experienced since her youth. Heart thumping, she took another look at the stern-faced guards, and then gingerly lowered herself onto the plush velvet seat. William grinned his approval and she beamed back. She glanced quickly at the guards but they stared straight ahead, seeming to take no notice. She gripped the arms and tried to set a regal pose. *Perhaps Queen Elizabeth herself once sat here!*

William placed his left hand over his chest and took the brim of his hat in the right, removing it in a sweeping gesture as he bent in a deep bow.

> *"Upon a great adventure he was bound,*
> *That greatest Gloriana, to him gave,*
> *That greatest Glorious Queen of Faerieland,*
> *To win him worship, and her grace to have,*
> *Which of all earthly things he most did crave.*

"Do you remember, Lizzy?"

His smile was infectious. Eyes shining, she answered, "If I am Gloriana, then you must be my Redcross Knight."

"Just so, fair lady. And it shall be my task to see you safely from this evil realm, and escort you back to your own lands of faerie. I shall not rest until the thing is done. You have my promise."

For just a few minutes they were children again.

"William, I—" The sound of muffled voices made her leap from the throne straight into the air, and William almost choked on his laughter. A rotund, harried-looking man swathed in brocaded velvet and chains of office burst into the room with several people carrying reams of paper scurrying behind him. He stopped halfway to the north exit, turning to glare at them, fixing them with a frosty look that made clear his disapproval. His mouth opened and closed several times, as if he were about to say something, and then he harrumphed and stalked from the room.

William took her by the arm. "Come along, Lizzy, before your outrageous behavior gets us both into trouble. I swear for a little bird you move as quick as a cat when caught doing mischief."

Elizabeth was mortified. "Stop laughing! It's not funny. Who was that man?"

"Why that was Chancellor Hyde, love, now Lord Clarendon. It would seem the king is not in the mood for business." At her look of horror he started laughing again.

The doors to the privy chamber from whence the chancellor had just come were guarded by six grooms arrayed in the gold, blue and red of the Stuart coat of arms. They passed through and stopped at the doors to the withdrawing room.

"This is where we'll find Charles. Unlike his father, the king is an informal man who mixes business and pleasure freely. He will sign state documents with a mistress on his lap and conduct his business, including formal audiences, even in his bedchamber. This is *not* an audience. It is simply an introduction. How formal he is will depend upon his mood. Let me do the talking and do not speak unless spoken to. If he attends to you just follow his lead. If he tells you to call him Charles, then do so. Should he hold out his hand, curtsy and kiss his ring."

"But I will have the opportunity to ask about my lands?"

"No. I will make mention of it, but you'll not ask him for anything today."

"But what if I don't get another chance?"

"I know what I'm doing, Elizabeth. I promise that you will. He is essentially amiable, always practical, and generally self-serving. He needs time to think. His better nature will wish to reward you, while practicality reminds him no matter who seized your property or why, your lands represent a valuable asset to the crown. If you press him too soon he will do what is easiest and speak to you most kindly, promise to consider it, and never think on it again."

He tapped her gently on the nose, smiling as he spoke. "We must tip the balance in our favor, by appealing to his baser nature as well. Charles is like a raven. His gaze is caught by bright and shiny things. He is insatiable when it comes to women. They don't have to be beautiful, there are far too many here like that, but they do have to sparkle in some way, be it wit, beauty or originality. He is very generous to those who catch his fancy and once we've fixed his attention we will get you back your lands."

"And just how am I to stand out, William?" She was reserved and plain, a quiet and simple woman. What possible appeal, other than honor, did he think she might have for his jaded king?

"Mmm?" He frowned and began adjusting her clothes until she pushed his hands away. He turned his attention to her hair, shushing her impatiently when she made to stop him. "It shan't take a moment, Lizzy. Stay still."

His knuckles gently brushed her cheek as he loosened a flame-red curl from her bonnet and lay it artfully against her throat and neck. She colored fiercely, his nearness making her head spin. He lifted the tip of her chin with one finger, and his gaze caught hers in a smoldering caress. Trembling in anticipation, she gave a soft moan, closed her eyes and parted her lips. His mouth touched hers like a whisper.

"De Veres? Is that you?"

"Go away, Buckhurst," he growled.

Oh, dear Lord, please make me disappear! One day in this licentious court and she was already a strumpet, cavorting in front of strangers with a notorious rake. Her face burned with humiliation but there was nowhere to hide. William was the only thing shielding her from the other man's stare.

"Uh…His Majesty is in the next room if you seek him. I tell you, William, he seems devilishly bored. It would be a good time to—

"I said get out."

"Yes, quite!" There was an offended sniff followed by muffled footsteps, and the soft exhalation of a closing door.

"Now where were we? Oh yes. How will you appeal to the king. Today you will stand out because you are with me. He will be diverted and intrigued and not content until the mystery is solved, but he will have to invite you back to court to do so. Once I've taught you how to dress and how to appeal to him properly, you will stand out on your own."

The casual manner in which he was treating their kiss made her wonder if she had imagined it. Obviously it was of so little significance to him she could safely pretend it never happened. She was both distressed and relieved. It took her a moment to catch the last part of what he said. "What? You think I—"

"But in order for that he really *must* see you shine. Have you truly nothing better to wear?"

He was fingering her clothing with a look of distaste and she slapped at his hand. "Of course I wore my best! Do you think I chose my worst suit to come to the palace? Your clever plan will come to naught if it depends on my clothing. I haven't the means for anything else."

"No matter, Lizzy my love. I will take care of it. We'll see to it over the next few days. I expect it's for the best that I help you with it. You are a country lass after all. I'm bound to have a better idea than you what impresses at court."

"I cannot allow it, William."

"You can and you will. Never mind my promise, Elizabeth, or that your aid may well have saved my life. I have cost you your father, which is something I cannot address, and your lands, which is something I can. It is not aid I offer, but recompense. You *must* allow me to do this. It would be the height of incivility and keep me forever in your debt should you refuse. Now hold tight to my arm, be mysterious, don't speak unless spoken to, and smile."

She knew he was enjoying himself—his self-satisfied grin had never faltered since they started on his plan. She didn't want to trust to stratagems and she was afraid to trust in him. This might be just a game to relieve his "hellish boredom" but her future and that of those who depended on her were at stake. *He has brought me this far. I am but one door from my goal. I can only pray he doesn't abandon me if he loses interest and—*

The door to the withdrawing chamber flew open and she clutched his arm and smiled.

"WILLIAM, BY GOD! Haven't I banished you yet? I meant to. That last was certainly an impertinent piece of verse!"

Elizabeth rose from her curtsy uncertain what to expect. The words were spoken by a tall, vigorous-looking man with long black hair, a thin mustache and full sensuous lips. Though far from conventionally handsome, his eyes glinted with intelligence and humor and he was exceedingly well made. Lines of weary cynicism etched his face, giving him a wolfish look. *This must be the king!* He was magnetic and arresting and she could hardly look away.

He sat at a table, toying with a lovely woman perched in his lap, her head resting on his shoulder. He was drinking and gaming with more than a dozen other men. A handsome young page warbled French love songs in the background and a bank of at least two thousand pounds in gold lay on the table. She recognized some of the men from broadsheets and knew that at least three of them were dukes, including the king's brother, the Duke of York, and Monmouth, his natural son.

"Perhaps Your Majesty has been too busy with wine and whores to give the matter the attention it deserves." William lifted a glass of wine from the table and downed it in one shot.

"Do not test me, Will. I am in a foul mood." Charles eyed Elizabeth with curiosity as he spoke.

She blushed and ducked her head, then took a step

back when the man nearest her tried pawing her bodice with an unsteady hand.

"What are you hiding under that sack, Rivers?" the drunkard mumbled, "Is she naked underneath?"

"I'd advise against that, Jermyn." William grabbed his hand in a viselike grip, forcing his wrist over backward until the man winced in pain.

"Why, is she poxed?" Not easily cowed, Jermyn pulled his arm away, rubbing his wrist and eyeing Elizabeth with a lewd grin. A moment later the tip of William's walking stick lodged tight against the base of his throat, making him sputter and cough.

"No. She is offended. Tender your apologies and off you go."

"Enough, gentlemen! I will have no brawling in my presence. Jermyn, go for a walk. Madam, my apologies on behalf of Lord Jermyn. William, at least it was not your sword, but you know better than to draw any weapon in the presence of your king. Now put that thing down before I call my guards and have you exiled in truth. If the lass is not meant for diversion, then who is she and why is she here?"

Elizabeth tried to disguise her annoyance, but her lips thinned and she couldn't help but clear her throat. William gave her a warning look and she tossed her head.

"Your Majesty, might I present Elizabeth Walters, a childhood friend, and a great friend to Your Majesty, as well. It was Lady Elizabeth who sheltered me when I was pursued and wounded by Cromwell's soldiers on one of my forays from France."

"Is it so, madam?"

"Yes, Your Majesty. I am pleased to see you returned to England and looking so well." Elizabeth curtsied again, giving him a grateful smile, relieved that at last *someone* addressed her directly. She was tired of people speaking of her as if she weren't in the room. It might be an elegant court but it certainly didn't seem like a mannerly one.

The king removed his hat and made her a courtly bow. "Then I owe you my thanks, madam. During that difficult time when I was sorely disheartened, it was the help of people such as yourself that kept my will and spirit strong. You must be William's Puritan miss. He spoke of you on more than one occasion, but we had no idea that he knew you as a child."

Surprised, Elizabeth looked in William's direction, unable to suppress a broad smile. He gave a slight shrug in reply.

"You are very welcome in my court, madam. You should have made your presence known to us long before now."

William spoke for her before she could reply. "She would have, Your Majesty, but as punishment for aiding you, Cromwell stripped her of her lands."

There was a hint of wariness in his voice now. "Walters is the name?"

"Yes, Majesty. Her father was killed in the fighting."

"By God, Will! General Hugh Walters? That was your doing, wasn't it?" He looked from one of them to the other with curiosity, and then waved over a page and whispered something in his ear. The boy returned immediately with pen and paper.

"I find this story quite interesting and would like

to hear more. We shall have to have you back to court, madam. Make me a list of your properties and we shall think these things through. I make you no promises, Lady Elizabeth. Though we are clearly in your debt, I have no idea of the current conditions of these properties, and of course the state is always in need of funds, but we might be able to do something for you."

As he spoke his female companion leaned against him and smiled, fingering her jewels. "You shall remain here at court while these matters are decided. We will see that you are assigned somewhere to stay. As for you, Lord Rivers...I demand a forfeit to forgive your impertinence. If you are to be a damned nuisance you must at least entertain me. Let us see how skilled you are at impromptu amusements. Make us a verse using men at this table."

William looked about the room, his eyes lighting on the handsome but vacant Monmouth, the toadlike Lauderdale, the king's imbecilic pox doctor Frazier, and the dismal and prickly Duke of York. "Very well, my lord, as you command it...

"Here's Monmouth the Witty
and Lauderdale the Pretty
and Frasier, that learned Physician
but above all the rest
here's the Duke for a jest
and the King for a grand Politician."

"Here now, Charles! Why do you encourage such impertinence?" the Duke of York protested hotly. "Allowing it in those close to you can only encourage it amongst the rabble!"

The king was laughing so hard he nearly choked on his wine. When he finally caught his breath he tried to soothe his brother. "What is the problem? He compliments us all, does he not? Don't worry, Jamie. No one will kill me to make you king. Off with you, Will. Unless you intend to join us at cards."

As they left the room, the voice of the king, clearly amused, rose above the general chatter. "What is that rogue de Veres up to now? He has a history of poaching but it's the first time he's pimped, and the woman covered from head to toe like a harem concubine!"

"Perhaps she is exactly what she seems and he simply wishes to aid her," an earnest Monmouth replied. There was a moment of complete silence, and then they all roared with laughter.

CHAPTER THIRTEEN

WILLIAM WAS disturbing in so many ways. He aroused fears and uncertainties she'd thought long overcome. Once she'd believed in chivalrous knights, true love and happy endings, but that had been hard to hold on to when her mother died, harder still when she lost her father, and nearly impossible after Benjamin. *Mother Goose tales!* Now here he was again, like a comet that came out of nowhere, challenging all of her careful defenses and threatening her hard-won peace. He was a jaded libertine. Mercurial and insouciant. How could she trust him when he'd likely be gone from her life as quickly as he'd come. *He's no Prince Charming, and I'm no Cinderella.*

"Elizabeth! Elizabeth, come quick! Come and see! There's a carriage at the door, Lizzy. I think it's here for you!" Marjorie was almost squealing with excitement.

Elizabeth rushed over to join her and Sam and Mary, all of them craning to see out the window to the street below. A gilded black carriage with four magnificent horses took up most of the road. They watched as a footman jumped down from the rumble and opened the footstep outside their door. Unlike the footman or driver, the man who stepped out wore no livery, and his clothes matched neither the coach nor team. A moment later, there was a polite knock at the door.

"Good morning, milady." The towheaded young man swept off his hat and bowed. "Thomas Ayers, if you please, ma'am, and here to escort you to my master, Lord Rivers, at the exchange."

"But this is most unexpected!"

"Is it?" He sighed and pursed his lips. "I feared as much. But he insisted you'd be moving to the palace today and would know what it was all about."

"Yes, I am, but—"

"Excellent then! He should've let you know what time we'd come around, but no bother. It is always a pleasure to wait on a lady. We'll be just outside the door when you are ready."

"But you're blocking the street."

Tom looked over his shoulder and grinned at the elegant coach and its growing crowd of onlookers. "That's all right, ma'am. We don't mind."

Trailed by Marjorie and Mary, a flustered Elizabeth hurried from room to room gathering her pitiful collection of personal belongings. Besides the dress she was wearing, she had a brush, a small mirror, a few hairpins, and her much maligned wool suit. She'd been putting off her return to the palace, had almost talked herself out of going, uncertain if the king's words were invitation, joke, or command. She had no idea where to go or what to do when she got there and it was clear from her adventures yesterday, she would not be well received if she had nothing suitable to wear. William de Veres's aid would certainly make things easier, but she couldn't help but wonder what would be the price.

She looked at her women with their careworn faces and threadbare clothes. She watched as Mary bustled off in search of her wrapper, noting how her hands were crabbed and twisted, and how she favored her left side. *They've grown old. They deserve better. What does any of it matter other than that?* If William should buy her an acceptable suit she would wear it. It was recompense as he himself had said. When her lands were returned she could sell it, and buy them all coats instead. As for her heart, she was a widow and not some moonstruck girl. Despite giving herself a stern talking-to, a worried sigh escaped her.

"Here now, Lizzy girl. What's the matter?"

She stepped into Marjorie's arms, and the old woman gave her a motherly hug. "Am I wrong to accept his help?"

"Nonsense, girl! It's only right that he should help you after all the trouble he's caused."

"But he's…he drinks and writes scandalous poems. He's an infamous, womanizing rake. You should have seen him, Marjorie. He's handsome and seductive. Your eyes can't help but watch him. He says the most outrageous things but they make me laugh. They are all so sophisticated and beautiful there, the men and the women, and I am naught but a little brown wren."

"Are you? We shall see."

"But what if…"

"He is still your William, girl. I am certain of it. I knew if he saw you he would take you under his wing."

"Marjorie…he *kissed* me. And I very much fear he might try to again."

"Did he now?" Marjorie raised her brows, but her eyes were amused. "And you didn't like it?"

"No…I…yes. It was very confusing and it happened so quickly. He hardly seemed to notice he had done it at all. I don't think he's bothered much by delicate scruples. They are all so casual about such things, even the king."

"Lizzy, my dear. Your life has been hard, with little enough joy in it. A widow is allowed her pleasures. She can kiss who she pleases so long as she's discreet." She lowered her voice. "They even say that's why those widows who can afford it hire handsome footmen."

"Marjorie!"

"It's true enough, dear," Mary piped in, returning with her wrapper. "Did you think keeping your money is the only reason a widow is a good thing to be?"

"I have to go now." A red flush stained her cheeks. "I'm not sure how long I shall be there, but I will let you know soon. The silverware is gone but we still have some china. Sell what remains if you need the funds."

"Should you not take one of us with you, Miss Lizzy? To tidy your room and do your hair?"

"I was not told that I might, Mary, and I've no idea where I'll be lodging. I shall just have to make do as best I can." She received another hug from Marjorie and one from Mary, and Samuel nodded sadly as he waited by the door.

Lord Rivers's man moved forward when she stepped out the door.

"I will take that, my lady."

"Thank you, Mr. Ayers." She handed him her small valise and he took her hand, helping her into the plush interior. In less than a minute they were on their way. As the coach lurched forward she clutched the leather strap and peered back through glass windows to watch Southwark roll away. Much like the day she had walked out on Benjamin, she knew something irrevocable had just taken place. For better or for ill, she was stepping into a new life.

CHAPTER FOURTEEN

ELIZABETH HAD NEVER been to the New Exchange before. Dispossessed widows had little use for hobby-horses and singing birds, jewels, perfumes, sables, or curds and cream. What she needed she found in her garden or purchased from a street vendor, not here on the Strand. This road was lined with palaces and great houses, most with river gates and landings that backed on the Thames. By the time they pulled up to a large stone-fronted building, she couldn't help feeling she didn't belong.

She clutched her valise tight to her bosom, craning her neck as they walked through the mall. Two floors of long doubled galleries were crowded with rows of luxurious shops. There must have been close to a hundred different places selling exotic goods from all over the world. Wig makers, confectionaries, bookstores and drapers, tailors and milliners lined its broad walls. Most of them were tended by well-dressed women, and the courtyard bustled with a cosmopolitan crowd. She saw men in turbans and Muscovite merchants walking amongst fashionable ladies and elegant lords.

"Mr. Ayers, I will hazard my cloak and bonnet that in my woolens I am the rarest flower here."

"Please call me Tom, my lady, and you might well

be right. Lord Rivers will meet us at Mademoiselle La-vallette's. It is just over here."

WILLIAM LOUNGED negligently in a gilded chair, twirling a glass of wine. His coat lay open and long strands of slightly tangled hair curled against his collarbone. He stretched out his legs and sighed, crossing his booted feet at the ankle, and mentally cursed any endeavor that robbed him of his sleep. His irritation proved fleeting. A moment later his cynical eyes softened as Elizabeth came into view.

She looked almost comical in her shapeless dress and ridiculous bonnet, with her bag held in front of her as if it were a shield. There was nothing comical about the powerful jolt that had shaken him last evening, though, when he had finally remembered who she was. There was nothing amusing about the unexpected stab of tenderness he'd felt when he kissed her.

She hadn't spied him yet; she was far too busy looking around. Her obvious fascination with the world was a welcome balm to his jaded soul. He passed his thumb over the thin white scar that was all that remained of childhood promises, and smiled as he wondered what direction his life would have taken if things had been different. Lizzy Walters. *We built a raft together and sailed it all the way to the river.* Her kisses still lingered, the one last night and even the one in the meadow. It was the only innocent kiss he had ever known. What if there had been no war? What if there had been no Giffard? What if she had come?

He flicked away a sudden memory of the pastor, crawling in bed beside him. *"I am just here to warm you, boy,*" and motioned for a drink. The mademoiselle slid across the room in a rustle of silk and placed a brandy in his hand. He tossed it back and relaxed in the armchair, watching as poor Tom did his best to herd Elizabeth to the mercer's door. She had given him a brief taste of childhood. She had brought him sugar cakes and laughter on a late spring day. Because of that, because of her help in the forest, because he had killed her father, he was going to transform her from a curious little bird into an elegant swan.

He gave his head a quick shake and banished the past to where it belonged. There was no need to wax sentimental, or to confuse friendship with more complicated emotions. He owed the girl some recompense for all her help and that was all. Besides, he *had* been bored of late and she certainly was a novel diversion. Transforming her from shy country abbess to a jewel of the court should prove entertaining. He inclined his head and Marie Lavallette leaned over him, placing her hands on his shoulders as he told her what was required.

THE GOSSIP SHEETS TOUTED the first floor of the exchange as a place for romantic assignations, but the sight of an overdressed harlot slouched against William, as he whispered in her ear was a good deal more than Elizabeth expected. He looked like an overgrown tomcat relaxing after a long night on the prowl. She narrowed her eyes and stopped so suddenly that Thomas bumped into her from behind.

"Have a care, Tom." William was out of his chair in one stride, catching her as she stumbled, steadying her with a wicked smile.

He held her just a moment too long, one hand steadying the small of her back as his lean body supported her curves. Her breath quickened and her cheeks warmed. She clutched her valise defensively, embarrassed and annoyed. When she caught the shopkeeper eyeing her with bemused curiosity, she took a step away from his arms.

"Good morning, Elizabeth. I thought it was metaphorical when they said all of London falls at my feet."

"Good morning, William. I am sure that it was." She used his name deliberately. A not so subtle challenge to his overfriendly French miss. *She* was the one he had invited here, and for the rest of the morning he was hers.

"Elizabeth, this is Mademoiselle Lavallette. I've had Tom bring you here as you're in immediate need of some suitable clothes." His eyes flicked over her attire dismissively. "You'll find that Ma...the mademoiselle, has an ample collection of ready-made suits suitable for wearing at court. She is also an excellent tailor, abreast of all the latest fashions from France. Marie, perhaps you would bring us some chocolate while Lady Walters and I examine your wares?"

"But of course, my lord, my lady." Much to Elizabeth's surprise the woman didn't seem to object to being used as a servant. She gave them both a curtsy and went into the back with a satisfied smile.

William placed a warm hand on her shoulder, squeezing gently as he murmured in her ear, "You will find the mademoiselle most accommodating, Lizzy. She has booked no other appointments and hopes to sell a week's worth of business today."

Every time he touched her she found it harder to concentrate on anything else, but there were things she needed to make clear. "William, I am not sure about this. I do not like being in anyone's debt and I'm not in a position to repay you."

He sighed. "Elizabeth, I have few expenses, other than wo...er...servants and drink. It is I who am in your debt, and as I told you last night, I do not care for that feeling, either. If you permit me to help you now, then we shall both be quit. You lost all you owned on my behalf, whilst I have been richly rewarded. I fully intend to see your lands returned. For that to happen, you need to be seen at court. Surely you haven't crested the hill and found the gates of the city open before you, only to slink away in defeat?"

"Well, no, I—"

"Good! We're of a mind then. Neither have I."

He snatched her worn valise from her hands and tossed it to Thomas. "Take this to the ragman, Tom. Or find a charity that needn't be bribed to accept it."

"How dare you! Give that back at once! I might not have much, but those are my possessions!"

"And none of your possessions are suitable for court. When you return to the palace it will be as an elegant lady. You will take the king and the court by surprise. I can't have you wandering about carrying an eastside ragbag. For this to work, Elizabeth, you must leave the past behind."

Like you did me? "I have servants. People who depend on me. I will *not* leave them behind. The past few years they have had no wages. My clothes might be a joke to your vain and shallow friends, but they can be sold or fashioned into other garments. Very few of us can use things and just casually throw them away as you do. Why the proceeds alone would—"

"Enough!" He held up his hand in a gesture for silence. "Tom."

"Yes, Master William?"

"I have annoyed Lady Elizabeth. I fear she means to kill me and feed me to the poor. Sell the lot for the best price you can and take the proceeds back to her servants. Lest they are as ferocious as she is, buy them each a ribbon and hat besides." He turned back to Elizabeth, stilling her protests. "Your life has changed, Lizzy. You will never wear those clothes again. You are like Britomart about to enter faerieland. You must don the finest armor to face the perils that lie in store."

"You are as fanciful as ever, but that's very much what Marjorie said." She paused and took a breath, and then blurted out what was really on her mind. "People will think I am your mistress!"

"Sweetheart, they already do."

"What?" Her mouth dropped open.

He shifted uncomfortably. "You needn't sound so horrified. 'Tis not so bad as that. I have somewhat of a reputation, Lizzy, as you are well aware. We had a long private conversation in a public place and then you were escorted through to the privy chambers without having waited in line."

"Somewhat of a reputation? You mean just talking to you—"

"Can set tongues to wagging, yes, love. You noted it yourself. It's pure speculation now, but all courts thrive on gossip, and it is the appearance rather than the substance of things which matters most. They will think you belong to either myself or the king, and your clothing a clever disguise. Do you come to stay at court, dress as a lady, and continue to appear at my side they will be certain of it."

"Why didn't you warn me?"

"I am warning you now. If I help you it will be assumed you are my mistress and everyone, Charles included, will be immensely diverted and completely enthralled. It will get them all talking. They will wonder what it is that makes you different."

"No doubt that suits your plans."

"Yes, it does. But it's not too late to turn back. If you do not return to court you'll be quickly forgotten. I'll purchase you a cottage and give you five hundred pounds. That should keep you in comfort for some time to come. But, Lizzy, should you chance it… I am fair certain we can get your lands returned."

"This is all a game to you, isn't it, William."

"Yes. And one I intend us to win. Why should you care what people say? It never stopped you as a child."

"I've grown up even if you haven't," she snapped. She didn't know if she should laugh or cry at his admission. Well, she didn't want his charity, she wanted what was hers, and she could learn how to play games, too. What *did* she care of what strangers thought? All that mattered were the people she cared about, and she knew they would support her whichever path she chose.

"We speak of Charles Stuart's court, Lizzy. There's no dishonor in a widow making merry there. 'Twill do no harm to your reputation, though it might do some to mine."

She shrugged off the coaxing finger trailing down her sleeve. "Why should it capture anyone's attention? What can be so different about one woman among so many?"

"But that is just it, my love. You are not." She looked at him curiously, surprised to see a faint flush stain his cheeks.

"I am known for taking an interest in women, but not for settling on any particular one. Such is the way of the rake. We move from flower to flower. I've yet to take a lover or keep a woman past the conquest. You will appear a great novelty."

"And the king will reward me for that?"

"He will want to meet and know you for that."

"I heard what they said as we were leaving his presence. Do you intend that…" Her voice trailed off.

"Perhaps I intend to keep you for myself." There was mischief in his voice, but his eyes darkened dangerously.

She snorted, dismissing his words. "You would not expect me to—"

"Of course not."

"I've yet to take a lover." What a curious thing to hear from a noted libertine, and yet when she thought about it, amidst all the gossip and pamphlets and broadsheets, she'd yet to hear or read anything coupling his name to someone else's. She felt curiously lighthearted for a woman contemplating a road she'd been taught led to ruin.

"You are not afraid, are you, little bird?" He took her arm in his and leaned companionably against her. His voice was low and husky as he whispered in her ear, "I dare you."

She tossed her head and turned to glare at him. "I am *not* going to do it for your amusement or for the sake of whatever mad game you're playing. I am doing it to get back my lands."

His face split into a wide grin. "Then let us begin."

His good humor was infectious and Elizabeth put her reservations behind her. He wanted her to join him in his sport? Very well, she would. He might play for amusement, but her stakes were much higher. She would let him teach her the rules of this game, and though her heart danced with excitement whenever he smiled, she would keep her eyes fixed firmly on the prize.

The mademoiselle returned with an ingratiating smile and a tray of hot chocolate and pastries. The rest of the morning passed in a cloud of silk and lace and ribbons. William bought her three fine cambric shifts, two petal-soft chemises with voluminous sleeves made from Holland linen, and two richly colored morning gowns of green and gold. Whatever lust the mademoiselle might have felt toward William was long forgotten. Her goal was to please Elizabeth and make her shine.

Elizabeth had never worn bright colors in her life. As she was draped in golds and greens and shades of burnished ochre, both William and the tailor shushed her murmured protests, assuring her repeatedly they knew what was best.

"These colors will complement your hair and eyes and subtly enhance your skin tone, my lady. You must always trust a man's taste in this. They judge with their eyes, and are attracted to women much like a bee to flowers. You can trust Lord Rivers's taste in this. He is a connoisseur when it comes to beautiful women," Mademoiselle Lavallette said through a mouthful of pins and measuring tape.

Elizabeth wondered how many women William had brought to the mercer's, but her mild annoyance was overshadowed by a growing excitement. She remembered watching the beautifully dressed lords and ladies from a distance as she hid among the branches in the old oak in Kent. She did feel a bit like Cinderella even as she ignored the thought that William might yet be her Prince Charming. Which reminded her, she needed shoes.

She stifled any further protest as the mademoiselle brought her several pairs of gloves, embroidered silk stockings and garters, and jewel-colored shoes in satin and kid. Petticoats were ordered to match her skirts and bodices, with brocaded panels and hems trimmed in silver and gold. To complete it all, there was a dainty purse to wear between shift and petticoat, a suit of riding clothes, and a warm velvet cloak. Having decided to relax and enjoy it, she was just a little disappointed when it seemed they were done.

"I'll send my man to fetch what's ready. Send the rest to Lady Elizabeth at the palace, mademoiselle, once it's done. I've an errand to do, ladies." He reached out his fingers and plucked off Elizabeth's cap.

"William!"

She reached for it back but he crumpled it in a ball and stuffed it in a pocket. "Have no fear, Lizzy. I will be certain to give it to a worthy orphan. Marie, find her a dress or two ready now and do something with her hair. Ladies…" He bowed low and a moment later he was gone.

Elizabeth could see the woman's eyes were full of questions, and lord knew she was full of questions of her own, but it hardly seemed appropriate to discuss William with a stranger, so she smiled and talked of weather and the dreadful London fog. She gasped in delight when her hostess showed her a ready-made moiré silk of a rich burnt India yellow, and a sarcenet petticoat trimmed in black Italian lace braided through with gold. She followed that with a deep sapphire gold-edged lutestring skirt and bodice, and a petticoat of embroidered robin's-egg blue. Elizabeth tried the moiré first, but Mademoiselle Lavallette would not allow her to look in the mirror until she'd seen to her hair.

"You have glorious hair, Lady Elizabeth," she said as she combed it out carefully. "Hair like this is a greater adornment than clothing or jewels. If properly presented, it frames your eyes and shoulders, and draws attention to your graceful neck and your décolletage. Men are like moths. There's not one of them breathing that is not drawn to flame." When she was finished, she clicked her tongue and looked about. "Ah!" She marched away and returned a moment later with a jaunty black three-cornered plumed hat that was a smaller and daintier version of William's. "You must insist that Lord Rivers take you to the milliners and gets you a hat to match each of your suits." She steered a bemused Elizabeth to a full-length mirror and stood back proudly, smiling at the transformation she had wrought.

Elizabeth stared in fascination at the elegant stranger standing before her. Her full skirt was open down the front and gathered behind to show off her elaborate petticoat, and her slashed sleeves were caught with amber clasps over the voluminous sleeves of her chemise. Her hair was drawn into a bun at the back of her head, but a cluster of curls framed her face, and masses of gleaming ringlets hung artfully about her shoulders, caressing the dropped shoulders of a long and narrow low-necked bodice, which plumped her breasts and showed her curves in a most unseemly way. She turned to one side, and then the other. Despite herself, she grinned.

"My lady is pleased?"

"Yes, my lady is pleased!" She was more than pleased; she was giddy, thrilled and delighted. She could hardly believe that she was the glamorous creature in the mirror and she couldn't wait to see William or, more to the point, have him see her. Both he and Marjorie had referred to clothes as armor, and at last she truly understood what they meant. Dressed like this, she felt ready to take on the world.

CHAPTER FIFTEEN

WILLIAM DIDN'T SEE Elizabeth when he returned to the shop. Marie looked up from the counter and smiled, nodding toward the back. He could hear a lilting melody coming from a draped room in the corner. She was humming to herself, too engrossed to hear him, and he folded his arms and watched her as he leaned against the wall. *By God, she's beautiful!* His heart hammered as it hadn't since he was a boy. He had never seen her as an adult in broad daylight, unguarded with her hair unbound. Marie had served her well. With her flame-red hair and molten dress she might have been a goddess of the sun.

His eyes crinkled and his lips twisted with amusement as she flattened her palms against her dress, holding it back and wiggling her toes so she might admire her underskirt and shoes. He felt a stab of tenderness at her childish delight, followed by a stab of guilt. She was such an innocent. Despite her obvious wariness, she had blithely put her fate in his hands. *She trusts me. She still thinks of me as her childhood friend.*

He was unaccustomed to moral qualms. He'd had the world figured out to his satisfaction for some time now. But it seemed that as of last evening he no longer knew himself. He should have packed her up in her best woolen dress and sent her back to the country. It would eliminate the danger to her and to him. This was no place for her. She didn't belong. They would do what they could to corrupt her, not content until she was just like them. *And if I let her gain a hold inside me I'll no longer fit, as well*.

She sat down and he watched in fascination as she slowly eased her lacy petticoat partway up her calf. She stretched her leg, admiring her stocking, and he felt a hunger so fierce it stole his breath. His eyes roamed her body with frank appreciation, traveling from the toes of her shoes to her rakish black hat. *It's not too late. I can still send her away*. But then she turned to him with a dazzling smile…and it was.

"William!" She spread out her arms and turned in a circle. "I don't know about you but I rather like it."

"You are as lovely as a summer's day, little bird. Now close your eyes and turn around."

He stood so close she could feel the heat of his body. Something smooth and sleek slid across the sensitive skin between her neck and bosom, and cool fingers skimmed her collarbone and shoulders, lingering as he fastened a clasp.

She opened her eyes and touched a finger to a lustrous pearl necklace. "William, I can't."

"Elizabeth, you must," he said with a low chuckle. "No lady leaves home without at least a pearl necklace. I've not been extravagant. It is the minimum accoutrement for appearing at court and can be worn with every dress you own. You see. I strive to economize."

He brushed her cheek gently with his knuckles and then slipped a pair of matching drop earrings in her hand. "Now your outfit is complete."

She could feel his uneven breathing on her cheek and she lowered her lashes as she fastened them. She looked back at him in the mirror, hypnotized for a moment by his penetrating gaze. His eyes seemed to undress her, sliding slowly from her lips to her shoulders to her breasts. She flushed and ducked her head. "All I need now is powder to cover my freckles."

"No." His voice was rich and husky in her ear. "They are but a light dusting, and suit you much better than powder or patch. You look natural, unaffected, as if the sun himself came down to rain kisses on your cheeks. It stirs a man's senses, and makes him want to follow in their path." His hands slid up her arms and he turned her to face him. Encircling her waist with one strong arm, he pulled her close.

Her knees weakened as his mouth descended. She parted her lips and arched into his embrace, shutting out the voices that questioned her eager response. His mouth covered hers in a hungry kiss and she reached her arms around his neck with a breathy moan. He cursed and lifted her, almost roughly, and backed her hard against the wall. The weight of his arousal pressed heavy on her belly, insistent through layers of fine linen and silk. A delicious shudder heated her body and she squirmed in his arms as his knee parted her thighs.

She leaned back against the wall and he leaned into her, cradling her face between his palms. His kisses gentled, growing slow and tender and his lips on hers were sweet and warm. A soft sigh escaped her as he nibbled at her bottom lip and his tongue traced the swollen contours of her mouth. Teasing and coaxing, he implored her to open, giving a heated growl when she did. Elizabeth whimpered and melted against him as a smoldering fire began to burn. He struck a vibrant chord within her, bringing all her senses to life. Something deep inside her was thawing after years of being frozen in a cold, dark place.

A scratching at the curtain made her spring back in surprise. She'd been so intoxicated by his kisses she'd lost all track of place or time.

"What?" William snarled.

Mademoiselle Lavallette poked a curious and careful head into the room. "I do beg your pardon, my lord, my lady, but 'twill soon be nightfall and the exchange is about to close. If you wish to arrange delivery to the palace today, we need to do so now."

As THEY WALKED through the exchange, Elizabeth was aware of all the eyes that watched them. It brought a red stain to her cheeks, but the memory of William's kisses was still singing in her veins. Every time she cast a nervous eye in his direction, he smiled his approval, and she was sure that no one could fault how she was dressed. Proud of his attention and how she looked, she clung to his arm possessively, her eyes shining and her plumed head held high. If they faulted her as a woman of loose morals at least she knew she wasn't. She was a widow after all, and as everyone kept telling her a kiss was just a kiss.

I am a widow who accepts presents from notorious rakes. She felt a twinge of discomfort. "Is it true what they say, William? That this is a place used to arrange assignations?"

"Yes, indeed, love. It is almost as bad as St. James's Park. And yes, there will be those who speak of us.

"Much wine had passed, with grave discourse,
Of who fucks who, and who does worse.

"That is from a little ditty of mine," he said modestly.

She smiled slightly and almost asked him about Mademoiselle Lavallette, but he'd said he kept no mistress and she stopped herself in time. A light drizzle started to fall as they waited for the coachman by the steps to the exchange.

"Does it bother you?" he asked.

"That people will talk, or that you write filthy verse?"

"I write *satiric* verse. Does either bother you? Or both?"

I am twenty-seven years old, a lonely widow, and I am on my way to the palace in a beautiful dress after kissing my childhood love. "No, William. I've made my choice. Write what you please and let people talk if they must."

He took her hand and pressed a lingering kiss in her palm. When he looked at her his eyes were bright with mischief and his teasing smile made her blush. "If we're to be damned for it anyway, little bird, what say we take full enjoyment? I am not only renowned for my poetry. You know you are curious. I can show you delights you've never imagined. What happened in Sussex was only a prelude."

The words were playful but his meaning was not.

"I thank you for your kind offer, Lord Rivers. How noble of you to devote such patience and effort to a drab little country mouse. I am honored, of course, but I beg you to accept that I've no desire to be eaten by one of His Majesty's tomcats."

Much to her surprise she was flirting. It was something she'd never expected. She had told herself those who did it were frivolous, but the truth was she'd never had occasion before. He made her feel pretty, desirable and witty, and she found herself responding and wanting more.

"You are a tasty little mouse I think, Lizzy Walters. I've yet to decide if I shall eat you or let you go, but whatever I do, I intend to play with you first. Not tonight, though, I'm afraid. I've matters to attend to and must be on my way."

She looked at him in surprise and disappointment. She'd been expecting him to see her safe to her quarters and had no idea how she would find her way in the dark. As he handed her into the coach, his hand squeezed her waist and his breath stirred the fine hairs feathering her ear. "I've never forgotten Sussex, Elizabeth," he said in a seductive whisper. "I've wanted to kiss you again ever since. I swear I'll be kissing you like that again soon."

She settled back against the cushions, physically and mentally exhausted. She'd had more excitement over the past two days than in the past two years. She had been to the palace, acquired a fine wardrobe, ridden in a grand carriage, and met the king and his brother and son. She'd met her childhood sweetheart and been thoroughly kissed by a notorious rake, and the thought of it curled her toes. Now she was on her way to live in a magnificent palace and it seemed she'd been abandoned, no doubt for a French seamstress, on the eve of entering a brand-new world. She wondered if anyone had ever had two more strange and wonderful days. She touched her fingers to her lips. *"I'll be kissing you like that again soon."*

She woke from her reverie as they clattered into the palace courtyard. It was full dark, bitter enough to see her breath and the cobblestones were slick with rain. She shivered from cold and anxiety as she stepped from the carriage, at a loss as to what to do next.

"Lady Elizabeth?"

"Tom!" Relief made her voice a bit shrill. Seldom had she been so pleased to see a familiar face. William's man greeted her with a warm smile and she had to stifle an urge to hug him. He and the footman unloaded her bags with her plunder from the strumpet Lavallette's. Perhaps she wasn't a strumpet, but if she didn't want to be accounted one she best keep her hands off William. They traipsed in and out of courtyards and up and down stairs through a warren of twisting corridors. She would never have found the room on her own. Even though William wasn't with her, he'd made sure she was taken care of, and for that she was grateful.

"Master William thought you might like to settle into your rooms in private, milady. There are easier routes, but this one's seldom used. One of us will show you the others tomorrow."

They stopped in front of a carved oak door and Tom pushed it wide. Elizabeth stepped into a luxuriously appointed sitting room, and made a soft *oh* of surprise. The walls were covered in rich wood paneling, inlayed with carvings of roses and vines. The design carried through the whole of the apartment, sculpted into the moldings and beams. Beautiful tapestries added warmth and color, and a blazing fire crackled in the hearth. A tall mullioned casement window overlooked a small garden, and comfortable furnishings made it seem like a home. A very luxurious home, with a large desk, a table suitable for cards or dining, two plush settees, and comfortable armchairs set facing the fire.

"This is meant for me?" Elizabeth turned in a circle looking all around her, noting the silver goblets and wine flagon gracing a small marqueted table, and the book-lined shelves set into the far wall.

"Yes, my lady. The rooms were assigned by the chamberlain after he consulted with my lord. You will find that Master William's rooms are situated close by. He felt you would like a garden view to remind you of your home, and thought it best for you to have a friend close by."

"I…well, I…it's really quite lovely, Thomas. Did he supply the furnishings, too?"

"Some of them, milady. He took a look and saw what was missing and him and me and Allen," he nodded to the footman, "reconnoitered, so to speak."

"Do you mean to say you stole furnishings from other rooms?"

"Oh, no, ma'am. Certainly not. There was no one living in them. We, ah…rescued them from obscurity, is what the master would say."

Her snort of amusement made Tom a little defensive on his master's behalf. "'Twas just a few things. A desk and trunks and a bookcase and such. The linens and candles and the books and wine he supplied himself."

"And I am extremely grateful, Mr. Avery, to you both. And Allen, too, for taking the effort to make things so comfortable for me. It was most thoughtful and very kind."

Tom beamed, straightening to his full height. "There's more, ma'am. The door to your left leads to a bedchamber and a dressing room, and off that is a room for your woman."

At that very moment the door to the bedchamber opened, and an apple-cheeked flaxen-haired woman poked a diffident head in the room.

"This would be Nell, milady. She's fresh from the country. She's not French, but she's the best we could do on short notice."

Elizabeth cringed for the girl. Just yesterday she'd been mocked herself for her country dress. It seemed all of London had a disregard for anything not French or from the city. She gave the girl a warm smile and beckoned her forward. "You are a blessing indeed, Nell! I was just wondering how I was going to manage and poof, here you are."

The girl gave her an awkward curtsy and squeaked an inaudible reply, then scurried to the dressing room with the overburdened footman and a precarious mountain of packages.

Elizabeth raised her eyebrows and looked to Tom, who grinned and shrugged his shoulders. "She is said to be good with hair, ma'am. Would you care to see the rest of your lodgings?"

If anything the bedchamber was more opulent than

the sitting room. The walls were papered in a rich teal, enhanced here and there by the touch of delicate gold-leaf acorns. An enormous oak-carved bed was hung with dark green gold-embroidered curtains. The desk and cabinets shone amber-hued in the light from the small marble fireplace, as did the clawed feet and carved backs of a matching set of a sea-green-striped settee and chairs. Her father's home in Kent had been prosperous and comfortable, but she'd never seen anything like this.

Eager to have the place to herself, Elizabeth thanked Tom and Allen again and dismissed them. She let Nelly comb out her hair and help her into a bed gown and then dismissed her, too. A modest repast and glass of sack waited for her on a small table. She bit into some cheese and wandered her rooms, sipping from her wine. A delighted smile lit her face when she stopped by the bedside table. A small gold pocket watch lay beside an elaborate dressing case with a mirrored lid. She opened it carefully. Inside was a set of tortoiseshell combs and hairpins. Behind it, half-hidden, was a book. She reached for it curiously, wondering why it had been left by her bedside.

"Oh, William," she said with a happy sigh. He had thought of everything! It was the third book of Edmund Spenser's *The Faerie Queen*. The book in which Britomart's adventures in faerieland began. *The book where she finds her true love*. Clutching it to her chest, Elizabeth lay back in her feather bed, and fell asleep, a dreamy smile on her face as the feel of his slow, drugging kisses still percolated through her veins. The last thought she had before she drifted away was that she had never kissed anyone else.

CHAPTER SIXTEEN

WILLIAM WOKE with the distinct feeling there was something he was supposed to do, but the room was spinning in dizzying circles and it felt like a dull knife was splitting his skull in two. He could hardly remember what he had done last night, let alone what he was supposed to do today. Something to do with Lizzy, he expected. He covered his eyes with the back of his forearm, cursing the cheerfully efficient Tom for opening the bed curtains and rudely hauling him from a restless sleep. Once again it seemed he'd had a bit too much to drink. He did have a hazy recollection of carousing with Killigrew, Sedly and Sackville, and he vaguely remembered stopping at Oxford Kate's. He groaned and sat up on his elbows, searching the room for Tom. The least he might have done was have coffee ready.

He knew he was drinking too much, though he barely kept up with his companions. Drinking was a must at court, much like keeping a mistress. It was one of those rituals, along with dueling and reckless gambling, that proved to the world a man had bottom. There was no shame in a fine lord or lady sliding arse-first drunk under a table. But he didn't drink to fit in. He drank to drown his discontent, and he didn't keep a mistress, favoring casual encounters.

When he felt the need, he preferred to enjoy the

lovelies of his generous monarch. They tended to combine the four cardinal virtues he looked for in a sexual partner. They were beautiful, sexually experienced and adventuresome, had the morals of a cat in heat, and were free of disease. Women, alcohol or danger, he needed a constant swirl of sensation, for whenever it began to creep and stutter to a halt he was gripped by a powerful ennui that bordered on despair. Ah! But here was Tom with coffee, just in time to save the day.

"Good morning, Master William. You'll be pleased to know that Allen and I saw your lady comfortably settled."

"My lady? I'm quite certain I'd have remembered if I brought one home. Have you been drinking, Tom?" He peered at his man suspiciously.

"Lady Elizabeth, milord," Tom said with infinite patience.

"Ah! Yes…Lizzy. She's not my lady, Tom. Think of her more as a project. Or a protégé, if you will." Somehow it didn't feel right to lump her in with the parade of interchangeable and easily forgettable warm bodies that eased his nights. If it had, he'd not have gone to Oxford Kate's. He eased upright, cursing as shards of pain stabbed his temples. "God's blood, man! Have you nothing to ease my head?" He edged gingerly out of bed and moved to his desk with his coffee, yawning and trying to wake up.

He was simply trying to do a good deed. Keep a promise. Repay a favor with a favor, but with a few quick brushstrokes his Puritan miss had made a startling transformation. He'd intended to escort her back to the palace last evening, but her passionate response to his kiss and the feel of her lush body molded to his had forced him to make other plans. She was ripe fruit ready to be plucked, and if he'd gone with her he would have taken her right there in the carriage.

Truth be told, he'd hungered for her even when she'd been swathed from head to toe in dark wool in her little cottage in the woods. She was a jewel that he alone had uncovered. A score of women had come and gone since then, many of them celebrated beauties, but she was the only one to linger in his thoughts. How much more so now? God, to see her yesterday in a dress that clung to every curve. Even now he hardened at the mere thought.

It had been three short days since she'd walked back into his life, but it felt like he'd been wanting her forever. How could he not have known her as the only real friend of his youth? Perhaps because he tried to avoid thinking back to those days. Memories of his tutor's drunken pawings were always certain to intrude. *Ah well, I was a pretty child.* His lips twisted in a sardonic grin.

"Tom! Bring me wine." The chaplain's nocturnal fumblings had been the end to childhood innocence he might have claimed. It had made him sexually precocious, and an early initiate into the joys of wine. Giffard, his loving father, and his mother's refusal to hear him, had taught him a cynicism well beyond his years. It served him well at court, and was reinforced each day.

A snippet of verse sparked in his brain and he reached for a pen and his latest composition. As he wrote, the pain in his head was replaced by a pleasant buzz, a prickling sensation, not unlike that which he felt when under the influence of wine. As his thoughts hummed faster, his excitement grew and his hand flew across the page, the words flowing almost too quickly to capture.

It evaporated as suddenly as it began. Sliding away like a receding tide, taking his brilliant insights with it. His brain was left sharp and clear and well awake, but whatever had been powering it had just abandoned him. He leaned back with a sour smile, and read over what he'd just written.

> *But if in Court so just a man there be*
> *(In Court a just man, yet unknown to me)*
> *Who does his needful flattery direct,*
> *Not to oppress and ruin, but protect*

He nodded his head, testing the cadence of the words and was pleased with his finishing argument.

> *Whose pious life's a proof he does believe*
> *Mysterious truths, which no man can conceive*
> *If upon the earth there dwell such Godlike men,*
> *I'll here recant my paradox to them,*
> *Adore those shrines of virtue, homage pay,*
> *And, with the rabble world, their laws obey.*
> *If such there be, yet grant me this at least*
> *Man differs more from man, than man from beast.*

Tom placed a goblet by his elbow and he tossed it back. Poetry and wine always defeated a black mood. Deserted by his sulking muse and lacking wine to tempt her back, his thoughts returned to Elizabeth. He'd promised her a tour. It was hard to be cynical when thinking of her. What was he to do with her?

You know damn well what to do. Help secure her lands and send her on her way. It was a noble thought, but hard to do when his mind kept returning to visions of her naked in his bed.

He had a quick mouthful of bread and cheese and slipped a package in his pocket. "You did well yesterday, Tom. You made the lass feel comfortable. I knew I could count on you last evening to act in my stead."

Tom reddened and cleared his throat. "Thank you, milord. It was a pleasure. She seemed a kind sort of lady. Very gracious."

"Aye. She is." William sat down to pull on a pair of boots.

"Nice…she was…sir."

"Yes."

"Not like your usual ladies."

William stomped his boot on the floor to force his foot past the heel. "No, Tom, she is not. I quite like her. She is amusing. Not deliberately comical, of course." He caught Tom's worried look from the corner of his eye and relented with a grin. "She's not a dalliance, man. She is an old friend."

"Indeed, sir?" Tom looked both astonished and relieved.

"Yes, Thomas. Contrary to popular myth, I did not spring from the earth, a satyr fully formed. I had a childhood. She was a part of it. Now, no more questions if you please. I promised Elizabeth a tour of the palace and grounds so I will not be needing you the rest of the day. Take this." He flipped a guinea in the air and

Tom caught it with the ease of long practice. "Take your Janet—"

"Jeanine, milord."

"Yes, her. Take care of your lady today, as thanks for taking care of mine."

WILLIAM SAUNTERED into Elizabeth's apartment twenty minutes later. If he wasn't careful, he was going to get in the ungentlemanly habit of starting his day before noon. The first thing he saw was a chubby little maid who bobbed her head and scurried away. The next thing he saw was Elizabeth. His entire body tightened at the sight of her. She was wearing her new lutestring skirt and bodice. Her hair, defying the current fashion, was tied back by two thin braids, and tumbled loose about her shoulders in an artful fall of curls. He swallowed back his hunger. *How is it no one else has recognized this prize?*

"Good morning, Lizzy," he said with a slightly crooked smile. "My, how you've grown."

"Since yesterday, my lord?"

"Since first you fell like manna in my lap. Are you quite settled in?"

Flustered, she ducked her head. "Yes. Thank you. Your man Thomas, and Nell here, were a tremendous help. It seems I've you to thank for all the personal touches that make it feel like home." Elizabeth watched him from beneath her lashes as he ambled over to the fireplace and sat down. He sprawled on the settee in negligent splendor, looking just like the tomcat she'd called him last night. She wondered what he'd been up to on his nocturnal prowl. His long hair was a bit disheveled, his face a little haggard, and when Nell rattled the coffee cups, he winced and rubbed his brow.

"Consider it recompense for your sugar cakes and biscuits." He caught her look and returned it with a dazzling smile. Her heart beat faster. His smile was devastating, the very air around him seemed to crackle with excitement. *Oh, Lizzy, be careful! No doubt he was out carousing last night. It's all a game. Like widows and footmen.* She choked back a startled laugh at an image of William as a virile footman, smiling as he laid packages on her bed. He patted her back solicitously as her coffee made her cough.

"Are you all right, Lizzy?"

"Yes! Yes, thank you," she managed, her face hot. "I... It... I...was just thinking of something Marjorie said...about footmen." She stifled another fit of giggles and drew a deep breath, then stiffened her spine and straightened, resolving in future to practice more restraint.

Regarding her with a rueful smile, William's gaze darkened. Her eyes sparkled, her cheeks flushed, and her full lips quivered with laughter. If it weren't for the presence of the country maid he would have kissed her right there. "Enough of this, love. I think we both need air. Shall we out and about and explore your new realm?"

"Oh, yes, please!" Elizabeth leaped to her feet with an eager grin, her resolution already forgotten.

Holding his hat in one hand, William performed a gallant bow, then offered her his arm.

"Tho to their ready steeds, they clomb full light

*And through back ways that none might them
espy.*

"Will you go adventuring with me, Lizzy?" Her face
lit up as she took his hand and his smile widened into
a grin. "We shall not rest till faerieland. *'Forth rode
Britomart.'*"

CHAPTER SEVENTEEN

THE COURTIERS' LODGINGS were tucked into a maze of courtyards and passageways and at first Elizabeth despaired of ever being able to find her way through them alone. If William walked away and left her she was certain she would expire from hunger before she found her way back to her apartment. Not that he would. He was more than kind. He might call it a game, but his care for her since she'd arrived had been astonishing. Not three days ago she'd searched his face trying to find her trusted and familiar friend William. Now she had to remind herself he was Lord Rivers, too. A charming, rakish, dangerous stranger. Which man was he really?

He is both, and neither can be trusted with my heart. William forgot both me and his promise, and Lord Rivers makes none, other than to help me win my lands.

Still she knew him in a way that no one else did, and at least a part of him, the best part, was hers, and unlike Sussex, when hurt, awkwardness and surprise had left her mute, she intended to keep reminding him.

To that effect she had allowed Nell to work her magic. She knew William liked her hair. He was always commenting on it, in Kent, in Sussex, and yesterday. Little Nell really was good with hair and though he hadn't remarked on it, or on her dress, he looked at her often. His slow smile was like a caress, sending delicious thrills through her body as surely as if he touched her with his hands. She'd been in a state of anticipation ever since he'd entered her apartment, remembering his promise to kiss her.

She clutched his arm, holding him tight, savoring the feel of banded muscle beneath his velvet sleeve. As they wandered the grounds and twisting corridors of the palace, several people stopped to stare. She stared back, glad to be seen with him, so they might mark and note her possession.

He stoked her excitement as they walked. As he pointed out the servants' quarters in Scotland Yard to the north, he leaned against her on the balustrade, his big body crowding hers. He led her around to a hidden entrance on the edge of St. James's Park, and held her hand to help her up the stairs to the long privy gallery leading to the royal chambers from the south. As they walked, his thumb ran seductively up and down her palm.

A light stroke along her forearm drew her attention to the windows facing west. They looked out over a grand garden, divided into squares of colored gravel like a chessboard, with statues as a centerpiece in every square. To the southwest were the tennis courts, the bowling lawns, and the park. There was the banqueting house and there the cockpit theater, and through the east-facing windows spectacular views of the Thames. A private landing stage jutted into the river and William told her it allowed Charles and other monarchs before him, as well as "private" visitors, to leave and enter discreetly by barge.

"Those are the queen's chambers bordering the river to the north." His hand rested warm on the small of her back.

"Queen Elizabeth's chambers?" She'd been fascinated by the redheaded Tudor Queen ever since William had first spun his tales.

"Gloriana's herself at one time, yes. For now they lie empty, though much work is being done to prepare them for Catherine, Charles's Portuguese bride."

"Can we see them?" The excitement in her eyes ignited a spark of mischief in his own.

A charming smile and a silver half crown saw them down a hidden passage to a padlocked door. The housekeeper produced a key and after William thanked her, they slipped down a dusty passage, slid back a wall panel and stepped into a glittering chamber.

"Perhaps the virgin queen wasn't so chaste after all," William said with a chuckle.

Elizabeth shushed him. The room was hung with cloth of gold and magnificent tapestries. A mural on one wall with cherubs and winged chariots stretched from the floor, over a door, up the wall, and onto the ceiling. She turned around slowly, taking it all in. William was well accustomed to such splendor. He had spent many a day in the rooms of his king. He'd yet to visit the queen's chambers, though, and wasn't likely to after Catherine of Braganza arrived. He ambled to the muraled door and peeked around the corner.

"Lizzy. Come. You'll like this."

She hurried over to stand behind him, rising on the tips of her toes to try to see over his shoulder. He turned and tweaked her nose, then stepped aside, guiding her through the door with a gentle squeeze of her waist.

"Ohh! Oh, William, how beautiful! I've never seen anything so wonderful! This is truly something from a fairy tale!" Water poured from oyster shells and rocks, splashing down into a large marble tub carved with sea beasts and dolphins. It was fixed to be filled with hot water from a small furnace hidden behind one of several gilded mirrors along the wall. It was guarded by armed and bearded Poseidons sculpted into four pillars, and gold-trimmed marble tiles graced the floors. The tub was situated so the bather enjoyed panoramic views of the river, and of a mural that took all of one wall. The mural showed an arched and columned walkway with a shy, half-naked maiden being importuned by a hand-some dark-winged angel as she sat by a pool.

"That might be you and I," William said with a chuckle.

She shushed him again, but allowed him his place close behind her.

He grinned at her obvious pleasure, put his hands on her shoulders and murmured, his breath feathering her ear. "I promised you something magical, didn't I?"

She looked back at him, beaming. "Yes, you did, Sir Artegall. You are a most mighty and resourceful knight. Once you set upon a quest the thing's as good as done. Can you imagine what it must be like to bathe in it?"

"If you wish to, my queen, you shall."

She looked at him in amusement. "I'm afraid that's a bath meant for real queens, not fairy-tale ones." She turned impulsively and reached her arms around him, giving him a warm hug. "Thank you! For everything. You've been so g—"

His arms tightened around her waist and he cut off her words with a searing kiss.

She murmured something incoherent. It was this she'd been waiting for all of her life. Rising on her toes, she pressed eagerly against him. He grabbed her hips, pulling her closer, and a thrill ran through her at the feel of his body pressed hard against hers. She could feel his arousal, potent and probing, as she gave herself over to his soft whispers and skillful tongue.

"I promised you this, too, little bird. I thought of kissing you on waking, I thought of it last night, and I wanted to kiss every inch of you when I saw you in this dress."

She pressed her palm against his chest, feeling solid muscle and the steady beating of his heart. He gave a soft groan at her touch. His hands slid up her waist, his fingers trailing over her rib cage, and her breasts swelled as she leaned into his touch. He took one hand and spread his fingers through her hair, cupping her head and holding her close against him as his burning lips claimed hers.

Alive with sweet sensations, she threaded her fingers through his hair, unable to stop a moan of excitement as he deepened his kiss. She gasped when his fingers brushed her tightly bound nipples causing rock-hard peaks to strain and tighten through their thin layer of silk.

"Sweet Christ, Lizzy, I swear—"

An urgent scratching at the panel in the other room made them both jump.

"Bloody hell!" Laughing in frustration, he helped her straighten her hair and smooth her dress. There was nothing to be done about their obvious signs of arousal, and all he could do was shrug his shoulders. He spread his hands in a helpless gesture and grinned. "It's cold?"

Elizabeth glared at him, "That doesn't explain you," she hissed, edging over to hide behind him.

The panicked housekeeper was waiting at the passage. "Hurry, my lord. The workmen are on their way."

By the time they exited the hidden corridor, Elizabeth had regained her composure and was feeling more herself. William was nonchalant, just as he had been after the last two times he kissed her, as if nothing unusual had happened at all. Well, he had said he would teach her the ways of the court. "Do people kiss like that all the time, William? Is it expected?"

"A gallant gentleman alone with a lovely lady might be expected to make the attempt. When she agrees to keep his company he assumes she has entered the lists."

"You make it sound like jousting. Some kind of combat or challenge."

"It is, my love. To many here. Women as well as men. For the man to win, the lady must surrender. For the lady to win she must hold him at bay until he comes as supplicant, not conqueror. That and hunting are considered the finest sports at court. The greater the battle, the greater the glory and the more valued is the prize."

"Then I have played the game poorly. I offered no defense and presented you no challenge, allowing your kisses as though I were a common wh—"

He silenced her with his lips. "Hush now, Lizzy. You are not a common anything. You play no game. Your heart is in the thing and that is most uncommon. That makes your kisses something priceless and rare. What would you do if someone else tried to kiss you?"

"I'd take a pin from my pocket and stab them."

He threw back his head and laughed in delight. "You see? One would expect no less from Britomart. Artegall was the only one to ever best her spear, and even then it seems she let him. There's much you need to learn and understand, though. And I mean to teach you."

"About kisses?" she asked with a yawn.

"About kisses and more. Come. It will be dark soon. I'd best get you back before I have to carry you. Should you like to see my lodgings on the way?"

"Yes, please. I fear without a visit to the lair of the infamous Lord Rivers, no tour of Whitehall could ever be complete. I expect nothing less than a den of darkest iniquity, with the smell of sulfur seeping from hell's own gates."

CHAPTER EIGHTEEN

"WILLIAM, I am exhausted!" Elizabeth flopped down on his settee with a grateful sigh. They had just shared a jug of wine and a cold capon for supper. She had no doubt they had walked for miles, up stairs and down stairs, along gravel paths and through secret corridors. He dropped down beside her, wedging himself in so that they sat shoulder to shoulder. The air had cooled sharply since the sun went down and her stiff muscles and chilled skin relaxed against his warmth. "This is really not what I was expecting. Your reputation is larger than you are."

"Sadly that is the fate of many an infamous legend, but I hope it isn't true in all respects. What *were* you expecting?"

"Naked nymphs, amorous statues, naughty pictures. There were more of those in the queen's bathing chamber than here."

"And are you disappointed?"

She looked around the room carefully. The opulent bed with its silken sheets and mound of pillows looked suitably rakish and decadent, but the rest of the room was devoted to globes and maps, stacks of books, and endless reams of paper. "No. I'm relieved." She shifted position and twisted her neck from side to side, trying to ease strained muscles. The shoes she'd worn were beautiful confections, but hardly made for walking.

"I've naked nymphs chained in the back room," he offered, once she'd stopped squirming.

"Pah! You lie, sir. It's probably filled with clocks and strange rocks and unicorn horns and other curiosities."

William chuckled appreciatively. The wench was sharp and still knew him better than anyone else did. In fact, she might be the only person who knew him at all. She was certainly the only one with whom he shared any sense of camaraderie.

"I like your wine, William. We only drink ale at home. I've never had such a fine beverage." Her eyes sparkled, her cheeks were flushed, and her movements were uninhibited and languorous.

"It's imported from Spain and is a favorite of the king. You are drinking wine fit for royalty."

She shifted again, trying to get comfortable.

"Come here. Turn around." He pulled his knees up, making a backrest for her, and began to knead her shoulders with a soothing circular stroke.

"Mmm...William, that feels so good. It reminds me of when we used to sit in the old hollow as children." She sighed and closed her eyes, a sweet smile on her face. She was exquisitely aware of every place his body touched hers, and she allowed herself to relax and enjoy it. His solid warmth and skillful fingers and the heat cast by the fire lulled her back to a simpler time.

"There's something I forgot to give you this morning. I think you'll find it suits this dress." His gentle nudge brought her back from her daydreams. "Hold up your hair." She held her hair back off her neck and gasped in pleasure when he dipped a magnificent sapphire necklace between her breasts. It was a luminous collection of vibrant blue stones, set amongst two intricate ropes of gold. A delicious thrill coursed through her, thrumming in time with her heart as warm fingers caressed the silky swelling that escaped her décolletage, lingering there a moment before drawing the cool stones slowly up her chest. His hands rested on her shoulders, and his knuckles brushed the sensitive skin of her collarbone as he fastened, then smoothed and straightened it.

"You look stunning," he whispered against her throat as he placed a box with matching earrings, bracelet and sleeve clasps in her hands.

She was rendered momentarily speechless by the richness of the gift, and by the power his merest touch seemed to have over her. *He brushes my arm and my whole body aches for him.* At a loss for words, she fingered the necklace, holding each jewel up to the light. Their satin sheen reflected the firelight and six star rays danced across each gem. "William it's…it's beautiful! I've never worn anything so lovely! But—"

"No buts, Elizabeth." He squeezed her waist. "You mustn't count this as a gift, love. It is simply a part of this ensemble. A woman without the proper jewels is only half dressed, yes? Besides, I didn't buy it. It came to me with my inheritance. What use have I for such a bauble? You wouldn't want me giving it away to some theater actress on a drunken whim, would you?"

"Well, no, but—"

"Ah! What did I tell you? A beautiful jewel deserves a beautiful setting, little bird, and a well-mannered guest does not refuse a gift. Did I quibble when you offered to sew up my arm? Did I say you could ill afford to feed me or keep me, or waste your thread? Did I cavil at putting you in danger or accepting the…comfort you offered?"

Elizabeth blushed furiously.

"No, I did not. The necklace is a family heirloom. Mine to give where I choose. I'll hear no more about it." He cocked his head and regarded it with a critical eye, and then adjusted it slightly. "Do you know, Elizabeth, when I first saw you in Sussex with your sea witch eyes…"

"Sea witch eyes?"

"Yes, rather like a siren's, the color of the ocean as the wind whips up a storm. When I saw you then, I imagined you wearing this and nothing else, sitting by a fire with your hair unbound. It's funny how things turn out." He gave her hair a gentle tug.

"Your life is rich with amusements and diversions, William. Why do you concern yourself with me?"

"I've told you why."

"You know what I mean."

"I dreamed of you after Sussex and I didn't know why. You do remember that night?" His fingers continued to work their magic and his voice beguiled.

"Mmm. *Yes*." Her voice was a dreamy whisper. "Perhaps it's because of the friendship we had as children. Yet you've changed so much. What happened after you went away?"

He shrugged and downed his drink. "I went to school, I went to war, I went to France, and then I came home to England." He filled another glass, and adjusted his legs so she lay against his chest.

"Mmm." She snuggled down a little to join his silent study of the fire. The pop and crack of burning wood was a peaceful sound in the hushed room. She watched the flame dance in rivulets of orange, red and blue, caressing the log with greedy fingers even as it destroyed it. *That's what happens when you let the flame embrace you.* She giggled. "William?"

"Mmm?"

"I think I'm sizzled…no…sozzled…no…"

"Drunk?"

"Yes, that's it!"

His glass clinked against hers. "I find myself in good company then.

> *"Cupid and Bacchus my saints are,*
> *May drink and love still reign*
> *With wine I wash away my cares…"*

He leaned closer, his breath warm against the soft nape of her neck. "And then, my love…"

"That's very nice, William." She moved back a bit and patted his thigh approvingly. "What else did you do? Besides school and war?"

"Well, Lizzy…I wrote poems and drank and fucked a lot."

She elbowed him in the side. "You never used to talk that way. I want my William back."

"I am what I've always been. Your William never existed. He was a dream that lived awhile in your imagination."

She turned onto her side, accidentally kneeing his groin and making him spill his drink.

"Damn it, Lizzy, have a care! You can emasculate a man that way."

"I know," she said smugly. "*My* William taught me that. That hurt because he *is* real." She laid her head on his chest. "He's right here."

William sighed in frustration even as his fingers combed through her hair. "There's no point in discussing the distant past, love. It has little purchase on my memories or my mind." He reached for the wine jug to refill his spilled drink.

"You drink too much."

"*I* drink too much?" He arched his brows and gave her an incredulous look. "One hates to be unmannerly to a guest, but 'tis not I who am stretched in reckless abandon, completely…ah, yes…sozzled…aboard the lap of one of London's most renowned libertines."

Elizabeth sniffed and replied with some asperity. "*Notorious* libertines, you mean. It's not something to be proud of. Nor is being ill-mannered."

Impertinent chit! She was not so judgmental when I had her in my bed. "Manners can be used for good or ill. Lord Rivers uses manners to entice his prey."

"Pfft!" She gave a flip of her hand. "Silly women perhaps. What care I? My William will protect me from the likes of Lord Rivers."

He burst out laughing and she answered with a mischievous grin.

"You are a saucy chit, Lizzy Walters."

"Would you have me believe you are soulless?"

"I am honest. I appreciate women like a fine wine

or a warm fire. They are comfort. I need nothing more from them than that. Why can't people just have sex and enjoy it without having to pretend to be in love or going through the pantomime of making an acquaintance?"

She sat up, drawing away from him, and leaned back against the far bolster, poking him with her foot as if he were something vaguely disturbing she'd found rotting on the beach. "You don't really mean that, do you? It's a joke. Like the nymphs?"

"It's a lesson. I promised to teach you the ways of court. You may take your first lesson from me. We are just animals, Lizzy. Lusting, greedy, hungry animals."

"You make it sound sordid and ugly."

"It *is* sordid and ugly. It is also sublime. The ritual that propagates life. Dogs fuck, cats fuck, why must people make such a fuss about it? Why pretend it's anything else? It's scratching an itch, a release and a heady pleasure when done well, an irksome burden when not. There's no need to dress it up."

She was biting the end of her thumb, watching him closely. "Is this what you tell all the ladies who come to your chamber? I shouldn't think it's very poetic."

His shout of laughter rang off the walls. "Lizzy Walters, you are a treasure and that's the truth. I tell only you." He shrugged. "Perhaps it is William doing his duty."

"So it's true what they say about you, then."

"Only some of it. Well…quite a bit I suppose, but I'm not so bad as others paint me. I've always appreciated my enjoyments. A man doesn't know how long he's got or what's coming next in this world. If he can find a moment's pleasure why shouldn't he take it?"

"You see women as playthings. They are disposable assets to you, not meaningful pursuits. They give you their innocence and you repay them with scorn."

He bit back a laugh, wary of her frown. "You are in the court of King Charles II. There are no innocents here, Lizzy, except perhaps, yourself. The little lambkins stay at home. To venture here makes them fodder for the wolves."

"Like you." She shivered and hugged herself.

He picked up an apple from a side table and bit into it. "Yes."

He knew he was presenting himself in the worst possible light, but he couldn't seem to stop himself. He had no idea if it was test, a warning, or a challenge.

Fatigue and wine had lowered her defenses, but not so much that she didn't feel a keen sense of loss. It seemed he was saying he would never love her, *could* never love her. Not in the way she'd dreamed of for years. She'd known it, of course, though part of her refused to accept it and her treacherous heart leaped with hope every time he looked at her a certain way. She knew it the night he'd stumbled upon her in the woods and hadn't remembered her. She'd given herself to him anyway, and he'd made her dream of other things. Things she'd never known before and wanted to feel again no matter how the aftermath might bruise her heart. She sighed and blinked away her tears.

"To be soulless is to be dead inside."

He shrugged.

"There are people who love each other. There are people who are true to each other and live happy lives together." Her tone was almost accusatory.

He gave her a pitying look. "Too many fairy tales, my love. You have started to believe them. If you want to know Lord Rivers, you need to understand this." He stood and cleared his throat, holding his hand over his chest in the manner of one about to expound, and looked toward the ceiling.

> *"All my past life is mine no more;*
> *The flying hours are gone,*
> *Like transitory dreams given o'er,*
> *Whose images are kept in store*
> *By memory alone*
> *The time that is to come is not;*
> *How can it then be mine?*
> *The present moment's all my lot;*
> *And that, as fast as it is got,*
> *Phillis, is only thine*
> *Then talk not of inconstancy,*
> *False hearts, and broken vows;*
> *If I by miracle can be*
> *This live-long minute true to thee,*
> *'Tis all that Heaven allows."*

She threw a pillow at him. "You are an ass!"

He caught it and gave her a clipped bow. "A poetry-spewing soulless ass. Perhaps you should put a rope around my neck and exhibit me at the Southwark Fair." She moved to give him room and he sat down beside her.

"Why so much? So many women. So much wine? Such cynicism in your verse?" she asked, trying to understand.

"I should have known this was a trap." He tried to sit up but her arm held him back. "A brawl with a Puritan housewife, even in my cups, is far too undignified even for me." He surrendered with a drawn-out sigh. "I don't know, Lizzy. I seem to have a great deal of empty space I need to keep filled. With words, alcohol, adventures, pleasures. I enjoy the taste of my wine. I enjoy the taste of a woman. I can't seem to feel deeply, so I content myself with touch. Of course, according to you I am dead inside, so that would explain it."

"Perhaps sleeping with all these people keeps you from sleeping with your thoughts."

"And what do you sleep with, my dear?"

"There's nothing wrong with me just because I don't change men more often and with less thought than I would give to choosing a new pair of shoes."

"Indeed, you are country bred. It's to be expected. It's a failing you can work to overcome. Pass me the wine, Lizzy, there's a dear girl."

"You are country bred, too. How can you drink so much and not get drunk?" She handed him his glass.

"I ask myself that selfsame question. I work so very hard at it, too. Wine is a magic elixir. Drink enough and you forget the past, the root of all life's misery. Without the past each day would be a new beginning. Wouldn't that be grand?"

"I don't think so. I should think it was a curse. You would forget who you were. I would have forgotten I ever knew you."

"And well you should, Lizzy girl." He reached out and tweaked her nose, and then he sat up and turned to face her. "These bloody perches are too damned small. I am falling off. It reminds me of the one at your cottage. Shall I take you home now, little bird? Or will you lay with me by the fire and learn another lesson?"

Her heart swelled and she couldn't seem to find the breath to answer. She knew what he wanted, and she had heard and understood every word he'd said, each note of his warning. She watched as he slid to the floor and stretched full length in front of the hearth, his hands caressing the soft fur rug, his back warmed by the fire. He was silhouetted by the flames. Tongues of fire and shadow cavorted in a macabre dance about him, and flickering light and gathering dark sketched a wolfish smile, coal-dark hair, and blazing eyes alive with challenge and invitation. She was reminded of the words one of his fellows had used to describe him. *I know he is a devil, but he has something of the angel yet undefaced in him.* Why pretend when they both knew what she wanted? Mesmerized, she slid slowly to the floor. "What lesson would you teach me at this late hour, William?" Her voice was barely a whisper.

He patted the rug beside him. "Come closer, love, and I will teach you how to resist a man like me."

CHAPTER NINETEEN

SHE KNEW he might forget her in a fortnight, but she loved him and she always had. Her journey had taught her that life changes in an instant, bad to good, good to bad. One had to seize the moments when they were offered, and so she had in Sussex without expectation or regret. The memories she had stolen then had fed her till this moment, and now life offered the opportunity to reach for something more. She hadn't regretted it then and she wouldn't now. Besides, she told herself, *I am a widow,* and it's allowed. She settled close beside him, her gaze intent upon the fire, her knees drawn up and wrapped tight against her chest.

Reaching out a questing finger, he captured a gleaming lock of silky copper hair, and tugged gently. "I have loved your hair since we were children." His voice was a warm caress. His eyes caught hers and held her spellbound, and like a doe caught in a hunter's sights, she couldn't turn away. "Do you remember how you would hide it?" He rubbed it between his fingers and raised it to his lips, kissing it softly as he inhaled her scent. "Even then I wanted to kiss it. I used to think about it all the time."

His knuckles brushed her cheek, leaving delicate thrills of sensation, and his fingers stroked the sensitive hollow just below her ear. A small gasp escaped her and he curled his fingers around the back of her neck, lacing them through her hair. "In Sussex, when I first saw you, 'twas your lips that held me captive. You were so severe, so serious, but they were full and soft and so inviting." As he spoke, he nibbled hot, wet kisses along her jaw and around her ear. Her breath caught in her throat and her heart fluttered as a teasing finger traced a slow path along her décolletage. She closed her eyes and shivered, knowing she should slap his hand away, but the light caress left her melting, and as her breasts swelled and nipples hardened, she moaned and leaned into his touch.

He cupped her chin, guiding her mouth to his, silencing her helpless whimper with a lazy kiss. It was lush and unhurried; it teased and invited, a luxuriant exploration that curled her toes. She turned into his arms and he eased her down onto the thick rug, one hand entwined in her mass of curls. She allowed him to gather her against his length, and slid unthinking into his arms.

"Christ, Lizzy, I have dreamed of this," he murmured into her hair.

She rested her head against his heart, listening to its soft pounding, having yet to say a word. With each beat she felt her body come alive. Her dress felt too close, tight and constraining, the friction of her stockings a torture on her skin. She needed no lesson. He had made it clear he wasn't her William; nor was he the man people spoke of. He was something completely new. *And so am I.* She pressed closer and placed a tentative hand on his chest.

He growled low in his throat, and pulled her mouth to his in a devouring kiss. She sighed and squirmed as he pushed her back into the silky furs, covering her body with his own, pinning her beneath him with a groan of pleasure and pain. His fingertips gently traced her face and the column of her throat. His lips followed the trail he blazed with soft breathy kisses, and when his teeth tugged on her ear she arched against him, her entire body jolted by a sharp bolt of desire.

"Oh, God, William," she breathed against his cheek. He gathered her tight, his arm around her waist, skilled hands shaking as he pulled her supple body hard against his own. His tongue prodded her lips, impatient and insistent, and when she parted her mouth he plunged inside. A thrill coursed through her body, pulsing from her center and she gasped and wrapped her arms around him as he plundered her mouth. Intoxicated by his scent, reveling in the feel of his quickening pulse and heated skin, she opened herself to him with a breathy sigh.

He thrust his tongue deep in her mouth, exploring every recess, and she met him eagerly, her senses all on fire. They spent a small eternity lost in drugging kisses as he slowly dragged his burning mouth back and forth against hers. His lips embraced hers, teasing and caressing, and naught was said between them but what was in each tender touch.

Relaxing against the furs, her limbs felt loose and liquid. Her body, warm and pliant, was eager for his touch. It was William, not the wine that caused her sweet intoxication and she was eager to follow wherever he led. She could feel his arousal, hard and insistent, eagerly prodding as it pressed against her thigh. Her body responded with exquisite twinges that tugged at her nipples and pulsed and ached between her thighs.

She moaned, restless and bothered, and his sure hands skimmed her body, roaming her back and waist.

Nuzzling her neck, he placed a series of warm kisses, as soft as the flutter of butterfly wings. "Tell me what you want, little bird," he breathed against her throat.

"I want you to love me, William. Like you did at my cottage. If only for this night, I want to be yours, and you to be mine."

"I am more yours than anyone else's, Lizzy Walters," he murmured against her temple. "I want to drive you senseless and make you cry out my name." He bent her forward, steadying her with a hand cupped over the firm swell of one breast as he plucked at her stays, tugging one by one until each was unbound. She held her breath as cool fingers deftly loosened her bodice, sliding under the straps of her sleeves to ease it off her shoulders.

His warm breath fanned her naked skin and she shivered in spite of the fire. He guided her back against the cushions, wedging one long leg between hers. At the feel of his thigh pressed hard against her, a twinge of liquid heat moistened the valley between her legs.

His fingers traced her contours, softly exploring, and he drew his thumb across a cambric-covered nipple, watching with a smile as it stiffened proudly. His palm plumped her curves, squeezing and caressing, and the fire in her loins spread to every nerve. He caught her eyes, his own filled with molten teasing, and then he lowered his mouth to cover her breast. She gasped and jerked against him when his hot mouth found her nipple, flicking and lathing it with a hot wet tongue. She whimpered and shifted, pulling his head closer, and he bit her gently, making her moan.

He growled low in his throat and pealed back the wet material, and the cool air on her naked breasts made her tremble in his arms. His finger circled her nipples and gently flicked the tips as his mouth sought hers. She moaned in pleasure, drugged by his touch, clinging to his shoulders as his fingers tugged and teased and his tongue danced with hers. She arched her back, thrusting her nipples forward and he twisted them gently as he blazed a trail of kisses down her throat, along her collarbone and the plump underside of her breast. She quivered in anticipation, gasping when his tongue rasped her naked peak. He pinched each nipple gently between thumb and forefinger, tugging the rigid tips with his fingers as he kissed and sucked with lips and tongue.

With a soft moan of pleasure, she laced her fingers through his hair and he sighed and lay his head against her chest, listening to her heart. "What shall I do with you, Lizzy Walters?" One finger absently circled a nipple as he spoke. "You are too winsome to resist, too innocent to keep, and far too delightful to easily let go."

Her breath hitched slightly. "Kiss me."

He needed no further invitation. He rose over the length of her body in one fluid move, his mouth stealing her breath in a hungry kiss. His hand slid over her shift, tugging and pulling at her clothing, expertly freeing her from the confines of her skirts. When she shivered and colored, his hands stroked and soothed her as he murmured soft endearments and kissed her face. His hands roamed her body, calming and soothing, and then more demanding, bunching her shift and rasping it across her breasts and belly as inch by inch he freed her from her clothes. She gasped and arched into him as it brushed across her nipples sending an exquisite throbbing thrilling to her core.

When he was done, she lay before him clothed in jewels and firelight and her stockings and a curtain of lustrous hair.

His eyes lit with a feral hunger and his bold gaze raked her from head to toe. Stiff nipples rose and fell with her breath, dark against her pale skin. Her stockings teased her upper thighs, bound tight by confining garters. The fire burnished her hair, making it dance like the flames behind her, and shadows clothed the delta hidden deep between her thighs. His nostrils flared, his teeth flashed in a wolfish grin, and he placed a knee between her legs and lowered his body to cover her.

> *"License my roving hands, and let them go
> Before, behind, between, above, below."*

Drunk with passion, his body raw with wanting, he nudged her legs wider and she opened to welcome him, arching her back, cradling his head, and spreading her thighs. His tongue plunged in and out of her mouth in an urgent rhythm, matched by the movement of his rocking hips.

She met him eagerly, cradling his arousal against her stomach and thighs. She moaned and whimpered, too inflamed to be embarrassed, even though she was naked and he fully clothed. All her senses were heightened and her world had no meaning beyond his murmured words, his kisses and his touch. The silky fur smoothed her back and caressed her bottom, and reached to tickle the back of her knees and her inner thighs.

His hands and tongue spoke of ancient raw emotions no poet could describe. Wanting to speak in the same language, she trailed her hand down his side, tracing his waist with her fingers, and brushing his ridged belly with her palm. He moaned and shifted so she could find what she was seeking, guiding her fingers to the massive erection straining against his breeches. She smiled when he groaned and bucked against her, running her fingertips back and forth against it, and then giving an experimental squeeze.

"Christ, Lizzy!" His body jerked up off the floor. She tugged at the buttons on his breeches, grown bold by this gratifying demonstration of her power. He chuckled and played with her hands as he helped her, tugging her fingers and tickling her palm. His arousal sprang forth, released from its bondage, waving proudly beneath her inexpert caress. Closing her eyes, she held it, stroking its smoothness, enjoying its feel and weight in her hand. He grasped her hand, showing her how to hold and rotate it, and then sank back as she experimented on her own.

"Enough, my sweet, or you'll unman me. I'll spend in your hand like an overeager pup."

Delighted with her power to please and arouse him, she hid her smile against his shoulder, purring when he rewarded her efforts by massaging her buttocks and the small of her back. Marjorie had been right. It was nice to be a widow, at least when one had William rubbing one's behind. He leaned against her and bit the back of her neck, and then he kissed and licked her breasts, her stomach and sides.

His hands slid expertly over her body, caressing her belly and slowly descending to the tops of her thighs. He plucked at her garters, sliding a finger under them, frowning to see how they had left a red welt on her skin. He grunted his displeasure and inserted a careful finger, hooking one and slowly drawing it down her leg. As he did, he caressed her thigh, calf and ankle, warming and kneading them between his palms.

Dazed, Elizabeth pointed her toes and arched her leg to help him, and as he peeled away her stockings, her breath came in sharp little gasps. She felt as though she'd been seduced by some otherworldly magic. His touch and her body's responses held her in thrall. When his supple fingers began stroking the welts left by her garters, petting and soothing, she threw back her head, gasping as a slick sheen of moisture coated her thighs. This was the Lord Rivers people spoke of in hushed whispers, the man so dangerous to women that none he wanted could resist.

His fingertips moved in easy circles, massaging her tender flesh, eliciting a long wavering sigh. "Oh, William…"

"Mmm." He moved up alongside her and bit her ear gently, while his fingertips stroked the crease between her legs. His mouth claimed her lips in a slow and lazy kiss as his middle finger gently probed her, dipping in her warmth. He circled his finger slowly inside her and she whimpered, her head thrashing from side to side. He drew his finger out, licking it like nectar, and she blushed and turned away.

"Don't be shy, Lizzy. Look at me. You taste like honey. I'm going to taste every inch of your body and leave you begging, and then I'm going to fuck you with my tongue."

His words should have shocked, sent her fleeing from his chamber, but instead they made her breath catch and her limbs begin to melt. She didn't know who this person was, this careless flowering wanton, who seemed to spring into existence and possess her whenever he was near. His voice compelled, his touch cajoled, and though his stark words reminded her of all he'd told her of Lord Rivers, his smile was enticing and his eyes were warm and full of promise.

He slid down her body, nibbling and sucking, and buried his face in the curve of her belly, grazing her soft skin with the stubble of his jaw. His hands claimed her thighs and parted them. She felt awkward and exposed for a short moment, for he still wore his coat and boots, but then he lowered his head and kissed her wet and steaming curls, and when his fingers spread her open and he parted her with his tongue she lost all coherent thought.

She was moist and swollen, soaking from his mouth and her own juices, and she gasped and gripped his shoulders as wild bursts of pleasure rocked her to her toes. She moaned and writhed as he stroked her slowly, swirling to explore her folds, flicking up and down, and sliding in and out. "William…oh, God."

She was moaning his name, over and over, and her breath was coming in short hard pants. Unthinking, unable to stop, she dug her heels and hands into the thick fur carpet and raised her bottom, lifting her aching body to his face. He did what he had promised, sliding his hands underneath her beautiful bottom and fucked her with his tongue. She bucked and twisted, her hands pulling his hair, her thighs quivering on either side of his head. He raised his eyes to watch her, her pale skin flushed and rosy, her lips gently bruised and swollen, the imprint of his hand still on her hip. Damp hair spilled over her shoulders and breasts in streaming fire-hued rivulets and the mark of his unshaved cheek still lingered on her breast.

He sought and found her eyes as he gave her pleasure. They gleamed with an otherworldly silver-blue glow, catching the light from the fire against the backdrop of her morning sky necklace. *Like Venus at the break of dawn.* They were luminous and haunting, filled with passion and abandon and a sweet and dangerous hunger that arrested and disturbed. Still watching her eyes, he gave her a long slow stroke that caressed her folds and circled the center of her pleasure, breaking the spell so unexpectedly woven and replacing it with one of his own.

He knew what she dreamed and he knew what he could give her. He grasped her buttocks tighter, his fingers almost cruel, and pulled her hard against his hot seeking mouth. She cried out his name when his tongue teased her nub, gasping as he sucked and licked it, delirious as wave after wave of pleasure coursed through her.

She was bucking against him, her hands gripping the back of his neck, trying to pull him closer, deeper, not sure of what she wanted, but wanting more. "Please, William! I want to feel you inside me."

He kissed his way up her belly as she moaned and rubbed against him and then knelt between her legs. She tugged at his shirt, wanting naked skin, and he shoved down his breeches, his arousal swinging arched and potent as he flexed his hips. She gave a quick intake of breath and a quiver ran through her body, pinching her nipples as if he'd touched them, sending delicious twinges through her thighs and groin.

"Your body is a work of art, your flesh a living sculpture, Lizzy Walters. Your every round and hollow is fitted to my touch. I've been longing to hold you like this since I first saw you in your dress. Nay, since you came to me in shadow on a stormy night." He removed his shirt and coat and flung them to the floor then, trapping her wrists above her head, he bent to plunder her mouth once more.

Completely enthralled, Elizabeth followed where he led, no smallest part of her making any attempt to deny that she was his. All that mattered to her now was his lifelong minute. When he pressed his palm against her, stirring her with his thumb, waves of desire coursed through her body and her legs spread wider as she arched into him, pushing up against him and crying out her need. He ground his hips against her, his heavy shaft straining, bouncing and sliding against her slick heat.

"This is what you want? You are certain, little bird?"

His voice was hoarse and labored and she could only answer, "Please." She reached for his shaft, squeezing it firmly, and guided it into her molten heat.

She sighed and her heart fluttered as he eased into her carefully, stretching her passage and filling her tight. With every nerve in her body singing, she clamped her legs around his hips, pulling him deeper as their bodies joined. At first he rocked her with a gentle forward stroke, gauging her response and varying his depth and speed, but when her hot inner muscles tightened around him he plunged into her, rocking hard against her with a guttural cry. Their groans and cries echoed though the chamber as her taut velvet muscles squeezed and released repeatedly, in wave after wave of exquisite bliss. Shouting her name, he clutched her to him, kissing her wildly as a dam broke inside her and waves of exquisite pleasure rocked her to the core.

Sated, he sprawled atop her, nuzzling the tender skin under her ear as his fingers stroked, and braided, playing with her hair. Her skin was covered with a thin sheen of perspiration, and when she shivered he gathered her in his arms, kissing her cheeks and nose and wrapping her snug in his coat. They watched the fire in silence for a few gentle minutes. "Tonight I have claimed every part of you, Lizzy. For this moment you are mine."

"It would be foolish of me, wouldn't it?"

"What would be foolish, love?"

"To let myself love you."

"Yes, Lizzy. Very foolish indeed." She moved him like a lovely poem, and he wished he had one to give her, but all his poems were mocking, angry or profane. He kissed her then, with tenderness and care, and rocked her in his arms.

Elizabeth laid her head back and rested against his shoulder, lulled by his even breathing and the warmth thrown by the fire. When they had made love in her cottage in Sussex, he hadn't known her. She was just a stranger he'd happened upon, hidden in the woods. This was their first time as William and Elizabeth, and she knew in her heart he was the person she remembered. He was still her William and it was special for him, too.

"Are you all right, Lizzy?" His voice was warm and gentle.

She didn't speak, but nodded, her head against his chest.

"We can love each other, can't we? In the time we are together. I know that I can manage that if 'tis something you'll allow."

"Of course we can." Her voice was barely a whisper. What else could she say when she loved him even now. *At least for this moment I am his and he is mine.* Who knew how long the moment might last? The truth would be there for her and all the court to see, whether he kept her close or sent her home.

"I love you then, Lizzy, for as long as this moment lasts." He hugged her and kissed the top of her head, and somewhere between waking and sleeping, she sighed and smiled.

She fell asleep, cuddled in his arms. He stayed with her like that awhile, watching the fire, lost in contemplation. He had meant to teach her about men like him, to warn her and prepare her. As sensual and open as she was in bed, despite the harsh hand life had dealt her, she had remained an innocent. She didn't fit into this shallow sharp-edged world and the sooner her business was done and she left it the better. It was the only place he'd ever fit, though. It welcomed his bitterness, applauded his cynicism and allowed him pleasure and release.

He rose and gathered her in his arms and carried her to his bed, slipping in beside her, curling up against her with his arm around her waist and one hand tucked between her breasts. As he yawned he reflected how pleasant it was to fall asleep beside a wench one would recognize and not regret in the morning. He smoothed her hair and watched the rain as it battered the window, spattering fat droplets that clung to the pane before sliding down in thick rivulets.

What would you think if you knew what I really was, Lizzy? If you knew how Giffard made me puke and made me moan? If you knew how I lust. For women, for wine, for revenge that can never be mine. She wanted fairy tales. She yearned for love and romance. He had told her he loved her years ago. *And I meant it at the time.* He still did, he supposed. God knew in all the intervening years there was no one he'd valued so much or to whom he'd ever felt as close.

He'd wanted to steal her from her home and marry her before he left for Europe, though she was but fifteen and he a year older. *If she had I would have ruined her as she tried to save me.* How could she understand hatred and craving? How could she understand the emptiness that made a man want too much, and never have enough. And what now? Here she was lying in his arms. Despite his warnings, she would make him her hero, and when her eyes shone like starlight, he wanted to be one. He leaned his cheek against hers, whispering the poem he should have given to her earlier, now she was safe asleep.

"Oh my America! My new-found-land,
My kingdom, safeliest when with one man
manned,
How am I blest in this discovering thee!
Then where my hand is set, my soul shall be.

"Whatever shall I do with you, Lizzy Walters?"

CHAPTER TWENTY

LORD RIVERS HAD a mistress. It was the talk of London. No one knew who she was or from whence she came. No one could claim a prior acquaintance. No one had kept her, discarded her, married her, kissed her or courted her. She seemed to have sprung from the earth with no past or connections to speak of. She was fresh, with a faint sprinkling of freckles that she didn't hide with powder or paint. She had unusual eyes that glowed silver and blue, flame-and-copper hair that tumbled in tousled abandon down her back, and an air of calm dignity that was unusual in the frantic gaiety of the court. She was novel, she was interesting, and she was a mystery.

Some said she was an actress, though no one had ever seen her onstage. Some claimed she was a famous courtesan, newly arrived from Italy or Spain. Some said she was a common whore that Lord Rivers had brought as a joke, to dangle in front of the king. Everyone was curious, including His Majesty, who loved gossip as much as the next man, and half-hoped the last claim was true. Most preposterous of all, the Duke of Monmouth stoutly proclaimed she was a Puritan housewife, a widow who had once been Lord Rivers's childhood friend. The only thing certain amongst all the speculation was that she had fixed the dissolute earl's attention in a manner no one else had before. Whenever she appeared, he was there beside her, and the stunning necklace she wore clearly marked her as his.

What magic did she possess to captivate the elusive earl? What wit? What unique quality? What erotic skill? No one dared try her while she was under his protection. The king's poet could destroy equally well with pen or sword. So for now she was welcomed, studied and left alone. There'd be time enough to taste her when de Veres grew bored of her, and plenty of sport in wagering on how long that would take.

Elizabeth was well aware she was a novelty. People murmured excitedly and heads followed her with curiosity whenever she entered a room. William had been right, though. Being publically accounted his mistress hadn't done her social standing any harm. Every day her desk was flooded with invitations from court functionaries, courtiers and the most respectable of private homes. No doubt they sought to snare William, whose wit and unpredictable behavior was guaranteed to make any event a success, but together, they were a much coveted prize.

Life at court was proving full of surprises, but it was William who surprised her the most. If it were all a game he could not have played the thing better. He was a tender and considerate lover, generous and attentive and eager to show her his world.

They saw an Egyptian mummy of a Libyan princess at Mr. Savage's at the Head and Combe on The Strand. He took her to the royal menagerie in the Tower of London to see lions and elephants, and to India House to see birds of paradise and a serpent almost twenty feet long. She felt her youth returning. Every day was a new adventure. She was in love with life and in love with him.

William found her passion and enthusiasm somewhat alarming and did his best to temper it. Tonight they were expected in the Great Chamber for an evening of dining and cards and she'd been thrilled when he told her that her presence had been specifically requested by the king. "You mustn't be too trusting, Lizzy, or expect too much. You have to be careful. He'll be far more interested in what you might give him than in what he might give you." He was sprawled on her bed, watching her dress.

She looked over her shoulder at him as she stood in front of the mirror. "But isn't this what you wanted? Your plan is working."

"Perhaps. I am just trying to armor you, Lizzy. To teach you to be wary and protect yourself."

"I know, William. You did the same when we were young, but you needn't worry so. I have learned how to fight. You taught me. You also taught me how to dream. You can't have forgotten."

He didn't have the heart to tell her that life had stripped him of his dreams before he'd ever met her. What he'd shared with her was false. A fragile refuge constructed of lies he had used to soothe and entertain her. He had never believed good triumphed over evil, kindness was rewarded, or the strong protected the weak. He had always known that wasn't true.

"How do I look? Am I presentable?"

"You are stunning, but if I may…" He rose from the bed and came to stand behind her.

*"A sweet disorder in the dress
kindles in clothes a wantonness.
A lawn about the shoulders thrown
into a fine distraction.
An erring lace which here and there
enthralls the crimson stomacher.
A cuff neglectful, and thereby
ribbons to flow confusedly.
A winning wave deserving note
in the tempestuous petticoat.
A careless shoe-string, in whose tie
I see a wild civility.
Do more bewitch me than when art
is too precise in every part."*

He tugged here and there as he spoke, loosening ties and undoing ribbons, trailing a little bit of lace suggestively along her wrist, and ruffling her hair. "*This* is the Lizzy who fell in my lap. A fairy-child all grown up." His knuckles skimmed her décolletage and his breath raised the hair on the back of her neck. "Like this a man wonders what if I pull this?" He grinned appreciatively as the soft silk of her chemise slid off her shoulder. "Or this?" He slid his palm down the back of her stockinged calf, reaching for a ribbon, but she tapped him smartly with her fan.

"I shall never be done dressing if you keep undressing me, William."

"When he sees you he will be enchanted."

"Why do I feel so false? As if I was an impostor? If he stops and speaks to me he'll know I don't belong."

"Aye, my love. And like you the better for it. You've

a quick wit, but it's neither vicious nor malign. You're a redheaded beauty as fresh as the first day of spring. We are all impostors when we first stretch our wings. We don't know if we can do a thing, but we pretend we can. I feigned bravery when first I rode into battle, but when I rode out I owned it. Do you remember how fierce and strong you were when you played at being Britomart? You became her, and she became you. It was a game, but by playing it you found the warrior inside you. That which the game awoke was real. Now we need to find Gloriana, the fairy queen, whom no man can resist. It's not false to let loose what's locked within. Your head was always full of dreams, Lizzy. They weren't of being a little mouse."

He put his arm around her waist and squeezed her affectionately. She swung into his embrace, resting against the warm lines of his body, sheltered a moment in the circle of his arms. His lips brushed hers as he spoke. "You needn't worry about a thing. I'll guide you. You will dazzle him." Between each sentence he planted kisses on her shoulders, nose and face.

"And this game of love *we* play? Will *it* wake something real?" Her eyes searched his and he looked away.

The propitious arrival of Tom, bearing a summons regarding preparations for the night's entertainment, rescued him from having to answer. He backed from the room, bowing and smiling, as Tom tugged at his sleeve.

"Tell me not, Sweet, I am unkind
That from the nunnery

Of thy chaste breast and quiet mind,
To war and arms I fly.

"My deepest apologies, lovely Gloriana. Duty calls. But I give you my word I will attend you this evening, and together we shall storm the palace gates."

Elizabeth snorted, unimpressed. Even though the sound or sight of him made her pulse leap, his scapegrace charm wore thin when he used it to avoid any serious discussion of what lay between them. She was a straightforward person, unused to dissimulation, which she was fast learning more than French, Latin or English, was the preferred language of the court. Nevertheless, she had a woman's instinctive understanding that in order to catch a man one didn't chase him, one made him chase her. She watched him leave through narrowed eyes, giving him a curt nod of farewell.

"I seem to have annoyed her again, Tom. That was a close escape. It's all rather unsettling."

"Oh, I daresay, sir."

"Did you hear the chit? Next she'll be wanting marriage. I am entirely unsuitable. Frankly I thought she had more sense. There's a great deal about me she doesn't know. Nor do I have any intention of turning my life upside down to please her. I would make her miserable and she me."

"Then why do you continue to—"

"I made her a promise. I owe her my aid. The rest just…happened. I can't help these things. It's in my nature."

"But I've seen you turn women from your bed before, milord. You always do as soon as you tire of them."

"Alas, that's in my nature too. It's not the point, though, is it, Tom? She's not used to our world. That would hurt her feelings. I am trying to help her not hurt her." He stopped and threw up his hands. "What in God's name am I to do with the wench, Tom?"

"You said yourself she's very nice, milord, and not a dalliance, and it's not just women you've been leaving alone, Master William. It's been at least a fortnight since you've been overshot. You're coming on thirty years old. Maybe it's time you—"

"Damn it, Thomas, when I want your opinion I'll ask for it! Go and tend to your own lady fair and leave me tend to mine." He waved his hand in a dismissive gesture. "Go. Go away. You're a worse meddler than that magpie Oxford Kate." Coattails flapping behind him, William stalked off down the hall.

ELIZABETH SURVEYED the Great Chamber. It looked nothing like the imposing vestibule that had separated her and other lesser mortals from the glory of England's king just six weeks past. She had only to close her eyes to see herself, fighting her way through a crush of people in her sober black dress and bonnet. Then William had swooped down like some dark angel, and carried her away to the inner sanctum.

Tonight it had been arranged for an evening of entertainment. Fragrant beeswax candles were set in wall sconces; gold and silver candlesticks and glittering chandeliers lit the room with a golden glow. Tables were set for cards and dicing and long tables lined the far walls, piled with gold and silver plates. Crystal flagons and drinking vessels surrounded silver wine coolers housing a vast array of bottles, and for those not inclined to walk to a table, liveried servants trod the black-and-white marble floor with trays of drinks.

She watched from a corner column, still a little uncomfortable mingling without William by her side. Heads craned to catch a glimpse of her, the men with predatory interest and the women with cool assessment or a pitying gaze. No doubt they thought she had already been abandoned by the fickle Lord Rivers and had yet to realize it. She sighed in exasperation. Perhaps she had been. Despite all the attention he had paid her recently, he certainly hadn't liked her earlier question.

There was a respectful nudge at her elbow and she turned to see a footman bearing a tray of drinks. She couldn't resist a wry smile. Every time she saw a handsome footman, Marjorie's words came to mind and she found herself sizing up his manly attributes.

Unfortunately she couldn't help but compare everyone to William. Was he as handsome as William? Did his eyes hold hidden mysteries? Did he have William's lopsided grin or insouciant walk? Did he make her shiver inside? No and no and no and no. Let other widows settle for their handsome footmen. Ever since the day she had fallen in his lap, her heart had been set on William.

She wandered over to a card table and sat down to play. Gambling was a serious business and it was a place she wouldn't be disturbed. William had insisted she have money for gambling, and in truth, she rather enjoyed it. Along with dancing, it was one of the social necessities for upper-class women as well as men, be it cribbage, ruff and trump, backgammon or piquet. She seemed to have particular good fortune at one and thirty. William was a good teacher and she was a quick study and though she wagered only small amounts she won far more often than she lost.

Indeed, over the past few weeks she had made enough to buy new suits for Marjorie, Mary and Samuel, along with winter coats and new galoshes. She had been to visit them just yesterday, with beeswax candles, a sack of coal, a barrel of wine and a lovely haunch of venison. That and a tidy purse of coins should see them nicely through the winter. It had been a rather difficult visit, though, because she had also made a point of seeing Captain Nichols.

He had been very formal and rigidly polite. She'd been prepared for his disapproval, but not the naked hurt she'd seen in his eyes. She had never once encouraged his suit, telling him she was content to be a widow and had no desire to marry, and never suspected he harbored any great depth of feeling for her. He had always been so reserved she'd assumed his interest was based on chivalry and misplaced loyalty to her father. His reaction to her liaison with William was the first passion he had shown.

"This man is a rake and a libertine of the worst sort, Elizabeth. He is debauched and dangerous and can only do you harm. He uses women and then discards them. I cannot bear to see you hurt."

"He does not wish to hurt me, Captain Nichols. He has been a great help. But I deeply regret if I have hurt you."

"For God's sake, Elizabeth. For once call me Robert!"

"I am sorry, Robert. I know what you must think of me."

"You have no idea what I think of you. If you did you would have turned to me for help instead of trusting a man with dishonorable intentions. He is charming, and you are trusting and grateful. Can you not see how he takes advantage of you? How much he has cost you already? Let *me* help you. I care for you, Elizabeth. I offer you all I have and I would never hurt you as he will do. As he has done. You don't know what men like him are like."

She reached out and took his hand. "But I do, Robert. I know him better than anyone."

"No, you don't," he said earnestly. "He uses charm as a weapon. He uses your innocence against you. He tells you he will help you because of the trouble he caused you and makes you believe you know him to put you under his spell."

"Robert…I have known him since I was eleven years old. We were best friends as children. I helped him in Sussex because he was my friend, and because I am his, he helps me now. I…I do not expect he will long be my lover, but our friendship has lasted these many years. I hope yours and mine will, too." She hadn't meant to share so much with him, but he deserved a full explanation, and it struck her suddenly that she very much wanted to keep him as a friend.

"You will always have my friendship, Elizabeth. And I will always do for you what I can. I promised it to your father but I meant it for myself. I watched you grow up from afar. It always made me smile to see you. I was

waiting for you to be only a little older and then the war
came and I lost you. I came too late."

"Oh, Robert, I am so sorry. I never knew. But it would
have made no difference. The day I met him it was
already too late."

"Then I pray he deserves you and makes you happy,
Elizabeth. And I wish you well. If he ever disappoints
you, if you ever need me, you have only to say."

A polite tap on her shoulder startled her from her reverie, bringing her back suddenly to the glittering Great
Chamber.

"My lady? My lady, will you place your bet?"

They were all waiting for her and after a quick glance
at her cards, she doubled her wager. She sighed as she
raked in her winnings. The conversation with Captain
Nichols had been hard, but honor demanded it, and in
the end it had also been a relief. *I truly am a fallen
woman. The kind of widow Marjorie and Mary talk
about by the fire. I drink and gamble, I ogle handsome
footmen, I accept gifts of jewelry and have a rake for
a lover.* She knew she should feel guilty, but she was
honest to a fault, and the truth was, except for once,
many years ago, she had never been so happy in her life.
She tossed her head, sending copper tresses tumbling
in winsome disarray. Humming to herself she picked
up her cards and smiled.

A moment later she reached for her fan to slap the
fingers of the rude fellow who wedged himself in beside
her. A warm hand on her shoulder stayed her, and a
familiar voice teased her ear. "If that's how you greet
your lover, I shall have to hide all your hairpins. It seems
you have an admirer, love."

She made a face and looked over William's shoulder. The king had entered unannounced, and was motioning for everyone to carry on about their business. His arm was around the waist of a pouting doll-like blonde. He caught Elizabeth's eye with a bold smile and winked right at her! She blushed and hid her burning face against William's shoulder, pretending she hadn't seen.

"Well done, my love. Your blushes are artless and charming, quite the novelty here at court. He is entranced. I wager you two to one he comes this way."

"Oh, hush!" She elbowed his encroaching ribs. "Why must you be so cynical? That's not Mistress Palmer with him, is it?"

"No, my love, though she does look vaguely familiar." William gave the king's latest toy a closer look.

"Has Mistress Palmer been supplanted then?"

"God, no! She's made Lady Castlemaine now. She knows he likes variety and she handles him as adeptly as a first-class bear-leader with a randy charge about to embark on the Grand Tour. Doubtless she picked the girl herself. While he enjoys her presents, she's busy playing with the Duke of Monmouth, and no doubt her footmen, too." Elizabeth blushed a deeper hue, and reached for a nonexistent bonnet to hide her face.

William regarded her with curiosity as he leaned back and casually pilfered a gold and crimson feathered fan from the table behind them. "Here. Use this, love. It serves the same purpose and to greater effect."

She was too embarrassed by visions of William as a naked footman to object. "They say you and he ofttimes share the same women."

He shrugged and lifted a glass of sack from a passing tray. "On occasion. He's not jealous. His women are healthy, mercenary and clean. There's no fear of entanglement and little fear of the pox. What more could a man want?"

Captain Nichols wanted a wife. She fanned her cards and regarded him with a sour look. He avoided any meaningful discussion of their relationship, yet he responded to all her other questions with surprising candor. At times, he almost seemed to use it as a weapon to keep her at bay. "So it's not a contest between you? I needn't fear he mistakes me for a pawn in play?"

"You do me too much honor, Lizzy. A lowly earl is no competition for a king, but if by chance he does, I've no fear you shall soon set him straight. If our plan is to work, though, you *do* need to arouse and use his interest. You could learn a great deal from Cousin Barbara in that regard."

Elizabeth raised her brow and signaled for another card. "Really? Yet just hours ago you were warning me against him. What special tricks would you have her teach me?"

William eyed her warily, careful of the frosty tone in her voice. "Well…by keeping other lovers, she never allows a man the certainty of conquest. She never allows herself to be his and his alone. Rather than show jealousy when his attentions wander, she treats him with coolness and finds a lover of her own. She doesn't make the mistake that is fatal in the contest between lovers. She doesn't give him the power by allowing herself to fall in love."

"So, to you, love *is* a contest then."

He sighed and put down his drink. "It is here at court. A game if you prefer. The first one to suffer loses. The first to refuse takes control. Charles's first mistress, Monmouth's dam, Lucy Barlow, had no talent for strategy. She lost any faint hope of managing him by falling in love, something no other of his mistresses has been so careless as to do. She became an embarrassment and was discarded long ago. I do *not* counsel you to become his lover. In fact it is something I warn you against. Be coy, be careful, and capture and hold his interest, just long enough to sue for your lands."

"How do you know so much about her as a lover?" Elizabeth folded her hand, ignoring the play. "Was she one of those that you shared?"

"Barbara? Most, if not all of us in the exiled court did, Lizzy. She is a common shore." He tugged at her sleeve. "Look you now, I told you. He comes our way."

CHAPTER TWENTY-ONE

THE KING WAS indeed coming their way with his pink and blonde confection poised like a decorative trinket on his arm. William and Elizabeth both rose as he stopped by their table, though he made a good-natured effort to stop them. "There's no need to rise, dearest William! We are all family here. I am, after all, the father of my people."

"Certainly a good many of them, Majesty," William replied.

There were snorts of laughter throughout the room and the king smiled in amusement. "You've been far too scarce in our chambers of late. I had to inquire of my lord Buckingham if I hadn't banished you again." He let go of his strangely agitated companion and bowed to Elizabeth. "Madam, if you are the reason for his neglect then I must forgive him."

"You will remember Lady Walters, Your Majesty."

"Ah, yes! Though last we met she was encased in robes like a desert princess, I could never forget those lovely eyes. How are you enjoying our court, my dear?" His eyes were merry, his smile engaging, and Elizabeth felt the same stir of interest as she had when they first met.

"I am constantly enchanted and amazed, Majesty."

"Mmm. 'Tis often said our William has that effect

on the ladies, though you seem to be the first to have an equal effect on him." He turned his attention to his impertinent companion, who was insistently tugging at his sleeve. "What is it, my dear?"

"That man is a vicious criminal, Charles! He kidnapped me and stole my jewels. He...he..." Her lower lip was trembling. "He assaulted me and then he bound and gagged me!"

"I distinctly remember you enjoying the first part, Jane," William said with a slight bow. "And as to the last, I am amazed His Majesty has not done so yet himself."

"William! That is hardly chivalrous."

"She was most annoyed with me, Majesty, because I declined to leave her a likeness for posterity. As that will not be an issue for you, I am sure you will enjoy each other mightily."

The lady in question gave an outraged gasp and slapped him hard across his face.

"Jane! Apologize to Lord Rivers at once." But the king's command fell on deaf ears. Mistress Shore had already stalked from the chamber.

"Odd's fish, de Veres, but that was ill done! 'Twill cost me a necklace to placate her. I shall have to claim your own lady for the first dance. Lady Walters?" The king held out a fine-boned hand and Elizabeth had no choice but to take it. She hadn't danced since childhood, though William had hired a dancing master to give her a couple of lessons. Charles Stuart was one of the finest dancers in Europe. As the music started she needed all her concentration not to make a fool of herself.

"Lady Elizabeth?"

She looked up, startled. "Yes, Your Majesty?"

"I asked how you enjoyed the music."

She gave him a chagrined smile. "I confess I have scarce paid attention. I have never danced at court before, indeed I haven't danced since childhood. All I hear is my own voice saying 'Step onto the left foot. Step onto the right foot. Step onto the left foot *and* rise up on your toes. Close the right foot to the left foot as you lower your heels.'" She spoke in a singsong voice in time to the music and he laughed delightedly as he swung her into a right double turn, finishing the last sentence with her.

"How well I remember those very words. You are doing beautifully, my dear. And please, call me Charles. Now relax and enjoy the music. You can trust I will not lead you astray." His smile was contagious and his sure hold gave her confidence as they moved around the floor. He used his skill to hide her small mistakes rather than highlight them, and by the time the dance was done she was flushed and beaming.

He offered her his arm again and she took it, waiting for him to lead her from the floor, but he pulled her into a country dance instead. "You'll not abandon me just as I'm getting the hang of the thing, will you?" he asked, before guiding his laughing partner through a set of intricate figures. She was more confident the second time around, and by the third she had stopped counting and was thoroughly enjoying herself, the music and her charming partner. *I am dancing with the king of England!* Her eyes shone and her smile lit the room.

William watched from the edge of the dance floor, irritably brushing aside those who sought his attention.

His face was expressionless, his eyes stony, and a muscle twitched along his jaw. *Has she listened to a word I've said? He holds her too tight. Her smile is too warm and one dance should have been enough. She should be cool, distant, elusive, damn it!*

When Charles finally deigned to return her, William met his silky smile with one of his own, but king or no, his eyes flashed a warning only a blind man could miss. His stare followed his majesty's retreating back until he left the chamber.

"William, is something wrong?" Elizabeth asked for the third time.

"What?" He turned his attention back to her.

"Is something wrong?" Her eyes still sparkled and a becoming flush stained her cheeks. She was a little out of breath, her clothes and hair were slightly disordered, and she had a happy glow about her he found unaccountably annoying.

"No, of course not," he said sourly. "Though in the future you might try to heed my advice. You do your cause no favor by throwing yourself at him. If you wanted to dance you had only to say so. I can't be expected to read your mind."

"Throwing myself at him? I thought you wanted me to encourage his attention. In any case, what choice did I have after you were so rude to his lady? Whatever were you thinking?"

*"When she has jaded quite
Her almost boundless appetite
She'd still drudge on in tasteless vice
As if she sinned for exercise."*

He bit out the words. "Jane Shore is no lady. She wanted me to sire a child she could pass off as her husband's. When I refused she would have turned me in to the authorities. It was still Cromwell's England at the time. Was I to sit quietly by as she accused me of rape in front of you and my king?"

"So you refused to have relations with her?"

"No, Lizzy. I refused to complete the act."

"Then you also sin for exercise. It seems very hypocritical to me. Change she to he and the poem might be about you."

"You are right, of course. Though I've yet to give you cause for complaint. You can't say I haven't changed my habits to better suit you." He stood up abruptly.

"William, wait!" She jumped to her feet and clutched his arm. "You've been wonderful. That wasn't fair. I should judge you by what you do, not what others say, and I have no right to be jealous about women from your past. I apologize."

And I've no right to blame her for what passes between me and Charles. Of course he would pounce. I need to prepare her better. He put his hand on her shoulder in a possessive gesture and drew her into his embrace, heedless of the eyes that watched them. "Elizabeth." His voice was tender. "Don't apologize to me. It *was* fair. You speak no more than the truth. You do well to be wary, and I should point out you've forgotten all the lessons I've taught this night. You should have danced with the king and laughed in my face, been cool to my jealousy and harsh over my past mistakes. But I ask you to put it all aside for tonight. I planned an adventure, and this is not it."

"An adventure of our own?" Her eyes glowed with excitement.

"A magical one." His smile promised hidden delights. He slid his mouth along her cheek and whispered soft in her ear. "Close your eyes, love. And let me guide you."

She did. They left the babble of voices behind them and she trusted to his touch. His fingers interlaced with hers as his arm encircled her waist. It was cold in the passage and at least once they stepped out into the chill night air, but he wrapped them both in his cloak, enveloping her in his warmth. Without her sight, the thrill of his body next to hers brought all other senses to life. A shout of laughter rang in the crisp night air and muffled voices argued from a passageway. The loam from the gardens was perfumed by rain, and a wild salty musk drifted up from the river. Underneath it all, right next to her, was the sound of his breathing, the scent of his skin, and the steady beat of his heart.

When he told her to open her eyes he spoke in a husky whisper. She stared in wonder. "Oh, William! We shouldn't be here. You are madder than they say!"

"Possess these shores with me,
The winds and seas are troublesome,
And here we may be free.

"I promised you would bathe here, Lizzy."

They were in the queen's bath chamber. A silver wine flagon and crystal goblets sat on the ledge next to the window. Oil lamps and scented candles surrounded the tub, bathing the chamber in a soft flickering glow.

Otherworldly shadows danced on the walls as steaming water trickled through rocks and scallop shells, shimmering in the candlelight. The chamber seemed to float above a golden path carved by the full moon over the inky river and into the night sky beyond.

His hoarse whisper broke the silence. "Shall I be your lady's maid?"

Elizabeth's heart pounded with excitement. It was so beautiful. So magical. So daring and outrageous. *So William.*

"Please."

He came up behind her, breathing in her scent as he loosened her stays. With each tug her body swayed against him. Her breath was shallow, his nearness an intoxicating erotic drug. He smoothed her hair, and then he brushed cool fingers over her shoulders, hooking the straps of her gown and slowly sliding it off. It gave a soft sigh as it slid down her body and pooled on the floor. She sat down on the edge of the tub to peel off her stockings, and he watched, his eyes glittering with hunger as she arched her calves and pointed her toes. When she rose, she wore only her shift.

"Shall I guard the door for you?" His breath caught in his throat as he spoke.

"Why? Aren't we safe from discovery?"

A devilish grin played about his lips. "No, little bird," he whispered. "We are not. If you're too frightened…"

She closed her hand over his and stepped backward, pulling him with her toward the tub.

He caught at her shift, bunching it with his hands, baring her legs and rubbing it slowly up the length of her body, past her thighs, her hips, her belly and breasts, then pulling it off over her head. She shivered, though not with cold, and helped him shrug out of his shirt and coat. Blushing, her eyes downcast, her fingers strayed to the buttons of his breeches, fiddling with them and twisting them between her fingers. He cursed softly and his hands joined hers, opening the buttons one by one.

Elizabeth ran her hands across the taut ridges of his stomach, delighting in the power to make him shudder beneath her light caress. She slid her hands inside the band of his breeches, and her fingers moved over the smooth muscled curves of his buttocks as she worked his clothing off his hips. The feel of his flesh, warm and firm between her fingers cast a seductive kind of spell, for where once she had been shy, now she was bold.

He kissed the hollow at the base of her throat and guided her hand to his straining erection, closing his fingers around her own as he stifled a groan. "Feel what you do to me, Lizzy."

She squeezed his length and he moaned her name. His breath was soft against her ear and his heart beat next to her own. She caressed him with her thumb and forefinger, lingering wherever he arched or groaned, and then she did the thing he had done to her, covering his chest with hot fluttering kisses, blazing a path from his throat to navel and kneeling on their heap of discarded cloths. He was hard as iron, soft as velvet, and when she took him in her mouth his breath came in a groan.

He gripped her arms and pulled her up his length, grabbing her hips to jerk her tight against his belly, inserting his thigh between her own, almost lifting her off the ground. "Good Christ, Lizzy, I want you so badly. Nothing ever seems to be enough." Splaying his fingers through her hair, he took her mouth in a searing kiss, his tongue seeking hers as he walked her backward to the tub.

He swung her into his arms, lifting her off the floor, and then carefully lowered her feetfirst in the water.

She gripped the edges, easing slowly into the hot water, lowering herself until she lay stretched full-length. "William, this is bliss!" Grinning, he flicked his fingers in the water, splashing her lightly as he pulled off his boots. Steam dampened hair curled around his neck and his eyes shone with the familiar delight of grand adventure and a promise both tender and wild. *Oh, God, I love him so.* Her lips burned to kiss him, her arms ached to hold him, and a lovely thrill heated her thighs. He handed her an ice-cold glass of wine and she marveled that he'd thought of everything. She refused to break the enchantment by asking questions such as how and when or why, but as if reading her mind, reached down to his pocket and held aloft an ornate key on a ribbon of gold, then put it away with a wink.

"You pocketed that from the housekeeper! I am imprisoned by a thief and scoundrel! William de Veres, you are a very bad man!"

"And do you like bad men, Lizzy?" His voice was pitched low, deliberately seductive, and it raised the small hairs on the back of her neck.

She snorted and splashed him with her toes. "My name is Gloriana, and you should worship me, knave." She chose to ignore his ill-mannered chuckle in favor of admiring his naked form. How could anything bad look so good? He was stretched along the wide marble outer ledge, leaning back on his elbows with one leg bent. If she lifted her head she could just make out a dark thatch of hair, and a thick, heavy—

"Lizzy Walters! You're ogling me! You're every bit as much a knave as I!"

"I am not! I was merely admiring the mural that graces the far wall."

The sound of faraway music drifted in the window, perhaps from the Great Chamber or perhaps borne across the river by an evening breeze. Though much of her life had been austere, enveloped in warm liquid and surrounded by candles while listening to music and drinking cold wine, her sensual nature was breaking free. *With a beautiful dark angel just a hairbreadth away.* She regarded him, her eyes bright with anticipation, a warm smile of invitation curling her lips. "You look as though you just stepped out of that painting. All that's missing are your wings."

"I'm more often referred to as a devil than an angel."

"The devil *was* an angel. Do you think he intends to molest that poor girl?" Her voice was a playful combination of sultry seductress and wide-eyed innocent. She put her glass on a ledge and closed her eyes, sinking below the flower-strewn water with a soft sigh. It took only a moment. A soft splash, and water rippled round her knees and shoulders. Strong hands encircled her ankle, drawing her foot to rest on a hard stomach as his thumbs drew circles in light patterns across the bone.

He adjusted his position, holding her foot tight against him as he began a deep and methodical massage. Something firm and heavy stirred against her arch and she moaned in pleasure. She opened her eyes to his heated look, and a delightful ache pulsed between her thighs.

He turned his attentions to her calves, though his eyes still held hers as he caressed and massaged them with long sure strokes, sliding his palms over every hollow and curve. He hooked her hips and pulled himself closer. "Every part of you is made for me, little bird. Every part of you is mine." She didn't deny it as he began to knead her thighs. She spread them open slightly, in anticipation and invitation, and she moaned when his body settled over hers. His penis brushed her thigh, hard and insistent, and when it nudged the juncture between her legs her body ignited like liquid fire.

His hands roamed her body as his lips bruised hers and his bristled jaw rasped her cheeks and chin and the soft skin of her breasts. He claimed her with his hands and mouth, each touch a sweet sensation. There were no words spoken, nothing but moans and sighs and gentle splashing, and the muted music drifting from a place far away. As he settled deep between her thighs his kiss was urgent and demanding. She ran her hands along the ridges of his arms and explored the hollow of his back, the tight curve of his buttocks, and the iron column of his thighs, afraid that it was all a dream and if she opened her eyes he would be gone.

He deepened his kiss, his tongue stroking hers, and one arm encircled her waist while his hand tickled her inner thighs, feathering her curls. He spread her with his fingers and she moaned her need. The water swirled around her, warm and liquid, while his fingers stroked and teased her, strong and sure. She whimpered and shifted, inviting more. He obliged her, spreading her wider with his fingers, massaging her swollen nub with his thumb.

As his fingers flicked and danced and played, his teeth grazed a nipple, and delicious waves of sensation pulsed and gathered, building at her core. His mouth captured hers, hot and seeking, and he entered her in one fluid move. The water sloshed back and forth, spilling over the side of the tub. It was slow, exquisite, but her need was hot and urgent, and she arched up against him as her fingers dug into his flesh. He lifted her legs over his shoulders, thrusting harder and deeper, slamming into her again and again and again.

His head snapped back and a growl tore from his throat. Her nails raked his shoulders as she rocked against him, gasping in sweet agony at each sharp throb of pleasure, surrendering to exploding waves of blissful sensation and all that mattered was centered on his breathing, his being, his touch.

She buried her face against his chest, not wanting to ever leave the refuge they'd created, but he called her back by tipping up her chin and showering gentle kisses around her mouth and along her jaw. His lips left hers to nibble her earlobe, and then he gathered her, weightless in his arms, easing them both around so his back lay against the marble tub and she was cradled between his legs. She sighed in pleasant exhaustion, relaxing into his embrace, laying her head in a perfect fit in the hollow between his neck and shoulder.

"What was that, William?"

"I don't know, love," he murmured.

She was blissfully happy, basking in the warm glow

of sated passion and her lover's arms. "Where did we go? Where are we now?"

"I don't know that, either, Lizzy," he whispered in her hair. "Though I only go there with you."

She smiled contentedly and kissed his shoulder and then shrieked, nearly jumping out of his arms as a series of loud bangs and long sibilant whistles sounded outside the window. He hugged her tight and pulled her back down, his warm laughter rumbling in his chest. "'Tis the fireworks, Lizzy, from a barge out on the Thames. Many a dinner ends this way. When you're an old woman you shall brag to your friends, *When I made love there were fireworks.*"

She grinned and accepted the wine he passed her, settling back in his embrace to watch the show as rockets of light exploded into the air, spiraling upward in the shapes of geysers, plumes and fountains, and floating down as chrysanthemums, spirals and bright glowing suns. It was a magnificent display accompanied by music and the cheers of the populace who had lined the banks of the river to watch. She lay quiet in his arms after it was over, content just to be on such a wonderful night.

"Are you sleeping now?" William asked softly, nuzzling her ear.

"Mmm, I suppose I must be. For what is this if not a dream?"

"Lizzy, we need to talk."

CHAPTER TWENTY-TWO

IT WAS HARD to think with a naked young woman, slippery and smooth, wriggling in one's lap, but William did his best. "You certainly caught Charles's attention this evening. He danced with you three times. It was a great step forward, and sooner than I expected, though in the future, you'd be well advised to seem less eager."

"And I thought you were jealous." Elizabeth pouted and took another sip of wine.

"Why would I be jealous? Securing his attention is a part of our plan." *Just as long as he keeps his hands to himself.*

"He is a very good dancer, much better than you."

"Lizzy…" His voice was warm and rueful as his fingers stroked her shoulders. "You can't know that. You've never danced with me."

"He's taller than you, too, and very, very charming."

He bit at her ear and earned a giggle. "Only because his heels are taller than mine."

"His hands are nice and long, and his feet are bigger than yours are, too. Some women say that means… mmph!" He smothered her words with a kiss.

"Well, you certainly know that can't be true," he said smugly, then took her drink from her fingers and set it on the ledge. "You are getting tipsy, Lizzy Walters."

"Mmm-hmm. It's hardly fair. You drink twice as much as I do."

"Thrice I should think, love, but I am bigger than you and I've been doing it for a very long time."

"You make me tipsy and fuddled."

"Then I shan't give you any more to drink."

"No. I mean *you* disorder my senses. I can hardly think straight when you are near. I feel carefree and merry, and I don't seem to care what anyone thinks."

"Hmm." He rested his chin on top of her head and reached to cup her breasts. "I wonder why? Perhaps I shouldn't give you any more of me."

"Nooo," she moaned, and stretched, arching back against his chest.

"I need you to be careful and attentive now, love."

"I am paying attention. Tell me." She shifted again. The water should be chilled by now, but she felt warm all over, enveloped in a languid heat. She moved to straddle him, sending water sloshing over the edges of the big tub, and reached around his neck, drawing his mouth to her breast and running her fingers through his damp hair.

He nuzzled her, taking a nipple between his teeth and flicking it with his tongue before kissing her throat and whispering in her ear, "He will summon you soon, love. He will want to meet you in private, likely his bedchamber. He always does with pretty women, but don't be alarmed. 'Tis his habit to mix business and pleasure. There's many an ambassador he's met there, too."

She pushed at his shoulders, her voice rising in anger.

"Is that what you brought me here for? To teach me how to prostitute myself to the king?"

"Hush! You know better than that, Lizzy." He pulled her back into his lap, soothing her with soft kisses across her nose and cheeks. "I've had this planned for a fortnight, but as he singled you out so decidedly this evening it has to be dealt with, for he's certain to summon you soon. You're a beautiful woman who wants something from him. He will attempt to seduce you, and you must be prepared."

She swallowed hard, biting back tears. The night had been so lovely and she wasn't going to cry. "So your clever plan has worked too well and now he wants to eat me. Or am I to give him whatever he wants so I can get my lands and you can be free of me and send me home and not have to feel guilty about it anymore?" Uncertainty made her voice harsh.

Her low opinion of him stung. "You'll want to keep that waspish temper. It's something that he dotes on. Perhaps my plan *has* worked too well, but I certainly don't want you hurt, and it's not my intention to feed you to Charles. My plan is for you to charm and divert him long enough to get his attention and secure your lands. I don't expect you to prostitute yourself to do so. How can you think that, Lizzy? You brought me sugar cakes. You gave me refuge from my enemies and the storm. Do you really believe I'd repay your kindness that way?"

"No, William, I don't. But everything is so strange here. I don't… I'm not at all sure I'm equipped to handle a king. It makes me very anxious. And I'm not always sure I know you when you're being Lord Rivers. Sometimes I wish…"

"That you never came to court?"

She sighed and relaxed back into his arms. "That I never grew up."

With a low chuckle he gathered her close and kissed the top of her head. "Well, I for one am very glad you did. Now close your eyes and listen, love, while I teach you a lesson that will keep you safe. I know this king well, and if any woman is fit to handle him it's you. Under our clothes, no matter how fine, we are each of us, naked and alone. The king is just a man, no wiser, smarter, or more worthy than you. The man is trapped behind his scepter, buried by the robes of state. No matter how he tries to breathe, people only see the king.

"You were always a perceptive child. Respect the king, but find the man and make him respect you. He's isolated and lonely and he wants to be seen. Be proud as you should be. He is far too used to women falling at his feet. Both king and man are lazy and self-indulgent, but he does have some honor. He may not give you what you ask, and if you refuse him, he may increase his efforts to capture, but he'll never force you or do you harm."

"Mmm." Her fears calmed for the moment, she let him tug her pins and combs. Her hair tumbled loose in a coppery mass and he gathered it in his hands, combing it with his fingers before lathering a bar of fine castile soap scented with roses and sweet balsam, and slowly massaging her scalp and washing her hair. "I don't have a waspish temper."

He bent her head over to rinse her hair with warm

water. "I've been stung by it a time or two. I assure you, little bird, you do. The problem with many women is they seldom harness or shape it. They drown in it or keep it buried until it explodes. By then it has no subtlety to direct or manage, and is far more likely to simply repel." He reached for a spigot that released more water and she sighed in pleasure as a liquid cloud washed over her.

"And what should one do with one's anger, William?" Her voice held a hint of mockery, but she was curious as to his response. She had buried mountains of anger while living with Benjamin, alongside despair, depression and fear.

"One should hone it, let it energize, use it as a tool, to alter one's circumstances the way that one wants. My mother was very good at that. Her tools were religion and lawyers. They made her a formidable and dangerous woman with influence beyond that generally allowed her sex."

"And how do you hone and direct your anger?"

"It's called poetry, my dear. I use it as my muse."

"Now that makes a great deal of sense. I have read some of your poetry. I find holding on to anger most unpleasant. Rather than using or burying it, I try to let it go."

He soaked her hair again in a thorough rinsing, and then began to twist it into a braid. "Mmm. Sometimes a pointed verse will do that for me. Charles seems to enjoy the explosions, though. He loves a temper. He must or Barbara would never have lasted so long. For that matter neither would I. But make no mistake, hers are carefully orchestrated. She is the dramatist, he the enthralled audience to her play.

"Perhaps she reminds him of his virago mother. That blasted woman could never be pleased. Do you know she charged him for his meals while he was in exile? And the coldhearted bitch refused to visit his youngest brother Henry as he called for her on his death bed just one year past. He was but twenty years old and still she punished him, for following the dictates of his brother and king instead of hers."

"So he rewards you both for venting your anger on him?"

"Mmm." He nodded into her hair, trailing her thick braid across his lips. "Perhaps it is some kind of inner victory that protects him. Where once he was hurt, he is now entertained, so there's nothing left that can harm him. Do you understand why I take pains to warn you, Lizzy? We are a dark and twisted little family here."

She turned around and looked at him closely, her eyes searching his face. Her fingers traced his lips. "Why do I think you speak as much about yourself as of him?"

"Because you are a strange and whimsical creature full of fancy and a healthy dose of a very fine sack." He growled and bit her neck as if he were a sea monster and she shrieked in delighted protest, her legs splashing water over the floor.

He pulled her down against his chest, drawing her into a lazy kiss, but she was determined to get some answers, and after an intoxicating moment, she pulled away. "Seriously, William. Who is the man beneath your clothes?"

"Why, you are sitting on him, my dear. Your lovely bum is in direct contact with—ow!"

Elizabeth let go of the strand of dark wet hair she had just yanked, patting it solicitously back into place.

"Ah! You speak metaphorically. I don't know that myself. Whatever insight I may have only works on other people. I can't seem to apply it to myself, except when I am feeling maudlin and deep in my cups. I am something in between the William you remember and the Lord Rivers you've heard so much about, I suppose."

She curled herself around him. "It doesn't matter. I don't care. I love you whether you are a stranger or the William I adored. I intend to keep you as long as I can, Lord Rivers. Unless of course I become smitten by your charming king. You have covered all eventualities but that."

"That would never happen," he scoffed, though the thought of it annoyed him mightily. "You would never be content as one of many and you are already smitten with me."

"Yet you only promise me a minute at a time. I daresay he can do the same, and make me a duchess besides."

"Perhaps we should marry."

"What?" She jerked upright so suddenly water sloshed over the sides of the tub and onto the floor. The warmth of his laughter sent shivers up her spine, but it was his words that held her complete attention.

"Maybe we should marry." He spoke the words tentatively as if testing the idea. "I didn't mean to startle you, little bird."

"Nor I you. Surely you know I was jesting, William…. Are you?" Her heart hammered so loudly she could hardly hear past it. It was the last thing she had been expecting. She felt a strange mix of trepidation, caution and joy.

"I don't think so. If one gives it due consideration it makes a great deal of sense. It is I who has cost you your home and security and we are embarked on an elaborate charade to see you made whole. You're clearly not comfortable with it and, to be truthful, neither am I. As Thomas delighted in pointing out earlier, I am thirty years old and not getting younger. Sooner or later the deed has to be done. You'd certainly do as well as another. We like each other well enough and it would give you my lands in Kent. In truth I should have offered as soon as I knew your situation."

Soaring hopes plummeted. Her mouth flapped open and shut several times, before setting in a stubborn line. "Is that the best you can do? For a renowned poet your proposal is singularly lacking in originality, sentiment or romance." She lay back against the far corner of the tub, facing him, feeling that something wonderful had just been snatched from her grasp.

"I am simply presenting an idea, an alternative for your consideration. And you know very well I don't write that kind of verse."

"Of course you don't. I've read several." What he said was true. Perhaps he was as anxious and uncertain as she was and had simply used a poor choice of words. She needed to be certain. Her very happiness depended on it.

"Out of mere love and arrant devotion,
Of marriage I'll give you this galloping notion.

*It's the bane of all business, the end of all
pleasure,
The consumption of wit, youth, virtue, and
treasure.
If you needs must have flesh, take the way that
is noble,
In a generous wench there is nothing of trouble.
You come on, you come off—say, do what you
please—
And the worst you can fear is but a disease,
And diseases, you know, will admit of a cure,
But the hell-fire of marriage none can endure.*

"That is yours, I believe."

"Ah, well yes. But you must put it in context, Lizzy. It was a little ditty I composed for a friend, on the eve of his nuptials. It is traditional to frighten and abuse a fellow on such an occasion."

"I see."

"What is your point, love? You object to my verse? It offends you? What you've quoted is actually rather mild."

"No, my lord, your satire is sublime."

"Do not mistake me for my poetry."

"Does it not reflect your views and opinions? Who you are?"

"Perhaps it reflects who I'm not and what I lack."

"If you're not jesting I need to know, William. Is that really how you see marriage?"

He groaned as if he were in pain, and reached out to draw her back. "I can think of more profitable avenues of discourse, little bird."

"William, please." She pushed his questing hand away and drew her knees up to her chest, hugging them against the sudden chill that gripped the room.

He let his hand slap the water as it dropped. "Very well. You will be serious. Yes. In general, that *has* been my observation, but I am certain 'twould be different between you and I. Where there is honesty, friendship and respect, there's no need for anger and jealousy. I can give you all three."

"So if we were to marry, things needn't change much."

"Exactly! We should continue to enjoy each other's company, you could live on the estate in Kent, and who knows? We might even manage a little Elizabeth or Will." He gave her a coaxing smile.

"And you would continue as you have in the past? You would have lovers?"

"You've been my only lover, Lizzy. I have sex, not relationships. Before you I've never kept a woman past a night or two, though I might revisit them on the odd occasion and some few have become friends."

"All right," she said patiently, as if talking to a child. "Would you continue to have women?"

"Not when I have you to hold, Lizzy my love."

"And what if I was not about? Off visiting or in the country and you were alone?"

He sighed unhappily. Why must she insist on having the kind of conversation he strenuously avoided? *I've offered her marriage, for God's sake! Why can't that be enough?* He refilled his wineglass and downed it all in one swallow.

"William?"

"I see you are determined to bring the fox to ground. You want to know if I would be faithful. The answer is no, Lizzy. I would not."

Her face whitened. She was genuinely taken aback. Any foolish dreams she harbored had just been crushed. He offered no future she could accept. She should have been prepared for it, he had warned her often enough, but the pain in her chest was as keen as any blade. She gripped the side of the tub to pull herself to her feet, but her limbs would not obey her. Unable to escape, she surrendered to a wave of sadness and fatigue. Dropping her lashes to hide her hurt, the pain in her voice barely perceptible, she asked the only question she had left.

"Why?"

"Sweetheart, every man does it. It's for pleasure and enjoyment. Like playing cards. It means nothing. If a man does not indulge he's regarded with great suspicion."

"That's a poor excuse. You don't care what others think. You make a point of flaunting your contrary behavior in everyone's face. You asked me to marry you. You say you are serious. I want to know who you are. I want to know why you would marry me if you see it as a trap and have no intention of being faithful. Is it just from obligation? As soon as you grew bored would you pack me off to the country?"

"But you *like* the country. Besides, who knows? Perhaps I'd stay there with you."

"That's very kind, but it's not kindness I want. If I wanted that I would marry the captain."

"Eh? What captain?"

"Never mind. It doesn't matter. Who are you really, William de Veres? What have you become?"

He sighed and reached for more wine. "You've read my poetry. You think it gives you some insight. What does it tell you?"

She reached carefully for her own glass, relieved to find she had control of her limbs again. "It tells me you are a contradiction. A royalist who hates monarchs, a libertine who rails against sex and vice, an atheist who feels compelled to challenge God and an idealistic cynic who vents his spleen for want of a worthy man. It tells me you are jaded and angry and uneasy in yourself."

"Well, then…it's told you rather a lot."

"It doesn't tell me why you can't love. *Shouldn't* you love me, William? At least a little?"

"After six weeks by your side, Lizzy, I suspect I do."

"Just not enough to be faithful."

*"Since 'tis nature's law to change
Constancy alone is strange.*

"Why must love and fidelity be one and the same? I was debauched well before I was twelve, Elizabeth. Well before you ever met me. It's not for want of caring that I can't pledge to be true. It's my nature. How can I promise to avoid something I can ill control? Would you have me lie to you, sweetheart? You ask who I am? I will tell you. I am a man who has no center, but travels back and forth between extremes. I am always betwixt despair and delight, Lizzy. When I riot and drink and sing I delight. When I find the right phrase I delight. I delight when I am with you. But the nights are long and lonely and in their depths a man has only his thoughts.

"'Tis then I fear that nothing we do has meaning. It's then I despair, unless a warm body is close to bring me some heady new pleasure. Life has to be lived somehow. Drink makes it endurable, writing purges dark thoughts, and foolish adventures make one forget. I can promise to take no mistress or lover. I can promise to be true to you when you are by my side, just as I've done these past several weeks. But I can make no promise as to what I'll do when the drink takes me and something warm awaits me when I find myself alone."

The candles had burned down to sputtering pools of wax, flickering and failing, and through the eastern window from across the Thames came the first glowing fingers of dawn. The water was cooling quickly now, and a chill crept up her spine. "I always wondered when we were children. The way you spoke of your tutor—"

"If you don't mind, I'd rather not slip into fond remembrance. Let's leave the past where it belongs and speak of the future. Shall we forgo this charade with Charles and play a new game? Will you marry me and stun the court?"

"I suppose when you play with your women I might occupy myself with handsome footmen. Marjorie says that many women do."

"Does she? That explains a great deal. You've yet to answer my question. It's not a shabby proposal. I can well take care of you and your servants, including your impertinent and scandalous cook. You will be back in Kent just as you wanted, only a stone's throw away from where you grew up. I've yet to go back there since Charles returned it, but perhaps with you in residence I would. It was a fine estate, little bird, so far as I remember."

"Yes, I know. I used to watch it from the branches of the oak."

"Good! It's settled then. Let's finish here. I can hardly have my wife to be expiring from a cold."

"William, no. It's not settled. At least not the way you assume." A part of her wanted to say yes more than anything. To be married to him would be a dream come true. She had imagined it, wished for it, and joined their names together since the day he had rescued her and seen her safely home. But it wasn't this passionless, practical proposal she had imagined, nor was this future, filled with other women, one she was prepared to accept.

Taking a deep breath, she sat up straight, steeling herself to face the man who'd so casually broken her heart. "Given all you've said, I will not marry you, William. I cannot. Perhaps you remember my views on being a widow? And now I am of course, familiar with yours on wedded bliss. It's very chivalrous of you to offer such a sacrifice. I know you mean to help me, but given your views I feel the burden would be unfair. As foolish as it seems, it is a fairy-tale husband I want, and unless I find him, I fear a merry widow is my lot."

William blinked, unable to mask his shock. When he had planned the evening he'd had no intention of offering marriage. It was the furthest thing from his mind. Still, the chit should have been thrilled and grateful that he had even mentioned it. He had seen Charles's intent from the moment he asked her to dance. The king had been stung in the past when William poached his women, and that trollop Jane had only made things worse. Revenge, a contest, or simply a diversion, William had no intention of using Elizabeth as a pawn in court games. He had seized on marriage as an honorable solution, to return her to her proper place and guard her from a far too interested king.

"I should hope we might continue as very close friends though, for as long as it suits," she ventured.

"I am not sure I have the talent for it, my dear," he said sourly, unable to keep the bitterness from his voice.

"Neither am I," she said with a defensive laugh.

"You insult me, madam, when I offer you the best I have?"

"Please don't be angry, William. I mean no insult. I count our friendship no small thing, but what we expect from marriage is so very different I fear we would make each other desperately unhappy."

"I don't understand, Lizzy. You want to be friends, you want to be lovers, but you don't want to marry? Frankly it's the last thing I expected of you."

Though on the verge of tears, she managed a rueful grin. "A proposal of marriage was the last thing I expected from you. I do love you, William, very much. But I don't hold my friends to the same standard I would a husband. They, after all, have no more control over my life than what I choose to allow them. I won't become one of those sad, abandoned creatures who is packed away and never sees her husband."

"You think I would control you?"

"I don't know you well enough anymore to say. You would have the right. The man who *was* my husband… well, never mind that. It's not that complicated. I will not marry you if you can't promise to love me and be faithful."

"It's amusing, don't you think. First I didn't know you and now you don't know me?"

"Yes. Very amusing." Her voice was cool and steady, but she lacked the strength to stop from asking, "Can we continue as we have been doing? These past two months have been the happiest in my life."

"Of course we can, Lizzy." He stepped from the tub and offered her his hand. "'Twas naught but a foolish notion. You know how fanciful I get. You should never listen to a word I say when moonstruck or drunk. We shall speak no more about it." They were both damp and chilled, he dressed himself quickly, and then gathered her clothing and wrapped her in his coat.

"It was a wonderful surprise, William. The bath, I mean," she offered as he hefted her in his arms and carried her through the hidden passage.

"You've sat on her throne. I thought it only fitting you soak in her tub."

"You're not angry?"

"Why would I be angry? I have just escaped the fires of hell without being burned. Now hush, love, unless you want to alert the guards to our presence." He carried her back to his room, but despite his studied insouciance her words had stung. He had never offered himself to anyone before. No talent for love, no talent for friendship. He had a talent for fucking, though. He had yet to hear her complain about that.

CHAPTER TWENTY-THREE

WILLIAM KICKED open the door to his chamber, the sudden move jolting a slumbering Elizabeth awake. She looked up at him with a tentative smile.

"Hello, William. I thought you were never coming home." An auburn-haired violet-eyed beauty, naked but for a strategically placed pillow, was artfully posed in his bed.

Elizabeth's smile faded. William let her slide to the floor and stepped past her, as if she weren't there.

"Goddamn it, Barbara! What are you doing here? Tom! Thomas!" A barely awake Thomas stumbled into the room, fastening his bed gown, looking first at the white-faced Elizabeth, then the purring Barbara, and then his clearly discomfited master. "Bloody hell, Thomas! How did *she* get in here?"

"I assume she had a key, Master William, or you left the door unlocked. You often do when...er...ahem."

"Escort her out. You were not invited, Barbara. Thomas will see you to your chambers."

Barbara Palmer pouted and stretched and her pillow fell to the floor. "Why so surly, William? You were far more welcoming the last we met." She ran her hand slowly down her body, lingering so her fingertips just brushed her nipples before sliding over a softly rounded stomach to cover a thatch of thick auburn curls.

Elizabeth bristled with indignation, looking from William to the bed, every inch of her rigid with anger. Barbara leaned on her elbow, exposing her whole body to view. A round-eyed Thomas stammered, clearly uncertain as to how he was supposed to perform this new and daunting task, while Barbara peered around him to give Elizabeth a cold smile.

"Oh, William, how charming! This must be your little Puritan housewife!" Her voice dripped sweet poison. "Charles has told me all about her. She's every bit as amusing as he said."

As Thomas seemed frozen in place, William reached down and picked up the lady's discarded silk bed gown, flicking it to her with a look of mild distaste. "Up, Barbara. Now! Lest I throw you out in the hall naked."

"You swine! You wouldn't dare."

"One...two..."

Barbara snatched the gown with a moue of annoyance and stood up, flaunting her glory before fastening it about her waist. "You are so very attractive in one of your moods, William." She gave Elizabeth a false smile as she approached him, winding around him and clutching one arm as her fingers trailed across his cheek. "Don't you think so, dear?" she said to Elizabeth. "It's always a pleasure to meet one of William's playthings. Perhaps we might all play together sometime." She purred and passed her palm over his crotch. He growled and grabbed her by the wrists.

"You may call me *my lady, ma'am,* or *Lady Castlemaine,* and you should curtsy. I see William has neglected to teach you your manners yet," she called to Elizabeth over William's shoulder as he hauled her unceremoniously to the door.

Elizabeth returned her cold-eyed smile with one of her own, and though her fists were clenched and a muscle twitched along her jaw, she managed a cool retort. "You are not a duchess yet, madam, despite the rumors, just a woman who cuckolds her husband and the plaything of a powerful man."

Lady Castlemaine pulled herself free from William's grasp. She smoothed her hair and adjusted her clothes and turned to give Elizabeth a venomous look, but when she spoke it was to William. "You will trample that girl within a month and then come back to me."

They both watched in silence as Lady Castlemaine swept down the hall, an anxious Thomas trailing behind her. Elizabeth couldn't unclench her hands until the woman had rounded the corner and was out of sight. When she looked at her palms there were marks where her nails had dug into her flesh.

"That wasn't wise, Elizabeth. You don't need her as an enemy. She's known for her temper, and for her influence over Charles."

"First this Jane person, now that witch. On a night you made romantic plans for the two of us. It's a good thing I said no to you, William, for it's clear to me now how things would be if we were married. You let her… she…had her hands all over you!"

"Come now, love. Why so upset? I swear I didn't invite her, and I threw her out into the hall directly." He ran his fingers distractedly through his hair. "What else was I supposed to do, Elizabeth? They are always climbing into my bed whether I will it or no."

She shot him a withering glance. "Perhaps you might have locked your door."

"But that would be rude. Wait! Elizabeth! Come back! 'Twas only a jest!"

An iron grip on her wrist stopped her halfway to the door. She turned and stared at him, her icy gray eyes demanding he release her. He let go of her suddenly, as if she had grown too hot to touch. She rubbed her wrist, though his grip had left no mark. "What if you had been alone and found her there, Lord Rivers? What if I had not been with you?"

He studied her thoughtfully for a moment, but he didn't answer.

She slammed the door with such force it reverberated through stone walls. He was right. She, too, had a temper, and when pressed she could use it to great effect. If she'd had any doubts about turning down his proposal they had just been washed away. She stalked to her room, her whole body vibrating, her cheeks flushed, her skin pricking, and her breath coming in deep pants. Anger was energizing. He was right about that, too. It was much better than disappointment, or hurt.

As it happened, he was right about something else, too. After a restless sleep a timid Nell woke her to inform her that she was summoned to attend the king that night after dinner.

CHAPTER TWENTY-FOUR

GIVEN TIME TO reflect, Elizabeth reconsidered her anger at William. It was true an overbred, underdressed strumpet had been waiting in his bed but he'd clearly been surprised and he'd sent her packing quick enough. *The nerve of that woman! The trollop had her hands all over him.* The stab of possessiveness and jealously she'd felt had been fierce. Still he hadn't actually done anything, and she had stormed out before he had answered her question. Perhaps she'd been a little harsh, still angry at his disappointing marriage proposal.

But this was the moment she'd been waiting for since she came to the palace, and he was her trusted guide. This might be the most important interview she would ever have in her life. It certainly would be the most exalted one. Everything he'd said had been right so far. Now she wanted him to come with her, to tell her what to say, to tell her how to dress. She wanted to share her excitement with him, and have him ease her worries and dismiss her fears. He was her only friend at court after all, and he *knew* the king. He was a gentleman of the bedchamber who spent a week each quarter in his majesty's chamber. *Dear Lord, here I am, Lizzy Walters from Maidstone in county Kent, and I have been summoned for a private audience with the king!* She shooed

Nell out the door to go and find William, and danced around the room in nervous glee.

Unfortunately, Nell returned with the news that Lord Rivers had already left for a prior engagement, and was not expected back before nightfall. They had been so close these past several weeks that despite the events of last evening it still took Elizabeth by surprise. He really should be helping her; it was his plan after all. He might at least have sent a message. It looked like she was going to have to prepare to meet her sovereign on her own.

She decided on the blue lutestring dress with her sapphire necklace. No one else had seen her in it. William had liked it well enough, and failing his presence, she must rely on her own good sense and all his tutoring. Let the king, as he should, shine as the sun. She would represent Venus and mystery, and that aristocratic doxy and everyone else, including the king, would see the de Veres jewelry and assume that she was his and he was hers.

Truth be told, she was not as confident of that as she had been a week ago, but he *had* proposed marriage just last night, which she knew for him, despite his words, was no small thing. In fact, the more she thought about it, the more it heartened her. *Perhaps…given time…* She gave her head a shake. *No more of that, Elizabeth Walters! You've given him every opportunity and you've both said all there is to say on the matter.* His patronage and protection at this juncture was no small thing though, and the necklace proclaimed it.

Nell dressed her in a robin's-egg blue silk shift that matched her petticoat and showed through the slashes of her sleeves. Elizabeth looked at herself curiously in the large glass once she was done. With her gold-embroidered dark blue overskirt and bodice and her hair loose about her shoulders in a shining mass of tumbling curls, she didn't recognize herself. Her jewelry trapped and reflected the candlelight, from gathered cuffs to neck and ears. The necklace and earrings drew attention to her breasts and throat, and when she moved she glittered like the nighttime sky.

She nodded her head thoughtfully, remembering what both Marjorie and William had said about wearing armor, and then she remembered the poem William had quoted yesterday. She pulled one curl free to caress the curve of her breast, and another to brush her temple. Then she loosened a ribbon here and there, arranged the lace of her cuff just a little askew and, despite Nell's anxious squawking, twisted the hem of her petticoat into a slight disorder. She examined herself carefully in the mirror one last time, and her face broke into a satisfied smile.

WILLIAM HAD GONE seeking escape and entertainment, both of which were deuced difficult to find before dinner. He settled for a round or two of drinks with Sedly at Oxford Kate's, exchanging gibes and barbed witticisms with old cronies, and rudely fielding scathing comments as to whether his sanity had at last returned and his fascination with Elizabeth Walters finally come to an end.

The way she had stormed from his room had been completely unexpected. Usually he walked away from a woman; she didn't walk out on him. It was a surprise that had both rankled and relieved. When Elizabeth

had asked what he would have done had she not been
with him, he'd been unable to answer. The truth was he
honestly didn't know. The sight of Barbara had raised no
hunger, just anger that she dared meddle in his affairs.
Nevertheless, she was an old habit. And apparently he
didn't meet Elizabeth's exalted expectations. According
to her, he was only fit to be considered a friend, which
left him under no obligation in regards to his sexual
partners that he could see.

The chit refused my offer of marriage! Let her see
if someone else offers her anything better. *Charles
well might. His interest is unmistakable. Could that
be why she refused me?* No. Not his little bird. It was
some childish romantic fantasy that stopped her, even
though he'd promised to take no lovers or mistress, and
be faithful when they were together. For him, that was
extraordinary and it was a good deal more consideration
than most men offered their wives.

In order to sleep he needed sex and liquor, something
wired into him since Giffard's tutelage, yet he hadn't
felt the need for any other woman since Elizabeth had
come back into his life. He certainly hadn't sought one
out. Barbara had seemed unbearably coarse and vulgar
next to Lizzy, and he'd been proud of the way Lizzy
stood her ground.

Who could blame Elizabeth for being annoyed about
Barbara? Given his reputation it was a scene that might
easily be misconstrued. Perhaps all she needed was reassurance and explanation. He would have one more
drink, then go back to the palace and seek her out.

It was Thomas who told him she'd been summoned
by the king. Trust Charles to wait until the cat was away.

He had expected to accompany her, marking her as his, but he had been careless and left her unguarded out of pique. *Iacta alea est.* The die had been cast. There was nothing for it but to wait.

ELIZABETH SAT waiting in the king's privy chamber on a plush upholstered walnut chair. She kicked her heels back and forth as her hands rubbed up and down the smooth grain of its ornately carved arms. Cocking her head back, she admired the beautifully painted ceiling with its mythical flying chariots and cherubs, and goddesses and gods. There was always something spectacular to admire in the palace, a welcome distraction when one had to wait and wait. She took several deep breaths, trying not to think of this meeting's importance, though if Charles refused her request there was no further appeal.

Her feet stopped in midswing, defying gravity, as she was struck by a sudden horrible thought. What if he hadn't called her to discuss her property, but to chastise her for insulting Lady Castlemaine and send her from court? All hope would be lost.

Not true! her practical self countered. She was already well ahead of where she'd been. She would sell her new dresses and all of her jewelry, except William's necklace, which she would keep or return. The proceeds from her dresses would provide all they needed to live on for many years to come.

Calmed, she returned to kicking her heels and contemplating the winged deities on the ceiling, relaxed for the moment and lost in thought. A slight squeak made her look to her right. The king stood watching her with a bemused look. He was dressed somewhat informally, in white silk with a blue robe and a crimson sash and ribbons. It seemed he had come to fetch her himself.

"By God, madam! I scarce remember you looking like this, and I saw you just the other day. You look like Ishtar herself, descended from heaven. How utterly charming!"

Elizabeth blushed and rose to her feet, performing a deep curtsy. "Thank you, Your Majesty, you are very kind."

"Nonsense, my dear. It is you who grace us with your presence. There's no need to be so formal. Please call me Charles." His manner was easy and familiar. William had said the late king's maxim had been "I mean to be obeyed" while Charles preferred "To women you cannot be too civil," and at the moment he seemed more charming gallant than illustrious king. He offered his arm and she took it, trying to keep her wits about her and remember William's coaching.

He is broad-minded and curious with wide-ranging interests and loves a quick wit. He likes independent women with forceful characters, feels the whole world is governed by self-interest, and the only creatures he trusts completely are his horses and his dogs. He befriends enemies and abandons friends as he finds necessary, and has the greatest art of concealing himself of any man alive. He can pass from business to pleasure and pleasure to business and no man can tell what his true thoughts. If you wish to succeed, find the man beneath the king. Just how was she to do that?

"What is going on beneath that lovely brow, Mistress Walters?"

Elizabeth couldn't help but notice that he'd not called her Lady Walters, and she wondered if Lady Castlemaine had turned him against her already. "I am trying to remember all that William, I mean Lord Rivers, counseled, my lord...um...Charles."

"Ah! Then you *are* his creature. Tell me, my dear, what has our Will taught you?" Before she could answer, the door to his bedchamber swung open and they stepped inside.

I am in the bedchamber of the King of England! How did little Lizzy Walters ever find her way here? Elizabeth gaped in wonder, forgetting for the moment to be an enigmatic goddess of the night. Charles II was entranced by two things besides women—his beloved spaniels and his clocks. There were no fewer than six clocks in his chamber and one sounded as they entered the room. He grinned when she jumped, pleased with her obvious amazement, and explained that they were all set to chime at different times. There were long case clocks, table clocks, pedestal clocks and wall clocks, some with mechanical automatons that moved as they counted the hours. There were birds with moving parts, mechanical otters catching fish, and one of Chinese monks begging girls to sing.

Delighted with her interest, Charles proudly showed her his favorite, a mantel clock of gilt-edged silver with a tortoiseshell veneer that depicted Venus at her toilette, Venus and Diana, Venus at the forge of Vulcan, and Venus with Mars. His arm brushed her shoulder as they examined the intricacies of its pendulum movement, and she felt the same magnetic animal charisma she'd felt when she had first met him, and later when they danced.

He moved now to stretch out on his bed, patting a place beside him, then folded his hands behind his head. The bed was placed in a deep alcove, decorated in the French style with a parquet floor and muraled ceiling, and a gilded rail separating it from the rest of the room. He was surrounded by a pack of playful black and tan spaniels, with silky coats, long floppy ears and bushy tails. They growled and cavorted about him, some playing together, one curled up on his chest. One licked his face, and one tugged obstinately at his shoe.

"Do you like dogs, Mistress Walters?"

"Indeed, Your Majesty, I do." She settled herself comfortably in a large masculine armchair with plush velvet cushions by his bed. He gave her a rueful look she pretended not to notice. "But I was not allowed puppies as a child. My governess thought them too noisome, though I had a kitten for a space before she ran away. I told her all my secrets and she took them with her." She smiled mischievously "I wonder what stories your dogs could tell of you."

"By heavens, there are none, madam. I've yet to meet a dog that couldn't be trusted, provided one took the time to befriend it."

Another clock chimed and she squeaked in surprise. She wondered how William performed his quarterly duties as a gentleman of the bedchamber, with all of that racket going on. No wonder he drank so much.

Her supine monarch raised his brow suggestively and again patted the bed. "I assure you, my dear, there is room for all of us, and your mighty sovereign will protect you from striking clocks."

"'Tis most kind of Your Majesty to offer to guard me, but I fear that in this I must show fortitude and protect myself."

His lips twisted in mild annoyance as he gently ruffled his closest companion's head. "I confess I am confused, madam, though generally I am rather fond of games. William's pretty friends tend to be more... affectionate. Are you de Veres's creature or a Puritan goodwife? For I swear you cannot be both."

"I like to think I am my own creature, Your Majesty, as I suspect does everyone else."

"You suspect wrong, my dear. Being someone else's creature takes a good deal of the worry out of life, as *all* of my pets well know."

"I beg to differ, my lord. I was married once, and now I am widowed. I worry a good deal less since I've been on my own."

"Ah! I have offended you. Puritan goodwife it is, then. Still, one wonders what you are doing wearing his necklace. It is not my intent to offer insult, but I have no inclination toward your beliefs. I have always admired virtue, but I can never seem to imitate it. Rather like your William, no? It is my belief that all appetites are free and God will never damn anyone for allowing himself a little pleasure. I enjoy the company of beautiful women. If you are a selective Puritan miss we might get along."

"You make up your mind too quickly, Your Majesty. You had already analyzed and classified me before I sat down."

He chuckled, pulling on one of his spaniel's ears. "Now it is I who beg to differ. I analyzed and classified you when you chose that chair. Tell me what I have decided."

"That I am sanctimonious and judgmental, though passably attractive, a hypocrite who wants to be cajoled to your bed."

"Ah! Well! God's teeth but you're damnedly good at this game!" He waved a negligent hand in her general direction. "You certainly look like one of de Veres's creatures, but hang me if you sound like one. What will it take for you to call me Charles?"

"You might try calling me Elizabeth or Lizzy. Am I to be insulted or pleased, Charles? I've no idea what his creatures are like."

"Beautiful, petite, with flame hair and freckles seem to be his favorites, though it's clear he's not choosing them because of their wit."

He's been choosing women who resemble me! Charles sat up and poured two glasses of wine and handed her one. She accepted it with a grateful smile.

"So, madam, here you are at last, and very much changed from when first I saw you. That is that rogue William's doing, no doubt. If you're not William's creature, you are certainly his creation. What exactly are you seeking here at court?"

"I seek the return of my lands, Your Majesty. Lord Rivers spoke of it when first we met."

"I'm afraid you'll have to refresh my memory, my dear. I confess I was self-indulgent that evening, and other than he had you wrapped in a sack, which was most entertaining, I don't recall much of the conversation at all."

"My properties were seized by Oliver Cromwell—those of my father, my late husband and my dower lands. You had me write down a list of what used to be my holdings, told me you would look into it, and told me to wait here at court."

"So I did. It was taxing and boring and I quite forgot why I agreed. To please Will, no doubt. Yet you deny being his creature. Why would he help you where there is no gain?"

Her heart fell as she remembered William's warning, *"If you press him too soon he will do what is easiest and speak to you kindly, promise to consider it, and never think on it again."* Nevertheless, she was annoyed. "Are you always so cynical and mistrustful…Charles?"

"Oh, my goodness, yes!" he said with a delighted laugh. "I have been schooled in exile. It's the one thing that has kept both me and my brother alive. I trust no one, my dear. Every one wants something from me, your sweet and prickly self included. There are some who like me well enough, but none, with the possible exception of our reckless Will, are sincere. His poetry and his spite are honest, no matter the consequence. It's one of the reasons I love him so well. That and he makes me laugh. But none of the rest can divorce me from what I am. Most think my job is to suckle them and they are a greedy lot—titles, jewels, lands, a post, an annuity or commission."

His wolfish gaze caught hers directly. "All of you seek to use me somehow. I've learned to consider each request with care, and with an eye to my throne and my own gain. I expect at the very least to be entertained. So let us be frank, a quality I admire. What do you offer in return for these lands, madam? How will you repay me if I grant your request? Don't be shy and I assure you I shan't be shocked."

She supposed she should feel insulted, but he was so amiable and charming it was difficult to take offense. "My thanks, my gratitude…what more *can* I offer?"

He grinned and patted his bed again. "If you are not Lord Rivers's creature you've no reason to deny us both pleasure, and if you are, then you know that we often share and he wouldn't mind. Don't be shy, my pet. You won't be the first to sell your honor to get back your lands. I've done it a time or two myself."

"I've no intention of selling myself and yes, he would mind!" She was fairly sure he would at least. She tossed back her wine and held her glass out for more, slightly affronted but exhilarated, too. Call it flirtation or contest, the man was a master, and she was enjoying the game and holding her own.

"Then why are you here by my bed?" His voice was rich and inviting. He lay on his side, elbow bent, with his head resting on his palm. His free hand patted a puppy, long sensuous fingers caressing its silky hair. "If you are here for lands, but you offer nothing in return, why would I inconvenience myself?"

She dragged her gaze away from those hypnotic fingers and looked him in the eyes. "Out of nobility, chivalry, a sense of fair play, Your Majesty?"

"Come now, Elizabeth. You promised to call me Charles." His lazy smile was pure seduction. "Would you have me believe that's why William helps you?"

"I know that's why. He feels responsible for my current situation. He made a promise before he went on his way to help me should I need it."

"Mmm! His little brown wren. Yes, I remember. You did make an impression on him. He spoke of it often in France, and when he first introduced you also, as I recall. He went to find you, but your house was empty. He's a conscienceless rogue when it comes to women, and he borders on treason when he writes of his king." Charles reached for an apple from a silver bowl and took a bite, waving it at her as he spoke. "But he does keep his promises, it seems. How diverting. It seems very unlike him, but I have noted at times, that between bouts of drunken abandon he has a decidedly puritanical streak, which he loves to sharpen on verses about me. How difficult it must be to detest what one so thoroughly enjoys. He is no hypocrite. He is a divided soul. Don't you agree?"

"Your Majesty is clearly not bothered by such an affliction."

"My majesty knows a great deal more of what lies in the hearts of men than some green slip of a girl."

"Men perhaps, but apparently not women."

He gave her a slow, wicked smile. "Oh, but I do know, and I have offered to show you. Tell me though, your father was Hugh Walters, which means you are neither whore nor actress but a lady in truth. It doesn't bother you to seek help from a man who killed your kin?" His question wasn't rude, it was simply curious.

"I've never blamed Wi…Lord Rivers for my father's death. It was war, as you know. He could not have known who he fought in the heat of battle, and there was naught

else he could do, even if he had. You have forgiven those
who took up arms against your father."

"Have I? I have made the necessary accommodations.
Perhaps that and forgiveness are one and the same."
Charles shrugged. "In any case he has helped you. You
are here now, just feet away from an indulgent king.
You dress to stimulate and attract. You've caught my
attention. Come! Claim your reward."

"It's true I dress to lure your attention, my lord, as I
have been waiting your notice for over six weeks. Lord
Rivers is convinced you are much like a raven, your
attention caught by bright and shiny things."

"And did he tell you of my generosity to those who
please me?"

"He told me you were kind to women, and more so
to pretty ones."

Charles sighed and gave her a crooked grin. "I am
when they are nice to me, but you're not going to be,
are you? At least not in the sense I like best. What a
pity. I should be very nice to you indeed. I assure you
no woman has left regretting my generosity in my habits
or my parts."

"To demand payment is not generosity," Elizabeth
said primly, taking a bite from an apple herself. Her
tongue swirled over her lips, trapping the sweet juices as
she tilted her head and gave Charles an innocent look.

"And to offer nothing in return is to plead a favor.
Making you one of many beggars here at court."

Elizabeth scoffed and sat up straight. "I do not beg
favors. I seek ju—"

"Justice?" Charles interrupted mildly. "I admired
your father. He could have been a very great help to

mine, but please correct me if I am wrong, madam. Didn't he work hand in glove with that devil Cromwell? Did he not seek and support my father's death? Do you have any idea how many Royalist supporters lost their lands and fortunes in defense of me? My parliament refuses me money to repay them. I return lands where I may, where it will do no harm, but I cannot do as I please lest I subvert the peace we have now. Do you know how many wait, hand extended, praying for justice and the return of their land? Why should I turn from them and give to you? They have families to support."

She had lost the man, but found the real king, and he was right. "I am sorry, Your Majesty. I have presumed too much."

"No, my dear, you haven't. But I will accept your apology anyway, if you'll come and sit with me. I promise to behave. This bed has room for six. Some nights I am in the mood for company and banter. We will chat and gossip and talk about William, and I will tell you what I am prepared to do about your lands."

Elizabeth looked at him uncertainly. In his eyes was an entreaty. *He's lonely, just as William said.* She rose and brushed out her skirts, then settled gingerly on the edge of his bed.

CHAPTER TWENTY-FIVE

ELIZABETH HAD barely sat down when she was swarmed by a pack of spaniels, clambering onto her lap and trying to lick her face. Charles shooed most of them away and she collapsed in laughter, clutching one of them close to her chest. She lay back on her elbows on the opposite end of the bed, as far away from him as she could get. He tossed her a pillow and another apple. "I shan't starve you for being a contrary lass, but if you want more wine, my dear, you shall have to come here and fetch it."

Effortlessly charming, attentive by nature, the charismatic Charles filled her ears with court gossip and told her some fascinating, hair-raising and uproariously funny tales of his adventures in exile. She was just a little tipsy, and she watched him wistfully, wishing he were William.

"What will you do, Elizabeth? If I don't give you back your lands?"

She patted her puppy with a thoughtful look, wondering why it was so much easier to talk to a man one wasn't in love with, even when he was one's king. "I think I shall open a bakeshop."

"A bakeshop? Whatever for?"

"Well, if I sold all my dresses and most of my jewelry, I'd be left with a reasonable sum. My cook Marjorie has been nursemaid, mother and friend over the years, but she's truly a marvelous cook. Her sugar cakes and jumballs are the finest in England. I'd wager my best dress on it. She's always wanted a bakeshop. She would keep it full of delicious smells while I read and drank tea by the fire. It would be a nice life, I think."

"That's very industrious of you. But aren't you afraid you'll grow very fat."

"Oh, I daresay I would, but it would be a happy life. And I could get a dog like one of yours and take it on adventures."

Charles's lips twisted in a wry grin. "I had an old servant like your Marjorie—Mrs. Wyndham, my wet nurse. She was more a mother to me than my own. Although she offered other things as I…ah, well, I gave her some property when I came into my own. I'm not terribly fond of paperwork, but I did take a look at your list before I called you. I am not so lazy as William thinks. I regret it, Elizabeth, but your father's lands in Maidstone I cannot return."

Her lower lip trembled. She dropped her lashes quickly to hide her dismay, and focused her attention on petting the puppy that squirmed in her lap. "These little fellows must be a great comfort to you."

"Yes, they are." He sighed, clearly unhappy. "The lands went to a man who lost his wife and family while he was with me, fighting for my crown. He was a loyal supporter raising money and troops, and it cost him all that he owned. If I dispossess him for you I must dispossess another to replace what I've taken, then another and another and on it goes. It can't be done." His voice was kind and regretful and she nodded her head, though she couldn't help feeling a keen sense of loss. Not so much for the property—it was not unexpected—but that the adventure was over and it was time to go home.

"It is not all bad news though, my dear. I *can* return you your properties in Sussex, both your dower lands, and those that were your husband's as he had no heir. They are still untenanted and reside with the crown. I will attach an equivalent title to the larger estate so you will remain a lady still. I wish I could do more. I have tried and teased you, but your actions in helping William were a direct aid to me."

"Oh, Charles! Thank you! Thank you! Thank you! You've no idea how much this means. If you weren't so attractive and you weren't my king I would kiss you." She took a deep breath as a warm wave of joy and relief flowed through her. It was enough! All their efforts, all their hopes, hadn't been in vain. They didn't have Kent, but they'd been given enough. They would never want again, never have to depend on anyone else again. They would have a home of their own.

"You might anyway," he said with his easy smile.

She laughed in sheer joy and bounced off the bed, moving up to his end and gripping his shoulders and kissing his cheek. He reached to put an arm around her but she stepped out of reach and wagged her finger. "You've promised to be good, and I'm here to claim my wine." She sat down beside him cross-legged on the bed, her face split into a wide grin.

"It's de Veres, isn't it? The reason you won't kiss me. Are you in love with him? You must be to turn down the attentions of a king."

"I hope I am not so foolish as that. He himself has

warned me. He says once a man captures a woman's affections she loses all her allure."

"Some of them and some of it. Why does he tell you all our closely guarded secrets?"

"Of rogues and rakes and libertines? He is almost as bad as Marjorie. He wants me to be armed and able to protect myself. He did the same when we were children."

"And yet he put you in my path. Did you not think he might have given you to me to nibble on?"

She couldn't help her burst of laughter. "You think he sent me to entice you for his own purposes? I can't imagine what that might be. It would be akin to sending a chicken to trap a fox... Oh! Foxes *like* chickens!" Their laughter rang through the chamber and carried through the walls to the hall outside. "You are still wrong, though, Your Majesty," she managed when she caught her breath. "He would never deliberately hurt me or put me in harm's way."

"Few women here would think being put in the path of the king as harm's way. Do you know, my dear, a more important quality than being honest with others is being honest with oneself. You are very quick to rush to his defense. I think you *are* in love with him."

She gave a sad sigh and leaned back on her elbows. "I loved him once, as a child. We were neighbors and we played together and had many adventures."

A teasing grin lit his face and he smoothed the place beside him. "Come, Lady Walters, and we can have adventures, too."

She made a face at him. "Not *those* kind. Were you never a child, Charles?"

"No. Never. Buckingham was my friend when I was a boy. He shared my nursery, but people change. I forgive him everything because of it, but one day I shan't." He looked at her with shrewd eyes. "Be very careful, my dear. Don't be a blind fool and fall in love with William. He is entertaining and handsome, but contrary to your fond memories of him, he is just like the rest of us, cynical and damaged and not very nice. He has but one use for women."

"He is not always that way."

"Oh, he has his moments. He has more idealism and honor than the average rake. But make no mistake, my dear, he's an irredeemable libertine. I have known him well these many years. You've fixed his interest in a way no one else has, and now that I've met you I'm not surprised. Still, he is what he is and it cannot last. You are nothing more than an after-dinner sweetmeat to him."

"A sweetmeat to him, a morsel to you. Women are disposable toys to you both. He has so much as told me he is no more capable or interested in love and fidelity than you are. You give little moments of yourselves instead of your hearts. You are intimate with women's bodies but not their souls."

"Oh, well…as for the souls of ladies, I never meddle with those." He sighed and stretched out his full length and shook his head sadly. "Pretty Puritans should not be allowed to dress as you do. It's very disappointing. Like receiving a gaily wrapped present, only to open it and discover a prayer book inside."

"I am not a Puritan. My father was in name, but not in strict adherence, and my husband cured me of any belief it had something to offer me. But I do know what I want from a man and a husband."

"I can promise you Lord Rivers will never marry you," the king said drily.

"He has already offered," she replied rather smugly.

"Be damned you say! Our William?" He sat bolt upright, spilling his wine and drawing protests from the spaniels resting on his chest. "When is the happy event?"

"I have not accepted."

"Why ever not? He's a very good catch. He's intelligent, handsome, I give him a healthy income and he has a fine estate."

"That is a matter between he and I."

"You might have told me sooner. Now you are out of bounds. He already pummels me with angry verse. Just imagine if I poached his intended bride!"

"How did Lady Castlemaine fix your attention, Charles?"

"I should think that would be obvious. If you don't know that, you've no hope of keeping Will."

"But you have been with her at least three years now. There must be something more to it than that. You must love her very much."

"I love her not at all, nor does she expect me to. She is beautiful, acrobatic, and has the morals of an alley cat. We share similar appetites. She knows how to please me and she's always entertaining. I enjoy her. That is all I ever ask of a woman. Don't look so shocked. I have affection for her. I have affection for many people. She gives me pleasure, which is all one can really trust in this world, and I reward her in turn. I love my sister and that is all. Lovers are for diversion."

Elizabeth cringed at a sudden onset of cursing and shrieking that grew louder by the minute and was clearly headed straight toward them. She looked anxiously at Charles but he only grinned and shrugged. "Speak of the devil." He stood up and offered her his hand, just as the door was flung open and the violet-eyed beauty who had dared lie on William's bed stormed into the room.

"You ungrateful, sorry excuse for a man! I have given you everything! My youth, my beauty, your children! And still you refuse me this one little thing." Elizabeth watched openmouthed with astonishment as the raging virago shook her fists and stamped her feet. "I *will* be a maid of honor to your queen. I demand it! I deserve it! I have earned it! If you do not make it happen I will tear your children limb from limb and set your palace on fire!" She was so enraged she had yet to notice he had a companion.

Charles bent to whisper to Elizabeth, "It is better than a play."

The lady halted midshout, and raked Elizabeth with a scalding gaze. Elizabeth lifted her chin and returned her stare for stare. *You tried to play with mine, and I have been playing with yours. How do you like it?*

"Good evening, my dear. Have you met Lady Walters?"

"Really, Charles! Please tell me this pathetic creature is not your latest plaything or I will be mortally offended. I can certainly find you something better than de Veres's latest trollop. He's already tired of her. It ill befits you to take his leavings."

"But I so enjoy *you*, Barbara."

She gasped in outrage, and for a moment Elizabeth thought she might have slapped him if she hadn't been present.

"Lady Walters?" The king offered Elizabeth his arm and she took it, looking over her shoulder to give Lady Castlemaine a cold smile. "Wait for me here, Barbara. I'll be back soon. Elizabeth, please allow me to escort you to the privy chamber. From there one of my pages will see you safely to your rooms." At the door to the privy chamber he bent and kissed her hand. "It was a great pleasure, Elizabeth, as was our dancing the other night. I will see that the papers are drawn up for your properties and title, though it might take a little time. I hope we become good friends and I look forward to having the pleasure of your company again soon."

She gave him a bright smile and curtsied. "Thank you so much, Your Majesty. I very much enjoyed this evening, and I hope we become friends, too."

Charles bowed and turned to leave, but then he stopped. "A last word of caution if you will, Lady Walters. Barbara knows she's the favorite of all of my beauties. Accepting men for what they are is how to make the thing work. William will not have passed the night by himself, but if he offered you marriage, he esteems you above the rest. Accept that, and he might make you happy."

She was too surprised to make a protest, and when he smiled and winked all she could do was nod. As she followed the page back to her chamber, she reminded

herself the king was the biggest cynic in London, and
when it came to William and marriage he was certainly
wrong. There was a light under the door to William's
chamber. It was the first time since coming to the palace
she'd not seen him all day. She was eager to tell him all
that had happened, the success with her properties and
the remarkable behavior of Lady Castlemaine.

She tried the door to his outer chamber and it was
open as always. She had been harsh last evening. It was
the lady she should blame. She'd just witnessed how
vicious and unstable she was. Perhaps she'd slip in his
bed and make an apology and—

She stood frozen in the doorway. A naked woman
she'd never seen before gasped, and stared back in surprise. They stood like that for what seemed an eternity.
Trapped in a frozen tableau. A sudden sickness drained
the blood from Elizabeth's face and she struggled to
breathe, feeling much as she had when an enraged
Benjamin had once punched her in the stomach. Tears
pricked her eyes but she was too stunned to cry. She
said not a word, just pulled the door closed behind her,
then withdrew to her room and leaned against the wall.
She slid to the floor and wrapped her hands around her
knees, shaking her head in dismissal to a confused and
worried Nell. It was Marjorie she wanted. It was to be
back in Kent and eleven again. Her throat ached and her
shoulders started shaking, and for the first time since
childhood she cried.

CHAPTER TWENTY-SIX

IT WAS WELL PAST NOON and William still hadn't gone in search of Elizabeth. More to the point, she hadn't come in search of him. He had sent Thomas to her rooms twice, only to be told she'd had a late night and was still abed. The irony didn't escape him. He, who used to sleep well into the afternoon, had been up since the crack of dawn, while his country miss now slept late as a courtesan.

He looked down at his paper. It was covered in scribbles and ink drawings of her naked, but for a sheer low-cut gown. He slid it into a drawer. The chit was clearly on his mind. He'd expected her to seek him out when she was finished and tell him how things went. It would have been courteous given all the efforts he'd put in to help arrange it. And here it was the next day and still he didn't know. He'd been worried about her since his return last night. What had happened in her meeting with Charles? Had he addressed her petition? Had he treated her well? What did she think of him?

A morning walk had attracted a steady stream of gossips eager to share the latest news and he already knew what the king thought of her, though it was already clear when he singled her out last night. He had talked of her at tennis, he had mentioned her at council, he had kept her in his chambers very late and Castlemaine was said to be furious, while His Majesty was well pleased. *What kept the two of you talking so late? Did he turn your head, Lizzy my love? Or did you turn his?*

Bah! He threw his pen across the table. She was supposed to turn his head and no doubt she had. He had seen Charles at work. The blend of charm, humor, charisma and power was almost irresistible when he directed it to conquer, but the little bird would have taken him by surprise. *And he likes surprises. It would please him to take her away from me, just as I've taken women from him.* But there was no danger of that. If anyone could steal her, it would be some romantic fool, chivalrous and true, with fanciful ways and a love of adventure that matched her own. *Who is this captain she spoke of?*

He reached for his discarded pen. In any case, she could never be bought or kept with lands and baubles, and what she valued Charles could never give. *The question is, can I?*

He knew he shouldn't have left without speaking to her yesterday. Considering how close they'd become and their heated exchange over Barbara, he should have sought her out and tried to explain. That was a problem one didn't have when a relationship with a woman wasn't meant to last past today. Surely she knew after a decade avoiding it, he wouldn't offer marriage to someone he didn't care for, but her expectations were alarming. Was he supposed to change his habits in a day?

He wanted to please her but, *because* she was different, he had tried to be honest, though 'twas far easier to lie. And how had he been rewarded for it? She had stormed out and slammed his own door in his face. He leaned on his elbow, fiddling with his pen, and sighed. His own words reminded him one was more likely to be rewarded for being a rogue and scoundrel.

Wronged shall he live, insulted o'er, oppressed,
Who dares be less a villain than the rest.
Thus, sir, you see what human nature craves:
Most men are cowards, all men should be
knaves.
The difference lies, as far as I can see,
Not in the thing itself, but the degree,
And all the subject matter of debate Is only:
Who's a knave of the first rate?

I am. He should use the skills he was best at. Tell her pretty words and promise to be true, whether he was certain he meant the thing or not. He was more than able to make her believe it, but he respected her too much to try. Perhaps if he tried reasoning with her. Barbara could put anyone in a state. And of course Jane hadn't helped. Still, things had been good between them over the past several weeks. Very good. Far from getting bored he had become more and more fascinated with her. Over all she was a sensible girl. If they made an effort he was certain they could work out some mutually acceptable agreement.

He looked up at the clock as Thomas came in the door. It was just past three. Unless she was ill, she should be awake. "And so?"

"So, my lord, it seems the lady walks and talks in her sleep, for though little Nell still swears she's abed,

I am certain I heard her talking in the parlor just before
I knocked on the door."

So her visit with the king had not improved her
temper. It seemed the girl insisted he pursue her. Why
stop now? He'd been doing it since she'd first come to
court. Besides, he thought with a grin, if it sweetened
her mood it would be well worth it. It would soon be two
nights since he'd held her in his arms. He tossed back
a glass of wine to fortify himself for battle, and with a
tomcat's swagger and an offering of very fine brandy,
he sauntered down the hall.

ELIZABETH GAZED from the window, her mood matching the weather. The wind sighed like a haunted thing,
dirge-like and moaning. It had started to rain, though
she supposed that wasn't possible since it had never
really stopped. It was simply raining harder. She could
hear it drumming on the pane and splashing on the
walkway below. She touched her finger to the glass,
tracing a fat gelid drop as it slid down the window. She
supposed it rained every bit as much in the country,
but somehow it didn't drain one's spirit like the endless
London drizzle.

She should be joyful. She should have gone today to
deliver the happy news to Southwark, but her head ached
and she was in no mood for celebration. She sighed
and leaned her forehead against the windowpane. It
was smooth and cool and eased her head like one of
Marjorie's cold compresses. She wondered if William
was warm in his bed with his honey-haired treat of the
evening. The girl had been every bit as surprised as she

had been. He might at least have done them all a favor and barred his door.

She wondered if the woman had told him of their encounter. If she had, he hadn't thought it worth explaining. She wondered if he knew about her meeting with the king. If so, it didn't seem to concern him. Perhaps his promise kept, his duty done, he had turned to other interests. She drew a heart with her finger in the condensation filming the glass, and then drew an *x* right through it, vowing to show him how little she cared.

A familiar voice interrupted her reverie.

"Elizabeth?"

She looked to the mirror to see him, paused just inside the door. As he entered, his well-muscled body moved with the easy grace of a practiced swordsman and courtier. Annoyed at the traitorous thrill of excitement coursing through her, she was determined not to reveal it. Nevertheless she couldn't stop her eyes from traveling his lithe form. The hair that kissed his collarbone just where she had done, his full lips, hooded eyes and aquiline nose, the remembrance of those skillful hands roaming her body, all quickened her pulse. Unconsciously, she licked her lips.

He faltered in the silence, then stepped forward suddenly, reaching out and swinging her around to face him. Her lips parted in surprise and she took a step back, but he halted her with a firm hand on her arm. Her nipples firmed instantly under his touch and she felt a wave of excitement. "I've missed you, Lizzy." His voice was hoarse, it caressed her every nerve. He wound a hand in her hair and pulled her close. In one motion she was in his arms, her soft curves molded to his body. She could feel him iron hard and wanting, pressed rigid against her. Her eagerness matched his. Her stomach fluttered, she ached between her thighs and, unthinking, she responded, wrapping her arms around his neck. Where Charles had kindled a fascinated interest, William ignited a raging fire.

He pulled her into a voluptuous kiss and she gave a soft sigh, closing her eyes as his hands trailed down her throat and over her shoulders and his fingers tightened over her lush curves. He gave a tormented groan as her body squirmed against his and his mouth covered hers hungrily.

She couldn't deny she craved his touch. Her own need shocked her, but she wanted something from him he couldn't give, and when he moved a hand to cup her breast she stiffened and withdrew from his arms.

"You were warmer the last time we met."

"Before you abandoned me for your new playthings?"

"So you *are* still angry about the other day. I thought I explained that to you, Elizabeth."

"Because you explain a thing doesn't mean I accept it. Why are you here?"

He was taken aback by her coldness. Her anger over Barbara had been heated and raw. The sign of someone who was hurt, someone who cared. This icy reserve after sultry kisses was unexpected. *Is this what I have taught her? Or has she been taught something new by somebody else?*

He put the bottle of brandy down on a table, certain it wasn't the time or the place. "One hears you met with Charles last night. Apparently he was quite taken with you. They say he has not stopped talking about it all day. I waited several hours last night to hear of your adventures. Understandably, I am interested. I thought to ask you today."

"Of course. You've invested both time and money. Your plan was a success, at least in part. He returns to me my dower lands and the property in Sussex, along with a title to replace that from Kent, which land I cannot have."

Was this what had made her so bitter and angry? "Elizabeth, I did spend part of yesterday out carousing with Sedly, but much of the day I spent deep in thought. We were both surprised by Barbara's mischief, and really did not have a chance to talk. Perhaps we might discuss this marriage thing again."

If he'd been paying attention he would have noticed her indignant bristling, but he was focused on getting his words out and plunged ahead, heedless of her angry glare. "I've been thinking perhaps I might try some accommodation, and we might test the idea again. Marry me, Elizabeth. You can live in Kent, and it shall be as yours. We can discuss the distinction between love and sex after, and perhaps come to some agreeable terms."

"Agreeable terms? I think not. I can't imagine any terms agreeable to me that would also be agreeable to you. I've told you before I am content to be a widow. I am well enough with what I have."

"Or perhaps you think to do better." His voice dripped with sarcasm. He wondered if he had been blind. As cynical as he was, he had held on to the memory of his little Lizzy as something—someone—innocent and sweet. Honest, straightforward and kind. She'd been the personification of what was missing in his own life. But why shouldn't she have changed as much as he had? She had known him in Sussex and not said a thing. Was that not a form of deception? She knew he was an intimate of the king before she ever came to court. Maybe she *had* come seeking recompense. Perhaps she was more skilled at manipulation than he'd thought.

"Better?" The word was spoken with deceptive calm.

He folded his arms and leaned negligently against the wall. "It seems Charles is quite taken with you. You have managed him expertly. As well as any seasoned veteran of the court. You were with him several hours last night. Many a fortune has been made by being the king's whore. He rules a flock of women with the scepter between his legs."

She gasped, her face white with shock, and slapped his face with a stinging blow. "You judge me by your own lax standards and those of your merry sluts? The pair of you are feebleminded! Proficient in sex with no understanding of love. Well, *I, sir,* am no fool. I would never tie myself to *either* of you!" She hurled the words at him as if they were stones.

A muscle ticked along his jaw and his eyes flashed a warning. "Damn it then! What do you expect of me, Elizabeth? In what way have I failed you? I have introduced you to the king. I have schooled you how to influence. I have worked to regain your lands. I have even offered marriage. Twice, for God's sake!"

She chose her words carefully, wanting to hurt him as his casual affairs hurt her. "From what I have seen, Lord Rivers, you have an exceedingly impulsive nature ruled by a craving for sex, drink and oblivion. You do not appear to have the talent to love, nor to be happy. I may have been as moonstruck as your other victims, but I hardly think I deserve to be tied the rest of my life to someone who would make me miserable!"

He stiffened as though she had struck him. *Impertinent, ungrateful baggage!* For once in his life, he floundered for something to say. "I am accounted a fine poet, though, madam!"

"And so you are, sir. Though a vitriolic and rather profane one. Your satire is sharp, your cynicism thought-provoking, but your work lacks any generosity of spirit, gallantry, or vision of real love."

He gave her a mocking bow. "I knew I should have used more pretty words. I should have realized you were no different from the others."

"You used to have a talent for friendship." Raw hurt glittered in her eyes.

"So did you, Lady Walters. There was a time you weren't so quick to condemn. It seems we are both disappointed."

"Did my Will ever exist at all? Did we meet in the summer down by a stream, or did I dream it?" Her voice was wistful now. In the sudden quiet they could both hear the snap of burning logs and the rain drumming on the mullioned windowpanes.

He sighed, his anger gone, replaced by another dark emotion she recognized but had never been able to put a name to. When he looked at her his eyes were tender and infinitely old. "He lived, Lizzy. For a summer or two. You didn't imagine him. He was real. *You* brought him to life with fairy magic." His quick grin was heartbreaking.

"But he couldn't survive long without you. I killed him. I buried him. So you see in a way I am dead inside. A part of me anyway. Lord Rivers is what remains."

"But why? He was so very much like you." She couldn't help a slight smile. "He loved poetry and adventure, and he was a hero."

"Was he?"

"He protected me. He came to my defense. He told me stories. He made me a promise once, I still have the scar." William stroked the base of his thumb unconsciously as she spoke. "He kissed me and I have never kissed another. I loved him, Lord Rivers."

"He was no hero, Elizabeth. He was a weak, pathetic, trusting fool. He lay abed half his life, frightened and frozen, waiting for Giffard to come."

"Your tutor? You mean he beat you? I remember you saying he claimed to do it for the good of your soul. I thought you very brave."

"No. I mean he fucked me, and taught me to do other things, as well. He crawled in my bed almost every night." He spoke without inflection. "You needn't look so shocked. Tutors beat their charges, masters bugger schoolboys, and many's the lord who makes free use of his page behind closed doors. I was a pretty and oversensitive child. Now I am big and mean."

A soft gasp escaped her. She was caught off guard, too surprised to speak. She'd always felt something was wrong, but she hadn't known enough of the world to even fashion a guess anywhere near the truth. Now her thoughts were flying and tumbling into place as piece after piece of things he'd said and hints he'd given finally began to make sense.

He gave her a wolfish grin. "Well, then. I think we've said all there is to say. I'll keep this, shall I?" He straightened up and hooked the brandy he'd brought her as a gift.

"William, wait, I—" But by the time she found her voice he was almost out the door.

He stopped and turned at the sound of her voice. "Don't bother looking for William again, my dear. He is long gone."

Elizabeth sat huddled by the fire after he'd departed. She wished he'd left his brandy. Wine didn't seem to have the strength to soothe her shattered nerves. She was still angry with him, with the casual way he had used her, but she supposed she could understand it a little better now. The secrets he had kept! He was right when he said part of him had always been a stranger. *That was why he was so eager to leave. I suppose it's why he never came back.* She thought back to her own fear and helplessness, the humiliation and the hatred she had felt for Benjamin. But she'd had Sam and Marjorie and Mary. She was an adult, and she'd had a place to escape to.

Pride and hurt warred with friendship and the need to comfort, and lost.

She couldn't accept his other women, but that didn't mean they couldn't go forth as friends. He had done so much for her that only a friend *would* do. She needed to find her way back to that friendship again. It wasn't until she had tried to have everything that things had gone so horribly awry. *He would never have told me if he still didn't trust me, but if I go to him now I'll end up back in his bed.* Well…what did it matter? Pride was a cold and joyless companion. A lover was certainly not the same as a husband, and once she had her papers she would soon be gone. *Besides. He has been there for me when I needed a friend. I don't think he'd have told me about Giffard, even in anger, if he didn't need one now.*

A slight tapping on the door made her raise her head. She watched in surprise as Nell led a red-faced and anxious Mr. Avery into the room. "This gentleman is asking to speak with you, ma'am."

"Of course! Please sit down, Mr. Avery."

"Tom, ma'am." He loosened his coat, looking decidedly uncomfortable.

"Sit down then, Thomas, and Nell will fetch us some biscuits and tea."

Her efforts at small talk went unrewarded. Tom Avery would do nothing but blush and fidget until Nell had brought biscuits and left the room.

"Ah…um. It's about last evening, ma'am."

Now it was Elizabeth's turn to color. No doubt he was aware of her late-night visit. "I don't see that we've anything to discuss, Tom."

"Please, ma'am. My Jeanine is afraid she will lose her position, and if Master William finds out I may have to choose between her and mine."

"Jeanine?"

"My sweetheart, Lady Walters. I'd not let just any girl into his rooms. She is lady's maid to Miss Temple, and she's not supposed to be courting, you see. Master William lets us meet in my chamber, but forbids her to wander anywhere else. But…well, she's curious is Jeanine. She stumbled from my bed and fancied a snack and a peek. She says a lady looked in and caught her. I'm figuring that had to be you."

"She was honey-haired and naked?" Tom's face flushed darker than his crimson ribbons.

"That would be her, ma'am. I guessed you hadn't told Master William and I'm grateful. He'd refuse her entry if she caused any trouble, but she's terribly afraid you might say something to Miss Temple, not on purpose, but because you didn't know."

"Well, she did give me a start, Tom. I'm not ashamed to admit it, but you are very gallant to come to her rescue like this."

"Thank you, ma'am, but I think any man goes to the rescue of a lady he loves."

She couldn't stop her grin, no matter how hard she tried to order her face. Charles was wrong. The woman William had been waiting for last night was her.

"You won't tell, my lady?"

"No, Tom, you may put her mind at ease. I shall be careful not to tell. You might warn her, though, that next time she might not be so lucky. Lord Rivers doesn't bar his door and anyone might walk in."

"He's not so wild as people make him out, my lady, though it suits him to let people believe he is. He would bring someone to his bed when the need took him, but other than that cold-blooded shrew the night before last, there've been no ladies in his chamber since he took up with you."

"Well, I'm sure that's no business of mine, Tom," she said primly. "Good luck with your Jeanine."

"Thank you, my lady. Tonight I'll be taking her to a play."

As soon as Tom left, Elizabeth started dressing in her best shift and petticoat, silk embroidered stockings, and an emerald dress. She left her hair unbound, the way he liked it. He had accused her of judging him by what others said, and she supposed that in part it was true. She felt terrible thinking of all he had done for her and how she had repaid him. His actions had been those of a man worthy of trust. He had been honest and forthright and kind to a fault. He had treated her to many wonderful surprises and come to her rescue time after time. Maybe she was so quick to think the worst because of Benjamin. Maybe it was because she didn't know where she stood. But Tom said men rescued the women they loved, and William said he was willing to make accommodations to be with her. He'd also given her a family heirloom. Though he hadn't made any great declaration, something she found a little disappointing from a poet, when one took a step back, it sounded a great deal like love.

Dressed in her best, at her most enticing, she set out to apologize, to mend their friendship, and to listen to what he had to say.

She stood outside his door taking several deep breaths. She wasn't certain of his reception. She had insulted him and turned his proposal down twice. Nor would she agree if he ever made another one. Not unless he could trust himself to be content with just a wife. She hoped they could find their way back to old friends and lovers again. She wasn't really sure how they'd lost that in just two days. She wanted him to tell her the rest of his story, and she wanted to tell him about Benjamin, too. She put on her warmest, most charming smile, and rapped on his door.

He was bleary-eyed and disheveled. His shirt was open to the waist and he hadn't shaved. She could smell the brandy on his breath from out in the hall, and though she'd yet to see him so drunk he didn't know what he was doing, there was a challenge in his voice and a wild look to his gaze.

"What do you want?" He stood blocking the door, and wouldn't move to let her in.

"I...I wanted to talk. I wanted to apologize."

"Now is not a good time."

"William, I know I was unfair and I said some things..." Her voice faltered then stopped. A feminine hand appeared on his shoulder and ran over his bicep and down to his waist.

"William?" It was a familiar throaty female voice. "I want to go back to my room, it's too busy here."

He looked back over his shoulder. "All right. Let's find your clothes." He turned back to Elizabeth, his gaze unreadable.

"Go away, Elizabeth. I'm not alone."

CHAPTER TWENTY-SEVEN

WILLIAM CLOSED the door behind her with a firm shove. She wanted to apologize. For what? Refusing to hear him? Mocking his proposal a second time and throwing it in his face? Or casting her lot with the one who could advance her furthest. It was the way of the courtier. *We are all whores here. Charles included. Why should she be any better?* He should be proud. He had taught her well. So well that the pupil outstripped the teacher. How amusing. While she had donned armor and become practiced and cynical, she had stripped him of his and left him naked and cold.

His lip curled in a self-mocking smile as he bent to retrieve Barbara's stockings and jeweled kid shoes. He tossed them to her. "Get dressed. Get out."

"But, William, darling, she'll just run to him. Let's show them both that we don't care."

"I *don't* care, Barbara, and you've nothing new to show me. I grew bored of you before we left France." He knew now why Elizabeth hadn't come last night. Barbara had taken malicious joy in recounting how she had found her curled in Charles's bed. Now the king's angry mistress wanted to revenge herself on both of them by fucking him. Let Lizzy gather her troubles and take them to His Majesty. It seemed his little bird would test her wings. Let her see how high she could fly.

Barbara came up behind him and wrapped her hands around his waist. "Come play with me, William, we'll forget them both."

"I'm not in the mood for fucking, Barbara, and you aren't built for conversation. You let yourself in, you can let yourself out."

He caught her wrist in a firm grasp as she lifted her hand to strike his face. "I'm not in the mood for that, either. Be warned. If you hiss or spit or scream or shout I will gag you and lock you in a cupboard for Tom to find in the morning."

"I meant the girl no favors but she's better off without you. You are a heartless whore-mongering rogue!" Gathering her gloves and her dignity, Lady Castlemaine prudently withdrew.

Cursing, William poured himself some brandy and let its liquid heat soothe his nerves. He cringed at the thought of what he'd revealed to Elizabeth. He'd trusted no one with it since he once told his mother and she'd starved him to try and force him to recant his filthy lies. But somehow he had always trusted Lizzy. He had thought…if she understood…if she knew him better… *What? That she would love you less or more?* As it turned out it didn't matter. Much like his own mother, it was her lands that she loved.

He tossed back another brandy. Whenever he thought of Giffard he sought distraction through sex and alcohol. He wasn't in the mood for Barbara, but after another tumbler full of brandy he'd be comfortably numb.

"I SHOULD NEVER have been with him, Marjorie. Not that way. I should have listened. I should have known.

He is not who I remembered." Elizabeth's glass sloshed as she thumped it on the table, and Mary discreetly took it away.

"Young Master William? He was a good lad as far as I recall."

"You remember what you want to, Marjorie, and don't think I can't tell. There's only Lord Rivers left now, and they are not at all the same."

"Master William or Lord Rivers, either way he helped you, dear."

Elizabeth nodded morosely, looking for her ale. "He helped himself to me, and now I'm unhappy. Do you let a man molest you, that's the price you pay."

"Oh, dear God, are you with child, Lizzy?"

"Of course not!" she snorted. "I never conceived with Benjamin, why should I with him?"

"Well, some would think that a lucky thing for a widow."

"Marjorie! You're a very bad influence. I should never have let him touch me that way at all."

"Nonsense, love! You're a woman with needs. You only pass this way once, my dear. Why, when I was a girl there was a fine young soldier. A sparkle in his eyes, he had. Turned all the girls' heads. But he had eyes only for me and…well, never mind all that. The point is I've some fine memories I'd not otherwise have. So long as you harm no one, including yourself, there's nothing wrong in taking a little enjoyment is what I say."

"That's what Charlie says, too."

"Charlie?"

"Mmm," she said, reaching for a biscuit. "You know. The king."

Marjorie chuckled and ruffled her hair. "You're muddledheaded with ale, girl. But you've done us all proud. We'll make a home in Sussex we will, by the ocean near Brighton. Now you sit here cozy by the fire and Marjorie will get you some tea. We can afford it again, love, and that and some biscuits will make you right again, you'll see."

Elizabeth didn't think anything would be right again until they left London behind them. If she could, she would have packed her belongings and left the evening Lord Rivers turned her from his door as if she were some stranger. Only a week before that she had been full of joy as she rediscovered her old love and made him her new love. She had held high hopes in regards to the future for her and her small family, and was thankful for all the adventures and gifts life had sent her way. Now she was heartbroken and furious.

Until William had come back into her life she'd been content with Marjorie, Mary and Sam. She always had someone to talk to, and she slept surrounded by people she trusted. Together they celebrated life's little joys, everything from Christmas and birthdays to the simple pleasures of a pint of ale and a game of cards.

Other than the captain, who'd been very good to her, she'd had no gentlemen callers and she'd liked things that way, but a day in William's company had turned her into a hungry wanton, kissing men in public buildings and melting at her lover's touch.

She hardly knew what had come over her. He had turned her into a creature that laughed and flirted, and ached and trembled, craving the feel of her lover's body next to hers. *I* shall *have footmen!* Strong handsome ones.

It had been two weeks since he broke her heart. She'd stopped waiting for an explanation just over a week ago. Lonely in ways she had never imagined, she pined for something she had never had or missed before. Why had he unlocked her closely guarded heart, only to break it so casually? Not that it had been difficult for him. Much of her life had been a bitter struggle. A smile, a joke, and a few kind words had her trotting after him like an eager pup.

How foolish to feel loss for something that had existed only in her imagination. He had treated her with the same shallow interest he treated all his women. She was so furious her throat ached at the thought of it. How stupid to think he had valued her as anything more than a toy. Well, she may have been his prize, but her lands had been her prize, and she'd won them, and they were far more valuable, dependable and useful than any man.

She didn't feel like a winner though. When Marjorie came with cookies and tea she started weeping, and the older woman took her in her arms and hugged her tight.

"Maybe it wasn't wrong to let him touch me that way, Marjorie. But I should never have let him touch my heart."

"Hush now, Lizzy. Not a thing you can do about that. That happened many years ago."

Elizabeth brushed the tears from her eyes and stood up. She hadn't come to cry on Marjorie's shoulder. She had come to see to the packing. Though she was still waiting for her papers, Charles had assured her the thing would soon be done, and once it was she wanted to be on her way. She would have gladly left today if she wasn't worried that with her absence and Lady Castlemaine's shrieking in his ear, His Majesty's promise might somehow be forgot.

APRIL CAME and her papers didn't. If she didn't know better she might think the king was taking his time to keep her in London. But the court was buzzing with preparations for the arrival of his Portuguese bride, Catherine of Braganza, and she assumed any delay was due to important matters of state. She refused to stay in her rooms and hide from Lord Rivers. Once she left for Brighton she didn't expect to return and while she was in London she wanted to see and do everything she could. The king seemed to turn up often where she did, at plays and games, or even walking in the royal parks.

William's desertion should have made her an object of pity, but Charles's obvious attraction made her interesting, while keeping most others at bay. Few were brave enough to attempt the woman who held the interest of both Lord Rivers and His Majesty. It was commonly assumed it was she who had left the handsome and acerbic earl in favor of a besotted king.

William showed up at the same gatherings, his wit sparkling, his coat undone and a drink in hand; the charismatic and oh so appealing center of attention, with his cronies Sedly and Buckhurst, some purring feline version of himself, or a starry-eyed breathless young matron at his side. He was handsome, bored and lonely, and beautiful women flocked about him.

They dueled without raising their voices, their weapons laughter, disinterested politeness, or an icy smile. He barely acknowledged her. Once he passed her and touched his forehead in mock salute, another time they exchanged a polite smile, and once his rapier glance passed over her for all to see, and then he turned and walked away.

She didn't understand his hostility. It was he who had injured her. She worried at how much he was drinking. It was the fashion at court, indeed all over England, and, as people said, it seemed to sharpen his wit. Other than a reckless disregard that had always been a part of him, it hardly showed in his behavior, but she worried it would eventually ruin his health. She tried to speak to him once, but his tone of bored impatience chilled her and she didn't try again. He spoke to her, though, if only through his verse. One night in the banqueting hall, just before a ball, he responded to requests for a verse by raising his glass high. Though he spoke to them all, his eyes were on her.

> *"'Tis not that I am weary grown*
> *Of being yours, and yours alone,*
> *But with what face can I incline*
> *To damn you to be only mine?"*

She walked out before she heard the rest. It surprised her then, when he rescued her from Lord Jermyn, who had tried to paw her the first time they met. He had approached her drunk and stupid a night Charles wasn't present, and stood staring down the front of her dress.

"Where His Majesty goes, his faithful Jermyn follows. I will be the next to spread your lovely thighs."

"I will spread your guts all over London, do you ever speak to her again." William's voice was cold and sharp with menace. He spoke from right behind her. His hand squeezed Jermyn's wrist with such force the man's fingers were white. He leaned closer, placing himself in front of her and spoke so only they could hear. "Or we can step outside and do it now."

Though a noted duelist, there was more hesitation than rage in Jermyn's eyes. The king had placed a strict ban on dueling but de Veres was known to be reckless, and known to be good. He was seldom challenged, and had never been bested. Drunk as he was, Jermyn managed to jerk his arm free and stumble quickly away.

"Stay away from him," William snapped, addressing her for the first time. A moment later he had disappeared into the crowd.

That was a week ago and he hadn't spoken to her since. Tonight there was to be a lavish court masque, a combination of drama, opera and ballet, and Charles had asked specifically that she attend. Everyone said it was to be the grandest entertainment of the year, and she was as excited as all the rest. She also had hopes that Charles might have news for her, and she could soon go to make her new home. She was weary now. Weary of watching William charm other women and ignore her with a palpable anger she couldn't understand.

She had refused his offer to share him with others. He had discarded her and moved on. Shouldn't that be enough? Why couldn't they be civil? A raw sorrow seemed to have settled around her, though she was skilled now at hiding such things. She knew from experience if she could get away it would soon grow dull, until all that remained was an old wound that ached from time to time. She'd had enough and was ready to go.

The king waved her over to sit beside him. She was glad for his company and a friendly face. The excuse for this grand frivolity was his upcoming marriage, though he had yet to meet his bride. He was as excited by masques and theater as any small boy and it was pointless to ask him any questions until it was done. The entire room descended into a rapt silence as the entertainment began. Elizabeth had never seen anything to rival it. No expense had been spared. The room was lit by a thousand candles, but it was amazement and wonder that lit her face.

Astonishing creativity and ingenuity had gone into creating a dream world that took form before her eyes. Exotically costumed courtiers danced over roads through plains and valleys, serenading the mighty knight who sought to rescue his kidnapped bride from incarnations of the seven deadly sins. Clouds of musicians passed overhead as his journey took him to magical realms, some heavenly, others hellish, and some in faerieland.

Astounding buildings appeared from nowhere, people and coaches trundled over elaborate bridges, and monstrous creatures prowled terrifying dens. It was a glorious spectacle and too much to follow, but she oohed and ahhed and screamed and jumped with the rest. At one point, when the hero entered the monster's infernal den in a final fight to rescue Virtue, his bride, she hid

her head against Charles's shoulder, only pulling away
when he tried to place an arm around her waist.

Despite her excitement, a bittersweet pang almost
made her cry. It reminded her so much of the story of
Spenser's *Red Cross Knight*. It would have been perfect
if it were William that sat by her side.

Charles offered her his arm when the entertainment
ended. "Come, Lady Walters. I should like to talk." It
was unseasonably warm for early April, and they set out
to the garden to take a walk. William caught her eye
as they passed into the courtyard. He bowed to them
both, wineglass in hand. He looked slightly disheveled,
he hadn't shaved and for a moment she imagined a flash
of hunger in his eyes. Her heart seemed to stop, and she
had to remind herself to breathe. *The sooner I leave here
and don't have to see him the better.*

"'Tis been too long since you entertained us, Will.
One of your verses before the dancing begins."

"Of course, Your Majesty." He spoke to Charles, but
his mocking grin was for her.

> *"Let us, since wit has taught us how,*
> *Raise pleasure to the top.*
> *You rival bottle must allow,*
> *I'll suffer rival fop."*

"Enough, Lord Rivers!"

"Oh, but there is more, Majesty." He gave the king a
wolfish smile.

"I don't doubt it, William. Don't press me tonight."

Lady Castlemaine came up and passed her arm
through William's. "Hello, Charles. Are you still wooing

William's Puritan? That can't be much fun! Come along, Will. The night is young."

Charles patted Elizabeth's hand as Barbara and William walked off together. "I did warn you, my dear."

"Yes, Charles, you did. I don't understand why he doesn't let it go now. Is it some contest between the two of you?"

"Oh, no, my dear. I've never seen him this way. He's jealous. It's an emotion I don't tolerate in myself or others. Life is much happier for everyone that way."

"William…jealous? Surely not!"

"Oh, indeed, madam. He seethes. I thought at first he'd given you to me to nibble, but he fair seethes."

"Yes, I'm sure he and Lady Castlemaine enjoy their seething very much." They were farther out in the gardens now. The building was lit up behind them, the pathways were lined with lanterns and torches, and the sky was thick with luminous stars that seemed suspended just beyond her reach. The music of twenty violinists carried out the doors and past them, escaping into the night.

"I have something for you, Elizabeth." He reached into his pocket and pulled out a packet. Elizabeth's heart leaped. Even though she'd been waiting for it, a soft gasp escaped her. "Is it…?"

"Yes, my dear. Congratulations, Lady Walters. You are now a Sussex landowner, and a countess in your own right." He gave her a deep bow and then handed her the papers. "In recognition for your service to the crown and king."

"Oh, Charles, thank you so much!" She threw her

arms around his neck and hugged him, almost dancing with glee.

"It is an insignificant property, my dear, or it would never have been allowed, but I am glad you are pleased. And now I suppose you will leave us." His voice sounded regretful.

"I shall miss you, Charlie Stuart. But I will get a beautiful puppy and name him after you."

She twirled around with her arms spread out, too giddy to care what he might think. She had set out on a quest, like the Britomart of her childhood, and she'd accomplished her task. *With the help of a handsome knight,* a small voice reminded her. Bah! Who believed in fairy tales?

"Or…you might put a steward in charge of your holdings and stay here at court."

"It has been a grand adventure. I went to London and loved a poet and danced with a king," she said with a soft smile. "But there's nothing for me here now, Your Majesty. I should love to come back and visit, but it's time for me to make my way home."

"There could be a great many rewards for you here, Elizabeth."

"I am grateful for my lands, Charles. But aside from that and your friendship, you could never give me what I need."

"You might be surprised. I am a generous friend when I am encouraged."

"What I need is a man who knows how to love," she said with a chuckle.

"Madam, I assure you, there are many who can attest—"

Laughing now, she held out a hand to stop him. "A man who can *love,* Charles. Who can open his heart and trust and share his world, and is content with only me."

"Well, I grant you I'm not the fellow for the last, but of all men, there is none who loves women better than I."

"I concede you the point, sir. But it's women you love, not a woman. You men like to think yourselves brave, but when it comes to women you are terrified and always take the safer course. With many women instead of one you run no danger of intimacy, other than the sexual kind, which for a man is no danger at all. I don't understand why powerful men fear women so."

"And love them, my dear. You've hit the thing square on. 'Tis true it's a dangerous trap. First she's in your bed, then she's in your head, and then you have no secrets left and next she would control you."

"You've never had a female friend?"

"I have no one I really count as friend. Not in the way you think. Not since my sister Mary died two years ago. We were very close. I have six children, though, and proud of every one of them. I claim them and name them and make them earls and countesses, duchesses and dukes. I feel you might be my friend though, madam, and my mistress. If I were as selfish as they say, I would hold on to your lands and title until you made it so."

"I am happy to be a friend, Majesty, but I could be nothing more. You have a mistress, several in fact, and now your new queen is on her way. I am certain you'll not miss me amongst such an illustrious bouquet."

"So you refuse the king?"

"My king would never ask. I refuse you, Charlie. I do not judge you, but being a part of your seraglio, along with your wife and many mistresses, simply does not appeal. My sympathies in these matters lie not with you, but with your wife-to-be."

"Pah! 'Tis the Puritan in you that won't allow life should be about pleasure."

"I have discovered I am as fond of pleasure as the next. I am just not inclined to pursue it at another's expense. If I seek a faithful husband it ill suits me to take a lover who belongs to someone else. Perhaps she will surprise you, Charles, and if you let yourself, you will fall deeply and madly in love."

The king scoffed and then broke into full-throated laughter. "What an odd girl you are, Lady Walters! But a charming one, nevertheless. I shall miss you dreadfully do you leave my court. But I've said it before. You are not honest with yourself. You refuse me for love of that rogue Earl Rivers. Admit it. If you think me incapable of this intimate love you seek, how much poorer a candidate is he?"

"I do not seek love from either of you, Your Majesty. Perhaps I shall do the same as you and surround myself with dogs that will kiss my cheeks and snuggle close when I settle down to sleep."

"And have you no kiss for your king, Elizabeth?"

She curtsied, like a loyal subject, then took his hand and kissed his ring.

He pulled her to her feet and into his arms, holding her snugly. He was a vibrant man, virile and magnetic, and she felt an immediate response. "And one more, madam. For Charles Stuart, to say goodbye." When she hesitated he whispered into her hair. "Do you deny the attraction? Are you not as tempted as I? One kiss. And when you are an old woman you can say that you were kissed by England's king who loved you, and I will say I held and released the one meant to be mine."

His voice was tender and his soft breath fanned her cheek. She could feel his heat pressed against her length, a welcome balm after William's cold disdain. She leaned into his virile strength for just a moment, and he brushed her lips in a tender kiss. She closed her eyes and her pulse stirred, but he wasn't William, and she stepped slowly back and sighed.

He gave her a rueful smile. "The answer is still no."

"With regret, Charlie Stuart, for somewhere deep inside of you is a man a woman could truly love."

"I thank you, my dear. You are always welcome here at court. Do not stay away too long." He gave her a deep bow and kissed her hand, then walked away with his easy long-legged stride, disappearing quickly down the path.

"You missed a fine opportunity there."

Her heart raced as she whirled around. The hoarse voice was William's. He stood behind her, somewhat worse the wear for drink. He was pale in the moonlight, his hair a dark halo, hard eyes glittering with some inner fire.

"What do you want, William?"

"I want you."

CHAPTER TWENTY-EIGHT

"I WOULD NEVER have guessed it." Her heart was hammering in her throat, but her voice remained steady. It was the first time they had been alone together in weeks. She wondered what he wanted. What game he played now. "How long were you standing there?"

"Long enough to know you will be leaving soon. I thought I should speak to you. I didn't think you would come to tell me. Would you have?"

"No. I wouldn't have expected you to care. You followed me?"

"Like a lovesick swain. Wherever you go, there am I. Haven't you noticed these past weeks?"

"I have seen you drinking and mocking with your jaded friends and your latest paramour on your arms. Or is it still Castlemaine? Have you no self-respect?"

"No. None." He shrugged. "Love is war, and feigned disinterest my armor. You wear yours too, love. It is sad I know."

"I am unused to seeing you without your acolytes."

"And here you are without yours!" He looked toward the departing king, already entering the great hall.

"I refuse to fight with you, Lord Rivers."

"Have you become a coward then, Lizzy?"

"No. I think I am finally becoming an adult. If you'll excuse me, my lord."

He caught her upper arm, refusing to let her leave, and when he spoke his voice was hoarse and pleading. "I respect *you*, Elizabeth. I have no greater respect for any other human being on this earth. Dance with me before you go. It's something we have never done."

Elizabeth sighed unhappily. "Must you play with me, William? It is cruel. Like a cat with a mouse. You pounce and toy with me and then lift your paw and I think I'm free, only to find you have me again."

"You'll never be free of me, little bird. Just as I will never be free of you." He held up his palm, pale in the moonlight. "We loved each other as children. It marked me as much as it did you."

"Then why—"

He swung her into the circle of his arms, stopping her mouth with a feather-light kiss. She didn't resist. The heat of the day was long gone and the night had turned cool. She felt such joy and relief to hold him again. She wrapped her arms tight around his waist and pressed closer into his embrace.

"Why do we hurt each other?" he finished for her. "Why couldn't we be content with the good fortune we were given? You must answer your own questions. I just wanted to see you again and touch you again and hold you close. I've made a wonderful mess of things, haven't I? But sackcloth and ashes don't suit me, love. Kiss me. Dance with me. Let's not think about the future, or talk about the past. Right now I don't care about who is right and who is wrong. I would rather have one touch of your hand, one kiss—"

"Don't!"

"Don't what?" he said, taken aback.

"Spew the same meaningless drivel at me that you do to all of your women."

"Am I to consider you one of my women, then?" he murmured against her throat.

"No!" Her body gave the lie to it. Her warmth yielded to him, pressing close against his hard frame.

He murmured something unintelligible and bracketed her face with shaking hands, bringing her trembling lips to his own. This was what he'd been wanting, this was what he needed, and this was what he'd been missing since he sent her from his door. He forgot where he was, the differences between them, his anger about Charles, and even why he came. His mouth descended, claiming her swollen lips in an act of passion and possession as he plundered her mouth in a bruising kiss.

She smelled like lavender and roses, cinnamon and spring, and he couldn't get enough. He wanted to taste her, tease her, own her, devour her. He wanted to take her right there on the grass and never let her up. A soft moan escaped her as she parted her lips and he sated his hunger, plunging his tongue deep into her mouth. The shrieks of revelers, the sound of music and laughter, the distant hum of conversation, all receded until there was only her heartbeat, her whispers, her breathing, her touch.

Elizabeth returned his kisses with reckless abandon, arching against him, meeting and parrying each sensuous thrust. He growled low in his throat, enjoying the feel of her as she squirmed against him. Wrapping an arm around her, he encircled her waist, jerking her hard against him and grinding his straining erection in the valley between her legs. She took a step back as some strollers approached them, straightening her skirt and adjusting her hair.

He groaned and leaned his forehead against hers. "You drive me mad, Elizabeth. I dream I am holding you every night. I wake in a sweat, aching and disappointed. Dreams of you have replaced my nightmares, but they leave me empty and restless and my body on fire. I can't even remember why we argued. I don't care how things went wrong."

"I do, though, William. You wanted to have me, but keep other women."

"And to punish me you turned to Charles?"

"I turned to Charles as you taught me to. To secure my lands and regain my home. He has become a good friend since the night you turned me from your door. Will we dance, Lord Rivers? Or make accusations?"

"We will dance in the moonlight, little bird." He seized both her hands, and twirled her in circles, faster and faster as the stars spun overhead. When he stopped, she tottered, unbalanced and dizzy, and he steadied her, his hands cradling her back and hips. They swayed to the music that drifted past them, and she nestled her head against his chest, wishing she could keep him like this always. That this night would never end.

"You have no idea, Lizzy, the things you make me wish for. Things that might have been. Things long dead." His voice was rough, aching with emotion. "If only…"

"If only what?"

"If only your fairy tales were real."

"Aren't they full of evil monsters? Both man and beast?"

"So they are, love. Evil is always vanquished. The just are rewarded and true love overcomes all. A man's actions have import for good or ill, and he can change things accordingly. We find meaning in stories because our own world has none."

"Your world may have none. Almost everything you write mocks or decries it." She raised her hands from his waist and wrapped them around his neck as she listened to his heart beating steady and strong, next to her cheek. "Why is it so important for you to prove that nothing matters? If that were true, you wouldn't need to numb yourself with drink. It's as if you are trying to ruin the gifts you've been given. Perhaps your world has no meaning because you refuse to see it, and to confirm it you surround yourself by petty, hollow men. Look up into the night, Lord Rivers. Tell me what you see."

"I see stars, brilliant and cold, glittering in the distance. Each a molten inferno surrounded by an empty void, stark and alone."

"That makes me think of you," she said with a little grin.

"You are not cheering me, madam," he whispered next to her ear.

She laughed and squeezed him. "I see the world in a different light than you do. To me it is a marvelous gift. It's not perfect. There has been sorrow and heartache and Benjamin in it. But there have also been wonderful summers and my days with you. Close your eyes."

He did and inhaled her scent. It soothed him, along with her voice and her touch.

"Can you not feel the breath of life blowing across your cheek? It's soft and sweet with the smell of spring, heavy with the river and sharp with the bite of the sea. We are surrounded by such gifts. Such bounty! The stars last for aeons while we have such little time upon this earth. They have always been there but it is *we* who give them meaning. Our world has meaning because of us. Without us there is no wonder, no magic…no poetry. Why deaden your senses, William? Why demean it and deny it? Why waste it in bitterness and liquor? I wish you could see the world that I see. It is by far a happier place."

He gathered her so tight against him they might have been one. His chin rested on her head. The first streaks of a pale dawn were rising from the east and he sighed. He wanted to tell her that he could see her world when she held him in her arms, but the words wouldn't come. "It's almost daybreak. The night moves too quickly. Everything seems to move too quickly since you have come. One reaches for something and it lasts but a moment."

"Life is full of moments, William. All you do is gather them one by one and string them together. Then they last a lifetime." She looked into his eyes. Hers glowed silvery in the gathering dawn, resembling the star that hung low in the sky behind her.

"When you look at me like that, I don't know what to say."

"Say nothing."

He bent his head and brushed her lips in a tender kiss. He was sad and weary and she tasted of hope and home. Reaching out a finger, he touched her shoulder, gently prodding as if testing to see if she were real. "Perhaps you were meant to save me, madam, as I once saved you." He tucked her head against his shoulder. "Please don't go, Lizzy," he rasped. It was barely a whisper. "You are the only one who knows me. If you forget me there is nothing left."

"Come with me then."

"Elizabeth, I can't go back there. My life is here. I am asking you to share it with me, here in London. I am begging you not to go."

Her heart ached for him, and for herself as a lone tear rolled down her cheek. She laced her fingers around the back of his neck and rose on her toes to speak warm against his ear. "I can't save you, William. I leave tomorrow. You need to save yourself."

He stepped away from her, taking all the warmth from what promised to be a fine spring day. She watched him walk away from all she had to offer. Returning to his glittering world of fine lords and ladies, fashionable cynicism and elegant excess. "God keep you safe, William de Veres."

WILLIAM WALKED back to the palace alone through a gray dawn. England's king was sitting on a bench, a pretty countess on his lap. He yawned and waved at William as he passed.

William waved back. "Let our Lizzy slip away then did you, Charlie?"

"No, Will," the king's voice rang out behind him, "that was you."

CHAPTER TWENTY-NINE

WILLIAM RETURNED to his room and barred his door. He was too restless and angry to sleep. He'd seen enough to know the little bird had eluded the king's pursuit. It had given him hope that she might reconsider his. In all his life he had never begged for anything. He had never known a father, his mother had turned him over to others, his king was a whoremonger, his tutor a predator, and his life was the stuff of farce. But he'd always had his pride. He'd let it go for her. Not once, but two times. The second time he'd offered her marriage and again last night. He *begged* her to stay and still she refused him. She would be gone from his life in a matter of hours, with what she had come for safely secured. He owed her too much to let loose his anger, but as always there was the tempting and more than meritorious target of England's most amiable and self-indulgent king.

THOMAS CAME IN with morning coffee just as he was putting the finishing touches on a poem he had started months ago. "What is it, Tom? You look like Jeanine's brothers are after you. What trouble have you gotten yourself into now?"

"I…my lord, did you know Lady Walters is leaving? They say the king granted her petition last night."

"Nothing that happens here escapes me, Tom. You should know that."

"But aren't you going to do anything to stop her? I thought that you loved her, Master William."

William yawned and stretched and took a sip of coffee. "It is true, Thomas, that I like her well enough, and if it makes you feel better I did ask her to stay. As you've heard she's leaving, you already know her answer."

"I am so sorry, my lord. I must beg your pardon. I fear it is on account of Jeanine."

"Have you been drinking in the mornings again, Thomas? Take my word, you haven't the head for it."

Thomas was wringing his hands and two bright red spots colored his white cheeks. "My lord, I was frightened to tell you. I feared you might tell me to give up Jeanine. The day after you and Lady Elizabeth were surprised by Lady Castlemaine, Lady Elizabeth came to see you and instead she saw Jeanine."

"What the devil? When did that happen? How do you know? Why didn't you tell me?"

"Jeanine told me, my lord. She needed to use the chamber pot and she was curious, so she decided to explore a bit before coming back to bed. My lady came in to see you on her way back from visiting the king and found her naked, my lord. After Lady Castlemaine the evening before, I suppose she assumed the worst. I didn't tell you but I did tell her, sir. Late the next day. At the time she seemed to be most understanding, but…it seems things have cooled between you since. I should have told you, my lord. "

"Yes, Thomas. You should have." So she *had* come

to see him after the king. It explained why she'd been so angry with him the next day. *And then she came to apologize and found me with Barbara again and I turned her away.* "The whole thing is as farcical as one of Charles's beloved plays. Well, it makes no difference now, though you'll keep your chit from my chambers in future."

"But, Master William, shouldn't you go and explain the thing yourself? After Jeanine and Mistress Shore and then my Lady Castlemaine, what was she to think?"

"That she'd be better off with Charles, I suspect. Though it appears he's failed to win her, too. Fetch me some wine, man."

Thomas stood fast, ignoring the order. "I don't believe it—"

"Yes. It surprised me, too. Particularly after Barbara's claims. But I saw her send him packing with my own eyes." *I also saw how she kissed him.*

"I *meant* I don't believe she has ever preferred the king to you. Since when have you believed anything Lady Castlemaine had to say? She is jealous of both you and the king and she hates Lady Walters. God bless me, my lord, anyone can see Lady Elizabeth loves you. Surely you know that."

"Do I? I swear to you, Tom, her last kisses were better than those I taught her. I think she has acquired some novel art."

"She turned down a king for you. You used to be quick-witted, Master William. I think the drink has finally addled your brain."

"And that's about enough from you, Thomas! Whatever she did or did not do with Charles is immaterial.

Whatever I did or she believes I did doesn't matter. I asked her to stay and her answer was no. Now out with you. Out…out…out!"

ELIZABETH LEFT to pick up Sam, Marjorie and Mary in a luxurious coach lent her by the king. She had tried several times to write William a letter, but last night they had said all there was to say. Except *I love you*. It had torn her apart to say no to his plea, but she couldn't stay and watch Lord Rivers destroy what remained of William. A hot tear rolled down her cheek, followed by another and another. As raw grief overwhelmed her, she cried for what was lost and what might have been, but by the time she reached Southwark she had dried her eyes. She was grateful for last night, and not surprised he had refused to come with her. She would never forget a single detail of his face. She knew she'd always feel the sharp ache of desire when she thought of him, and hunger at the memory of his mouth on hers, but it was time to go home.

I'll sell my dower lands, or rent them and invest the money, and let Marjorie, Mary and Sam settle by the sea. I don't know if I can live in the same house as I did with Benjamin. I suppose I shall just have to try and see.

THE PALACE WAS in an uproar, the king incensed. William de Veres had finally gone too far. This time the king intended to have him arrested and, after cooling his heels in the tower awhile, exiled in truth. The poem was bad enough. Within hours it was all over London, but he had even had the impudence to nail it to the palace gates. Charles stood there now, reading it alongside his brother James, his eyes flashing, a muscle jumping along his jaw.

I' th' isle of Britain, long since famous grown...

The first two lines had wet his interest; he was prepared to be amused...until he read the rest.

There reigns, and oh! long may he reign and thrive,
The easiest king and best-bred man alive.
Him no ambition moves to get renown
Like the French fool, that wanders up and down
Peace is his aim, his gentleness is such,
And love he loves, for he loves fucking much.
Nor are his high desires above his strength:
His scepter and his prick are of a length;
Poor prince! thy prick, like thy buffoons at Court,
Will govern thee because it makes thee sport.
'Tis sure the sauciest prick that e'er did swive,
The proudest, peremptoriest prick alive.
Restless he rolls about from whore to whore
A merry monarch, scandalous and poor.

It continued in that vein until it reached its scathing conclusion.

All monarchs I hate, and the thrones they sit on,
From the hector of France to the cully of Britain.

"'Tis treason, Charles," James opined from over his shoulder.

"He is to go to the tower. Then exile in Europe. I will not see him in London again."

But Lord Rivers was already gone, his servant with him. There was no one to question, no belongings to seize.

"Shall we chase him down, Your Majesty?" asked the captain of the guard. "He can't have gone far."

"No. Not yet. You'll not find him in any case. He's quite capable of hiding right under your nose. We shall wait and see when and where he turns up. Perhaps he's gone after the girl. One never knows. She's a deceptively strong-minded little thing. She might salvage the ungrateful rogue yet." He turned to his dour-faced brother. "What say you, Jamie? Do you care to take a wager?"

The king walked away with his long loping stride as his retinue of functionaries struggled to keep up. *We shall see, Elizabeth Walters. Perhaps, after all, there is something I can give you that you want and need.* The twitch along his jaw turned into a smile, and then he threw back his head and laughed.

CHAPTER THIRTY

ELIZABETH WAS TIRED. She'd been up all night and felt drained and hollow. Her eyes burned from all the dust thrown up by a heavy coach and four galloping horses. That was what she told herself at least. It pervaded her hair and clothes, drifting in through the closed glass windows. The carriage Charles had lent them, though not an official one, was plush, luxurious and well-appointed, with an advanced spring suspension that was a vast improvement in comfort and safety over the coaches she was used to. Nevertheless, as they sped farther from London it lurched and shuddered so violently over increasingly rutted roads that it rattled her teeth and bones. Thank God, it wasn't raining.

Her companions for the most part weren't doing any better. Marjorie sat white-faced and stoic, Mary clung to the leather strap with a fierce grip, and Sam's head was bent as he tried to read his almanac in the dim light cast by the lantern.

It was a day's journey to Brighton from London. Strange how quickly one's life could change. Tomorrow she would manage an estate where she had once been virtually a prisoner, and yesterday William had kissed her and asked her to stay. She'd given him a choice and was not surprised with the decision he made. London was the home of Lord Rivers. That's why he couldn't leave it and she couldn't stay. They each had a different vision of the future, and they both insisted on having it their way. She was glad to have seen him, though, glad to have danced in the moonlight, and she knew that she'd always remember the feel of his mouth on hers. She closed her eyes and traced her lips with her fingers. They felt full and swollen, as if she had been thoroughly and repeatedly kissed. *I was.*

She sighed and leaned back, bracing her shoulders against the carriage wall. She would never forget William, but she prayed she would Benjamin. It was going to be hard to excise his memory, his yelling and screaming, his threats and beatings, even his smell and the feel of him, from her new home's halls. *I will scrub and wax and polish. I will tear down hangings and whitewash the walls. I will sell all the furniture and burn his bed and hangings, until not the smallest bit of that man remains!* She blinked…a little stunned. She'd seldom thought of him since the day she left, but now that she was faced with it, she was surprised at how much bitterness remained.

The coach gave a sudden lurch and they all had to scramble to stay in their seats. When it swayed upright again, the coachman shouted and cracked his whip, and with a sickening jolt they jumped forward, thundering down the road.

"'Tis highwaymen!" an excited Samuel cried with thinly veiled enthusiasm.

"Get your head back in here, stupid man!" Mary grabbed her overeager husband by his collar and hauled him back in the window and Marjorie pulled it shut again behind him. They careened around a

corner and barreled down the highway as shots ran out
behind them.

"Bloody hell! Pull it over before you end up in the
ditch, you fool!" someone shouted. A figure flew past,
bent low over the neck of a lathered steed. Moments
later, the coach began to slow as the cursing driver and
the daring horseman both worked to pull the charging
team to a stamping, snorting halt.

"Quick, Marjorie, my bag!" Elizabeth's heart was
pounding so hard she thought it might leap from her
chest, but she still managed to find the flintlock pistol
she carried. With minimal fumbling and reasonably
steady hands, she primed it and made it ready. Samuel,
whose eyes were alight with the fire of a man forty
years younger, also had a pistol and he did the same.
No one had approached the windows or doors yet, but
they could hear the sound of feet crunching on gravel
as the horses were settled.

"You there! Driver! Down now! Here's half a crown.
Make your way to The Highwayman in Brighton in three
days' time and the rig will be waiting for you."

"You don't expect me to abandon my charges now,
do you, sir? I am the king's man. I'll not be leaving
the ladies unattended. What say you take what you be
needing and we'll give you no trouble. Then we'll all
continue on about our day."

The rest of the conversation was too muffled for
Elizabeth to understand it, but after a prolonged silence
she could tell they'd been deserted. What had the world
come to when even a king's servant could not be relied
on to protect defenseless women in his charge? Well, no

one was touching the hard-won deed to her lands. She hunkered lower and aimed her pistol at the door.

"Good evening, ladies," a pleasant voice said from the window. They all screamed including Samuel, and the sharp report of two pistols went off with a roar.

Coughing and wiping her eyes, Elizabeth watched as a nimble hand reached through the broken window and neatly plucked her pistol right out of her grasp.

"God's blood, Elizabeth! Someday I must show you how to manage one of these things properly. It really shouldn't be used as a toy."

Sputtering in rage and indignation, she scrambled back into her seat and brushed broken glass from her hair. "Fool! Imbecile! Samuel might have killed you! What in God's name do you think you're about?" Elizabeth's heart was pattering madly with shock, fear and elation. She didn't know if she wanted to kiss him or wring his neck.

A bullet lodged in the roof and one had shattered the window. He examined the damage, turned to Sam, removed his hat, and gave him a bow. "William de Veres, Lord Rivers, at your service. I am relieved to see the ladies well protected on these dangerous roads. Indeed, Master Samuel, 'twas bravely done. You're not going to shoot me, though, are you?"

Sam sat up, beaming with pride. "Not unless my lady tells me to, my lord."

Thomas looked in the window over his master's shoulder and waved at Elizabeth with a cheerful grin. Marjorie nudged her with an elbow in her side. "Oh, Lizzy, he has kidnapped you. How romantic. It's just like in a story! I always said he was a good boy."

"Samuel! Would you be so good as to keep your pistol at the ready and ride on the box with my man Thomas here? One hears these woods are full of highwaymen and villains, and with both of you on guard I'm sure we'll all feel safer."

"Of course, my lord! It was my intention all along but my lady wouldn't have it."

"Well, now she's had the opportunity to see you in action, I am certain that she's changed her mind."

"He's sixty-five years old, William," Elizabeth hissed.

"And 'twas his shot that just missed me and took out the window, my love. I've told you before, Lizzy, do you wish to be a widow, you must marry me before you kill me. For that you are going to have to be a better shot. Excuse me, ladies. Pardon me." He opened the door and hopped in the carriage, helping Marjorie into the seat vacated by Samuel, and dropping his lanky frame down next to Elizabeth.

"Ah! when will this long weary day have end,
And lend me leave to come unto my love.

"I hate to be a grumbler, my dear, but I must say I am exhausted." He leaned his head against her shoulder and though the feel of his warm body sprawled next to hers was delicious, she shrugged him off. He was wild and reckless and probably half-drunk, and besides, they had a rapt audience.

"Do you mind?"

"Apparently I have no mind," he said amiably. "According to Thomas, I am the village idiot."

"Well, I'm sure he is in a position to know. But do stretch your limited faculties, Lord Rivers, and try to tell me what this is about." She glared at Mary, who quickly pulled out some knitting, and Marjorie, who closed her eyes as if preparing for a nap.

"Why, I should think it obvious, my love." His presence seemed to fill the carriage. His folded arms and stretched out legs took up too much space. With each sway of the coach his elbow nudged the soft outer curve of her breast and his muscled thigh brushed her hip. "I told you one day I'd show you how I occupied myself while in exile."

"You were a highwayman?"

"Yes. A rather good one. Tom was my accomplice, though people of sophistication called us knights of the road."

"You held people up at gunpoint and robbed them?"

"Only those who were wealthy, and supported Cromwell instead of the crown. 'Twas my patriotic duty really, and how I met that greedy harpy Jane Shore. I can't say I liked my name much though. It should have been something all together more dashing."

She couldn't resist it. "What did they call you?"

"The tax collector," he said with a moue of distaste. "As if I were some bureaucratic functionary rather than the terror of England's roads."

Elizabeth snorted in disbelief and he shook his head vigorously. "I know! I know!"

"So that woman…?"

"Jane? I did steal her jewelry, but she chose to come with me. You'd be surprised how many women enjoy being abducted." He stretched and reached an arm around her shoulders. "So tell me, love, do you?" His voice was pitched seductive and low.

She refused to answer his question. The thrill she was feeling had far less to do with abduction than the excitement of having him just inches away. He was charming and insouciant, all his bitterness gone. The teasing laughter was back in his eyes. She hadn't seen him like this in several weeks, and the spark of exhilaration and challenge wasn't the look of the bored and jaded Lord Rivers, but that of the William who had dared her as a child. Once again his smile was her sunshine. Once again she was enthralled.

"So does this mean I am now your prisoner? Or is this just a new game until you grow bored?"

"What this is, is a happy compromise. You wanted to go to Brighton, I wanted to stay in London, so now we're going somewhere neither of us wishes to be. We are returning to my estate in Kent, though I haven't visited the place in several years. I daresay it's hung with cobwebs and haunted and overgrown. Fortunately, you have brought a veritable army, and I'm sure they'll soon set everything to rights."

"How long do you think you can keep me?"

"Forever I hope. I will bribe your Marjorie with handsome footmen and your Mary, too, once I discover her heart's desire." Neither Marjorie nor Mary looked up from what they were doing, but they both had turned a fiery red. "I shall keep you long enough for us to talk, Lizzy. Without games or artifice. Would you have this conversation wait another fifteen years before we finally say all there is to say?"

"Won't you be missed at court?"

"I hardly think so. I expect I've been banished. I left a love letter to Charles on the palace gates. I've been waiting for the right time to give it to him and as I was leaving anyway…" He shrugged and smiled.

Her eyes searched his carefully. Satisfied with what she found there, she closed her own and leaned back against the cushions with a tired sigh. He was here. He had come. He had chosen her and chosen William. That was all that mattered. "I, too, am exhausted and need to sleep. Wake me when we arrive."

A monotonous English drizzle had started, and the horses were now splashing and spraying up mud. William drew a leather blind down over the broken window, and despite all the recent excitement, it was relatively warm and cozy in the coach. They started drifting off one by one. First went Marjorie, then went Mary, and soon an exhausted Elizabeth was drifting in and out of sleep. Lulled by rumbling wheels and the steady sound of rain pattering on the roof, her muscles and her defenses relaxed, and with a peaceful sigh she melted into William's warmth.

She imagined that someone was touching her hair. It was a soothing gesture, gentle and reassuring, but the touch became more assured and insistent as it followed her into her sleep, slowly tracing her curves, tugging and teasing her nipples, and lightly skimming her buttocks and breasts. She squirmed and whimpered as her excitement grew, her breath coming in sharp little pants. Her hands fumbled and caressed, finding his fastenings, releasing him from his coverings to take him hot and silky, pulsing and arching against her palm.

His knuckles grazed her cheekbone and he growled low in his throat, spreading his fingers though her hair and pulling her lips to his, covering her mouth with a torrid kiss. Her feelings towards him were confused, her brain and emotions in a tumult. She loved him and she was wary; he filled her with hope and despair, and it was impossible to remember hard-taught lessons when he held her in his arms. But it was pointless to deny her attraction. She couldn't maintain the facade no matter how she tried.

She turned into his arms, straddling his lap with a hungry cry. Gasping, she rubbed against him as his tongue plunged in and out of her mouth in urgent rhythm. His hands reached behind her back, tugging and loosening the strings of her bodice, until he was able to slide it off her shoulders and down her back. Her nipples ached to feel his mouth. It had been weeks. It had been too long. Icy fingertips circled the contours of her breasts. She shivered and stiffened, and then warm palms clasped her ample curves and his hot mouth fastened on one throbbing orb. She moaned as sharp twinges of pleasure rippled through her core.

His hand skimmed her hip and thighs and he caught her shift with his fingers, pulling it halfway up her thighs and sliding his hand in between. She whimpered, her body turned to liquid heat and wanting, and her skirt crept up to her waist as she gripped his hips between her thighs. He eased her linen shift aside and steadied her hips, and vibrating and humming inside like a tautly wound bowstring, she lowered herself onto him with a desperate sigh. He grasped his penis and moved it around inside her, his knuckles rubbing her sticky heat as the motion of the carriage made them rock and slide.

Her breathing was coming faster now as the pleasure built inside her and—

"Elizabeth? Lizzy? Are you all right?"

Somebody was shaking her gently and she fought her way up from her dream, red-faced and flustered. Mary and Marjorie were watching her with concern, but there was a slightly mocking glint in William's eyes. She struggled to sit upright and pulled a fan from her bag. "Yes. Yes. I'm fine, thank you. Just a bad dream. I must be overtired."

She was panting, her chest heaving, and Marjorie reached across to squeeze her hand. "There, there, dear. We have Lord Rivers and Samuel here to protect us. There's not a thing to worry about. Go back to sleep, love, and all will be fine." Fighting it, wary and deeply embarrassed, she eventually succumbed to an exhausted, dream-free sleep.

WILLIAM SAT at a tavern in Maidstone with Samuel and Thomas. Both men deserved a hot meal *and* several rounds of drinks after spending at least five hours huddled on the coach box in bloody foul weather. They had left the women at the estate, not one of them interested in traveling one step farther. The skeleton staff had been amazed at their arrival after several years of having the place to themselves. Nevertheless, from what he'd seen all was in good order, though they *were* somewhat deficient in their liquor supply. He assumed most of the staff that remained after his mother had left and the estate had gone into attainder were Puritan like she had been, and not much inclined or accustomed to alcohol or disorder. Their lives were about to change.

Retrieving Lizzy had gone without a hitch. He supposed he had Thomas to thank for that one. But how was he supposed to get the blasted wench to listen? He had never imagined in his wildest dreams that one day he'd be begging a maid for marriage. Three times at that!

But he was an honest man, at least with himself, and he knew it was her or no other. He was sick of Charles and his court and sick to death of London. More to the point, he'd been in love with Lizzy since she'd fallen from that damn tree, even if he hadn't known her in Sussex with her hair bound tight, grown to woman from child. She'd captured him then, too. She'd remained in his thoughts. If he'd had a day or two more, those eyes, that hair, he was certain he would have known her. *I would have as soon as I heard her laugh.*

It was that which he'd enjoyed most about spending his days with her in London. Making her smile, hearing her laugh, and seeing the light return to her eyes. Well, perhaps not most. There was also her creamy skin, her luscious curves, that fiery hair and the way she couldn't say no when he dared her.

He knew what she'd been dreaming about in the coach just before he woke her. A slight chuckle escaped him as he imagined the look on her elderly servants' faces if he'd allowed it to come to fruition. It was a good sign, though. He knew by her blush it wasn't Charles she dreamed of.

He could forgive her the king if she *had* succumbed, though he was fairly certain she hadn't. It had seemed the only reasonable explanation for her cold disdain, until Tom had told him of Jeanine. Now he had to explain Barbara, accept the unaccustomed shackles of fidelity—though in truth they had yet to chafe—and find some way of living in a house that made his skin crawl. He had another fortifying glass of brandy. It was London without her or Kent with her, and he had made his choice. *I need to kill the ghosts that haunt me, before they kill me.*

Putting down his glass, he looked to his companions. One couldn't find a better man than Tom, and he was fast growing to liking Lizzy's Samuel, too. But though good wine, good food and good conversation all served a purpose, they tended to hinder once their limits were passed. Samuel had the hiccups and was talking to his mug, and Thomas was bewailing the loss of his Jeanine.

"Damn it, man! Marry the girl, if she'll have you, and stop your sniveling. I suppose I can give you both employment here if not in town."

Tom sat up in delight, knocking over a flagon. "You mean it, sir? My lady will need a maid."

"Yes, I suppose, if she stays and she likes her. If not, perhaps she can open a small shop in town. I caution you not to get too excited. There are few lady's maids who would be willing to leave court."

Cursing and swearing, he managed to trundle both his charges out of the tavern and set off for the place that had never felt like home. He dropped both men off on some straw in the stables. He wasn't their nurse. If they couldn't hold their drink then so much the worse.

His new…or old servants were eager to make an impression and they guided him to what had once been his room. They had pulled out hangings and furnishings fit for a master, but as he stood in the center his stomach was queasy and his blood ran cold. *What am I doing here? This was a mistake.*

He waved them away and walked to his mother's suite. It was the appropriate room for the owner of the house. A thick layer of dust covered a stark, ascetic room, devoid of any personality and chillingly austere. He stepped out and closed the door behind him. He decided to see if Lizzy was settled, but the door to her room was closed and locked. His wanders in the dark elicited a wry smile. *Perhaps 'twas me all along that haunted this place.* Resigned to drinking and prowling until morning, he found a small side parlor and stood by the doors, looking out to the terrace with another brandy to help him get comfortably numb.

ELIZABETH LAY in blissful abandon, remarkably relaxed for a woman who'd just been kidnapped. She could stretch her full length, nothing rattled, and familiar childhood smells trickled into her sleep. Roses and wildflowers from gardens and meadows, the musk of the creek and nearby river, the green smell of trees and fresh spring grasses were released like a perfume by the gentle spring rain. It was some heightened sense that brought her fully awake. She gulped and caught her breath, almost panicked. She didn't need to look to know it was him. Thrilled but unsure what she wanted, she slowed her breathing and kept her eyes closed.

"Elizabeth?" His voice was caress, invitation and temptation. "Lizzy?" He stopped by her bed. "You can wake someone who is sleeping, but not someone who is pretending to be asleep."

Dropping the pretense, she rolled over to look at him. His hair was wet and tangled, his clothes disheveled, and he looked like the dark angel who'd watched grinning from Her Majesty's bath.

"It is I, William."

"Ah, yes! You. What do you want?"

"I want to finish what you started in the carriage. I watched you." His voice was hypnotic. "I know you want it, too."

"You give yourself too much credit." Her face flushed.

"Modesty is useless, love, save when feigned. 'Tis you who ignores the truth."

"You are sozzled!"

"But still fully functioning in all my parts, little bird." He moved closer to the bed. "If you think I am overshot, you should see your Samuel."

She sat up on her elbows. "You are *not* corrupting Sam!"

He hugged himself, shivering. "I assure you, my dear, he doesn't need my help. He's quite capable of doing so on his own. I also wanted to tell you I forgive you."

"*You* forgive *me?* For what? For mistaking Thomas's paramour as yours?"

"Ah! I forgot that! Yes! I forgive you for that, too. And for Charles."

"For Charles? Why you…you…you pompous, arrogant, witless ass!" She threw a pillow at him and began a frenzied search for something harder. A book, a goblet, a brush.

"Lizzy, stop!" He took advantage of her momentary distraction and sat down on her bed, pinning her hands by her sides. "Calm yourself, madam. You are overwrought."

"Don't flatter yourself, William. I am offended. If I were a man…"

"If you were a man this would not be happening," he said drily. "I merely wondered if you were the king's mistress. Barbara said she found you in his bed."

"Oh, Barbara did? The naked bitch for whom you barred me from your door! And you merely wondered? That is why you have been so surly and cold these past weeks. Hypocrite! Get out, William!"

"Was I in error?"

"I said get out!"

"Why? Would you prefer I never brought it up? It lies between us like some bloody wall. I have been angry! I have been jealous! If I am in error, tell me. And may I remind you in all fairness that as you've just noted, you believed ill of me, too."

Elizabeth flopped back down on the bed with an angry scoff. "It…is not…the…same! You have told me, warned me, that you will have other women when I am not available to you. I have never told you I sought other men."

"Except the footmen."

"William, I am serious!" Looking chastened, he edged closer to her, as if to hear her better, and reached out to touch her knee. She brushed his hand away. "And I have certainly never barred you from my door while I had a naked man there with his arms wrapped around me."

"I do take your point, Lizzy. I admit I was pleased to see you jealous, but I did not invite her, I did not partake of her, and I threw her out only moments after you left. Nonetheless, I shall endeavor to see it never happens again. But you have been cold, as well, madam. For all your kindness, your friendship does not flow deep. As soon as I give some small offense you throw me to the dogs. I offered you marriage. Twice! It is hardly an insult."

"I am not a woman who shares her man, William. That's no offense to you. As for the rest, it might seem like no great matter to you, but you have accused me of prostituting myself to the king. You might as well accuse me of being a whore."

"But this is the world I am accustomed to, love. Can you not make allowance? And I never seriously considered that you sold yourself to him. I know you better than that. I only pretended to think it when I was angry. But I couldn't understand your coldness. I thought perhaps he had charmed you. I thought that perhaps you were falling in love with him. I meant to accuse you of being his lover not his whore. It is not the same thing at all," he said with the hint of a grin.

She couldn't stop the slight smile that tugged at her mouth in response. "'Tis not a pretty apology, William. One might expect more from a poet."

"I thought you preferred honesty to pretty words, Lizzy. So you and he were never lovers?"

"Never. He kissed me goodbye before I left. That was all. What of you and Barbara?"

"We were never lovers, either. I had sex with her. But that was before we met in London."

She sighed. "How many women have you...? No, never mind. I don't wish to know."

He lay down on the bed beside her and she didn't object as he wiggled one of her toes. "So we are friends again?"

She gave him a warm smile. "Yes, I think we are. And I can't tell you how happy that makes me."

He was lying on his stomach and he pulled himself a little higher up the bed to lie on his side, drawing patterns on the blanket with his finger. "I know you are fond of me. I would have you to wife, Lizzy. What would it take to make it so?"

"I think you already know."

"You would have me faithful, whether we are together or apart. I suppose I can dream of you if you are too far away. It's what I do now."

"And I would see a curb on your drinking, sir."

"Eh? You'd stop me drinking? Are you mad, Elizabeth? I hold my liquor better than any man at court!"

"But will you five years from now? Ten? Curb it, sir, not stop. Water your wine. Drink one glass in the time you might have two. I daresay you'll hardly notice the difference. It should be no hardship for you at all."

"No hardship? Water my wine? I might as well drink piss!"

"You might as well, William. You don't expect me to believe it's the taste you care for. You've gone well past that."

"Why, madam?" There was a definite touch of annoyance in his voice. "You wish to show the world you rule me?"

"I care nothing if the world knows or not. I have no

desire to rule you. I seek to comfort myself. Surely you are familiar with that. My husband drank. He didn't hold it well. Rather than make him witty and creative, it made him mean. I don't fear that from you, but you've a dark side, William. You've had it ever since I've known you. I have no desire to bind myself to a man who is destroying himself slowly. Ruining his body and brain. You've seen it at court. You see it every day. The whole idea is hateful."

"Lizzy, there are things you don't understand."

"I believe those things are called excuses."

"The wine is my refuge and my muse. If you destroy my demons, my inspiration might die, too."

"Perhaps I can be your muse."

"No, love. You can't." He laid his head on her stomach and looked at the ceiling. "My muse is angry and bitter and raging."

"You haven't seen me when I'm really annoyed," she said grumpily, but her hand stroked his hair as she spoke.

"Can I sleep here with you tonight?" He raised her hand to his lips and kissed it.

"I love you, William. I've grown to love Lord Rivers, too. But you come and go and change so fast I don't know who is who. After all that's happened in the past few weeks I need to know you better."

"Please just hold me, Lizzy. You are the closest to happiness I've ever been and I don't want to leave you right now. I don't like this house. I never have. I can't ever seem to sleep here. It makes me feel like one of your cold and lonely twinkling stars. Let me stay, love, and I'll grant you a wish."

She harrumphed but reached for a pillow all the same. "You smell of brandy. I wish you to be quiet and keep your hands to yourself. If you snore I will box your ears and deposit you rump first on the floor." She pulled back the covers and he slipped off his boots and slid in beside her. He was still a little damp, but she pulled the blankets up to his neck and wrapped her body around him. "I love you, William de Veres," she whispered against the back of his neck.

He clutched her hand and pulled it to his heart. "And I'll lay you odds of six to four that I love you with all my heart, Lizzy Walters." The steady rise and fall of her breathing warmed his back and her heartbeat surrounded and comforted him. He settled deeper into his refuge of blankets, sheets and Lizzy. Within moments he was asleep.

CHAPTER THIRTY-ONE

THERE WAS no sign of William when Elizabeth woke, and she wondered if she'd dreamed him. A fresh breeze came in through the half-opened door to the terrace, bringing with it the soft, sweet promise of a beautiful day and a warm and pleasant spring. It lifted curtains and ruffled the silk morning gown draped over the end of her bed. She smiled and said a soft hello, just in case it might be fairies. As if in answer, a dulcet touch caressed her cheek and gently stirred her hair. She grabbed a wrapper and stepped out on the terrace, imagining that gentle hands propelled her forward. The air was soft, the sun warmed her face and the hillside glowed with vibrant color. She turned her head to the forest. A fox yipped in the distance, and the leaves and branches whispered excitedly of mystery and grand adventure. *Oh, how I have missed this!* She knew she was home.

She felt a lightness of heart she hadn't known for many years. Indeed, her life for the past several months had been the stuff of fairy tales. She had sat on a throne and bathed in a tower, danced with a charming prince and been captured by a highwayman. She'd been saved and protected by a handsome knight and stared down and bested the evil witch who tried to trap him. Now it was her turn to save him. He had left his soul-destroying evil kingdom to follow her. A huge smile

split her face. *There may be hope!* She knew she was
being fanciful but there was something about being
home again, and being with William, that made it all
make perfect sense.

Reality intruded as she tried to dress. She supposed
if she were to stay here or in Sussex she ought to find
a lady's maid. Some of her clothing was just too complicated to put on without help. Shy little Nell had been
horrified at the idea of returning to the country, and
given her justly deserved reputation for fixing ladies'
hair she had no fear of finding work and had elected
to stay behind. Both Marjorie and Mary suffered from
stiff fingers and were never comfortable standing for
long periods of time.

She rummaged through a trunk until she found a
simple day dress that fastened up the front. That and
a sensible pair of shoes were all she needed to go exploring. It made her slightly giddy to know she was in
the house she'd spied on from the trees. She wanted to
visit the old oak again, and she wanted to see the house
that had once been hers. She smiled as she remembered
simpler days, when she had put on breeches under her
clothes and hid her skirts beside the stream.

The house was magnificent, much grander than her
father's, but the halls were empty and it lacked light
and laughter and any of the warmth that made a house
a home. Her footsteps rang on the flagstones, echoing
down empty halls and corridors as she poked her head
into room after room of ghostly sheet-draped furniture
and colorless walls. It was no fault of the servants. They
were hardworking but few. The house was massive, but
the kitchen, parlor, library and the main bedchambers

had all been maintained. It still bore an air of neglect that made it seem unfriendly and cold. *It's no wonder he doesn't come here. It's a mausoleum, not a home.*

Things were better outside. The orchards were fragrant and lush with spring blossoms. Rows of greenhouses, though empty, seemed sturdy, well kept, and ready for fruit. *Oh, my! Wouldn't Sam be in his glory here!* A snorting and stamping and the jingling of harness turned her attention to the drive. The coach was being made ready for its return to Brighton. She hadn't seen William all morning and supposed he was in town. *Now is my chance to make good my escape.*

A sudden cry made her look up to see a peregrine falcon performing a series of intricate loops overhead. It seemed to look right at her, directing her attention to the crest of a distant ridge and what looked to be the head of a giant oak towering over its companions and the valley below. She took a deep breath, her heart thrumming with excitement, and set out to complete a journey started years ago.

SHE CRAWLED through the hedgerow on her hands and knees, cursing her cumbersome skirts and picking twigs from her hair. He was seated comfortably beneath the oak, just as she remembered, using it as a backrest, his hands folded behind his head and his long legs stretched out. "Have you been waiting for me?"

"All my life, it seems, Lizzy."

She brushed off her skirts, then settled down beside him, wrapping her hands around her legs before resting her head on her knees. "So this is the talk?"

"About anything and everything, yes. I'm glad you

decided to forgo the coach." She turned her head sideways and smiled, and he tickled her chin with a blade of grass. He reached for her arm and pulled her toward him, shifting his legs and settling her against his chest. When he had his arms wrapped around her, he continued, his voice husky and earnest, his words caressing her cheek and the back of her neck.

"I will start by telling you this. I have always known you, even when I didn't, and I am going to know you forever. I have always been with you, and I have *always* kept you with me, even when I tried to forget. I will not go away, even if you send me, and I will see you again even if you say no, and if you leave me I will follow."

"You mean if I'd left you'd have kidnapped me again?"

"Hush, child. I didn't kidnap you. I brought you home."

"You don't think you'll grow bored of me?"

"Never, little bird." He caressed her cheek with the back of his hand. "You are always new to me. It's been so since we were children. Each time we are together is a first adventure of some kind."

"William...I lost my mother before I met you. I lost my father and my home. Benjamin took my innocence, my trust and my faith. But I am proud of myself. None of it broke me. That was in part because of you. You taught me to imagine. To dream and dare, but...of all men, William, you alone have the power to hurt me. You have the power to break my heart. You are so fine and quick with words but you don't always mean them, and you don't always keep your promises. How am I to discern the truth in what you say?"

"My promises? I've kept every promise I've ever made to you, Lizzy. You may be the only one I can say that to. I promised you my help and I gave it. I came back from France and went to check on you even when I didn't know it was you. I promised to outfit you for court and I did. I promised to get you before the king and I did. 'Tis true I refused to make promises I wasn't sure I could keep, but what promise have I ever broken to you?"

She sighed and snuggled into his chest. "Perhaps it's not really worth remembering."

"Yet you do and it lies somewhere between us. I would have you trust my words, Lizzy. Tell me."

"You forgot me once before, William. You left me, but you said you loved me and you promised you'd come back." She lifted her hand and showed him her palm. He looked at his own and took her hand, pressing his scar to hers. "You were my friend, my hero, my childhood sweetheart," she said, her voice almost a whisper. "You were supposed to come and rescue me. I believed you would, until Benjamin. It was a good thing you didn't, though, I suppose, because that's how I learned to rescue myself."

"You were always good at that, Lizzy. Always strong and brave." His breath kissed her ear. "But I did come back, though it took some time. My mother didn't want me home from school and I didn't want to come. Not because of you, but him."

"Giffard?"

"Yes." He gave a heavy sigh. "Even though he couldn't harm me he was here. This place still reminds me. He's poisoned every memory of it but those I have of you.

My mother sent me up to Oxford when I turned twelve. And when the war began in earnest she decided we best all vacate to Europe. It took me three years, Elizabeth. But I came. I tried my best to see and speak with you before I left. I waited for you right here for three days in the rain, and then I walked through the mud to your back door. I was turned away several times, until I saw your Marjorie. She took my note to give you. And next time I returned she told me you wished me gone."

Elizabeth gasped and turned around so quickly she clipped him on the chin. "Marjorie told you that? Are you certain?"

"Yes, love, I'm certain. I thought it was you who wished to forget me. How could I blame you? I was hardly fit company for a Puritan miss, even then. And we were already at war. I tried not to think of you again, and after that, there was never any reason to return."

"Oh, William, I never knew! I came here every day I could unless I was ill or my father was home. How could Marjorie do such a thing? Why would she? She knew how much I cared for you and I thought she always liked you."

"I don't know, Lizzy. But look you just above my head. I left a message for you."

She turned to straddle him, kneeling in the grass, her body pressed against him as she examined the rough bark. He steadied her with his hands on her waist. It was there. Carved right next to their first promise. *April 1645. Where are you, Lizzy?* "Oh, William, I am so sorry!" She collapsed against his chest and he rocked her in his arms.

"You see, little bird? I've always kept my promises

to you. You made a promise, too. Never to forsake me. You didn't take the coach this morning. Does that mean you will keep yours?"

She snuggled tight against his chest. "I will never forsake you as my friend. I will always love you."

"But?" His voice held a note of wariness.

"You have known so many women and when you drink you can be reckless. How can I know you won't break my heart?"

"There have been no women since you came to London. Even after weeks of being without you there's been no one else. I've discovered that for you, I can be as faithful as an old dog."

"But when you drink you sometimes get hotheaded and restless. Can you promise the same if you're drinking, too? When you said you were debauched, long before I met you, you didn't mean you were irreligious and drank your mother's wine."

"No. Though both in fact were true. There is no power in childhood but imagination, Lizzy. For you it was a refuge, but for me it was a place I needed to escape. Drinking was a help, even as a child, and then I suppose a habit, but I've never been able to lose myself completely in it. I've always needed other forms of escape. Do you remember when we talked about feeling and touching?" He grinned and tweaked her nose. "I believe that's when you told me I was dead inside."

"Yes, and I'm sorry for it, though it's not exactly what I said. I'd never have said it at all if I knew it would rankle so." She hugged him and kissed his cheek.

"He made me sick, Lizzy. Figuratively and literally. I couldn't eat or sleep. I suffered from indigestion, fits of anger and depression, and my hatred gnawed away at me until there was little else left. You were the only thing William had to hold on to. Without you, that part of me would be long gone. I taught myself not to feel. It's surprisingly easy, and with the help of alcohol one can remain comfortably numb. With no feeling, it was just touching. Once I did that, the touching felt good. I liked it."

"Well, I don't know much about it, but I suppose that's normal. I know I feel very good whenever you touch me."

He chuckled and ruffled her hair. "God's blood, but I do love you, Lizzy Walters. But the difference is that you *like* me. Despite all your protests, I know that you do. I hated him. Yet after I escaped him, I found I wanted it all the time. The touch, the escape, the pleasure. Sex and liquor, the one to excite, the other to soothe and let one slip into easy indulgence. No guilt, no sin, no cares, just pleasure. There were willing maids and whores at school, and later lovely ladies and unsatisfied wives. The craving is still with me today. It's never stopped, it's just rested on you. If I can convince you to marry I shall keep you very busy, but I can promise you I'll never seek relief from anyone else. How can I when it's only you I crave?" His voice was unbearably tender, but something molten and fierce burned in his gaze.

"I will tell you true, love, when I'm forced to stop drinking there's nowhere to hide. I've been as empty and hollow as a bloody drum. All my life something has been missing, except when I have been with you. With you the world is full of light. You are my wine, love, and I would gladly drink you every hour of every day and none other."

His fingers bracketed her lips and he showed her what he meant, drawing her tongue into his mouth, drinking her kisses like a heady wine. She responded in kind, putting all of her love for him into each caress and warm embrace of heated lips and tongue, clinging to him as if he were life itself, exploring him as her destiny. It was a kiss to melt a frozen heart and soothe a restless soul.

"Without thy light what light remains in me?
Thou art my life; my way, my light's in thee.
I live, I move, and by thy beams I see."

His hands roamed her body as he spoke, unfastening her bodice, slipping inside the neckline of her chemise, stroking and soothing, fondling and teasing. His voice made her ache as sure as his touch. "You see, my love. I was mistaken. You *are* my muse."

His mouth trailed after his fingers, searing her skin with molten kisses. He cupped a rounded breast and eased it from her shift, the thin material rasping her delicate peak as he released it from its prison. He bent his head to take her in his mouth and his warm wet tongue teased her aching nipple, causing a chaotic swirl of excitement and relief.

She moaned and clutched his hair, a soft gasp escaping her, her bottom squirming atop his lap as she sought to allow him more. He groaned and hardened beneath her petticoats and her breath caught in her throat. Growling, he flipped her over and laid her back in the green bed of the meadow, in the hollow of the ancient oak. He slid a leg over hers and then she was under him, her red hair spilling across the verdant grass. He placed feathery kisses along her nose and her jaw as his hands tugged her robe, skimming it up her thighs to her waist.

The grass tickled her bottom and between her thighs, and the breeze joined with his fingers to caress her skin. She shivered and buried her head against his shoulder in embarrassment and delight. He stopped a moment to pull his shirt over his head and release his breeches, and then he lowered his hard hot body over hers. She moaned and gripped his shoulders, calling his name and rising to meet him. She had been missing him too long for delicacy or patience.

Her hands roamed over his sculpted form, feeling taut muscle and her aching breasts pressed tight against his naked chest as his knee nudged hers apart. The warmth of his flesh was intoxicating and shivers of delight followed his touch. His lips seared a path down her neck past her shoulders, and one hand slid down her taut stomach to the soft swell of her hips. He explored her thighs with soft butterfly kisses, and one hand came to play in her damp curls. He separated her gently with his finger, stroking her slowly in a teasing motion, then inserting two fingers inside her as she moaned her need, aching to feel him deep within.

"Ah, Christ, Lizzy there's nothing else for it." Abandoning the skillful dance of sensation, he reached for her hips in a raw act of possession and plunged inside. She arched her back and rose to meet him, grinding and bucking, her heels digging into the earth as she strove to relieve the aching longing in her heart and between her legs. Their groans and cries echoed through the meadow, joyful, passionate and unrestrained. As her hot tight muscles contracted around him, his thrusts grew wilder and deeper, spurring him to his own release. He collapsed against her in helpless wonder, and they cuddled together in a tangled heap of limbs and clothes.

"I love you, Elizabeth Walters," he murmured, nibbling her ear.

"I love you, too, William de Veres." She nestled in his embrace, sated and smiling.

"Do you like being kidnapped?" he asked, drawing circles on her tummy.

"Only by the tax man," she whispered in his ear.

"Fie on you, girl! You're a saucy wench!" She pressed her behind against him and sighed with content. "You know, we really *will* have to get married. If you refuse me a third time I will take it very ill."

She turned onto her back to stroke his cheek, greeting his remark with a worried sigh.

"Elizabeth?"

"William, I don't know if I can have children. If that is something you want, I would make you a poor bride."

He pulled her tight against him and wrapped them both in his coat. She could hear the wind rustling the leaves, and the trickle of the stream close by. The rumbling sound she heard was his laughter. "I've not wanted to leave a trail of fatherless bastards. I take care of such things, Lizzy. You've nothing to fear if you want a child."

"Benjamin wanted one, and it angered him mightily.

He was…a violent man. It might be that if I could, I can't anymore."

"Ah, Lizzy, I am so sorry. You would not have suffered him if not for me. I wish I'd killed the bastard for you. But understand, little bird, you are all I ask for or need. If you become lonely for something to pet or cosset we will get a herd of puppies and kittens." He leaned over her and kissed her nose, and they sank into each other, contented and at peace.

"I understand now why you don't like your house, and why you didn't want to return. I wasn't sure I wanted to live in Brighton. I was afraid somehow Benjamin would still be there. I really just wanted to get you away from London when I asked you to come with me. We can live wherever you wish to, William. Wherever you are will be home for me."

"Hmm." He gave her a thoughtful hug. "It might be different now that you're here. And I've always loved this tree."

"Do you remember how we used to play Britomart and Artegall, William?"

"Yes, my love. I do. We would turn into them by passing through yon hedgerow."

"I confess it's very long and I've not had time to finish it. How did their story end?"

"When first they met she bested him in battle. Naturally, he wasn't very pleased, so of course he behaved like an ass. By the time he realized how much he loved her, she was very difficult and hard to convince. Though very beautiful herself, she was somewhat jealous, particularly when he was captured by the beautiful but evil warrior Queen Radigund, who wanted her way with him. Still, he remained firm in his love and even though Britomart doubted him, she came to his rescue and set him free. He used all his skill to woo her.

"*With fair entreaty and sweet blandishment,*
So as she to his speeches was content
To lend an ear, and softly relent,
To be his love and take him for her lord,
Till they with marriage might finish that accord."

"She and I are very much alike."
"Yes, my beloved. You are."

EPILOGUE

MARJORIE HAD TAKEN over the kitchen within hours of their arrival and it was there William and Elizabeth tracked her down. "I know what you'll both be wanting," she said, sitting at the table with a hot cup of tea.

"Why didn't you tell me, Marjorie? And no pretending you don't remember."

"Oh, I remember it well, child. As if it was yesterday. So in love you were. And reckless with it, too. And both of you little more than children. Neither of you had any idea of the storm coming our way. It was war, and fate found you on opposite sides of it. Your William came right up to the front door, Lizzy. With him leaving for Europe and you not yet fifteen, his mother wouldn't let him have you, and your father wouldn't let you have him. I was afraid if I told you, you'd both run away. Too young for that you were. And your new governess was spying. Your father told me if you saw him again he would marry you on the spot to a trusted friend.

"I thought he meant Captain Nichols, which would have been a great improvement over Benjamin Horace." She spat on the ground. "But then, where would you and your William be now? I knew if it was meant to be, he'd find you again."

"Captain Nichols?"

She beamed at William. "A nice young man who

wanted to marry our Lizzy. I kept your note, Master William. You asked me to give it to her and I said I would, but I never said when." She walked over to her spice box and opened it, returning with a worn and fragrant note. "Take it, children! 'Tis time it were read."

They sat together, William's arm around her shoulders, and Elizabeth opened the letter that was a promise kept.

Lizzy Walters,
You are my laughter, my joy, my future and my life, and when this damned war is over I shall make you my wife. Meet me where you always do. I'm waiting.
Your William

"I clearly wasn't much of a poet at the time," he grumbled.

"Oh, William!" She threw her arms around his neck. "It's the most beautiful thing I've ever read!"

Though they were both adults and should have known better, at the first full moon they went to the meadow and carved new vows in the heart of the tree. And when the night air felt like magic, Lizzy donned her breeches and they crawled through the hedgerow and off to faerieland.

* * * * *

Author's Note

Libertine's Kiss is a work of fiction, but the character of William de Veres is inspired by that of John Wilmot, Earl of Rochester, who was court poet to King Charles II and generally considered the foremost libertine and wit of his day. He was also the top ranking satirist, second only to Dryden for his poetical works. The poetry used in this story as William's is in fact Rochester's, and their lives share many similar events.

King Charles was certainly one of the foremost rakes and wits of his time, as well. There is still much debate about his record. Was he canny or lazy, a great political survivor or a self-indulgent wastrel, an astute monarch with his finger on the pulse of his people or a jaded and dissolute rogue? It seems he was all of the above, and quite ruthless when protecting his own power and family, too. What is not in doubt is his addiction to women, and his large collection of mistresses, most of whom were content to share him, and were sometimes seen happily relaxing with him and his wife. He had at least sixteen illegitimate children, all of whom he was proud of, and he saw to their supervision and education, and awarded them lands and titles.

Despite his infidelities he sat for over a day by his wife's bedside when she was delusional and ill, chatting with her about the imaginary children that the poor queen could never have. Unlike Henry VIII before him, when his advisors pressured him to divorce his barren wife, he adamantly refused. He was certainly one of Europe's most amiable and informal monarchs and was well loved by most of the populace at the time. Interested readers can discover more about him in Antonia Frazer's *King Charles II* and J. P. Kenyon's *The Stuarts*. For a view of the times *The Diary of Sam Pepys,* Jeffery Forgeng's *Daily Life in Stuart England* and *Stuart England* by Blair Worden are all excellent books.

Other than the banqueting hall with its murals by Rubens, Whitehall palace was burned to the ground in 1698. The Whitehall of *Libertine's Kiss* is cobbled together from maps, plans, drawings and paintings, and various eyewitness accounts over a span of several years, starting when Henry the VII and Ann Boleyn stole it from Cardinal Wolsey. Its fascinating history is documented in the wonderful *Whitehall Palace* by Simon Thurley.

A story with a character who is a poet must have poetry, and I apologize to those who might find such devices, or the works chosen, not to their taste. As noted above, William de Veres's works are Rochester's, and of course there is a thread through the story from the longest poem in English, Edmund Spenser's sixteenth-century *The Faerie Queene.* Long before Zena, Ripley, Sarah Connor or Buffy, before Tolkien and C. S. Lewis and modern-day masters of fantasy, there was the Faerie Queen Gloriana, and the over-six-foot-tall, beautiful, invincible, armor-wearing, spear-carrying female knight, Britomart, who was never beaten and could take on six armed knights at once.

William quotes poets other than Spenser at times.

Though some of the poems are complete, most are snippets taken from larger works. All of them were written during or prior to the Restoration Period. These include "A Sweet Disorder in the Dress" by Robert Herrick, "Lucasta, Going to the Wars" by Richard Lovelace, "To his Mistress, going to Bed" by John Donne, "Ulysses and the Siren" by Samuel Daniel, and "Go, Lovely Rose" by Edmund Waller. In addition, the quote by Mrs. Hobart is a true one, and the playwright George Etherege wrote of Rochester that though he was a devil, he had yet a bit of the angel undefaced within him. And, yes, Charles's mistress, Lady Castlemaine, *did* threaten to tear his children limb from limb and burn his palace down around him. It was about that time he began to tire of her.

Some may have noticed the references to fairy tales. Mother Goose was well-known at the time. Some say she was a real figure, the wife of a fifteenth-century monarch, but by the seventeenth century, a *mother goose tale* was a common phrase. At the end of the century many of the stories were published in a volume by the French writer Charles Perrault. They included the familiar "Sleeping Beauty," and "Cinderella" with a fairy godmother and Prince Charming in the form we know them today.

People often ask where the ideas for stories come from. For some reason I find myself fascinated by the seventeenth century and the host of colorful characters that peopled that time. King Charles II, Samuel Pepys, Lady Castlemaine and the notorious Captain Blood, but certainly one of the most fascinating was John Wilmot, Earl of Rochester. Like the fictional William, John Wilmot's mother was a staunch Puritan and his father, who left as soon as he was conceived, was a cavalier. Much like William he had a tutor named Gifford who seemed to have formed an unnatural attachment to the point that he slept in the boy's bed for years "to keep him safe."

Debauched by age twelve, according to historians, Rochester graduated Oxford at the age of fourteen, tall, brilliant and surrounded by older men. There are reports that as a child he had difficulty sleeping and other ailments that would make a modern-day social worker sit up and take note. As a psychologist curious about the complexities of this fascinating man, that made me think *aha!* I should stress, however, that the connection between his overzealous tutor and his later behavior is mine and mine alone, and hence belongs in the realm of fiction.

So why not write a novel about the man himself? He was a war hero and poet, a faithless but good-natured husband, an inspired acting coach and fearless social commentator, not to mention devilishly handsome and charming to boot. Unfortunately, due to his lifelong promiscuity and untimely death caused by every form of excess, this fascinating man is not himself a viable subject for romance, but he certainly makes one ask "What if? Aha! and What if?" These three words are the cornerstones of many a story. Hence William and Elizabeth were born. I hope you enjoyed reading their story as much as I enjoyed writing it. Readers who are interested in reading more about Wilmot might enjoy Graham Greene's *Lord Rochester's Monkey,* James Johnson's *A Profane Wit* or Jeremy Lamb's *So Idle a Rogue.*

REQUEST YOUR FREE BOOKS!

HARLEQUIN® HISTORICAL:
Where love is timeless

2 FREE NOVELS PLUS 2 **FREE GIFTS!**

YES! Please send me 2 FREE Harlequin® Historical novels and my 2 FREE gifts (gifts are worth about $10). After receiving them, if I don't wish to receive any more books, I can return the shipping statement marked "cancel." If I don't cancel, I will receive 6 brand-new novels every month and be billed just $4.94 per book in the U.S. or $5.49 per book in Canada. That's a saving of 20% off the cover price! It's quite a bargain! Shipping and handling is just 50¢ per book.* I understand that accepting the 2 free books and gifts places me under no obligation to buy anything. I can always return a shipment and cancel at any time. Even if I never buy another book from Harlequin, the two free books and gifts are mine to keep forever.

246/349 HDN E5L4

Name	(PLEASE PRINT)

Address		Apt. #

City	State/Prov.	Zip/Postal Code

Signature (if under 18, a parent or guardian must sign)

Mail to the **Harlequin Reader Service:**
IN U.S.A.: P.O. Box 1867, Buffalo, NY 14240-1867
IN CANADA: P.O. Box 609, Fort Erie, Ontario L2A 5X3
Not valid for current subscribers to Harlequin Historical books.

Want to try two free books from another line?
Call 1-800-873-8635 or visit www.morefreebooks.com.

* Terms and prices subject to change without notice. Prices do not include applicable taxes. N.Y. residents add applicable sales tax. Canadian residents will be charged applicable provincial taxes and GST. Offer not valid in Quebec. This offer is limited to one order per household. All orders subject to approval. Credit or debit balances in a customer's account(s) may be offset by any other outstanding balance owed by or to the customer. Please allow 4 to 6 weeks for delivery. Offer available while quantities last.

Your Privacy: Harlequin Books is committed to protecting your privacy. Our Privacy Policy is available online at www.eHarlequin.com or upon request from the Reader Service. From time to time we make our lists of customers available to reputable third parties who may have a product or service of interest to you. If you would prefer we not share your name and address, please check here. ☐

Help us get it right—We strive for accurate, respectful and relevant communications. To clarify or modify your communication preferences, visit us at www.ReaderService.com/consumerschoice.